THE GIRL IN THE LOCH

ANDREW JAMES GREIG

Storm
PUBLISHING

Ebook ISBN: 978-1-80508-476-1
Paperback ISBN: 978-1-80508-478-5

Cover design: Aaron Munday
Cover images: Shutterstock

Published by Storm Publishing.
For further information, visit:
www.stormpublishing.co

Tha mo chridhe-sa briste brùite,
'S tric na deòir a' ruith om shùilean,
An tig thu 'nochd no 'm bi mo dhùil riut?
No 'n dùin mi 'n doras le osna thùrsaich?

My very heart is broken bruised,
Often tears run from my eyes,
Will you come tonight or will I expect you?
Or will I close the door with a heavy sigh?

From Fear a' bhàta (The Boatman) traditional Gaelic

PROLOGUE

The house rests uneasily in the landscape. Three concrete blocks carelessly dropped at an architect's whim, one on top of the other like discarded Lego. White geometric shapes reflect brokenly in the loch's dark troubled mirror, sharp edges transformed by nature's restless algorithm into complex fractals. A woman's voice is calling – the word Lilybet repeated cuckoo-like in the soft summer air, then rising in pitch as the first chill of panic enters her voice. From his eyrie window a man listens with irritation, leaning back in his seat to view the garden more clearly. She half runs, swiftly crossing the wooden decking to lean over the thick glass panels that delineate house from loch. She senses him, shooting a worried look towards his glazed lookout, then turns back to scan the water. She calls again. Lilybet. LILYBET! The loch doesn't answer, save for muted splashes as a warm summer breeze drives miniature waves against stone foundations. She's running now, towards the treehouse standing new and polished on the lawn. His irritation fades as he catches sight of her crossing the long meadow grass, moving like a skiff across an impossible green sea and seeing poetry in her legs, in her movement. Lily would be lost in a world of her own or asleep in the treehouse, three-year-old limbs stretched out on cushions warmed by the afternoon sun. He is unconcerned. What harm could happen here? The woman disappears into the treehouse, and he waits for the two of them to reappear, the girl held tight against her mother's chest and sent skipping back to the house for her tea. But when the woman reappears, she is alone. This time he can hear her cry their child's name, more a banshee's cry than anything remotely human. His blood freezes at the sound, and he swiftly stands, scanning the grounds and the fields beyond, searching for any sign of movement with an eagle's intensity. There is nothing. No vehicle on the track leading to their isolated home, no traffic on the single-track road winding along the glen, no sign of his daughter. Now the first doubt enters his mind, allowing fear to take insidious form.

Outside the triple-glazed windows, the world carries on as if nothing has changed. The same warm breath ruffles the loch's chill surface, the same swifts cut precise acrobatic paths, screaming at each other like impatient teenagers in their eagerness to feed. Only something had changed. Their only child was missing, and nothing would ever be the same again.

ONE

COLD CASE

Teàrlach Paterson knew the background to the case; indeed, it would have been difficult *not* to have known. The young girl's disappearance from her isolated Highland home had been the only news item to be given prime cover that summer, eclipsing wars and political scandals as the nation took the search for the missing child to its collective heart. A massive police search involving divers in the loch and dogs searching the moorland and mountains had failed to find her. The news channels' repeated footage of the tear-stained mother and her husband maintaining an icy-cool presence at her side led many to conclude he'd done it – whatever 'it' was.

That was three years ago, and the world had all but forgotten the blond-haired girl with the big blue eyes. Everyone except her parents and the red-tops desperate to keep the story alive with increasingly outlandish theories and salacious gossip.

'Show him in.' Teàrlach closed the box file on his desk, fingers unconsciously drumming a brief tattoo on the matte-black cardboard surface as he waited. The man about to enter his office had a reputation that preceded him, as someone you handle with the same care as a stick of sweating gelignite. If

Glasgow's criminal class had a hierarchy, he was the undisputed king.

Lilybet's father looked much as he did on television, maybe a few kilos lighter. He strode into the room as if he owned it, cold grey eyes observing everything they saw with the same detachment Teàrlach recollected from the TV interviews. His focus lingered on the row of old leather-bound books on the shelf behind Teàrlach – poetry for the most part. A recent bequest from the aunt who had taken a young boy to her home on Mull and made him whole again. They were her last message to him from beyond the grave, final words of advice or comfort – he wasn't sure which. Teàrlach wondered what the Glasgow hard man would make of the displayed works by Wordsworth, Keats, Blake. Would he see any man owning such books as emasculated? He watched him as he read the spines, eyes flicking from one to the next without a change of expression. When those eyes finally met his, he fought the urge to look away.

'Teàrlach Paterson.' He stood to introduce himself, offering a hand which was ignored.

'Let's get straight to it, shall we?' He sat without invitation.

Teàrlach Paterson returned to his desk, openly appraising the man opposite whilst inwardly questioning why he felt the need to look away. Tony Masterton didn't have the look of an apex predator; he was just a few years older than Teàrlach and in his early forties, dark hair beginning to grey around his temples. He wore a tailored suit cut so accurately it would show any excess weight in folds and creases of expensive material, open neck shirt devoid of tie. He had a few centimetres on Teàrlach, but then the PI knew how to handle himself. Gold cufflinks showed under jacket sleeves. Everything about the man spoke money and an effortless confidence. Teàrlach gave up psychoanalysing himself and re-opened the file on his desk. He didn't bother reading the copious notes, they were all committed to memory. The layout of house and gardens, images taken from police forensics, reports from the investigation. He waited for Tony Masterton to make his move.

'I've come to you because I'd heard Charlie Paterson is meant to be one of the best. You weren't my first choice.' He added the qualification without any emotion.

The backhanded compliment landed without any effect. Teàrlach ignored the anglicisation of his name – Teàrlach should be pronounced *Charr Loch*. Only in the Western Isles were there still people comfortable enough with Gaelic to pronounce his name without it sounding alien to their ears.

Tony Masterton continued, oblivious. 'You'll know the police found no evidence of any foul play; her body has never been discovered. I had my own security look at everything as well. Their findings are in the file.'

He gestured with a well-manicured finger towards the open box file.

Lilybet had been playing in the garden on her own. The last reported sighting was at four o'clock on the decking, then nothing until half past four when her mother called her in for a teatime that never happened. The live-in nanny had Thursday afternoons off. Her alibi was rock-solid, an afternoon with other nannies in Inverness. They were taking so many pictures of each other that there was an almost unbroken timestamp for every five minutes she was away. That hadn't stopped her getting the third degree. The poor lass would never be able to work with children again – not with that on her CV.

'No ransom demands, no contact of any kind?' Teàrlach asked dutifully, knowing what the answer was going to be.

'No.' Tony Masterton used words sparingly, almost as if it pained him to speak at all.

'And you can't think of anyone who might have had reason to take your daughter?'

Tony raised one eyebrow in response. 'I didn't get where I

am today without leaving some resentment behind. But someone stupid enough to take my child?'

The question remained unanswered, as it had since the day she'd disappeared.

'So, why come to me? What do you think I can do that the police and your own security have failed to do?' Teàrlach asked the question with real interest. Any trail that might have existed would be long gone by now. Three years of intense media scrutiny and eye-watering financial rewards for information leading to Lilybet, or her remains, hadn't resulted in a single step forward from that summer day.

'Because of this.' Tony reached into an inside jacket pocket, produced a photograph and laid it face down on the desk.

The picture was a screen grab from a monitor, the image low enough quality that Teàrlach had to hold it closer to his eyes to confirm first impressions. A young woman was tied to a chair. Plastic sheeting covered the chair and the floor, stained red with blood. It looked like she was being held in an industrial shipping container. She was dead – he didn't require a pathologist report to confirm the gash running from one ear to the other as the likely cause of her demise. The cut was so deep that her head was almost hanging off. Unless she had a twin, he was looking at the missing kid's nanny.

'Where did you get this?'

'One of my security staff. She's handy with computers. She's been searching every day for anything that may lead me to my girl. This popped up on an image search. She thinks it's somewhere in the Middle East, can't be sure.'

Teàrlach considered the photograph. It was possible the thing was a deepfake. Artificial intelligence was easily capable of creating a graphic so perfect it would fool an expert.

'What makes you think it's real?'

Tony's expression didn't change. 'Because this is a still from a live execution. My security team have the live video footage – and the audio.'

Teàrlach remained unconvinced. 'It could still be a fake.'

'Maybe so. In which case someone wasted £10,000 buying a film of her having her throat slit.'

Tony Masterton suddenly stood, looking impassively at the photograph before staring directly into Teàrlach's eyes.

'I want to know why that is, Charlie. And I don't trust the police or security forces to come up with an answer. I'll have my security consultant contact you. It may be via unconventional channels.' A thin smile fleetingly appeared. 'I don't care how much it costs. Find out who killed Jane Whiting and that will lead you to whoever took my daughter.'

Teàrlach held Tony's gaze, unsuccessfully searching for a shred of shared humanity. What kind of man could coolly discuss his daughter's disappearance without showing any emotion? His own concerns about taking the case were outweighed by Tony's need to know what had happened to his child. No matter the guy's reputation, or apparent absence of empathy, he deserved help in finding the truth the same as any desperate parent.

'You know your daughter, Lilybet, is probably dead by now?' Teàrlach felt duty-bound to pop the man's bubble before he took the case.

Tony Masterton's expression remained neutral. 'Oh yes. I fully expect that she died the same afternoon she was taken. I want vengeance, Mr Paterson. Pure and simple vengeance.' He paused with one hand on the door handle. 'They would have been better advised to take my own life before touching a single hair on her head.'

As the door closed, Teàrlach Paterson sat staring at the photograph in search of a clue, and finding none, added it to the file.

'What did you do to deserve this, Jane Whiting? Who did this to you?'

The rhetorical question hung in the air. Any answer would require a load of effort, and the client had just presented him with a blank cheque. Teàrlach closed the box file, newly undecided whether to take the case or not, following Tony's casual declaration of desiring vengeance. The girl had been missing three years now. The original and extensive investigation had failed to find any leads or suspects, and now that trail was stone cold. Even a million-pound reward had failed to encourage any new witnesses, any new information. His client was a dangerous man, and if he uncovered something that Tony Masterton wanted kept silent, then he knew how that might play out. Countering all that was the infinitesimal chance that Lilybet Masterton was still alive, waiting to be found. The thought of turning his back on that small girl, if she was still alive, was something he knew he couldn't live with. Whilst that vanishingly small hope remained, Teàrlach had no real choice.

'Clear my appointments, Chloe, and find out everything you can about the missing girl's nanny. Check her family, background, contacts, the last confirmed sighting – the usual.'

'You're taking the case?' His PA appeared in the doorway, doubt showing in her eyes. Her long fingers unconsciously played with newly braided hair. 'I thought we steered clear of outright criminals, especially the dangerous ones?'

Teàrlach smiled inwardly. It wasn't that long ago that she was a missing person herself, messed up with drugs and wanting an end to it all. He'd turned her life around, offered her a job, and now she was being protective of him. Chloe was a living reminder that what he did made a difference, that he could make things better – given a chance.

'He needs our help, Chloe. Same as anyone. We'll do what we can – although his girl's been missing for so long...'

She sighed acceptance. 'I'll get on it.'

He stared out of his office window at the Clyde far below, coiling like a black serpent with streetlights reflecting off its oily skin. Now that he'd met Tony Masterton in person, the impression he gave of being more ophidian than human had only been substantiated.

The time was 3:20pm, November 22nd. For the third time that day, he opened Google Maps and zoomed in on the futuristic building jutting out into the waters of the loch. Instinct born of investigating similar high-profile cases made the sea loch the most likely route in and out of the Masterton estate.

The house might have looked an easy target: isolated, no obvious security. Tony Masterton relied on his reputation to keep his family safe. But whoever took the girl never issued a ransom, never tried to contact anyone at all. That single fact alone all but convinced him Lilybet was dead – either on purpose or as the result of a botched kidnapping where they overdid the anaesthetic and stopped her breathing. The simplest scenario was that she simply climbed over the glass balustrade and fell into the deceptively peaceful water to be taken away by the current. His eyes returned to the window, catching his own reflection in the glass. There were worse ways to die.

TWO

WHATSAPP

Dee Fairlie stretched out in bed, all 173 centimetres of her, and brushed red curls out of her face. A few strands remained stubbornly stuck to her forehead, glued there by sweat.

'You can stop now.'

A guy's head appeared above the covers, a surprised expression forming as she levered herself from under him, swinging her legs over the side of the bed to stand.

'Do you want me to call again?' He pulled himself up into a sitting position, adjusting a pillow to make himself more comfortable.

Dee heard the questioning tone, knew his male ego needed reassurance, couldn't be bothered.

'I've work to do. See yourself out.' She spoke whilst dragging on leather trousers, a green T-shirt and a plain black jumper.

He shrugged, observing as she completed her attire by pulling on a biker's jacket, then grabbing a black motorcycle helmet as she exited the hotel room. At reception, she asked for her valuables to be retrieved from the safe, taking possession of a battered laptop before heading down to the underground car park.

The black Kawasaki Ninja 300 roared into life at the flick of a switch, and she exited into busy Glasgow streets slick with rain. It had just turned five, and the sun had set almost an hour ago, leaving the city to the harsh mercy of sterile white LED streetlights and the more welcoming yellow glow from shop windows. Dee weaved through the rush-hour traffic, wiping her visor clear of rain as she waited for stop lights to turn green. She automatically gave the car pulling up beside her a once-over. A young girl stared at her from the passenger window, wiping the glass clear of condensation to obtain a clearer view and smiling with delight when she saw Dee's red curls where they showed from underneath her helmet. The novelty of seeing a woman riding a motorbike had caught the child's imagination, and she gestured urgently for her mother to look as well. Dee gave them a friendly wave as the lights turned and accelerated into the open road ahead, towards her riverside apartment in Partick.

The apartment had been a gift from Tony Masterton, who'd paid upwards of two hundred thousand as a bonus for a job well done. Dee headed up his cyber security team – unofficially. Any inspection of personnel records would show no trace of a Dee Fairlie, nor the £5k/month retainer she was paid from one offshore account into another. It was an arrangement that suited them both.

She had started working for him a year ago, responding to a request in a hacking forum. It had looked like a phishing attempt by GCHQ, so she'd played along, tweaking the tiger's tale. Only the tiger had turned out to be a rich businessman needing someone to lift incriminating evidence from a secure server. By the time she knew who Tony Masterton was, it was too late to back out. Now she knew too much about him and his business for her own good. This wasn't going to be a problem if she danced to his tune and didn't look too hard at his activities.

On the positive side, turning an obsession with hacking online games into a career of sorts was now providing her with a comfortable existence, if a lonely one. Loneliness she was equipped to deal with – a lifetime in care makes an individual uniquely equipped for self-sufficiency in that regard. It was certainly better than the string of dead-end jobs that had kept her going before Tony appeared in her life.

Dee stopped off at the local store, picking up a couple of ready meals and a bottle of wine, exchanging good-natured banter with the guy at the till asking to see her ID even though she'd been a regular customer for at least a year. She left the shop with a lighter tread. The young girl in the car window had reminded her too much of her own childhood – passed from one care home to another like an heirloom nobody really wanted but were reluctant to throw away. During her one chance at adoption, she'd been unable to reciprocate the love freely offered; overjoyed to be welcomed into a family yet frightened of being hurt, she could give nothing in return. The final look in her new mother's tear-streaked face had stayed with her down the years, staring distraught through the car window as Dee was taken away by a social worker at the end of her wits. The husband had held her back when she lunged after the car, a final despairing wave sending Dee away.

Once back in her flat, Dee shrugged off her leathers, slammed a meal into the microwave and poured a large glass of white wine. She sank into the oversized sofa that dominated the modern apartment and turned to face the wall of glass overlooking the Clyde. The few people Dee had invited into her flat described it as 'sparsely furnished'. The only decoration was an expensive TV screen with a soundbar mounted directly underneath it.

The same tribute to minimalism continued throughout the open-plan kitchen and into the master bedroom. Dee couldn't see a problem with it. It wasn't as if she collected much detritus on her journey through life, and she could see no good reason to make a start now. No family photographs to display, no record of her own life she wanted to remember. A lifetime spent living out of a single suitcase tended to impart that aesthetic. The only place Dee's character was allowed expression lay in the second bedroom. Here a desk groaned under the weight of computer screens and associated hardware. A subdued hum pervaded the room as if a hive of electronic bees prepared for their next foray into the metaverse.

A ping announced her meal was ready. Dee took it back to her seat and ate straight out of the container, washing down the contents with another glass of wine. She briefly considered watching something on the TV, a soap or documentary to provide an impression that she wasn't alone, then decided to play music instead. The soundbar responded to a command from her mobile, and Billie Eilish's vocals declaring 'I'm not your friend' filled the cavernous space. Dee finished her second glass and left it with the others underneath the TV, walking in time with the music into her bedroom and stripped off for a shower.

Once her hair had been towelled dry, she pulled on an old T-shirt and pyjama trousers and padded through to the second bedroom. Dee nudged the mouse as she sat in her gaming chair, and her face was illuminated in the glow from three screens facing her like an electronic triptych. It was time for the queen bee to have a closer look at this private investigator that Tony Masterton had just hired. A few lightly tapped commands on the keyboard and the hive went in search of nectar.

THREE

GANGSTER

Tony Masterton relaxed in the back of the black Bentley Continental as his chauffeur expertly weaved a smooth course through stop-start Glasgow traffic. Outside the tinted windows, office blocks stretched pillars of light into a darkening November night, pedestrians leaned into a biting wind like figures in a futuristic Lowry painting. He caught glimpses of Christmas decorations, wrapped around lampposts, or suspended across streets like mutant mistletoe. It wasn't the convenient grafting of Christ's birth onto an existing pagan celebration that weighed heavily on his mind, but the cold fact of having to celebrate Christmas without a child.

Teàrlach Paterson had struck him as competent. The preliminary background checks had come back favourably, plus he'd managed to find missing children when every other agency had failed. There was less than a fool's chance he'd find Lilybet, not when Tony's own security had combed every square millimetre of ground searching for any sign of her. How had she been taken, from what was meant to be a secure location? The question lay in ambush for him at quiet moments such as these. She'd been playing unattended. He'd seen her on the decking, sitting cross-legged and fully engrossed with something that lay in her lap. A scattering of daisies had marked the spot, white petals already withered, green stalks twisted and limp. They hadn't been allowed to keep this last thing her small, nimble fingers had touched. Taken, bagged, destroyed by the forensics tests searching for DNA, fibre particles – anything that could lead to her abductors.

Lilybet had left an open wound. He had dismissed the phrase a broken heart as exaggeration, a poet's whimsy. The reality, the pain of losing a child... A broken heart could not encompass the rawness of emotion that had riven their marriage, leaving the two of them living but not alive. Greeting each day with the diminishing hope she'd be found, ending each day with that hope broken and unattainable. As days turned into weeks, weeks into months, the pain turned into an empty acceptance.

In an uncertain world, one unshakable conviction remained. Whoever had taken his child would pay.

'Take me home.' Tony released the intercom button before his chauffeur could offer an acknowledgement. He couldn't face returning to work – then another night alone in the penthouse flat. The short meeting with the PI had unsettled him more than he had expected. It had been the practical manner and flat delivery of Teàrlach Paterson's warning that Lilybet was most likely dead. He knew this. His imagination had provided all too-detailed graphic images of how she could have died. Images that ran as a sickness in the darkest corners of his mind – the door opened just a crack before being slammed shut again and leaving those horrors curling around each other. Black thoughts writhing in the snake den.

The Bentley noticeably picked up speed as it filtered onto the M8, traffic parting like the Red Sea. Tony closed his laptop with irritation, emails unanswered and work unfinished. His mind was too distracted to focus on anything other than his own thoughts, seeing his own reflection in darkened glass. Street-lights slid past in stroboscopic silence, just the faintest whisper of wind noise reached him in the isolation of his polished metal cocoon.

It was the not knowing that twisted the knife. Most parents had a body to grieve, something more substantial than elusive memory. He had the scent of her hair when he held her close to his chest, the softness of her skin, her laughter on the air – all of which inevitably faded as time callously eroded Lilybet from existence.

Samantha had blamed him for her disappearance. They'd taken what comfort they could from each other as the police and security first searched the house, then spread further afield with tracker dogs over hills and forests, divers for the loch. The long day turned into an even longer night, and at some time in the early hours, she'd pulled away only to glare at him in open hate.

'You've never even loved her. You have no capacity for love. You should have been watching her.' He could see Samantha so clearly in memory that she might have been standing in front of him now. The words spat out in pain and still ringing in his ears, her eyes accusing his. Their joint loss opening an unbridgeable chasm. He had no words to offer her, the time for physical comfort abruptly gone.

She had left him then, moved into one of the spare bedrooms, and for three years, they had warily circled each other like hyenas around a kill, unwilling to acknowledge the other in case they turned and feasted on the shared hurt and impotent rage in a frenzy of self-destruction.

He focussed on his image reflected in the smoked glass, searching for emotion, feeling his cheeks with fingertips for the tears that never came. Was he unable to love? There was no easy answer to that question. When Samantha had accused him of never loving, he knew she'd really meant her, rather than

Lilybet. Even she must have been able to see how much he loved his child, how deep and visceral that feeling flowed, how her loss had all but broken him.

Tony took comfort from poetry, a fact that would shatter a great many people's preconceptions of who and what he was. Not the Romantics he'd seen in the PI's office, although he could quote them from memory. Wordsworth, with his lines composed walking a few miles above Tintern Abbey – *The best portion of a good man's life: his little, nameless unremembered acts of kindness and love.* His was never going to be a good man's life, but you take the cards you're dealt. He favoured the more nihilistic side of T S Eliot's outpourings, the reduction of all human life to birth, fornication and death. There was a purity to that simplification of a human's messy existence. We have no choice in being born, sex is pre-programmed and exploited for reward or entertainment. Death though... death can be made to dance to his tune.

His mobile screen lit up, someone important enough to make the cut when he'd demanded privacy.

'Hello, Dee.'

'I've had a look into this Teàrlach Paterson. Clean, as far as I can tell. Spent five years working in military intelligence after the army funded him through Glasgow University. Healthy bank balance, couple of women he sees on a regular basis, no more porn in his search history than anyone else. Physically he's in good shape, last health check came back clear, except he drinks more than the three units he claims. His history has a gap of eighteen months where I've been unable to find anything, maybe he was living as a hermit somewhere? He was out of the country, otherwise I'd have picked up a trace – nothing doing on his bank accounts except for standing orders.'

Tony's interest was piqued. She hadn't drawn a blank before.

'What cases was he working on during that time period?'

There was the slightest pause.

'Only the one. The Saudi princess. He was paid over half a million sterling when the body was found, then went seriously off-grid for eighteen months. No internet, no comms, zilch.'

Tony nodded to his reflection. 'I want you to work closely with him. Do whatever he asks.'

'And report back, yeah?'

'When you find something.'

The phone screen blanked again, leaving Tony viewing it with caution. Dee was sometimes too effective for her own good. He couldn't be sure she hadn't taken over his mobile and was even now watching him from a laptop in her apartment. He resisted the urge to call security, check how secure his phone was. She'd run rings around them before. There were always the hidden cameras in her apartment, he could bring them up on screen? The thought was dismissed as soon as it surfaced – if she had compromised his phone, then he'd only alert her to the fact he kept as close an eye on her as she did on him. His lips curled upwards in a suspicion of a smile. Take surveillance too far, and it's like watching your reflection in two facing mirrors, multiple realities repeating until photons lose the will to live.

Dee was a problem best kept close to him. Valuable enough to make sure she stayed working for him and not against him. He had a copy of Sun Tzu's *Art of War* in his library, filed in the reference section next to The Bible. Only one of them had been read repeatedly, pages so thumbed that it required the pressure of other books pressing against it to keep the book fully closed.

Home was still an hour and a half away, too much time to waste in idle philosophising. He opened his laptop again, started on the emails that required a response. Work deadened the pain, made the unbearable bearable.

FOUR

MOVING GOALPOSTS

The isolated stone cottage stood adjacent to the main road. A young woman was upending a child's white plastic goalpost from the tended lawn, taking no interest in the car slowing down as it approached. Teàrlach Paterson turned into the drive, noticing a gap in the steel road safety barrier opposite the house, allowing access to the loch.

'Can I help?' She stood ten metres away, giving her time to judge whether he was a lost tourist or trouble.

'Teàrlach Paterson. I called earlier, about the Masterton child?' He motioned over the loch to the modernist building almost hidden by trees and distance. Just the top floor showed, hanging in space without any visible sign of support. From this distance, it looked like a child's discarded toy.

She took the few steps to meet him, hand extended in welcome and no longer hanging back in caution.

'Pleased to meet you.' She said the words as if she meant them, firmly gripping his hand. 'Come inside, I'll make us a cup of tea.' She turned, and an inopportune gust of wind played with her long, dark hair. She swept it out of her eyes with an impatient gesture.

Teàrlach entered the cottage, into a kitchen where he stood awkwardly whilst she filled an electric kettle, fussing over mugs and tea bags. Helen Chadwell had been the first police presence on the scene, before the city detectives took over, and scarcely merited a mention in the original notes. She'd left the force months later. He wondered if the two events were connected, the trauma of losing a young child hitting too close to home? Teàrlach ran a critical eye over the kitchen, seeing signs of her own child, the clean and ordered surfaces. His focus lingered on her until she turned around to talk.

'It's a terrible business. There's still no body. Who'd do such a thing?' She asked the question from the heart, shaking her head at the impossibility of such an event having happened on her patch. A patch he realised covered several hundred square miles of mountain and loch. The water must have been heated recently as the kettle clicked off before she'd finished placing a tea bag in both cups.

'There.' The word was spoken with the quiet satisfaction of someone who answered all life's curveballs with a cup of tea. She deftly scooped out the tea bags and dumped them in a pedal bin.

Teàrlach took the proffered cup, accepted milk and declined sugar. She spooned two generous teaspoons into her mug, stirring vigorously enough to prevent any conversation, giving him a cryptic look that made him feel he'd just failed some sort of test.

'Now, what can I do for you?'

What could she do for him? Contacting the local police was always his first move, bypassing the desk jockeys at head office to speak directly to the boots on the ground. He found it of more use than receiving a sanitised report third- or fourth-hand after being stripped of any contentious information – usually anything that could reflect badly on those in charge. In this case,

Teàrlach wasn't sure that he'd maybe started too far down the food chain to obtain anything of use at all.

'I just wanted to hear it from you.' He pulled out a kitchen bar stool, settled his frame onto the seat and attempted to make himself appear less threatening. Again, the cryptic expression.

'Aye, well. There's not a lot I can add to what's already in the report.' She looked at him hopefully.

'I'd still like to hear what you saw, in your own words.' Teàrlach attempted his most conciliatory smile as her mouth fleetingly turned down in an involuntary scowl.

Helen sat opposite him, nursing a mug of steaming tea in her hands whilst observing him from over the rim.

'There's not a lot I can add,' she repeated. A slight tremor showed in her hands, quieting as she lowered her elbows onto the table.

He waited patiently. The report had been thorough, in a stripped back police procedural sense. Time of first notification to the emergency services marked at 16:55, passed to PC Helen Chadwell arriving on scene at 17:37, escalated to missing person enquiry at 18:04. None of the usual delays before pulling out all the stops. Dogs had found no trail, covering the ground between decking and treehouse so many times the handlers had to call them off before they drove the mother insane. Divers found no body, air search saw no lost child, no abductor. No unusual activity in the area or strange vans patrolling the road that wound past the house and garden. The police had drawn a resounding blank.

'Who did you speak to when you first arrived at the house? Can you take me through it, step by step? I've read the reports, so I'm not so much interested in what you saw as much as your impressions at the time.' Teàrlach offered her another smile in encouragement. 'Even the slightest thing can be of help – anyone behaving oddly or something that struck you as peculiar. I want to hear what didn't make the report.'

Helen Chadwell thoughtfully sipped her tea as she processed Teàrlach's words.

He saw the slight nod, the understanding in her eyes before she placed the mug down on the workspace between them. The initial nervousness with which she'd started answering his questions began to fade as she relived the event.

'I'd not been to the house before. Seen it enough times, from this side of the loch. Caused a bit of a stushie when they started building it – bloody great eyesore to some minds.' She hesitated, wondering if she'd maybe said too much, then continued. 'The call came in that their daughter had gone missing. I didn't think much of it at the time. I thought she was just hiding, playing a game with them.'

'Did you treat it as an emergency?' he interrupted, noticed the guilt cross her face before she responded.

'As I said, I thought it was probably nothing. I just drove there, keeping an eye open for any suspicious people, vehicles – or the girl herself once I was close enough to the estate. They have electric gates at the end of the drive.' She mentioned the gates with a hint of scandal, pausing to add emphasis. 'The house looks a lot smaller from that side, more sunken into the ground.'

She drifted off as she replayed the memory.

'Tony Masterton was waiting for me. He'd just been dropped back at the house, climbed out of a helicopter.'

'How did he appear?'

'Calm. Unnaturally calm. You know he has that way about him, how events flow past him? He's like a rock in a river.'

She paused to take a sip from her mug, observing Teàrlach through a thin veil of coiling steam.

He visualised a helicopter perched like a dragonfly on the mown lawn, imagining the smell of cut grass – cut grass and kerosene.

'Tony told me he'd been looking for her, flying around the

house. He took me to talk to his wife. Said Glasgow were airlifting a team who'd be arriving any minute, so I left him to it.'

'How was his wife, Samantha?'

The ex-PC locked eyes with him, calculating how much to divulge.

'She was like any mother who's just lost her child, border-line hysterical.'

'You were the first on the scene. Anything strikes you now as being... unusual?'

She delayed, taking another sip from her mug and then looking over his shoulder to view the loch through the kitchen windows.

'Samantha, Mrs Masterton, was in one of the downstairs rooms. One that opened out onto the decking through floor-to-ceiling French doors. Their house was more like a film set than a home – you know, sterile. She was hunched over, holding a soft toy in her arms and rocking it like a child. She'd been crying. Another woman – the nanny – stood a distance away. She looked scared, really scared. I could feel the relief when she caught sight of my uniform. The place gave me the shivers to be honest, like something was about to explode.'

Teàrlach interrupted. 'The nanny was there when you arrived?'

'One of his people had picked her up from Inverness as soon as they realised Lilybet was missing. I think she was still in shock.'

Teàrlach swiftly calculated the driving time to Inverness.

'That's over three hours' drive. How did she get there so soon?'

'The helicopter. The family keeps one at Inverness Airport on permanent standby. It's just over an hour away if you fly. It was the same one Tony Masterton used to look for Lilybet.'

'Go on,' Teàrlach encouraged.

'I asked Mrs Masterton when the last time was she'd seen

her daughter. It's all in the report.' She spoke with an air of impatience, eager to be rid of him.

'I know, I'm just wanting to hear it from you. In case you can remember anything that could help me find her.'

She hesitated before answering.

'Samantha said Tony had seen her playing on the decking. There were daisies lying on the wood where she'd dropped them. One of his staff was standing at the edge of the loch, scanning the area with binoculars.'

'How many staff does he have at the house?' Teàrlach asked the question nonchalantly, but he watched her intently as she responded.

'Apart from the nanny, no one. This guy was the gardener – local lad. I never interviewed him; the Glasgow detectives soon made it clear that I was out of my depth.'

'Do you have a name?'

'Richard Tavistock'. She answered readily enough, but Teàrlach caught the tightness in her throat when she said his name.

He retrieved a notebook from his jacket, wrote something in longhand.

'What happened to the nanny after Lilybet's disappearance?'

She shrugged. 'I don't know. You'll have to ask them. I never went back there after that one visit – can't imagine there was much incentive to keep her at the house. Stable doors and all that.' She stood. 'Look, I'm going to have to end it here, Mr Paterson, unless you've anything specific you want to ask?'

'No, as I say, just wanted to hear it from the first professional on the ground.' Teàrlach stood as well, holding his mug and casting around ineffectually for somewhere to put it.

Helen took it from his hand and crossed over to the sink, staring out over the loch like a statue.

Teàrlach watched her as she stood with her back to him,

frozen into inaction. He wondered what he might have done to upset her, then saw the geometric outline of the Mastertons' home framed in the window behind her head.

'Were there any boats out that day, do you remember? Any way she could have been taken by water?'

She made a show of searching her memory, scanning the kitchen ceiling in search of that day.

'Nothing that I remember. There's always a boat or two out – fishing mostly, few leisure craft.'

'Thanks, you've been a great help. Do you mind if I contact you again once I've had a chance to look over the site myself?'

'Aye. No bother. But I have to get on now – the school run.'

'Of course. Thanks again for your time.'

He was acutely aware of her observing him as he climbed back into his car, taking the road north. The clouds had lowered in the short time since he'd arrived, covering the mountain summits in a dirty grey eiderdown. A chill wind gathered strength, carrying salt on its breath as it ruffled the loch's surface. He smelled snow, catching the back of his nose as he inhaled until the car's air conditioning took over.

Teàrlach's eyes were drawn to the Masterton house opposite, almost lost now as a fine mist began erasing the world. The loch waters reflected the darkening skies, becoming troubled as the wind picked up. What had made Tony Masterton build his home here, so far away from the city that was the source of his wealth? If he was looking for security, somewhere safe to raise a family, then that had spectacularly misfired.

The loch slipped out of view as the road curved away from the shore, hiding the troubled waters behind tree-clad hills until the house was no longer visible. Was that what Tony had sought, a means of erasing himself and his family out of the public's consciousness? The dangers inherent in raising such a young child on the loch shore would have been obvious, so why and for how long had she been left unattended before vanishing without leaving a trace? Neither of Lilybet's parents would welcome being faced with these questions, but he needed answers before his search could begin. Teàrlach checked the time; it would be dark when he reached the house. He pushed the speed as far as he dared on the unfamiliar roads, watching for the turn-off ahead.

FIVE

JAPANESE TREEHOUSE

I am the boatman
My fair-haired children lap
The shores of the loch

Teàrlach drove the thirty miles, following the road as it hugged the irregular shoreline of the loch towards the Masterton house. The loch waters appeared dark and foreboding under lowering winter skies, moving like oil where the chill wind was defeated by twists in the terrain. The ex-policewoman – Helen Chadwell – had answered his questions willingly enough, although twice he'd caught her watching him with a calculating expression, almost as if their roles had been reversed. As was often the case, it was the things that hadn't made the official record that sparked his interest – the admission that the modern building was not entirely welcomed or approved of by the local community. The fact that the nanny had been airlifted from Inverness almost as soon as the girl's disappearance had been noticed. Her anxiety to cut the questions short so she could make the school run.

This last concern was the easiest to explain away – he

hadn't needed to ask if she had children of her own with the football paraphernalia left lying around in the garden, scribbled drawings held against the fridge door with novelty magnets. Yet her home had the feeling of an unfinished jigsaw – no man's boots or coat in the porch, no sign that anyone other than Helen Chadwell and her child occupied the space. Teàrlach imagined becoming the missing piece, completing the picture.

Thoughts of family always brought back the same image. A mother and younger brother forever frozen in time, a father in prison, his aunt taking him to live with her in a small cottage on Mull, where she loved him like her own. Maybe they had completed their own jigsaw, just the two pieces locked together and making sense of the madness that had left him alone. Now she was gone as well, fading away whilst he travelled with the army. She'd never let on in any of the calls he'd made home, never told him she was dying. He felt as if she had betrayed him even though he knew she was trying to let him live his life without worry, leaving him alone with his guilt.

Teàrlach let the memories go. The past was a land best left untravelled.

He focussed on the case in hand.

The locals not liking the modernist architecture jutting out into the loch was predictable enough. Nimbyism exists every- where – perhaps never more so than in rural backwaters that rely on retirees and holidaymakers for dependable income. Not that he'd expect any lingering resentment to translate into child abduction, but he filed it away for consideration. The nanny being there when the policewoman had first arrived... that hadn't been mentioned in the original reports. Was that a purposeful omission? She hadn't been questioned originally, but then she wasn't at the house when the girl went missing, so Helen concentrating on the girl's parents made sense. The nanny was only mentioned when the Glasgow detectives came onto the scene, policework by numbers.

The car headlights came on automatically as the grey skies noticeably darkened. Teàrlach checked the time – 15:30. It was almost sunset. The satnav confirmed a turn-off at the next junction, and he concentrated on the route ahead. Deer were a problem on these roads, running from surrounding forest and meeting the twenty-first century full tilt in a two-hundred kilo explosion of blood, sinew, steel and glass. The tarmac resembled an abattoir some days: frogs as thin as parchment; hedgehog spines proving inadequate protection; bloated badgers and deer thrown too late onto the refuge offered by the verge. Ahead of him twin dark metal gates loomed out of the gathering dusk, LED lamps emphasising their geometric rigidity. Teàrlach unbuckled his safety belt, reaching for the door handle when the gates noiselessly opened. He drove on, following the curve of a drive illuminated by ground level lights that resembled a runway, then parked beside a black Bentley. A rectangle of light appeared in the otherwise featureless concrete, a figure standing in the doorway as floodlights erupted into life causing him to squint in pain.

'Mr Paterson. I was expecting you earlier.'

The figure in the doorway remained indistinct, but he recognised the voice. 'I made a detour. Is this an inconvenient time?'

Tony Masterton didn't answer, turning back into the house and leaving the door wide open in invitation. The place was a testament to minimalism, set in a building that could quite as easily have served purpose as a modern art gallery or mausoleum. Anything but a home.

'Do you want anything, tea, coffee – something stronger after your drive?' Tony's voice echoed off polished concrete walls as he led deeper into the house.

'No, thanks. Can you show me where your daughter was last seen?'

Tony abruptly stopped, turned to face him with the onset of anger in his expression. Anger or pain, it was difficult to say.

'Straight to business.' He nodded to himself as if in confirmation. 'Out here. She was playing on the decking.'

They approached their own reflections mirrored in a full-height glass wall. Teàrlach recognised the room Helen Chadwell had described – the mother sat holding a stuffed toy, the nanny stood frozen with shock. The glass wall slid open, and he stepped out onto the decking, where cold damp air blew into his face carrying a scent of the sea. Floodlights detected their movement, illuminating the decking and throwing the loch and surrounding hills into blackness. A glass balustrade caught the artificial light and threw it back, diffused in grey safety glass so that the decking appeared to be bounded by an insubstantial wall of fog. Teàrlach crossed over to rest his hands on the glass, half expecting the illusion to be real, but his fingers encountered a solid enough surface.

The balustrade was just over a metre tall; too high for a three-year-old to clamber over unaided? Teàrlach stared out over the loch, allowed time for his eyes to adjust to the artificial lighting. Pinpricks of light showed on the far shore where individual houses announced their presence, too dark now to make out anything other than the shape of the hills rising into charcoal skies. One of those distant lights held Helen and her child. He imagined her son drawing at the kitchen table, his mother chatting inconsequential nonsense as pots boiled, the absence of a father reminding him so sharply of his own childhood that he locked the thought down. Water slapped against foundations under the decking, a rhythmic wet percussion repeated along the shoreline with muted splashes. The temperature had dropped in the last hour. Teàrlach pulled his jacket in tighter, regretting not dressing more appropriately for December.

'Where's the treehouse?'

Teàrlach forced his eyes away from the featureless water,

almost fluid obsidian now the grey winter light had been absorbed by the rapid onset of darkness. From this angle, he could clearly see the three rectangular architectural blocks, piled up in stark white above his head. Tony Masterton stared at him as he took in his surroundings, his expression as featureless as the loch.

'Across the meadow. It's a short walk.' His features expressed irritation. 'Wouldn't it be better to look at this in daylight?'

'I have a torch.'

Teàrlach could feel Tony Masterton's eyes boring into his back as he turned away. The decking extended the width of the house before abutting seamlessly to lawn. He retrieved a small flashlight from his jacket, playing the beam across the grass. Dew was already forming, miniature jewels reflecting from each blade, so he had the impression of walking across a star-filled sky. Footsteps left an imprint in his wake, perfectly replicating the outline of each step. Water droplets, shaken loose by his movement clung to his shoes and trousers. He could feel the cold leaching into his skin and again berated himself for wearing city clothes, city shoes.

The treehouse held dark council ahead of him, visible more by an absence of light as if the timber building hungrily devoured the last of the dusk. Grass grew longer here – the meadow Tony had called it. Teàrlach could see no obvious path, so now the dew was soaking up to his thighs. In this miniscule jungle, cobwebs hung heavy with moisture, catching the torch-light as he swung it around. The incessant breeze picked up a notch once he'd cleared the shelter offered by the building, emphasising the cold in his lower extremities. Tony Masterton must have re-entered the house as the outdoor floods cut off, leaving him essentially blind except for a narrow cone of light. He couldn't shake off the conviction that the man was making a point. Leaving him to pursue a fool's errand in the darkness.

The treehouse was more substantial than he had pictured from the files. This was no ready-built toy building – a mock fort or cutesy cottage on stilts as he had supposed. The building bore more of a resemblance to the main house now that he circled it. From the angle he'd approached, same as the photographs he'd viewed, it was a standard geometric rectangle constructed from substantial wooden beams. From the sides, it resembled a Tetris puzzle or modernistic Japanese architecture, the joints refusing to submit to Pythagorean right-angles beloved of Western mores but hitting each other at angles more in keeping with Mikado. Looking more closely at the seemingly random joints, he could see they locked together in complex Tsugite shapes, a testament both to the ingenuity of the architect's vision as well as the woodworker's craft.

A circular door formed the entrance, green paint the only splash of colour on an otherwise natural wood exterior. The door swung open easily on his touch, easy enough for three-year-old fingers to operate. Cobwebs held guard in the passage beyond, proof enough that no one had been inside for a long time. For three years?

Teàrlach's question was answered as lights came on, triggered by his movement. The corridor opened out into a vaulted room beyond, blankets and cushions spread over the floor. A child's book lay open, a giant teddy leaning drunkenly against a wall where it had been carelessly left. Covering everything was a shroud of gossamer spun by a legion of spiders. Teàrlach was not a betting man, he left that to the desperate or those unfortunate enough to misunderstand what the odds were trying to tell them, but the webs confirmed the treehouse had been left empty since the girl's disappearance.

That simple observation raised the biggest question of all.

He pushed through the insubstantial curtains, trying not to think about the number of arachnids hitching a ride or their desiccated remnants catching in his hair. It was surprisingly spacious inside, the dimensions better suited to an adult than a child. Teàrlach only crouched to avoid the worst of the webs, arms covered in sticky white tracery. A staircase wound up against one wall, taking him to a smaller room above the main floor. This floor was covered with cushions, mould visible in the artificial light. This would be the den where Lilybet loved to look at her picture books or sleep warm afternoons away. This would be the last room her mother frantically explored before realising her daughter was missing.

Teàrlach gave one last glance around and headed back to the house. Tony opened the doors as he crossed the decking and triggered the lights into illumination.

'Well?' The question issued as a challenge.

'I'm not expecting to see anything the police and your security may have overlooked, if that's what you're asking,' Teàrlach answered evenly. Tony Masterton held his gaze for a moment, then turned away with a bored expression.

'I'm about to have a drink. Can I get you anything?'

'I'd like a word with your wife if that's possible. Then I must drive to my accommodation, so I'll pass on the drink, thanks.'

'You could stay here. There are spare rooms.'

'I find it easier to stay a distance from where I'm working. Keeps it... fresh.'

'As you will. I'll ask my wife to meet you here.' Tony made as if to say something more, but held back, issuing a brief nod as he left Teàrlach on his own.

Samantha Masterton appeared so noiselessly that Teàrlach started at the sight of her, catching her reflection as he stared through the French windows into the darkness beyond. She hovered above the decking at the exact spot Lilybet had last been seen, a Pepper's ghost. He turned on the spot to see her in the flesh, tall and willowy, wet blond hair cascading over her narrow shoulders like Ophelia newly risen from her watery grave.

'I'm sorry, I've just come out of the shower.' She began wrapping a towel around her head, bending down to fasten the ends into a knot so it stayed fixed in place like a white turban. 'Tony said you wanted to speak with me?' She fixed him with a stare that wasn't entirely welcoming.

'My name is—'

'I know who you are, Mr Paterson. Shall we just dispense with the pleasantries, and you ask your questions.'

'Of course.' Teàrlach retrieved his notebook and pen from his jacket, brushing away the cobwebs that still adhered. She and Tony Masterton shared similar characteristics. 'I was wondering if you could tell me about the day Lilybet went missing. Where were you whilst she was outside – when you first realised she had gone?'

'This has all been gone over countless times, I can see no cause to have me relive those moments again.' Samantha's expression veered from icy towards irritation. They faced each other across the room like two gunslingers, each waiting on the other to break. In the end, she acquiesced, sighing her displeasure and taking a seat that forced him to shift position to face her. Teàrlach remained standing, not wanting to leave damp patches on the furniture. He waited patiently whilst she fidgeted, her long fingers flexing in what he supposed was desperation for a cigarette.

'I'd left Lilybet playing outside. It was a hot summer's day – the French windows were wide open to the decking. She was playing with daisies. The nanny was teaching her how to join them to make a bracelet. She was far too young to manage, but they enjoyed being together.' Samantha's tone hardened as she made this comment and she paused, breathed deeply and focussed on her hands as she interlinked her fingers to stop them writhing.

'Tony could see her from his study.' She indicated the floors above with a tilt of her head. 'I had some things to be getting on with, so I left her playing and went through to my workshop at the back of the house.' She saw the flash of interest in his expression and answered before he'd had the chance to formulate a question.

'Bonsai, Mr Paterson. Like much of Japanese life they manage to combine art with intelligence, something so sadly lacking in our own culture.'

Teàrlach remained silent, thinking of the treehouse and its unusual design – the Tsugite carpentry.

'It was coming up to teatime.' She stopped, glared at him with anger. 'Is all this strictly necessary?'

'It can help me understand the picture, Mrs Masterton.' His eyes were drawn to the glass wall, the room mirrored back at him.

'What picture? In case you hadn't noticed that's a fucking blank canvas you're looking at!'

He met her eyes in the glass reflection. The floodlights had turned off, nothing but blackness outside with their insubstantial images looking back at them.

'You left her at 4pm, coming back to call her in for tea at 4:30. Is that correct?' he replied evenly.

He watched her face contorting, readying for a riposte. Then her features settled back into impassivity.

'That's correct. In that half an hour something happened. Something my husband would have seen if he wasn't so fucking involved in his spreadsheets.'

'You didn't see or hear anything? No response when you called her name?'

'No, Mr Paterson. If there had been, then we wouldn't have need of you.' She stood, announcing this meeting was at an end. 'You can find your own way out.' Samantha left as silently as she had appeared, soft shoes making no sound on the polished concrete floor.

Teàrlach made his way back to the front door, operating the

handle with some difficulty – a combination of pushing and twisting before the lock released. It was unlikely a three-year-old could have managed it unaided. The cold leached immediately into his trousers, causing him to hurry to the car before he literally iced up. Their stories appeared to match the statements he'd read, so why did he have a nagging doubt that something was being kept back? And why so keen to cut short their interviews when they'd hired him to find out what had happened to their daughter?

SIX

MIDSOMMAR IN MIDWINTER

Teàrlach reached his hotel at 18:00, a white-washed inn overlooking the loch. Chloe had taken care of the booking, finding him a comfortable yet anonymous location that clung onto an old-world charm. He threw his overnight bag down on the bed, opened his laptop and wrote up the little he'd been able to glean from the ex-policewoman and the Mastertons. The place had internet, almost as slow as dial-up used to be, but good enough for him to download emails.

The bar was empty when he made his way downstairs, taking a seat on a bar stool and selecting a Lagavulin twelve-year-old single malt. The drink was smooth on his palate, a smoky finish lingering much like the scent from the nearby open fire.

'You here on business?' The bartender interrupted his contemplation, forcing his attention away from the dancing flames to look at his interrogator more closely. The guy was in his forties, big ginger beard making his face appear twice as large. Judging by the red veins spreading out from his nose, he enjoyed the merchandise.

'Aye. I'm a private investigator, looking into the Masterton girl's disappearance.'

If the bartender was surprised by his candour, it didn't show.

'Only two reasons people come here out of season.' He picked up a glass, polishing it with the white cloth anchored to his belt before holding it up to overhead lights for inspection. 'Work or romance.' The glass rotated in thick fingers, passed muster and was placed back on a shelf. 'And you're here on your own, so that'll be work.' He smiled, somewhere under the facial hair, pleased to have made his own investigation public.

Teàrlach shrugged unconcernedly. 'Is that the menu?'

He was handed a sheet of paper, announcing he was in MacSween's Bar and Bistro.

'Unusual name.'

The bartender settled his elbows on the counter. 'You'd be interested in the story behind that name, being a detective an' all.'

Teàrlach made an encouraging noise, turning his attention back to the menu. The bartender continued, oblivious.

'Some centuries ago, a local laird – MacSween – had fallen on hard times and was reduced to stealing sheep. The punishment for this was hanging, and he was taken to Inveraray where he was summarily hanged, and his widow sent to collect his body. She fetched him in a rowing boat but spotted him moving under his shroud when they were halfway across the water and fed him a mixture of breastmilk and whisky.'

Teàrlach lowered his glass at this point, wondering if every customer was fed this tale.

'He immediately sprung to his feet as fit as a fiddle, and they landed not far from here. There's a cairn that bears his name.' The bartender added this defensively as Teàrlach's expression must have expressed incredulity. 'He couldn't be tried again for the same offence under Scots law, so lived for a good age before being buried locally.'

He observed Teàrlach shrewdly from under thick ginger eyebrows. 'An' that's no' the only thing that comes back from the dead.'

'I'm sorry. You've lost me?'

'The wee lassie, the Masterton girl.'

'What do you mean – do you know anything about her disappearance?' Teàrlach tilted his empty glass for a refill. The bartender filled a metal measure to the brim and upended it into his glass, golden liquid catching and reflecting the flames.

He leaned in, lowering his voice although they were the only two in the bar.

'Some say she was taken by a kaelpie, snatched from the garden by a spirit angered by the building of such a modern monstrosity.'

Teàrlach processed this unlikely information with equanimity. 'And this is a common explanation for the missing child?'

'I'm no' the only one. That loch is deep, man. There's no telling what creatures inhabit the depths.'

'You've not been to Glasgow then?' Teàrlach countered.

The bartender nodded seriously. 'I'll give you that. But not everything can be explained by recourse to logic. That girl will come back, one way or another.'

The sound of a motorbike intruded. A throaty roar as the throttle was given a final burst, gravel spraying outside the window as it slew to a halt. They watched the door open. A diminutive biker closed the door, crossing the room to face the open fire. Two hands lifted off the helmet, revealing a cascade of wavy red hair which she shook until her hair regained volume. She shrugged a backpack off her narrow shoulders, placing it and her helmet down on a table, adding leather gloves so her fingers could benefit from the heat.

'I'll have whatever Teàrlach's drinking.' Her eyes fixed his with amusement, watching as he tried and failed to recognise her.

'I'm sorry, have we met?'

'Dee Fairlie. We both work for the same guy.' She called out to the bartender. 'I've a room booked for the week.'

He placed a whisky glass down next to Teàrlach's. 'Water, ice?'

'As it comes, thanks.' She touched glasses, downing the measure in one. 'Same again. Have you eaten?'

Teàrlach handed over his menu.

'Venison pie.' She made the decision instantly. 'Which room am I in?'

'Three, overlooking the loch.' The bartender's eyes had adopted a restless up and down motion, scanning her with obvious interest.

'Key?' she asked.

'Room's open, waiting for you.'

'Great. Be back down once I've had a chance to wash off the road and then we can talk.' This was directed at Teàrlach. She downed the second glass as quickly as she had the first, following the direction indicated by the bartender's finger. He watched her until lost from view, then reluctantly returned his attention back to Teàrlach.

'Have you decided – from the menu?'

'I'll have the same.' Teàrlach scanned the tables, identified one far enough away to talk without being overheard. 'We'll be sitting over there.'

'I'll have the chef bring it over. Should be thirty minutes or so.'

Dee made a reappearance just as two plates of food were delivered to the table by a young lad dressed in whites with a blue apron. He balanced them on one arm, leaving a hand free to first place a stainless-steel vegetable dish on the table before flourishing plates in front of them.

Teàrlach waited until their waiter had gone, focussing on the woman piling her plate with carrots and broccoli. Her hair was that shade of red that is common on the West coast of Scotland, a genetic remnant from the earliest settlers travelling north from Asia in search of a weaker sun. Freckles scattered across her nose, dividing two grey-green analytical eyes that met his in amusement. She was above average height, maybe five foot eight, and slim, but she had to be strong to handle the bike. It required strength merely to rest it onto its stand.

'Good for you.' Dee spoke through a mouthful of food, gesturing encouragingly at the remaining vegetables.

'How did you know I was here?'

'Tracked your phone.' She gestured to the bartender whose attention hadn't shifted from her since she'd first arrived. 'Bottle of red. You have merlot?'

Teàrlach frowned, unconvinced she was able to track him and yet here she was, arriving scarcely an hour after he'd booked in. No, it was more likely someone had fitted a tracker to his car. He made a mental note to have the car scanned as soon as he was back in Glasgow.

'You don't think I can do that, right?' Dee's eyes danced with amusement.

'Track my phone? I think it unlikely.'

She stopped eating for long enough to pull her mobile out of a pocket, keying a few rapid movements before placing it down between them like a gauntlet. The conversation he'd just had with the bartender played through the speaker until Dee cut it off.

'Ooh. No telling what creatures inhabit the depths.' Her eyes grew large, flicking from side to side in mock horror. 'It's all a bit Midsommar.'

Teàrlach's confusion must have been plain as she elaborated for him.

'Wicker Man. Pagan horror stuff.' She continued emptying her plate, shifting forkfuls like someone who hadn't eaten for days.

'How long have you been spying on me?' Teàrlach asked tersely.

Dee cleared her plate before responding.

'Since Tony Masterton asked me to keep tabs on you.' Her head tilted slightly as she watched his response.

Teàrlach held back the words waiting on his tongue, replacing them with the polite version.

'Aye. OK. He let me know you'd be making yourself known.'

She nodded, then took the wine bottle from the bartender before he'd had the chance to attempt the pantomime of a tasting, filling two glasses and pushing one over to Teàrlach.

'Well, good to meet you in the flesh. Sláinte.' She raised her glass expectantly, waiting until Teàrlach's glass touched hers. 'Here's to finding the girl!'

'I don't wish to be rude, Dee. But I prefer to work on my own. Without someone listening in to my every conversation.'

'Oh, I'm not intending to hang around with you as you interview the whole glen. And if you leave your phone behind, then I can't keep tabs on you. No, I'm just here to introduce myself and make myself available. In case you need anything.'

He met her eyes, read her like a book.

'I don't think you've anything I need.'

She laughed at this, throwing her head back so her hair flowed around her face like a red veil, settling back on her shoulders as she leaned towards him. 'You sure of that?'

They regarded each other across the table, taking measure. A flicker of disappointment crossed her face as she broke eye contact.

'OK. To business then.' Dee fetched a battered laptop out of the bag she'd placed at her feet, checked the bartender was unable to see the screen and then tapped a staccato tattoo across the keyboard.

'I've sent you the video.' Her voice had dropped to more of a whisper. 'It's not pretty. You can draw your own conclusions, but someone paid to have her tortured. You find out who that was, and I'll find the evidence to put him away.'

'Do you have a geographical location for where this happened?'

'Still working on it. Looks like Rotterdam, but I can't be sure because they routed it via zombie servers.' She caught his puzzled expression. 'They tried to hide the IP address which would help me find where this originated.' Her face brightened. 'I like a challenge, though.'

They were interrupted by the bar door being flung open, a wild-eyed man blinking in the sudden light.

'I need a drink. Make it a double.' He brushed lank hair away from a pinched face, offering a cursory glance towards their table and headed straight for the bar.

'What's the matter, Jamie? You look like you've seen a ghost.' The bartender poured a generous measure, only for it to be snatched out of his hand and downed by the newcomer.

'Worse than that. There's a dead guy sitting at Moses' Spring.'

'Hell's Glen?'

The newcomer nodded, pushing his glass for a refill. 'I stopped to see if he needed a lift. Saw him in the headlights.' Jamie shook his head, unwilling to believe the evidence of his own eyes. 'I thought he was asleep, or maybe unconscious or something.'

A second double followed the first down his throat. 'His face had been beaten to pulp. Then I saw the hole in his chest.

Jesus! There was a gaping hole in his chest!' He shook his head in denial again.

'Do you want me to call the ambulance?' the bartender offered, only to receive a look of pure incredulity.

'An ambulance? He needs a fucking undertaker! Set up another, I'm going to call the polis. The shit's about to hit the fan big time.'

Jamie left the bar, opening a door into a small cubicle that contained a public telephone.

Teàrlach viewed the meat on his plate with a sudden loss of appetite. Dee tucked into hers without any hesitation, eyes intent on the newcomer as he returned to the bar.

'And there I was thinking this was going to be a total waste of a week.'

Dee's eyes positively sparkled.

SEVEN

HEARTLESS

PC Catherine Roylance played the beam of her torch over the figure slumped on the bench. She shivered, hugging her arms closer to her chest to counter the chill mist rising from the ground, sending the torchlight on an erratic journey, then hastily aimed the beam to encompass the corpse once more. The sound of water spilling from a carved lion's mouth into a stone basin supplied the only soundtrack – that and Sergeant Jock Daniels being sick just a short distance away, and he wouldn't appreciate being floodlit during that performance.

The call had come in just after 7:00pm. A garbled description about a half-eaten body found by a local roofer on his way back from a job. They'd dropped PC Spence at the pub to interview the witness, but she didn't hold out any hope of gaining anything useful. The guy was already three sheets to the wind and working determinedly towards passing out completely. She thought wistfully of the bar with its open fire whilst the sergeant spat the last remnants of his stomach contents into the burn. He had taken a closer look than she'd risked, angling his flashlight into the body cavity. Even from a distance she could see a gory mess where the guy's heart should be, a ragged circular hole taking the place of ribs and sternum. Now the sergeant was bent double over a stone bridge parapet, the car's rear lights catching him in ruddy hues.

Catherine risked another look at the body. She was no detective, but someone must have taken a power tool to his chest, cutting through flesh and bone with a circle hole cutter. The sort of thing a roofer might have in his toolkit. She tried to imagine someone doing that to another human. Was the victim alive when it happened? The bloodied mess where his face should have been implied he was at least unconscious if not already dead. Would anyone remain unconscious with a hole saw cutting through their sternum and rib cage? It was beyond her understanding. The press was going to have a field day with this – murder in Hell's Glen.

'I'm going to call in the Major Investigation Team.' Sergeant Jock Daniels called out, wiping his mouth with the cuff of his uniform before climbing back into the patrol car.

Catherine didn't respond. She didn't entirely trust the bile rising in her throat not to continue its upward journey if she opened her mouth, so remained silent. That meant she was stuck here for the rest of her shift until they sent someone out with a forensics team. True to form the rain started, caught in some indeterminate state between ice and water and carried on a strengthening wind pulled down from the surrounding mountains. Her uniform was insufficiently insulated for this and the body on the bench wasn't going anywhere. She joined the sergeant in the patrol car, both staring into the black void that lay beyond the reach of the car sidelights. Almost as an afterthought, the sergeant switched on the blues – casting the crime scene in stroboscopic flashes, so the corpse appeared to dance on his seat.

* * *

PC Spence – PC Simon Pence as he preferred to be known – received the update from his sergeant with equanimity. He'd drawn the long straw, dropped off at the pub to interview Jamie Coughlan whilst the other two were freezing their arses off in the hills. So far, he'd not managed to obtain any more information than they had already been given over the phone. Jamie's speech had descended into slurred syllables, devoid of any meaningful content. Now he slumped at a table, surrounded by a sea of shot glasses and grinning inanely at the couple eating dinner by the fire. He'd tried to take Jamie away to somewhere less public, but by the time they'd arrived, he'd already lost the use of his legs. PC Spence was aware he was the focus of attention – the redhead at the nearby table was lapping up every word. Her partner found the content of his laptop screen of more interest, plugging in earphones to drown out the theatre playing out in front of him.

'Do you mind if I just check your van, Jamie? Have you used any power tools recently?'

Jamie searched his pockets, frowning in confusion until his fingers encountered a bunch of keys, dropping them on the table and causing a shot glass to roll towards the table edge. PC Spence stopped it before the glass made the floor, spared a glance at Jamie's stupidly pleased expression and left the bar.

The van was slewed across the car park, carelessly covering two parking spaces. PC Spence triggered the remote before remembering to pull on his latex gloves, then shone a torch around the inside. The cab contained the usual detritus – *The Sun* newspaper on the passenger seat along with an empty sandwich box; coffee cups on the floor; big bottle of Irn Bru jammed in the dash. He opened the back doors, revealing a toolbox and work-clothes thrown in a heap. No power tools, just hammers, saws, chisels, a tin of sealant. Nothing with a speck of blood that he could see. From what the sergeant had let slip, he'd have expected the whole van to be covered in blood if

Jamie was involved. The PC lifted a fluorescent jacket off the floor, checked the crowbar underneath. No blood, just a dusting of rust proving it hadn't recently been wiped clean of incriminating evidence.

He returned to the pub just as Jamie folded face-first onto the table, avoiding every shot glass with the precision of the truly pissed.

'You're not gonnae be getting any sense out of him. He's totally bladdered.' The bartender's opinion fell on deaf ears. 'Can you at least give me a hand taking him through to the residents' lounge? I can't have him passed out in the bar.'

PC Simon Pence lifted one arm over his shoulder, waiting for the bartender to do the same, and they half carried, half dragged Jamie out of sight.

* * *

'This is fucking brilliant!' Dee enthused, pouring the last of the bottle into both wine glasses. Teàrlach was too late covering his.

'I don't want it. You have it.'

Dee shrugged, pulling both glasses to her side of the table.

'What do you think of that, Mr PI? A murder in the neighbourhood. Do you think it's some kind of vampire?' She asked the question half-jokingly.

Teàrlach closed the screen, slid the laptop back to its owner.

'I don't really have an opinion. If there's no connection to the missing girl, then I'm really not interested.'

She considered him, finishing one glass off.

'What of the video then? What do you make of that?'

Teàrlach pursed his lips. The video was graphic, only too real. He could still hear the woman's screams, abruptly stopped as her airway was cut and replaced with wet bubbling. Her executioner had taken care to cover his face – there was little doubt it was a man. The method and knife were those favoured by ISIS although copycat murders left that analysis open to question.

'I need the audio cleaned up. Is that something you can do?'

'I just find the material. It's up to you what you do with it.' Dee started on the last glass as the bartender and PC returned.

Teàrlach nodded. 'I'll deal with it.' He stood, towering over her. 'Text me your number. If I need your help, I'll be in touch, otherwise enjoy your break.'

Dee took the dismissal without care, although several whiskies and the best part of a bottle of merlot probably helped with that. She'd been expecting him to have a Glaswegian accent, his slow and deliberate delivery owed more to the Western Isles. The musical cadence of his words spoke of the sea and sky, not of that Dear Green Place. Dee stood unsteadily, headed towards the bar.

'What shots was your man on?' Her head tilted in the direction of Jamie's table, still festooned with shot glasses.

'Kamikaze. It's a mix of vodka...' The barman wasn't given the chance to finish.

'Doesn't matter. I'll have one as a nightcap.'

'Excuse me, miss, but haven't you had enough?' The PC felt duty-bound to intervene, especially as he was in uniform.

Dee fixed him with a look that would have withered a more empathic individual than PC Spence, then called out to the bartender. 'Make that two.' Her eyes remained locked firmly on the constable who looked away in confusion.

'Can I ask whose body you've found?' Dee pressed home her advantage.

PC Spence looked nonplussed. 'This is a live investigation, I'm not at liberty to provide any information.' The words sounded pompous even as he spoke. Behind the bar, a look of fleeting disappointment crossed the bartender's face as a potential source of gossip dried up.

'Doesn't sound much like a live investigation from what I heard.' Dee tipped the two shot glasses down her throat in swift succession, gave them both her sweetest smile and followed the direction Teàrlach had taken moments ago. 'Night all. Sweet dreams.'

EIGHT

LOCH DIVING

The sleet had cleared by morning. Weak sunlight illuminated the horizon at the head of the loch, catching hills dusted in snow and throwing them in sharp relief against a pale blue sky. Twenty miles away from the hotel where Teàrlach and Dee were staying, a group of four divers went through the buddy check ritual – air supplies, valves and masks – then clambered into a RIB moored against the ferry pontoon. The air temperature was hovering around zero, ice clung to each blade of grass. On days such as these it was warmer in the water.

Once safety checks were complete, the RIB took the divers a short distance offshore. The engine sounded like a submerged motorcycle, echoing across the surface of the loch. Cormorants lifted from vantage points at the sudden intrusion, taking to the air like black pterodactyls. Once in position, the coxswain cut the engine and coasted to a halt near a mooring buoy. The loch returned to silence as the RIB engine coughed its last, leaving the boat bobbing in the slight swell. After the dive leader gave the all-clear to his passengers, they followed him, tipping backwards off the side into the cold, dark water.

Overhead, a phalanx of geese cut the air with a perfect V, honking a warning as they plunged earthwards until hidden behind a row of trees. The coxswain made himself comfortable, legs stretched out to catch what little heat the sun offered whilst he waited for the divers to resurface. He set the timer for forty minutes, leaving sufficient safety margin for air reserves. The weather report had shown an area of high pressure providing ideal calm conditions for a dive, but this sea loch could change in an instant – turning from tranquil to ferocious in the space of mere minutes. He took a mental note of the green beacon position, marking the western extent of the Oitir – the shingle spit extending one and a half kilometres from shoreline into the loch – triangulated his position with the opposing red beacon off the western shore and waited.

As the most inexperienced diver, Meg had been paired with the dive leader. He'd taken a tangent to the rest of the group, leaving the other pair to continue some twenty metres down to the sea floor to survey sea grass. The plan was for him and Meg to dive nearer the gravel spit doing much the same, staying in more shallow waters to avoid the need for decompression stops. Once beneath the two-metre freezing freshwater runoff, they transitioned through the peat-infused thermocline, and she began to enjoy the sensation of gliding through warmer water. Her vision played tricks with her here as the water grew progressively more sepia, weird jiggles affecting her eyesight until they dropped beyond the freshwater layer and into salt-water proper. She was hoping to see starfish despite the generally dismissive comments from the rest of the team about the lack of any sea-life to be expected on the shingle.

The dive leader indicated a direction for them to survey and swam off a short distance away from her. He remained observant, watching her regularly whilst he worked away at noting how much sea grass, what types of seaweed and sea creatures made the transect he'd selected home. His torch remained mostly static so he could focus in on one small area, catching a scallop shell opening and illuminating two hundred shiny eyes lining its mantle. Meg turned her attention to scan the small, irregular stones forming the underwater body of this long spit of land. Her torch swept erratically, never staying long enough in one place for her to properly see the velvet crabs, scallops or colourful anemones clutching rocks hidden amongst the seaweed. The red of a starfish eventually caught her eye, anchored onto a white stone, larger than the others. She gently moved the creature with a gloved hand to reveal more of the smooth boulder, the water clouding with sediment. As it cleared, she could see that this wasn't stone and brushed away the gravel partly concealing it, scooping handfuls behind her until she saw the unmistakable outline of eye sockets.

Screaming isn't easy to do with a regulator clamped in your jaw, but she managed anyway. Alerted by her panicked reaction, the instructor closed in on her, taking a grip of her kit and making eye contact. Once he was certain she was breathing more normally, he motioned for her to be calm and pointed upwards to end the dive. That was before he saw what she'd uncovered. Displaying more calm than he felt, he tied the surface marker buoy to a rock near the skull and paired Meg as they both slowly followed the tethered line to the surface.

Two long hours later, the Dive and Marine Unit arrived from Greenock and had taken over the investigation. The divers were by now exchanging subdued conversations in the nearby pub, spread over the settees surrounding an open fire. The staff listened, piecing together the story of a human skull found embedded in the Oitir just half a kilometre away. Meg and the dive leader were briefly questioned outside and then allowed back into the warmth. By now, word had spread, and the bar started filling up with locals, noses unashamedly pressed to windows as the police launched a black RIB into the water. The crew of six police divers motored out to the location the coxswain had indicated, closer to the gravel spit than he had originally moored and commenced their dive.

A few onlookers even took binoculars, wandering out to stand on the edge of the pier to obtain the clearest view possible. Whatever occurred under the surface remained a mystery, but everyone's attention was drawn to the police coxswain as he heaved a black bag from a diver's hand. He replaced it with a new bag, lowering it over the side where it was pulled under the surface and out of sight. This procedure repeated over the next few hours, long after the most dedicated observer had taken refuge back in the warmth of the bar. The sound of an approaching outboard attracted everyone's attention once more, and they spilled outside to watch in silence as the black bags were packed away into the police van.

One of the divers crossed over to them, still wearing his dry suit.

'We've found human remains, buried by the gravel. Can I ask that nobody disturbs the site as this is now an active investigation and it may contain critical forensics?' The question was more of a warning. 'Anyone found to have dived in the vicinity of this area will be prosecuted to the full extent of the law. Am I understood?'

A sea of nodding heads responded.

'Good. We'll be posting a notice to that effect on the end of the pier, but I'd be grateful if you could make sure word gets out.' He made to turn away, hesitated before addressing the crowd again. 'You can expect to see some police activity over the next few days and a detective will be wanting to speak to locals. It would help us if you could think about any events that happened in the vicinity a year or so ago, anyone reported drowned or missing.' His eyes flicked downwards, voice quieter. 'Any child.'

He left it at that, turning away and unaware of the flicker of interest that shot through the crowd like wildfire. There was only the one child reported missing in the last few years, and she belonged to the Mastertons.

NINE

TEA WITH ANNIE

I am the mother
He held me as I gave birth
Hands red with my blood

Teàrlach pulled back the curtains, surprised to see the loch reflecting the blue of an early winter sky and light spilling golden on the hills. The view had completely changed from yesterday's heavy grey cloud. Overnight rain had lashed at these same windows when he finally turned in last night, running the video repeatedly through audio processing until he had isolated what he needed. His brows drew down in irritation as he pictured Dee's face replaying the conversation he'd had with the barman last evening, using his own phone to spy on him. She was good, he had to give her that, and so far, at least she was working with him and not against him. He toyed with the idea of removing the SIM card, making her surveillance of him that more difficult. But then he'd have to start afresh with a new laptop, replace all the IT at the office if he really wanted her tentacles prised off his business – and it would only take her a short while to get back in.

He emailed Chloe, explained Dee had compromised all the computers and mobiles and warned her to be careful what she shared. Her response pinged back before he'd finished shaving, acknowledging his warning and sending contact details for the Mastertons' gardener. His name had appeared in the reports as being present for the search immediately following Lilybet's disappearance, and Helen Chadwell had mentioned she'd seen him scanning the loch shore when she'd arrived. Something about the way Helen had paused when mentioning the gardener had caught his attention, sufficient for him to be added as a person of interest in his notebook. Chloe had turned up nothing of significance researching Jane Whiting's background. The nanny hadn't been able to find any other childcare jobs after the Masterton child and had drifted from one low-paid job to the next until her appearance in the video. Teàrlach fired off another email asking where she found the money to take herself abroad. Dee would be reading their exchanges – maybe it would spark her interest enough to hack Jane Whiting's bank account.

Teàrlach gave breakfast a miss, more from wanting to avoid Dee than any other reason, and he followed the road heading south along the east side of the loch. The gardener's cottage was a few miles past the entrance to the Mastertons' house, tucked away from the road along a rough track and hidden by trees. He wouldn't have guessed a gardener lived there. Shrubs had colonised the lawn, encroaching on a miniature Serengeti; a palm tree spread incongruous tropical leaves over a wintery Scottish vista. Concerned he may have driven to the wrong house, Teàrlach consulted his notebook. Annie Tavistock, Cuastaigh – that was the name he'd seen on the mailbox mounted at the start of the track. Maybe being a gardener was the same as other trades, do anything to avoid taking a busman's holiday.

The paint was peeling on the front door, strands of green hanging onto the wood like fine strands of seaweed. He knocked and stood back, waiting. The house was situated in a slight hollow, the Serengeti lawn sloping up behind his back and more untidy shrubs and trees stretching up the inclines to the side and behind the house. The loch must be just over the small ridge, but the view from any of the windows was bounded by dense vegetation. It had been carelessly hacked to keep a breathing space around the cottage, although he could feel damp in the air, smell the characteristic earthy aroma of rot. Give it a few years and the whole place would be drowned, devoured by nature.

'Come in. Door's not locked.'

The voice issued from inside. An old woman's voice.

Teàrlach turned the handle, pushed open the door and peered into the hallway beyond. His eyes took a second to acclimatise, focussing in on 1960s wallpaper and a threadbare carpet worn down to the backing. The only light came from the door he'd opened and a bare bulb hanging from the ceiling.

'I'm looking for Richard. Richard Tavistock?' Teàrlach stopped at the threshold, waiting for the owner of the voice to appear.

'You'll have to come here. I can't hear you.' The voice remained obstinately out of sight.

He followed the source, down the hallway and craning his neck to peer around a half-open door. There was a TV switched on but with no sound, so the room danced to the moving images displayed on the screen. In front of the screen was a bed, a woman propped up on pillows and turning her head in his direction.

'I'm sorry to bother you...' Teàrlach didn't have time to complete his apology.

'What have you done with Richard? Where is he? How am I meant to cope on my own for hours and hours?' Her voice was plaintive, querulous. 'Can you make me a cup of tea? I've had nothing to drink since yesterday. An old woman all by herself.'

'Where's the kettle?'

'In the kitchen!' She sighed in relief. 'Two sugars and not too much milk.'

Teàrlach turned away, back into the hallway and away from the sour smell emanating from her bed. He took the opportunity to explore the house under the pretext of searching for the kitchen. Another bedroom, deserted and not giving any indication that anyone had slept there last night; a lounge with curtains still drawn; bathroom and kitchen adjacent to each other and more likely than not in direct contravention of planning laws. He made the tea, opening more cupboards than was necessary as he gathered a picture of their lives.

'Here.' He returned to her side and handed her a mug. 'Is that how you like it?'

'You've given me the wrong cup!' The irritation left her face only to be replaced by a sweet smile so rapidly he wondered if she had mastered the Chinese art of bian lian.

'I'll manage. Thank you, dear.' She blew across the surface, taking a noisy slurp and slapping her lips together with satisfaction, then squinted at him as if surprised to see him there. 'Who are you?'

'My name is Teàrlach Paterson. I'm a private investigator working for Tony Masterton and his wife. I was hoping to talk to Richard about the missing girl. See if he could provide me with any information.'

She spluttered in response, spraying hot tea over her blankets.

'You think my Richard had anything to do with it? You think he's one of those pedal... paediatricians?'

Teàrlach understood what she was attempting to convey.

'No, I don't think your son has anything to do with the girl's disappearance. I'm asking everyone who was there on the day if they can try and recall anything that maybe didn't make the official reports. I'm not a policeman,' he added encouragingly. 'Sometimes, people can tell me things they wouldn't tell the police.'

Her eyes interrogated his. 'I need the toilet.' The mug was set down on a bedside table. Two sticklike legs poked out from under the covers, then a nightie came into view much to his relief.

'Give me a hand. I'm not so good on my feet anymore.' Two thin arms stretched out in supplication.

Teàrlach supported her as she stood, holding one arm as she shuffled along the hall to the bathroom.

'I can manage from here, young man. Thank you.' The smile slipped as the intervening door closed, leaving him wondering what mask she now wore. The sound of an approaching car intruded, engine killed as it parked next to his, harsh ratchet as a handbrake applied. Teàrlach left the woman, relieved that her son had returned to take over care duties and opened the front door just as a burly policeman raised a hand to knock. A policewoman stood behind him, craning around her partner's bulk to look Teàrlach up and down.

'Sorry to bother you, sir, I'm looking for Annie. Annie Tavistock?'

Teàrlach stood back, opening the door to its full extent.

'She's just in the toilet.' He waved a hand in the vague general direction. 'Should be out in a second.'

'And you are?' The policewoman was direct in her questioning.

'Teàrlach Paterson. I'm a private investigator working for Tony Masterton. I was hoping to have a word with her son, Richard.'

The two uniforms exchanged a knowing look, the policeman subtly adjusting his stance in readiness for action.

'And why did you want to have a "word" with Richard, may

I ask?' His partner's hand surreptitiously lowered towards her baton.

Teàrlach caught the past tense, read the response in their posture, guessed the reason for their visit.

'I'm looking into the disappearance of the Mastertons' daughter, Lilybet. She went missing three years ago from his house just a few miles up the loch shore.'

'We were part of the search party.' They visibly relaxed, not entirely at ease but giving him the benefit of the doubt. 'Why Richard?'

The toilet flushed; both police officers caught the sound but remained on the threshold waiting for his response.

'He was one of the first on the scene the day the girl disappeared. I'm asking everyone who was there to see if something previously overlooked may come to light.'

The bathroom door opened, a querulous voice asking for assistance.

'Can you wait in your car, sir?' The policewoman stood back, an invitation for him to leave.

'We'll be wanting a word with you after dealing with Annie, so stay parked where you are.' The policeman warned, also taking a step back allowing Teàrlach room to pass.

He nodded, leaving them to it. He'd seen enough to recognise they carried the burden of bad news – one they were none too keen to pass onto the mother.

Teàrlach heard the cry of pain from his car. There was a scale to a woman's anguish, from irritable to devastated. No shapeshifting expression could disguise a mother losing a child. It was a sound seared on his soul, and not one he could fail to recognise every time he heard it. The policeman came out, headed towards Teàrlach's car with an ill-disguised look of relief to leave the two women alone.

'What do you know about Richard? Have you met him recently?'

Teàrlach knew where this was going. It was a road he'd travelled before.

'I've never met him, officer. Just have his name and address, and I know he works for the Mastertons as a gardener.' He deliberately kept Richard's employment in the present tense.

A notebook was produced, biro laboriously transcribing his words onto paper.

'Can I see your driving licence, sir?'

He produced the licence, plus a business card which the policeman inspected with suspicion.

'And are you staying in the area whilst you do your "investigating"?'

'I'm staying at the local inn. Planning to be there for the next few days at least.'

The biro scratched in response. 'And you can be reached on this mobile number?' He lifted Teàrlach's business card into the air like a priest raising the Host.

'Yes.'

'The detective may want a word with you – about your movements last night.'

'I was driving from Glasgow to the inn, arrived about six. The barman can confirm I was there until we had a visit from your colleague around half past seven to interview your witness.' He locked eyes with the constable. 'I couldn't help but overhear a body had been found. Is it anything to do with Richard Tavistock?'

The constable's expression remained neutral. 'I'm not at liberty to provide any information whilst we investigate an ongoing enquiry. I suggest you keep any theories to yourself, Mr PI.'

Teàrlach gave an affirmative nod, wound up the window and backed away from the cottage with the policeman observing him until he was lost to sight. Something told Teàrlach the gardener was a dead end. Losing the nanny as one potential witness was careless, losing two... well, that started to look like someone was determined to keep the missing girl's location a secret.

TEN

BOBBY BAITING

His mobile chimed before he reached the end of the track, a number he didn't recognise.

'Teàrlach Paterson.' He continued reversing, slowing to a stop as the track met the road.

'They've found a child's body in the loch, well – skeleton really, down at some place called Oitir Ferry.'

He recognised Dee's voice.

'When was this?'

'Just now. The girl serving me breakfast was talking about it – news travels fast here! Thought you might want to look. In case...'

Teàrlach caught the pause, filled in the blank for her. 'I'll drive there now. It's not much further down this road I'm on.' He paused, checking the road was clear before pulling out. 'Are you going to let the Mastertons know?'

There was a humourless laugh. 'That's your job. If it's their kid's body.'

Teàrlach drove along the single-track road, following the irregular outline of the eastern shore. If the body *was* Lilybet's, then at least that offered closure to the parents. Tony Masterton had been fatalistic regarding the probability of ever finding his daughter alive, and her drowning in the loch was high on Teàrlach's list of likely scenarios. Could her body have been carried out towards the sea by the current? He'd need to talk to someone who knew the loch, a local fisherman would be a good place to start. It would take a while to confirm whether it was the girl's body – unless the age or sex ruled it out. Then he was back to where he started, except one, maybe two witnesses were no longer alive. There was little doubt in his mind the police were there at the cottage to tell Annie Tavistock her son was dead. He'd caught enough of the conversation in the bar to link the body missing a heart to the gardener who never came home last night. Was it purely a coincidence that this potential witness was murdered the night of his arrival? And why go to the macabre lengths of removing his heart? Teàrlach had no ready answers to any of his questions.

The folk at the ferry were congregating by the pontoon. A solitary policeman stood guard, fending off questions and looking like he wished he was anywhere but here. Teàrlach pulled into the car park, already busy with a variety of vehicles – half of which didn't look like they'd pass an MOT. He made for the bar, the hubbub inside lowering once they noticed a stranger, then redoubling in intensity. Teàrlach felt the eyes boring into his back as he approached the bar.

'Coffee, please. Single shot espresso.'

'You the polis?' The guy to his right had his face so close Teàrlach could see each individual pore in his nose.

'No. What's going on? Has something happened?'

The face fell back, surprised to find someone who hadn't heard about the body in the loch. Teàrlach took the opportunity to grab a more fragrant breath, reached for his coffee and held it under his nostrils to counter the inevitable halitosis-laden explanation of what had been discovered.

'Diving club found a child's skeleton on the Oitir first thing this morning.' He noticed Teàrlach's brows draw down in puzzlement – scarcely a difficult feat of observation from twenty centimetres. 'The Spit.' He accompanied his explanation with a sweeping gesture, ending up with his finger pointing out towards the strip of land curling away into the centre of the loch. 'Body's been there a few years, they reckon. Police divers have been and collected the bones. Now they're stopping anyone from going there until they've finished their investigations.'

He pulled back, awaiting a response. Teàrlach sipped his espresso, feeling better now he had his first shot of caffeine of the day and more fragrant air to inhale.

'Local kid?' Teàrlach added what he felt was a suitable level of compassion to elicit more information.

'Aye. They reckon it's the girl went missing from the big house up the water.'

'They don't know who it is,' the barmaid corrected. 'Don't go spreading rumours. Imagine if it was your kid had gone missing.' She glowered at them.

'I haven't got a kid.' The guy's hands stretched out in denial.

'No wonder,' she retorted, moving onto to service another customer before he was able to get in a comeback.

He took another swig from his pint instead, eyes narrowed in anger. 'That's who it is. Whatever she says. No other kids have gone missing around here in the last few years. Take it from me.'

Teàrlach inclined his head in acceptance. He caught snatches of conversation all of which mirrored what he'd just been told. The name Masterton being repeated from different corners of the room like an invocation – a charm to ward off evil. There was almost an air of relief in the bar, a release of pent-up worry now that a mystery had finally been solved. He'd felt the same gestalt at other gatherings when a child's body had been found, a sigh leaving everyone's lips in synchronicity. He knew this was partly because a ghost had been laid, partly because whatever evil had visited the community had been named and had lost its hold over them. A feeling of gratitude offered to whatever gods they followed that their community had been tested and found innocent of blame.

Whether this community was innocent had yet to be decided. Teàrlach moved through the press of bodies, out of the bar and over to the policeman and his questioning acolytes. The policeman had clocked him arriving, and now watched him approaching whilst fending off the same question asked in a myriad of different ways as if one specific cypher would break his secrecy.

'Sorry, sir, the pontoon is off limits.' He aimed this over the heads of the small crowd as Teàrlach drew close.

'I'm a private investigator working for the Mastertons. What can you tell me about the body they've found? Is it the girl?'

A pall of silence fell upon the group, turning as one entity to face this new novelty.

'I'm not able to make any comment. This is an active investigation, and any information will be made available as soon as the detective in charge deems appropriate.'

'Who's the detective?' Teàrlach asked. 'Based locally?'

'You'll need to call the police station, sir. I know as much as you.'

Teàrlach privately doubted that, but he knew which card to play next. 'Whose body did they find up at Hell's Glen last night? Do you have a name?'

The attentive crowd turned to face the policeman, his demeanour now distinctly uncomfortable.

'Like I said, sir. You'll have to talk to the station.'

'I'll do that.' Teàrlach headed back towards his car, seeing the group out of the corner of his eye as they began peeling away from the policeman and making for the pub. If they hadn't heard about the other body, then this would add to the day's excitement. The more these events were out in the open, the more likely it was that he'd come across someone able to join the dots.

As things stood, he didn't have a clue what was going on or whether the two bodies were linked in any way. It could just be a coincidence. 'Aye, right,' the voice in his head countered. Teàrlach entered the local police station into the satnav, twenty-two miles away but over a winding mountain pass. There was little point in making the slow journey only to be fobbed off by a more senior version of the bobby on the pier. He headed back to the hotel.

ELEVEN

HACKED

Dee had taken the bait, hacking Jane Whiting's online bank account from her hotel room. This was a challenge she'd enjoy. Now that banks had added biometric data analysis, opening Jane's account directly was too difficult. Instead, she worked on accessing the administrative portal, searching for openings in back-office functionality. A search of social media identified a woman working for the same bank, her online customer-facing role confirmed she'd have access to clients' details. Dee hacked one of her Facebook friend's accounts, sent a photograph of someone she'd recognise containing a viral package that included a keystroke tracker and waited.

The shift to people working from home, if only for part of the week, was having an enabling effect on phishing scams. Freed from the watchful eye of a protective IT department and lulled into a false sense of security in a home environment, the bank employee clicked on the link and viewed the photo. Seconds later and Dee was in. Now she was able to mirror the bank employee's screen, had a list of all the keystrokes used and could view each password as her target worked away, blissfully unaware that the bank's security protocols had been so easily subverted.

She composed an email, purportedly from the bank requesting Jane Whiting's last three month's statements be checked for any unusual payments and pressed send. Her mirrored screen displayed an email received. She watched as it was opened, saw Jane's bank details appear together with her log-on credentials. The scrolling bank statement stopped at a date four weeks ago, showing a credit of £5,000 on the 7th November. ZQUS Holdings was named as the origin. The screen changed to display a search for ZQUS Holdings, coming up with an address in Shoreditch, London. Dee waited as the bank operative did her work for her, searching for the directors and turnover. Her screen was being recorded anyway, but Dee took a screenshot as a name flashed up on her monitor. Peter Staffington, living at the same address ZQUS Holdings was registered to.

The details were copied and sent off as an email, ostensibly back to the bank except the address led back to a machine Dee could access. She sent an acknowledgement, thanking the operative for her fast response and stating that everything was in order. The bank operative continued working without realising anything untoward had happened, leaving Dee with a useful back door into a major bank. There was no knowing when that might become useful.

Dee now did some digging herself, using tools not commonly available and forcing her way into genealogical sites that were meant to be password protected. In under an hour, she had identified the person who had paid for Jane Whiting's holiday. Intrigued by what she found, Dee commenced digging into Peter Staffington's background and ZQUS Holdings' finances.

* * *

Teàrlach drove straight past the hotel, making towards the road to Hell's Glen. The identity of the child the divers had discovered would have to wait for forensics. From the little he'd been able to discover, all the police had been able to retrieve were bones – picked clean by scavengers and the corrosive effect of seawater. There was a good chance that major bones retained enough genetic material for them to confirm a match to the Mastertons' missing daughter, but until then, he still had a case to solve. The dead guy missing a heart was now very much in his sights following this morning's visit to the gardener's home. It didn't require a leap of the imagination to link Richard Tavistock to the heartless corpse, even before any official announcement had been made.

Moses' Well was an easy landmark to find, not least due to the blue and white police tape adorning the well and a forensics tent erected over the bench. Another bobby stood guard, his interest in Teàrlach increasing as he parked the car and walked towards him.

'Can I help you, sir?' The question was loaded with insouciance.

'I do hope so.' Teàrlach's forced smile had no effect on the bobby's willingness to engage. 'Is this where they found Richard Tavistock's body?'

The bobby's eyes narrowed, reminding Teàrlach of a scene from a spaghetti western.

'Why would that be of any interest to you, sir?' The title he bestowed on his questioner sounded anything but an honorific by the time the word 'sir' had left his lips.

'I've come all the way from Glasgow to see him. Just been to his house and a couple of your colleagues broke the news to his mum. Said he'd been found murdered. On that bench.' Teàrlach pointed helpfully in the direction of the forensics tent.

The bobby reached for his personal radio, hand pausing halfway in realisation that the signal wouldn't reach HQ. He turned his head towards the patrol car parked at the side of the road, contemplating the more powerful transmitter in the car radio. Teàrlach could see him visibly deflate. If someone had given out the dead man's name already, what was the point?

'Still waiting on confirmation. All we had to go on was his wallet and driving licence. Not much hope of identifying what was left of his face.'

'They found the heart yet?'

That gunslinger look returned. 'How do you know about that?'

'Cops at the house,' Teàrlach lied with ease.

'No.' The shiver that followed wasn't due to the cold. 'Seen some things in my time.' The policeman shook his head, then shifted his attention from Teàrlach to stare at the ground.

'Aye, well. It's a mad world.' Teàrlach made to return to his car.

'Just a minute, sir. Can I take down your details?' The question was issued as more of a command, the policeman taking back the initiative.

'Sure. I've just given my name to the two police at his house. Teàrlach Paterson – here's my card.' He handed over another business card, saw the policeman thinking things over – realising he may well have just been played.

'Are you staying locally, sir?' He viewed the card distastefully, a sneer appearing as he focussed back on Teàrlach.

'The local hotel.' Teàrlach returned to his car, seeing the policeman taking down his registration plate. There was a missed call from Chloe back in the Glasgow office. He waited until he reached the top of the hill before calling her back.

'Hi Sherlock. How's it going?' Chloe wasn't the first to use that aptronym, unsubtly mispronouncing his name.

'What have you got, Chloe? Be quick, the phone signal could cut out any minute.'

'Right. Looked into this nanny like you asked. Bugger all

income since the Masterton girl, few bar jobs, temporary secretarial work. Been living with her parents ever since and keeping herself to herself. Three weeks back she flew out to Amsterdam. One of her uncles took pity on her and gave her a wad of money to go off and enjoy herself. Guy called Peter Staffington.'

'How did you get all this?' Teàrlach questioned.

'Her parents. Told them we were investigating the case and made a big point of our trying to prove her innocence, then the floodgates opened. Gave me too much detail if I'm honest.'

'Have they seen the video?' Teàrlach imagined how that might have been received by her parents.

'No. They didn't mention it. Just said they'd been contacted by the local police about her disappearance. They said she's gone missing before, like it was a regular thing.'

That was something. At least the police had the sensitivity to keep the video under wraps – assuming they had that detail in the first place.

'Do the police have a copy of the video?'

'No idea,' Chloe responded. 'They're investigating her disappearance this end on behalf of Interpol. It's under Belgium jurisdiction – that's where she went missing.'

'Where was she last seen?'

'Some hotel in Bruges.' There was a rustle of papers as Chloe searched her notes. 'The Hotel DuBois, I'll send you the address.'

'How are the local police treating it? Random killing or do they believe she was targeted?'

'From what I can gather from the parents, they've only been told she's missing. The hotel reported her when she hadn't used her room after a few days.'

The road curved back down towards the waters of the loch; he could lose the signal at any moment.

'Book me a flight to Amsterdam. Tomorrow morning. And

see if you can book me into this Hotel DuBois for a couple of nights. I'll swing by the office later today.'

'Sure. How did you get on with...' Chloe's voice cut out as he moved out of range.

His phone signal returned as he joined the main road, exiting the twisting route through the mountains and Hell's Glen. He redialled his office, Chloe picked up the call and he continued from where he'd been cut off.

'I've just been to have a look at the site where they've found Richard Tavistock's body...'

'He's dead?' Chloe interrupted in disbelief.

'I wasn't completely sure until I'd spoken to the bobby looking after the scene. He confirmed it.'

'What's that about?'

'Wish I knew. May be because someone didn't want him talking to me.' Teàrlach paused as he swerved to avoid an oncoming lorry, crossing the central line as it rounded a bend. 'Can you do something else for me, Chloe?'

'Sure, what do you want?'

'Buy us a couple of burner phones so we can speak in private, take the old laptop and work from that – don't try and copy anything across from any of the office machines.'

'Is this because of your hacker?'

'Aye. She's more than likely listening in to us now.'

'Nosey bitch!'

Teàrlach laughed. 'Aye, right enough. One other thing before we meet, see if anyone's modus operandi includes removing hearts with a circular power saw.'

'Jesus! What are we dealing with here? I thought we were looking for a missing kid?'

'Wish I knew, Chloe. I wish I knew.' Teàrlach followed the road south back towards his hotel. He checked the clock – he should be there just after two giving him plenty of time to return to Glasgow and plan for tomorrow's trip. He again questioned the wisdom of taking on this case, working for a man whom he suspected had a part to play in the gardener's death for reasons that weren't at all clear. Tony Masterton had been implicated in at least two murders; business rivals found floating down the Clyde with their arms hacked off. Word on the street was that they were still alive when they entered the water – he'd heard a rumour there was a sweepstake on which body would reach the Millennium Bridge first. Teàrlach's instinct told him it was more than a rumour. Nothing ever stuck to Tony Masterton, though; he was human Teflon.

If the body in the loch was Lilybet's, then this case was closed – until that was confirmed, he'd continue the search. The added complication of having Dee watch his every move was something he could do without. She would be feeding everything he did and found back to Tony Masterton without him being able to filter the information first, and that could prove lethal – if not to himself, then to whoever he put in the frame for Lilybet's disappearance.

Winter sun glinted off the loch's surface, so it resembled a postcard picture, a touch of snow on the hilltops providing the icing. Was that Lilybet's body the divers had found, and if so, was her death the result of misadventure – a young girl climbing over the glass barrier and falling into the cold loch waters? She would have cried out in fear and shock, her voice muted from inside the house until it became just another wild bird's cry. Slipping beneath the surface and choking on salt water as death took her small body without ceremony. Teàrlach gripped the wheel more tightly, imagining Lilybet's final moments alone and frightened. Too small to save herself, too young to die.

TWELVE

SOMETHING IN THE LOCH

A notification appeared on Teàrlach's screen, incoming from Tony Masterton. He accepted the call and turned his attention back to the road.

'What's this about a kid's body in the loch?' Tony Masterton's voice sounded tight with anxiety.

'I've been down to the ferry, talked to some locals and the bobby they've left guarding the pier. Some divers uncovered a child's bones first thing this morning.'

Silence.

'There's no way of knowing if this is Lilybet until forensics have had a chance to look at the remains. This may not be her,' Teàrlach continued, hearing Tony Masterton's breath shuddering over the car sound system.

'What do you think?' Tony Masterton sounded more like himself, the question barked down the line and demanding a response.

'I think we should wait until we receive confirmation. Until that happens, I'm going to continue looking for her.'

The silence returned. 'I've had a call from the Major Investigation Team. About a body they found on the Hell's Glen road. Seem to think I might know something about it. Do you know who it is they've found?'

It was Teàrlach's turn to be silent. Tony Masterton was perfectly capable of having somebody murdered. There was always the possibility that the gardener had caused some offence – but sufficient for Tony to have his heart removed? That went so far beyond a typical gangland kill that they were into the realm of the truly psychotic. Could he be asking the question to throw Teàrlach off pursuing that line of enquiry?

'I'd heard about that – I went to Richard Tavistock's house to interview him when the police turned up. They let slip it was his body that had been discovered up at Moses' Well.'

'Why did you want to speak to my gardener?' Tony fired back.

'Same reason I want to speak to everyone I can that was there on the day Lilybet went missing. The more people I can speak to, the more accurate a picture I can make of whatever happened.'

'OK. Makes sense,' Tony Masterton reluctantly acknowledged.

'Only that's two key witnesses I can no longer speak with. Due to their being dead.' Teàrlach paused for a response which didn't come. 'You wouldn't know why two of the people present at the time of your daughter's disappearance should have been executed?'

'Are you accusing me of something?' His words were more menacing for being quietly spoken.

'No. Just wondering if there's something you're not telling me.'

'You have all the information you need, Charlie. I've provided everything that I can to help you find my girl. You concentrate on that. I'm not paying you to investigate any local difficulties. Understood?'

'I understand.' Teàrlach heard the faint chime announcing a

text had been delivered to Tony Masterton's mobile. There followed a period of silence as Tony digested whatever message had been received.

'Good. We'll provide DNA samples when forensics ask for them in case that is Lilybet they've found.' His voice changed to a questioning tone. 'Why are you going to Amsterdam?'

Teàrlach realised his phone must be leaking like a bloody sieve. 'Because that's where Jane Whiting went. If I can find where, why and who killed her, then I may be a step closer to finding out what happened to your daughter.'

'Waste of time if that *is* my girl they found in the loch.'

'Until we both know that for sure, then you let me do my job, Mr Masterton,' Teàrlach replied, keeping his voice as even as he could.

'We'll talk later. And keep me updated – I don't pay you and expect to have to chase you for information.' Tony Masterton ended the call abruptly, his name erased as the car display returned to show the time – 13:17.

'What do you make of that, Dee?' Teàrlach waited in vain for his phone to respond. Maybe she didn't listen in to her boss's calls or maybe she didn't want to advertise that she did. It would be safer that way – a man like Tony Masterton wouldn't want anyone knowing too much about his business. The woman was turning into a thorn in his side, eavesdropping to his conversations, reading his emails. He'd have to do something to keep her at arm's length. Teàrlach's thoughts returned to the gardener. Did he find out something that meant he had to die? And why remove his heart like a ritual sacrifice?

He picked a space in the hotel car park, reversed in-between sunken logs that delineated individual bays and switched off the ignition. Ahead of him the winter sun had reached its zenith, still low in the sky but sufficient to illuminate the loch waters in shades of aquamarine. If he was a painter, he'd be tempted to commit the scene to canvas; instead, he drank in the colours as an antidote to the dead bodies still vivid in his imagination. Richard Tavistock with his pulped face and open chest, slumped on the bench at Moses' Well; Jane Whiting's scream turned to blood; the tiny, bleached bones submerged under water.

Over the road was a rectangular stretch of sloping lawn, ostensibly for hotel guests to stretch their legs and view the loch. Teàrlach needed a moment to process the events of the last few hours, heading to lean over a wooden fence which sagged under his weight. The water was calm today, a gentle swell rocking a moored yacht as smoothly as a baby in a crib. Out in the centre of the loch a head poked out from under the surface, turning to stare back at him. It was too far away to make out any detail – could be an otter or seal. Perspective played tricks on the open water without any readily discernible object to compare against for scale. No, it was too big for an otter. The head rose out of the water, powered upwards by a strong swimming motion. It didn't look like a seal either, now that so much of the body was revealed. Teàrlach ran through a list of aquatic options, trying to fit whatever this creature was into a category that made sense. His unease grew as the list came to an end.

'Enjoying the view?'

Teàrlach span around, unaccountably startled by Dee's sudden appearance behind him.

'What do you think that is?' He pointed out into the centre of the loch, casting around ineffectually for the creature he'd just seen.

'It's a loch as far as I know.' Dee's amusement at causing him to startle was plain.

'Doesn't matter.' Teàrlach tried to shake off the feeling of unease, dismissing the notion that he'd been looking at a kaelpie or some other unworldly creature. 'It was a seal or something.'

Dee switched her attention from a bored scan of the loch back to the PI. 'Did you get anywhere with the gardener?'

So, she hadn't been listening during that part of the conversation at least. 'Turns out the gardener is the guy whose heart went missing last night.'

'No shit!'

'Aye. Not ideal for him.'

Her eyes remained on his, inscrutable. 'Bit weird that two of the people who were there when Lilybet went missing have both ended up dead.'

Teàrlach returned to looking at the loch, feeling the telltale prickle at the nape of his neck that told him he was being watched.

'Probably coincidence,' he replied, knowing neither of them believed that fiction.

'I've some information on the nanny that you may find interesting.'

'What have you found?' He needed something to go on. This case had supplied nothing but dead ends so far – literally.

Dee gave him an update as they walked back to the hotel.

He replied, 'So, this Peter Staffington character. He's already cropped up in our research as a person of interest. He's an uncle of hers, sent her some money to go on holiday—'

Dee interrupted him before he'd finished. 'Five thousand pounds. He transferred the money from his business account.' Dee made the unsubtle point that she had more detail than Teàrlach had been able to discover. 'And, even more interesting, his company is in financial trouble, which makes it unlikely that he'd bung her the money for no reason.'

Teàrlach reached for his notebook, wrote down the additional detail whilst Dee looked at him as if he was a relic from another age.

'Could be she was working for him. Drugs mule or something to raise ready cash? Then the deal went sour for whatever reason.' He dismissed the explanation as soon as the words left his lips. 'That wouldn't explain the method of execution or the paid-for video feed.'

Teàrlach's mind went into overdrive, searching for scenarios that explained the two deaths and how they could link to Lilybet.

'I'm heading back to Glasgow. There's no point in waiting here until forensics have confirmed the skeleton belongs to Lilybet. It could take days, and they haven't asked for DNA samples from the Mastertons yet.' Teàrlach wondered how much trust he should invest in this wild hacker. 'I'm flying out to Amsterdam, to have a look around the places Jane Whiting visited.' He decided; they were both working towards the same end after all.

'Can you send me any online receipts you find, hotels, coffee bars, public transport? Anything that I can use to follow her footsteps.'

'Yeah, sure. I'll send anything I find to your WhatsApp.'

'Thanks. Whilst you're at it, check if her uncle is the same guy who watched the video of her execution.'

Dee's shocked expression was in lieu of any other response. 'Her uncle?' She eventually managed to speak.

'Aye. If he's got financial problems, then he may have had her tortured to find out what happened to Lilybet to claim the reward.'

Dee shook her head in denial. 'But they've found her body – and you think her uncle would do that?'

'Until the body is confirmed as Lilybet, I'm still working the case, and Jane Whiting's trail is getting colder by the day.'

Teàrlach didn't bother trying to defend the dead woman's uncle. If it wasn't him, then someone else was going to fit in his crosswires eventually. Then God help them.

'Aye. I'll access any computers he uses. If he's watched the video, then he'll have left a trace.'

'You should see if he was stupid enough to pay the £10,000 fee for the video from one of his accounts.'

Dee's face lit with excitement. 'And if it was him, then I've a trail to whoever slit her throat!'

Teàrlach's tight smile was the only encouragement she needed. They split ways, heading to their individual rooms, and he packed his small overnight bag, lingering over the view of the loch with a new sense of unease before heading down to reception.

THIRTEEN

IN BRUGES

Schiphol Airport was quieter than usual. The recession had seen an uptake of increasingly desperate international sales representatives, dragging their wheeled wares across airport concourses with panic in their eyes. This close to Christmas they were being replaced by redundancy notices, doors shut tight, and windows battened in preparation for a harsh, financial winter. In their place came the students, far-flung family members looking for heat and comfort in an increasingly cold world. Teàrlach had the sense that the world was turning. The established order was under increasing pressure from ever more radical politics, restless populations, desperate refugees and wars. Even the climate refused to follow seasonal norms, giving way to flares of temper – biblical floods and burnings.

He cut an unhurried path through the crowds, made for the car hire and took the road south to Bruges. Dee had sent a detailed list of Jane Whiting's expenses, a JPEG copy of her personal bank statement. Chloe had booked him into the same hotel she'd stayed at in the town centre where he intended to base his search.

Following the signs to The Hague, Teàrlach felt the strands

of the mental web he wove, testing each fine thread. Three corpses caught, silk stained with spilt lives. Around them circled larger creatures: The Mastertons; Richard Tavistock's mother; Jane Whiting's uncle – each one too blind to see the web or convinced silk wasn't strong enough to bind them. He sensed other creatures moving in the dark, felt them by the smallest vibrations, willed them to touch a thread and be made visible.

Three hours after leaving Schiphol, Teàrlach pulled into the cobbled courtyard of the Hotel DuBois. The hotel stood out in an otherwise anonymous huddle of brick and concrete municipal buildings, wooden beams and crooked angles testament to its age. Utilitarian flats supported this old dame, lending a hand to keep the hotel standing. Somehow Hotel DuBois had survived two world wars, avoided the bombs that had levelled this ancient quarter of Bruges and offering an ingratiating welcome to invader and vanquisher alike. The eponymous name became even more apparent as he entered the foyer, from the parquet flooring stained black with age to exposed ceiling beams supporting three floors of accommodation above. Teàrlach's attention was caught by fire detection alarms set incongruously in the ceiling like alien artefacts, the sprinklers set in geometric accuracy and offering some small hope that a fire here wouldn't necessarily be an automatic death sentence. Above reception an unblinking camera stared at him, mirroring the expression of the male receptionist whose smile welcomed him with insincerity.

'Hello, sir, how can I help you?'

There had to be some cultural tell that identified the inhabitants of the UK – a common poor dress sense or weak pallor that shouted *we were once an empire, now we are the threadbare remnants scratching a meagre living on the edge of everything.* How else did Europeans with a mastery and choice of multiple languages seamlessly switch to English whenever he or one of his countrymen appeared?

'Teàrlach Paterson, I have a room booked for a couple of days.'

The receptionist angled his birdlike head down to observe Teàrlach over the distortion of glasses perched on a sharp nose. Whatever analysis he made wasn't positive, evidenced by the ghost of a sneer as he pretended to check the ubiquitous computer screen.

'Ah yes, here we are.' The registration book was spun around in preparation for Teàrlach's signature. 'And how will you be paying, sir?'

Teàrlach almost applauded the insult wrapped in an obsequious wrapper.

'Card. Would you like prepayment?'

A hungry look appeared. The glasses tilted down once more as a swift re-evaluation occurred.

'On checkout, sir. Here's your key, room twenty-seven on the second floor. Do you require help with your bags?'

Teàrlach held up a single overnight bag. 'I can manage, thanks.'

An eyebrow expressed disapproval at travelling light. 'Can I help with anything else, sir?'

'Yes, you can actually.' Teàrlach pointed to the camera. 'I'm looking for any information you might have on a Jane Whiting. She arrived here on the 9th November but went missing.'

He could see the shutters closing, an apologetic mask slip into place before the receptionist began speaking. Teàrlach reached into his coat pocket, held a bundle of two hundred euros in front of the reading glasses and under the sharp nose. It was close enough for his business card to be read, held to the bundle by elastic bands, close enough for the smell of money to change the receptionist's expression back to greed.

'Let me see what I can do for you, sir.' The words were accompanied with the first honest smile he'd seen.

Ten minutes later and two hundred euros lighter, Teàrlach had his first lead. Jane Whiting had booked a taxi just one hour after receiving a telephone call the first day she arrived. The number it came from was withheld, although the +44 code gave away the UK as point of origin. Her belongings had been taken by the Bruges police just yesterday after the hotel had informed them one of their guests had gone missing. Teàrlach didn't bother asking why it took them over three weeks – her room had been booked and paid for until then. What he did have was the number of the taxi company.

For a man who spent his life tracking ghosts, this trail was warmer than most. He dropped his bag in room twenty-seven, noting the furniture and plumbing was almost as old as the building, and checked WhatsApp for any new messages from Dee. Nothing yet. She'd be working on the uncle's bank accounts, searching for a £10,000 transaction and following the money. He deliberately removed the SIM card, shut his mobile in a heavy oak bedside cabinet and switched on the burner Chloe had supplied. He called her once he'd left the room.

'Chloe. Did you find anything on the power tool killer?'

Her voice came back with a slight echo, an electronic arte-fact from being bounced from satellite to satellite, mast to mast. 'Nope. Looks like whoever it is has cornered the market with that technique. Anything else I can do this end?'

His smile appeared at the sound of her voice. He couldn't think of anyone else, even hardened pros, who'd deal with the circumstances of Richard Tavistock's murder with such equa-nimity. Maybe it came from being so close to death herself, liter-ally snatched from the hangman's noose at the last minute. The smile disappeared as the scene of their first meeting replayed in his mind's eye.

He'd found her hanging around in Glasgow – literally hanging. Rope around her neck, feet en pointe like a dancer in a macabre ballet, desperately scrabbling to remain in contact with the floor. She must have been dancing on the spot for a while; poor lass was soaked through with sweat when he finally cut her down – although withdrawal symptoms may have contributed. She'd been one of his easiest jobs – parents desperate to find their missing daughter. The police weren't interested. A working-class lass over eighteen leaves home without a forwarding address – packed her clothes in a suitcase, taking phone and money with her – and no sign of foul play. Not their problem. He got that, but she left behind two bewildered and desperate parents whose imaginations filled in the blanks too readily.

It wasn't hard to track her down. Bung a few hundred to a guy working for the mobile company, triangulate her location to a couple of houses on Great Western Road, few more quid until one of the flat residents recognised her photo, and there he was outside the door to her flat. No answer to his knock, for obvious reasons, but he could hear muffled cries for help accompanied by a soft shoe shuffle going on without any accompanying music. She owed money for a nascent drug habit, going on the game to feed the need and managed to get pregnant first attempt. A pregnancy that subsequently miscarried. Fragile to start with, this pushed her over the edge.

Teàrlach wasn't a social worker, God forbid, but couldn't just leave her lying in a crumpled heap where she'd fallen on the floor, rope coiling around her like an umbilical after he'd cut it. She point-blank refused going to hospital, worried they'd section her under the mental health act, so he took her back to his place, patiently explained that he didn't want sex and gave her a meal. Then he discussed her options. She'd started helping out with the admin as a means of paying him back for his kindness whilst she looked for a job. Weeks turned into months until he wondered how he'd ever managed without her.

'See if you can get anything on the Bruges police investigation. Don't want to be chasing them all around Belgium.'

'Better than them chasing you!' Chloe shot back.

The sky was turning dark grey as Teàrlach waited outside the hotel, watching as a black Mercedes pulled up to the curb. The driver's window slid down, unhealthy driver looking as if his shift was already too long.

'Taxi?' The question issued from underneath a dark moustache, twisting upwards each end and reminding Teàrlach so convincingly of the actor who played Hercule Poirot that he had to do a double take.

'Sure. Mind if I join you in the front?'

'Be my guest. Where to?'

Teàrlach delayed responding until he'd settled into place, strapping into the seatbelt. 'Just take me on a tour, show me the sights.'

The driver brightened, seeing his chance to make easy money.

'First time in Bruges?' He pronounced it with a Flemish accent, elongating the r and elongating the soft g, reluctantly letting the word end before reaching the s.

'Yes.' The lie left Teàrlach's lips without thinking. 'I have some time to kill so thought it would be good to look around.'

The car pulled away from the kerb with alacrity, fitting in to a gap in the afternoon traffic. The driver managed the manoeuvre at the same time as setting the meter, euros visibly counting upwards as they drove.

'You looking for anything special?' The driver's balding head turned his way, a lascivious smile forming on blubbery lips. A wet tongue flicked out snakelike, licked them as if that might help with deciphering his meaning.

Teàrlach felt momentarily sick. 'You pick up all the guests at Hotel DuBois?' In common with most hotels, the receptionist had already told him they had an arrangement with this taxi company.

'Sure. We provide good service.' Poirot bared uneven nicotine-stained teeth as he exchanged a friendly grin. 'Know all the best places.'

Teàrlach retrieved a photograph of Jane Whiting, one where her head was still firmly attached. He held it up to the windscreen for the driver to see it.

'Did you pick this woman up from the hotel, it would have been three weeks ago?'

The driver gave the photograph a cursory glance, flicked a questioning look back at Teàrlach, then returned to negotiating the traffic.

'I pick up people all the time. They all start to look the same after a while.'

Teàrlach peeled off another hundred euros. Tony Masterton was paying for it all, he could afford the largesse.

'On 9th November, 3:20 in the afternoon.'

The driver's tongue made a reappearance at the sight of a roll of banknotes. He parked at the side of the road, put the taxi into neutral and reached hungrily for the notes.

'What can you tell me?' Teàrlach's hand pulled away, still holding the money.

The driver scowled, measured himself against Teàrlach's stocky frame and thought better of making a grab for the money.

'Let me think... 9th November?'

'That's right, 3:20. Someone from your firm picked her up. I just need to know where she went,' Teàrlach explained patiently.

A cunning look settled on the Poirot-lookalike's face. 'I don't know. Three weeks – it's difficult to remember with so many customers.'

Teàrlach added another fifty euros to the stake, letting his eyes do the talking.

'Ah, yes. Now I remember. I took her to 37 Rue de Bressons.' His podgy fingers extended expectantly.

'What's there?'

'A studio. Films.' The lascivious sneer returned. 'Easy money for pretty girls – and boys,' he added to show his open-mindedness.

Teàrlach gave him the money. 'Take me there.'

The driver pocketed the cash and nodded, pulling out into the line of traffic and attracting car horns and shouted curses in return.

'You can kill the meter,' Teàrlach stated simply.

The driver obeyed with an indifferent shrug.

'Did you pick her up again, afterwards?' Teàrlach asked as a formality, he already knew what had happened to the woman.

'Yes. Took her back to the hotel two hours later. Her hair was so wet I had to dry the seats. Must have worked up a sweat to need a shower.'

Teàrlach replayed the driver's words with disbelief.

'You sure it was her?'

Poirot looked at him with confusion. 'Yes, same girl, same hotel.'

They drove to the film studio in silence, arriving at a narrow lane and an unmarked door.

'Wait here for me.' Teàrlach ordered and left the taxi.

FOURTEEN

JE M'APPELLE CHARLIE

There was an illuminated doorbell, the name *Bresson Film Studio* printed on a rectangular piece of paper behind yellowing Perspex. Apart from a number '37', the door was anonymous. Teàrlach took in the blank brick walls, the lack of any windows even on the upper levels. It could have been a warehouse. He glanced back at the driver, counting bank notes and ignoring anything Teàrlach was involved with. He pressed the doorbell, silent as far as he could tell although the illumination dimmed as his finger pushed against the button.

'Oui?' The enquiry crackled out of a rusting grill set underneath the doorbell. Teàrlach bent down so his face was at the same level as the loudspeaker.

'I want to make a film. You came highly recommended.'

The speaker went silent. Teàrlach gave it a while before straightening, searching around for a camera.

'Who are you?' The heavily accented voice belonged to a man whose sales skills lacked any kind of finesse.

'My name's Charlie Paterson.' He didn't attempt the Gaelic pronunciation. 'Can I come in?'

'Let me see your face,' the voice demanded.

Teàrlach cast around, swivelling his head in search of a non-existent lens.

'The buzzer. Look at the buzzer.'

He looked at the buzzer.

'You alone?' the doorbell interrogated.

'Yes. I can pay good money.' Teàrlach made use of another roll of euros, holding them in front of the doorbell and feeling a bit like an idiot. As far as he could see, there wasn't a camera there.

The door gave a click followed by a rasping buzz from worn-out electronics. He pushed inside and climbed a set of worn stone stairs stretching upwards towards another closed door. The only illumination came from dim wall lights, scarcely sufficient to pierce the gloom pervading the stairwell. Each step edge had been roughly painted in white, potentially a health and safety measure to prevent people missing their footing and falling down an entire flight. The solid door blocking the top of the stairway opened, sudden bright light temporarily blinding him, so he had to reach for the wall for support. As his eyes adjusted, he made out the outline of a man blocking the newly opened doorway. Whoever these people were, they required a heavy on reception. Teàrlach hoped this wouldn't turn ugly – he was at a severe disadvantage on the stairs and didn't relish the thought of being forcibly pushed back down them.

'Bonjour.' Teàrlach attempted half-remembered schoolboy French. 'Je m'appelle Charlie.'

The doorkeeper snorted in derision at his attempt, stepping back a few steps to allow Teàrlach to climb off the stairs. He entered a cavernous room, laid out into film sets with cameras and lights randomly trailing cables across the floor. Technicians fussed around, being directed by a tall, skeletally thin man dressed completely in black, which only served to accentuate the unearthly pallor of his skin. A woman walked across the chaotic scene trailing a bathrobe which did little to conceal her curves. Their eyes met for the briefest moment, hers holding his with the trace of a smile playing on her lips before she shut herself away in what he took to be a dressing room.

'I'm Reynaert. What do you want? We're very busy, you should have made an appointment, Mr...?'

Teàrlach reluctantly took his attention away from the closed door. The tall man fussed nervously with scripts, rubbing them between blue-painted fingernails and taut with impatience.

'Paterson. Charlie Paterson.' He searched for a quiet corner in amongst the mayhem. 'Is there somewhere we can talk – in private?'

His request was on the brink of being denied until he pulled the euros from his pocket, nonchalantly counting another hundred from one hand to the other. Reynaert stopped shuffling scripts, hypnotised by the silken rustling of note sliding over note.

'My office. I don't have much time, Mr Charlie.'

Reynaert's office contained a desk strewn with more well-thumbed scripts, two mismatched filing cabinets and a red upholstered settee large enough to seat six. The red fabric held a patina of time – patches worn smooth, stains from unidentifiable liquids.

'You remember this girl?' He handed over the same photograph of the nanny that he'd shown the taxi driver. 'She came here by taxi, 9th November around four in the afternoon.'

A Gallic shrug together with a pointed look at a wall-mounted clock accompanied his response. 'We have so many girls. I don't remember.'

'Her name was Jane Whiting.'

If anything, the Gallic shrug was even more pronounced, elbows held tight to torso and hands upraised with painted nails spread apart as if time itself could not be held, slipping silently through open fingers like the finest sand.

'She had the starring role in a horror film.' Teàrlach laid the captured still on top of the piled scripts, her head hanging at an unnatural angle above a deep crimson gash.

Reynaert studied the image with no emotion, straightening up and turning towards Teàrlach with his hands already returning heavenwards.

'Maybe this will help your memory.' Teàrlach added another hundred to the notes already held in one hand, watching as Reynaert's hands ceased their upwards motion and headed south once more.

'What is your interest in this girl? Are you police?'

He held a business card towards Reynaert, keeping the notes in his other hand as bait.

'Ha! Private Investigator. Like Thompson in Tintin?' A smile of relief appeared as Reynaert visibly relaxed. 'We have a duty of anonymity to our clients, Mr Charlie. If you were police and had a warrant, then...'

'One thousand euros and you can tell me what I need to know. Otherwise, I may have to break your pretty fingers.'

Reynaert signalled his intent to make for the door so obviously that Teàrlach's arm had plenty of time to prevent him making good his escape.

'I just need to know what happened. It won't go anywhere else – unless you want it to.' Teàrlach's soft voice belied the threat inherent in his words. He could see Reynaert's calculations, working through the options and deciding on the easiest, least painful and most financially rewarding. The money changed hands and was tucked somewhere under Reynaert's dark clothing.

'This is between us, yes?'

'Just us. Nobody else needs to know what happened here.'

Reynaert motioned towards the red settee, taking a seat at one end and patting the space beside him in encouragement.

Teàrlach sat.

'I don't know who the client was, everything was done over

the phone from England. He wanted to have a scene where a young woman was interrogated, wanted it to look like the inside of a shipping container with low-quality video – like something filmed on a mobile phone.'

Teàrlach nodded in encouragement.

'It was all very, how you say it?' The eyebrows performed their own Gallic shrug, heading up towards his forehead in supplication.

'ISIS?' Teàrlach attempted.

'Exact! ISIS. He wanted it to look like an ISIS interrogation and execution.'

'What happened to the woman?'

Reynaert nodded excitedly. 'She came here, after we finished for the day. Just me and a cameraman. The set had already been roughed up. The lighting was deliberately low, so we didn't worry too much about dressing it. She knew what she had to do, what to say. The filming was over in under an hour.'

'But what about the woman? What happened to Jane Whiting?' Teàrlach's exasperation was clear.

'She showered off the blood and took a taxi. I don't know where she went.'

Teàrlach started to make sense of it all. 'So, she acted being tortured and having her throat slit?'

Reynaert nodded again. 'Yes. She was convincing. I could use that acting talent in some of my other work.'

'So, let me get this straight. This was a scene from your filming where Jane pretends to have her throat slit?' Teàrlach reached across to the desk, held up a still frame clearly showing the woman's head almost completely severed from her neck.

'Yes, yes. This is from the special effects we added. It's all made on the computer by our graphic artist. Quite realistic, don't you think?' Reynaert's pride was clear.

'What did you do with the footage?'

'With the finished film?' He waited for Teàrlach's affirmation. 'Sent it to an address on the web. That was it. That was all the client wanted.'

'An address on the dark web?'

Reynaert shifted uncomfortably next to him. 'We just uploaded it to the address that was provided.'

Teàrlach believed him. 'Do you still have the web address?'

The Gallic shrug answered for him. 'My client was most insistent that we destroyed all the paperwork after we had completed the work.'

'And you never knew who your client was?'

'As I told you. Everything was kept, how you say? Under wraps.'

Teàrlach made to stand, only to have a hand press down on his leg. Reynaert's face pressed close enough that he could tell what he'd eaten for his lunch.

'We kept an electronic copy of the video, though. I may be able to find it for you?' Reynaert's gaze focussed unerringly onto the pocket holding the remainder of Teàrlach's euros.

'How much?'

'Two thousand.'

Teàrlach counted out notes until one thousand euros lay on the chaise longue between them.

Reynaert's head tipped from side to side as if he was seriously considering the offer.

'Alright.' Reynaert sprang upright, crossed over to the desk and opened a drawer. Teàrlach's hand grabbed the wrist before Reynaert's hand had a chance to reach inside. 'Just a USB, for the video.'

Teàrlach's concern abated as the expected firearm wasn't there. He loosened his grip, watched carefully as piles of papers were shifted to one side of the desk to reveal a laptop. The memory stick was inserted, and a file copied across. Reynaert handed over the USB drive, then deftly pocketed the last of the money.

'Pleasure doing business with you, Mr Charlie.' Reynaert held the door open, inviting him to leave.

Teàrlach made for the exit.

'And phone before coming again, Mr Charlie.'

The heavy had made an appearance outside Reynaert's office, accompanying Teàrlach back to the exit and held the door open with a clear invitation to leave. The door closed with finality, the sound of a lock sliding into place echoing down the stairwell. The taxi remained waiting for him in the outside street.

'Take me back to Hotel DuBois.' This time he climbed into the back seat. Teàrlach needed to think things over without Poirot for company.

FIFTEEN

DIRECTOR'S CUT

There was a message from Dee awaiting him as soon as he'd replaced the SIM card in his stashed mobile. He read the WhatsApp text whilst his laptop rebooted.

> Found a payment from Peter Staffington's business account to an outfit called Bresson Film Studio, he paid them ten thousand the same day Jane Whiting flew to Amsterdam. See you've ditched your phone.

He didn't bother replying, but it was confirmation that he was on the right track. The laptop eventually came to life, then he spent the next thirty minutes getting to grips with an Apple Mac. He'd purchased the new machine at Schiphol Airport – justifiable expense for Tony Masterton seeing as how Dee had compromised the work laptop. It was a delaying tactic at best, Dee clearly had an exceptional talent for bypassing firewalls and passwords. Switching operating systems and making a new internet identity should slow her down.

He'd bought a few adaptors at the same time and was gratified to see the laptop transferring the USB file across without a hitch. The film started playing. The same poorly lit shipping unit, the same woman tied to a chair, the same hooded character standing behind her, but now the audio quality was clearer.

'You've been taken here because you know about the child that went missing. Tony Masterton's child. Lilybet.' The man's voice issued from underneath a black beanie pulled down over his face, just a slit for his eyes and mouth.

'I don't know anything about that. I wasn't there when it happened – who are you? Why have you taken me?' Jane Whiting sounded frightened but in control.

He clipped the side of her head with the back of his hand, the slap hard enough to pitch her sideways until she came up against the ropes binding her to the chair.

'I'm asking the questions. Tell me where the girl is, and you will be released.'

'I said I don't know.' Her voice cut off as another slap landed, a shout of pain her only response.

'You were her nanny. You looked after her every day. You know places she liked to hide – places she wasn't allowed to go. Where could she have gone that day, or did someone take her?'

Jane's eyes darted from side to side, frightened. 'I wasn't there. How could I know where she went?'

'Don't make me use other methods. You'll talk eventually. Tell me what you know.'

She bit her lip; tears left a trail on her cheeks, glistening in the harsh light shining on her and leaving her captive mostly in shadow.

'Her parents were meant to be looking after her that day. I only had one day a week off,' she said bitterly. 'It's not my fault they couldn't be bothered to even watch her for a few hours.' Jane started sobbing, chin down on her chest and tears falling like plump raindrops on her blouse. This at least was real.

'Tell me where she wasn't allowed to go.'

Her chin raised defiantly. 'She knew not to climb over the glass wall to the loch. I told her it wasn't safe.'

Her interrogator waited for more.

Jane took a deep breath before continuing. 'You'll let me go if I tell you all I know?'

'I don't enjoy torturing women.' Her captor unexpectedly stroked her hair, causing Jane to flinch at the first touch. 'Or killing them,' he added softly.

Jane froze at the words.

'I told her mother that I'd caught Lilybet climbing half over the glass wall. The decking extended on the other side, but it was a narrow strip, not enough to stand on safely.'

'Did you ever see her climb all the way over?'

'No. It's a metre high – taller than Lilybet. Sam... her mother didn't believe me; thought I was talking nonsense. But she was a determined wee girl, and strong. If she wanted to climb over, I know she could.'

'So, the mystery of the missing child is that simple. She climbed over the wall and fell into the loch. Why didn't anyone hear her cry out? Why didn't the search teams and the divers ever find her body?'

'The house is soundproof. Both her parents must have been inside when it happened. Her mother persuaded the search teams not to bother with the loch at first – said there was no way she could climb over the glass balustrade.'

'You could have told the police you thought she had climbed over the wall, was in the water. Why didn't you?'

Jane shook her head. 'I couldn't. Samantha gave me a look when the police asked me where I thought she could have gone. We both knew she would have drowned if she'd fallen in – the water's cold and deep there, and the tide can pull even strong swimmers away from the shore.'

She looked directly at the camera, staring through the spotlight fixed on her face.

'Tony loved that girl. If he caught as much as a whisper that Lilybet's death was anything to do with Samantha, he'd have had her killed for sure.'

Teàrlach stared into Jane Whiting's eyes. If some of this performance was acting, he'd swear these words were true.

'That's all I needed to know. You can go now.'

Jane's face flooded with relief, the tension left her body just as her captor pulled her head firmly back by grabbing a handful of hair. She screamed as he drew a blade across her throat.

There was a moment's silence, broken only by a voice off screen saying cut. The only difference between this clip and the one Dee had shown him was Jane Whiting was still alive, her neck devoid of the blood and gaping slit where her throat had been.

The androgynous character Teàrlach had met at the studio appeared in frame, directing another man to spread blood over her face and chest. Jane sat there emotionless, expectantly. A clear plastic pipe was placed by her throat, a pump sending red spurts of red liquid into the air.

'Now tilt your head back. No, not like that.' Reynaert held her face between both hands, pushed it back to one side, standing with his back to the camera to admire his handiwork.

'Cut her throat again, then walk around to stand in front of her. Make sure the blade has blood on it, and we can sort out the rest with FX.'

They repeated the scene, Jane's head obediently following Reynaert's instructions.

'Can someone untie me? These ropes are digging into my wrists.' Jane spoke like an accomplished actor after a wrap.

Her interrogator resumed his position behind her chair.

'If you want to leave here alive, you answer my questions.' His voice was muffled by the hood, but the meaning was clear enough. Now Teàrlach could make out a Germanic harshness to the accent that was previously concealed. Whoever had edited the film had deliberately reduced the vocals, made them so indistinct and overlayed with noise that it had been an effort to understand anything.

'What are you playing at? Come on, untie me.' Jane Whiting sounded frightened enough, her head whipping from side to side as she tried to see her captor.

'You used to work for Tony Masterton?'

'Yes, I was their nanny. Why do you want to go over this again?'

'You looked after their little girl, Lilybet.' This as a statement.

Jane nodded violently. She began sobbing.

'Speak! I can't hear you!' Her interrogator shouted so loudly he could see her visibly jump.

'Yes. Yes, I was her nanny. Please, I just want to go. You can have all my money.'

'What happened to the girl? Who took her?'

'I don't know. I wasn't there.' She began crying in earnest, heavy sobs coming from deep in her diaphragm, gulping for air.

The man in the hood casually slapped her hard across the side of her face, violent enough that the chair she was tied to rocked with the blow. Teàrlach knew this wasn't an act. Jane Whiting's face expressed real shock, real pain.

'Who took her?' His voice remained calm, quite at odds with the casual violence he'd just administered.

'I don't know. I told you I wasn't there when she went.' She spoke quietly. This time the sobs were for real.

'Why would someone take the girl?'

She drew a long, shuddering breath before answering. 'Tony has a lot of enemies, powerful enemies. Anyone could have taken her.'

'You know something, don't you?'

'I don't know who took her. I've already told the police, Tony's own security, everyone. I was in Inverness that day. I didn't even know she'd gone missing until my phone went mad.'

'Who are you protecting?'

Her silence earned her another hard slap, this time on the other side of her face.

'I don't know. I'm not hiding anything. Please... I just want to be let go.' Now she was sobbing in earnest, struggling against the ropes holding her tight.

The interrogator walked out of camera shot, returned with pliers in his hand. He held her hand, stretching the fingers out straight as she tried to make them into a fist. The pliers tightened on the first fingernail.

'No! No! No! I'll tell you what I know. Please.'

The pliers pulled almost playfully as she screamed.

'What do you know?'

Teàrlach watched the screen intently. This hadn't been on the footage Dee had shown him. Had she kept something back, shared it with Tony Masterton but kept it from his investigation?

'Richard. Richard Tavistock. It's his child. That's all I know.'

'This Richard Tavistock, he took the child?'

She sobbed, crumpled into her seat, the ropes preventing her from sliding onto the floor. He grabbed her hair, pulled her head back and thrust the pliers in front of her face.

'DID HE TAKE THE CHILD?'

'I don't know. I don't know! He told me it was his child when we...'

'When you what? I don't want to have to pull your nails out, but believe me I will do so until you tell me everything.'

'We were in love.' The words came as an anguished cry; this was no act Teàrlach was watching. She took another tremulous breath. 'I thought we were going to live together and then he told me that...'

'What did he tell you?' Her interrogator sounded impatient now.

Jane's voice broke with the pain of saying the words out loud. 'He told me that he'd had an affair with Samantha. It had been going on for years – he wanted to end it, but she threatened him. Said she'd tell Tony. Samantha told him Lilybet was *his* child.'

SIXTEEN

OSCARS ALL AROUND

Teàrlach sat staring at the screen long after the video had finished, his mind racing. He was all but convinced that Jane and her uncle had planned the whole hostage scenario to take Tony Masterton's substantial reward, convincing him that Lilybet had climbed over the glass divide and drowned. If she had been worried about reprisals for not telling Tony the girl wasn't safe to be left unattended on the decking, then having herself conveniently 'killed' should keep her safe.

The local police weren't going to commit resources to investigate a young missing woman, not without any evidence of foul play or a body to identify. In time, she could return home, and Tony Masterton would have forgotten she even existed. Her uncle was clever enough to place the video on the dark web, so there wasn't an easy path to identifying him – but he'd not allowed for someone like Dee tracing his virtual footsteps through the ether.

But then the second part of the interrogation – the part Dee hadn't shown him? Jane wasn't acting then. He didn't imagine for a second that she had wanted to implicate the man she loved, the gardener Richard Tavistock – much less imply Tony's wife had been, maybe still was, having an affair under his nose. It was bad enough saying Samantha had ignored her warnings about the dangers offered by the loch. Teàrlach could only imagine how a man like Tony Masterton would react to finding out about his wife's infidelity or Lilybet being fathered by Richard if the film studio had sold him the additional footage.

Suddenly, the gardener's violent death and missing heart started to make sense. It was time to talk to Dee again.

'What you got, Sherlock?' Dee sounded irrepressibly cheerful, but then she wasn't at imminent risk of a violent death.

He ignored her deliberate play on words. 'That video you sent me; that was all of it? You didn't leave anything out?'

'No, why ask?' Her interest raised a notch.

'It's just the film studio let me have their copy, maybe they gave me more than they bargained for, I don't know, but Jane Whiting's interrogation continued for some time after her throat was cut.'

Dee didn't have a flippant answer to that. Teàrlach waited until she processed his comment and came to the only conclusion that made any kind of sense.

'They faked it?'

'Aye. Fake blood and Oscars all bloody round.'

He heard her whistle in admiration. 'Fooled me,' she said simply.

'Did it fool Tony Masterton?'

She considered his question carefully. 'He wasn't exactly fulsome in his praise for finding out what she said happened to his daughter, but yeah – he believed it.' A computer chirruped in the background as she worked the keyboard. 'And they've found the girl's body in the loch so looks like she was telling the truth.'

'Have the police made a positive ID?'

'Nothing yet. They've been to Tony's house, taken DNA samples from him and his wife. He wasn't too keen on that!'

'No, I bet.' Teàrlach wondered how keen he'd be to find out if he was the father of his own daughter. At least that gave his wife some breathing space.

'You said the film continued after her death,' Dee asked curiously. 'What else was on it?'

Not for the first time, Teàrlach wondered how much he could trust her. Richard Tavistock's mutilated body decided for him – Tony must have already seen the entire film, yet Dee only knew about the first edit. The fact that she wasn't completely in step with Tony made his mind up for him. He explained what was on the second interrogation, the real one.

'Holy shit! You think the studio knew about the reward – decided to go to Tony direct?'

'I think there's a good possibility they did a bit of research themselves. It wouldn't be difficult to find the Mastertons' reward on an internet search and the incentive of earning a million would have been more than enough to interrogate her for real. Thing is, if he was sent the complete footage, I don't think your boss would have been too pleased.'

'That explains the gardener...'

'Aye.' Teàrlach cut her short. 'And it means Samantha Masterton is probably living on borrowed time – at least until the DNA comes back.'

'Someone has to warn her.'

Teàrlach knew there was only one person who could do that, and he'd be putting himself directly in the line of fire for whatever followed.

'We've some time yet. The police are stretched enough as it is. Be a good few days most likely before they run the sequences and come back with a positive match.' He spoke with more conviction than he felt, although if forensics identified a different father, that might throw enough doubt on the result to make them re-run the test.

'What about the nanny? Jane Whiting?'

'What about her? If Tony's seen all the film, he knows she's still out there, but he's bigger problems than an ex-nanny to sort. He's already made a start with the gardener, most likely tortured him to find out if he had any involvement with Lily-bet's disappearance before taking his revenge by removing the guy's heart.'

'I wouldn't put it past him,' Dee spoke quietly.

Teàrlach thought furiously. If Tony Masterton had already seen the footage before he'd announced he was flying to Amsterdam, would he have been so relaxed about his going there? Or maybe he thought that Teàrlach would find Jane Whiting's whereabouts – leaving him free to have her picked up at his leisure.

'I'm heading back. I'll catch a flight as soon as I can. See you back at the hotel. Can you see if Tony paid a reward to the film studio, or transferred anything across to Jane's uncle?'

'What makes you think I can do that – or be mad enough to even try?'

'It's up to you. It's not that important, just looking for confirmation that Tony's seen the full feature rather than the trailer.'

'I'll see what I can do.'

'One more thing,' Teàrlach quickly added before she cut the connection. 'Does Samantha leave the house at regular times – go to yoga or shopping or...' He ran out of ideas for what a married woman with expensive tastes might get up to in such a remote location.

'Now that Lady Chatterley's lost her gardener?' Dee replied, the sparkle returning to her voice. 'I'll try and find out. You want to warn her that Tony knows about her affair?'

'I think that might be wise,' he answered drily.

'I can track his phone. See when he's not at the house.'

'Ideal! Let me know as soon as the forensics report is ready.'

'May just be able to get on their network. Take a bit of work, but we'll know what they find out before Tony.'

'You know you're meant to be working for him, Dee? This could be dangerous if he ever finds out you're keeping things from him.'

'That applies to you as well, Sherlock.'

The call ended, leaving Teàrlach only too aware how accurate a summation that was.

SEVENTEEN

KAELPIE DREAM

I am the boatman
I stand where my child once stood
And see only death

Tony Masterton left the house without seeing Samantha, leaving long before she surfaced from her own bedroom. The Bentley and chauffeur were waiting. The engine growled in satisfaction as they accelerated along twisting roads towards Glasgow. Early sunshine strobed through pine trees, making it too distracting to view his laptop. He flipped it shut more forcibly than needed, the snap of metal hitting glass loud enough for his driver to check the mirror. One glance at Tony's eyes was sufficient warning to focus all his attention back to the winding road.

Outside the privacy windows, the loch slid by, glimpses of water turned aquamarine by the pale turquoise wintry sky above. The tranquil beauty was what had first attracted him to this place, away from the grime and noise of Glasgow. Somewhere to leave all that behind, to make-believe that the world wasn't as cruel and as evil as he knew it to be. But now that cruelty had followed him here as he realised it eventually would. His wife's affair with the gardener, he had shut away in a dark corner to be taken out and inspected when the time was right. For now, he'd lanced that abscess.

The rat gnawing at his mind and refusing to be silenced faced him at every twist and turn of the road. The loch had taken his girl. He'd insisted on building the house right next to the water, greased palms and threatened officials to obtain planning consent. Wanted the deck right up to the water's edge so he could stand there at night, drawn by a primeval urge to be near the water.

He'd dreamed last night, an unusual enough occurrence for the memory to lurk around the fringes of his consciousness. Tony lost himself in the scrolling scenery, dug deep to recall seeing himself standing on the decking at night. Even though it was winter, he'd felt warm. He had walked across the decking naked, feeling the rough wood through the soles of his feet. A full moon hung in the sky, surrealist and spilling a silver path across the loch's dark waters. He'd taken the notion to walk, Jesus-like across the loch and passed through the glass balustrade as though it were as insubstantial as mist. The silver path held him afloat, a sensation of needles pricking uncomfortably into his skin as each foot made contact. A feeling of power radiated from him, dominance over this liminal realm he crossed. He looked back, saw his house small and diminished. How had he travelled so far out into the loch with only a few steps? He moved effortlessly forward, the far shore staying resolutely distant. Under the surface, bioluminescence left blue sparks wherever his feet trod – forming an alternative universe of dancing stars. He stopped walking, entranced by the sight. Now he could see shapes indefinable under the water, swimming in slow circles. With mounting curiosity, he realised he was sinking into the loch. There was no feeling of cold, or panic, and as his torso descended into the water, his hands left trails of blue light as he instinctively began to swim. The experience was enjoyable, somehow sensuous as if the loch was giving itself to him.

Then the waters darkened, and he realised he'd sunk under the surface. Tony tried to swim back, long pulling strokes from his arms, strong kicks from his legs that should have propelled him upwards, but still he sank. He felt himself being pulled deeper and deeper into the voraciously hungry saltwater and started to panic, fighting against the instinct to draw a breath and surely drown. Unable to hold the impulse any longer, Tony took a gulp of seawater, expecting to choke as his lungs filled with the sea, but air filled his lungs instead. This was only a dream, he had reminded himself, and the panic subsided, arms and legs returning to a more languid motion underwater. He was aware of a creature rising from the depths, a change in the luminosity of the water until a woman swam up to meet him. Golden tresses curled and straightened with each surge upwards. Some trick of light or magic left her body indistinct, although he could sense the sensual shape of her.

'You left me an offering.' Her voice rang bell-like under the water, unearthly harmonics pulsing against his eardrums. 'And for that I am grateful.'

He realised her eyes were too oval, too far apart. There was an aquiline look to her features, a mouth too wide, lips too red.

'I don't know what you mean.' Tony was unsurprised to find he could talk underwater. She swam close enough that he felt the water pulsing against his body with every movement she made. He struggled to see her, an earthy need to see her naked flesh so close to his.

'The heart. It fed my hunger.' Unworldly eyes held his.

'You can ask me one thing, and if it is within my gift, I will answer you truly. Ask me another and you will have to pay.'

Tony felt deep malevolence seeping from this creature, an evil as old as time. He was not a man given to praying, or to a

belief in God in all its many forms. Pure goodness didn't exist –
the very essence of life was ensuring your own survival and that
of your offspring by whatever means necessary: teeth and claws,
force and strength, cunning and speed were the only tools
required. That and an understanding of why evil was always
stronger than good. Evil had taken Lilybet – he had to exact
revenge before he could rest.

'Is that my daughter, the skeleton they found at the Oitir? Is
it my girl?'

She swam around him. Now he was aware of the long,
sinuous length of her tail. No mermaid this, no selkie or other
folksy creature.

'The girl came to me; I did not take her.' The creature
almost sounded defensive, troubled. 'She is not your child.'

Tony felt a wave of relief flood over him, like a penitent
receiving a benediction. But then if that wasn't his child, whose
child was it?

'Who does the child they found belong to?' The question
left his lips before he heeded the creature's warning. What of it,
this was only a dream.

The woman's face twisted into an ugly smile, the lips
becoming reptilian. As she spoke, he noticed the teeth, narrow,
sharp – more shark than human.

'Your child's mother.' She laughed then, the sound as harsh
as fish scales scraped against a sharp blade. 'I'll collect my dues.
I always do.'

With that, she had sunk back into the impenetrable blackness of the loch, and Tony bobbed up to the surface like a cork.
That was when his dream had ended, and he had woken,
soaked with sweat in his own bed. What did it mean? Tony
wasn't a man who held any stock in dreams or premonitions.
This was simply his way of working through the discovery of
the child's skeleton in the loch. It had to be Lilybet, he was
braced for that. Maybe this was his way of preparing the ground

for the inevitable announcement, the police standing at the door with faces as long as a winter night and eyes unable to meet his.

What the hell. He'd met death enough times to know the smell of it. The cartoon character of the cowled figure with the scythe was pure imagination. Death came at you with a knife in the night, or as a car crushing flesh and bone and metal until it became one agonised whole. Death was the bullet's impact, the cancerous growth, the slow dance at the end of life until it was a fucking relief when you took your last breath.

'Your child's mother.' What sort of answer was that if he truly had entered a Faustian pact last night?

Tony snorted with derision at his own stupidity. Fairy tales were for children – or those whose children were still alive. Lilybet was gone, the only good thing he'd ever managed to produce in a life so starved of kindness and love these very concepts were alien to him until the day she was born, miraculous and free of sin.

Someone would pay. Once he knew who let his girl die – once he knew it was *his* girl. If Samantha knew Lilybet could climb over the decking glass. If Samantha had been screwing the gardener.

If.

Samantha's life hung on that simple little word.

EIGHTEEN
PUB PHILOSOPHY

The discovery of the child's body and horrific details of Richard Tavistock's murder spread like wildfire along the shores of the loch, setting up new conflagrations with every wayward spark of information until the entire community was ablaze with rumour and conspiracy. It took no time for the two events to become linked, a causality between Richard Tavistock's reputation as the local lothario and the young child's skeleton chewed over like a particularly rare and juicy steak. If there was an epicentre to this fire, then the ferry pub was ground zero.

Business was booming. Every table was booked for dinner, with a premium on those seats facing out over the Oitir and the site of ongoing police activity. Three settees formed a defensive perimeter around an open fireplace; dogs and children spread themselves; adults sat hunched over drinks.

'It's got to be the Masterton girl.' A woman, mid-thirties swung around to check her own child remained happily engrossed playing on the floor, oblivious to people walking around her small body with pints and plates. She was an accident waiting to happen.

'Whose else could it be?' Her partner spoke decisively, the mystery solved.

'Heard Tavistock was missing his heart.' Another man spoke through the beer froth lining his beard and moustache. He sounded personally affronted, as if it was his heart that had been ripped, still beating, from within his splintered rib cage.

'Still not found it. That's not natural, taking a heart.' An older woman, grey hair falling in unabashed waves down her long back.

The others nodded wisely. They contemplated the flames licking a fresh log, curling smoke reaching upwards in the chimney draft. A momentary companionable silence engulfed them as they drank. The murmur of conversation washed over everyone, waves of words churning into an indecipherable whole. The grey-haired woman imagined she was a stone on the shore, the tide pulling her one way and then the other. Disturbed at the prospect of being drawn into the cold water of the loch, she involuntarily gripped the cushions, anchoring herself to the settee. A shiver coursed through her even this close to the fire. One of the dogs detected the movement, raised a head to enquire with brown, trusting eyes, then allowed its head to fall back between two paws.

'That Masterton man. Wouldn't like to be in his shoes,' Mystery-Solver announced to anyone who'd listen.

They digested his words, unwilling to mention the name in public. Tony Masterton's reputation arrived a short time after the man himself. Rumours at first, hushed asides mentioning Glasgow and gangsters. There was an unspoken suspicion that Richard Tavistock's death and that of the girl in the loch were all connected to Glasgow and gangsters. It was best not to get too involved, ask too many questions. The inevitable march of cause and effect still powered the rumour mill.

'Was Richard... you know?' The mother took her eyes off

her child to unsubtly jerk her hips upwards. 'With his wife?' A guilty lasciviousness filled her face, replaced with yearning.

'What do you think?' Mystery-Solver made the question sound superfluous, as if the antics of the gardener were too much common knowledge to be asked after.

'Got what was coming to him then.' A fresh deposit of froth lined Beard's mouth. He wiped it away with the back of his hand, eyes looking for anyone brave enough to offer dissent. They settled on the mother, whose eyes returned demurely to the fire yet still retained a spark of heat.

'Don't speak ill of the dead!' Grey-haired Woman spat, fixing the heavily built man next to her with a look as hard as schist. 'And I wouldn't be too sure either death can be explained away that easily.'

Mystery-Solver cast a look heavenwards. He'd heard it all before.

'I'll get another round in,' Beard announced, weaving a path to the bar and avoiding assorted living floor debris.

'All I'm saying is that if that *is* their child, she's a long way from where she fell in.' Grey Hair had the benefit of old age and wisdom.

'Current could have taken her,' Mystery-Solver queried, unusually doubtful of the sound of his own words.

'Something took her.' Grey Hair declared, daring anyone to disagree. 'She's still there, in the loch.'

The others refused to meet her eyes. They knew of what she spoke. The kaelpie was a child's story, one they'd all heard – those that had been born and raised by the shoreline. A warning passed down from generation to generation until it became a fairy tale, a deliciously scary story to make a child pull the blankets in tight, snuggle down in safety and warmth. The adults on the settees exchanged knowing looks across the grey-haired woman's back – careful not to be seen. There was a time to leave such stories behind, especially in an age of technology and science. Even so, a nagging doubt remained. Cattle missing from fields, the sightings in the water that couldn't be explained.

Behind the mother's back, Beard cursed out loud as he tripped over the child on the floor, glasses spilling and shattering all around. 'Can you not look after your bloody kids!'

NINETEEN

LADY CHATTERLEY'S WARNING

Teàrlach arrived back at the hotel just after four. The sun had only set fifteen minutes earlier, western clouds stained red with its passing. The loch absorbed the colour, drinking in the dying sun until the water turned into blood. It reminded him of a biblical metaphor, the transmutation of day into night as inevitable as death following life. The sight unsettled him for reasons he wouldn't have been able to articulate. Blood turned to charcoal as the last of the daylight leached from the sky.

There was a knock at the door. He turned his back on the view as Dee entered.

'You decent?' Her expression was one of disappointment as she viewed him fully clothed.

'You ever wait to be invited in?' Teàrlach countered. He lifted his overnight bag off the floor where he'd left it, hoisted it up onto the bed and began emptying the contents.

She smiled, unconcerned by the rebuke and sat on his bed beside the bag, watching as he lifted each item out with the same curiosity as a cat.

'Did you find out if Tony paid the film studio – has he seen all of it?' Teàrlach felt uncomfortable under her inquisitive stare.

'Didn't go there. He made it clear what would happen if he caught me looking where I shouldn't be looking. Not worth the risk, sorry.'

He looked at her properly now, saw a young woman making her own way in a dangerous world. She hadn't started working for Tony Masterton willingly, she'd said as much. Now she was trapped, and the more she knew about him and his organisation, the more she was at risk. That at least they shared.

'OK. Doesn't matter. I think we can safely assume he's seen it judging by the state of his gardener.'

He removed the last items from his bag, took the toiletries and replaced them on the sink in the en-suite. Teàrlach stopped to look at himself in the mirror, saw the bags forming under his eyes, touches of grey in facial stubble like the first frost announcing the onset of winter.

'I need a holiday.'

'What's that, Sherlock?' Dee's raised voice rang around the tiled bathroom. She leaned on the doorway, inspecting her nails, then fixing him with an impish expression.

'I was talking to myself,' Teàrlach explained. He hadn't even realised he'd spoken the words out loud. Maybe he *did* need a break. As soon as this job was over, he promised himself. A proper rest from digging around in other people's shite lives.

Dee stood back to let him back into the bedroom. He brushed against her, opened his mouth to apologise, then closed it again. She'd deliberately closed the gap as he'd passed. A feeling of irritation flooded his veins, immediately followed by an unexpected desire as he caught her scent and the softness of her. Teàrlach frowned in confusion; he was too long in the tooth to be ambushed by a predatory woman. He turned back, searching for an appropriate comment that would leave her in no doubt that he wasn't interested. She still leaned against the door frame, posed like an actress in a fifties film waiting to be swept off her feet. Her smile would have confused the Mona Lisa – both mocking and welcoming at once.

Teàrlach's mouth opened and closed again. He had no words, so shook his head instead.

'What's the situation with Samantha? Is there some way I can speak to her when Tony's not around?' He took refuge in work. There was enough to deal with without letting himself become involved with his client's pet hacker.

'Now's a good time. That's what I came here to tell you.' She prised herself off the door, dropped the seduction like a mask. 'Tony's in Glasgow. He left first thing this morning.'

They faced each other, two players working out their next moves in a game without rules.

'I'll go see her now then. She needs to know if she's in danger.' He still had his jacket on, pulled open the door to leave. 'Do you mind?' Teàrlach held the door wide open, inviting Dee to vacate his room.

Dee had shown no sign of leaving.

'Aye, alright. Have some things I should be getting on with.' She smiled sweetly at him as she left, walking slowly down the corridor to her own room and secure in the knowledge that her opening gambit had left him off balance.

The gates to the Masterton house remained stubbornly closed this time. Teàrlach tried the car horn to no effect, the sound quickly absorbed by the surrounding trees. He remembered what the nanny had said, how the house was soundproofed, and clambered out of the driving seat to search for an intercom on the metal gateposts. He pressed the button and waited for a response, only then realising how quickly the cold had taken hold now that the sun had set. Hoarfrost sparkled on the floodlit gates, coated each blade of grass under his feet. Teàrlach shiv-

ANDREW JAMES GREIG

ered involuntarily, his clothes ill-suited to cope with the wind scything in off the loch.

'Who is it?' Samantha's voice queried tinnily from a speaker. 'Oh, it's you.'

Teàrlach searched for the camera, saw a small lens embedded above the intercom button. He bent down closer.

'Tony's not here. You'll have to come back tomorrow.' She slurred her words slightly.

'It's you I've come to see, if that's convenient?'

'No. It'sh not convenient.' She sounded like a female Sean Connery.

Teàrlach considered whether now was a good time. Samantha gave every impression of already being quite drunk, even this early in the evening. He didn't really have any choice. Tony could be back at any moment.

'I've some information for you. Something you personally need to know.'

Somewhere in the blackness of the woods behind his back a cry broke the silence. An owl hunting, or some small creature caught in its talons.

'Be quick then, I haven't got all night.'

The gates remained closed. She obviously expected him to tell her what he had to say over the intercom.

'I think it would be better if I could tell you face to face.'

There was an exasperated noise relayed metallically over the intercom, followed by the sound of whirring motors as the gates pulled back. He returned to the warmth of the car, followed the sweeping drive down to the house. She was standing in the doorway, much the same as Tony had first greeted him, a glass held loosely in one hand.

'Can I come in?' Teàrlach asked. 'I've not dressed for the weather.'

She looked him up and down, saw how his city coat provided little insulation for sub-zero conditions.

'Come on in then. Shut the door behind you.' She sauntered down the corridor, only slightly unsteady on her bare feet. They entered a room he'd not seen before. Huge TV showing a cookery program, chefs panicking in a kitchen in complete silence. Two wine bottles stood on a low table, one empty the other half-full.

'Want a drink?' She held her own glass up to him, shaped eyebrows raised in query. The temptation to drink from a glass held so close to her own lips became too great, and she tipped a generous measure down her throat.

Teàrlach's own throat felt dry. He'd had nothing to drink all day but coffees grabbed at airport lounges.

'Sure, thanks.'

Samantha's face thawed from its frozen aspect at the anticipation of having another drinker join her in what had become an increasingly isolated pastime. She retrieved a second glass from a cabinet, opening the sliding door to reveal bottles of whisky, bourbon and sherry, all of which had seen action.

'Cheers!' Her glass impacted with his a little too strongly. If he hadn't pulled his hand back, it would have certainly broken. She sprawled over a chair, her own glass remaining upright without spilling a drop.

'What do you want to tell me?' The words were spoken deliberately, an attempt at sobriety.

'I'm going to be blunt here, Mrs Masterton, so you'll have to forgive me, but it's for your own safety.'

Her eyes widened, followed by her lips curling up in a smile. She inclined her head, inviting him to continue.

'Have you been having an affair with Richard Tavistock, your gardener?'

Teàrlach was ready for almost any response but laughter. She laughed so hard, what little wine was left in her glass soon slopped over the sides in miniature tsunamis and left dark patches on her blue silk blouse.

'My gardener,' she repeated. The smile was wider now. She held her glass out towards him for a refill, indicating the bottle with a tilt of her head.

Teàrlach refilled the glass and returned to his seat, watching as she took another large mouthful.

'Yes. I've been "having an affair" with my gardener.' She repeated his words with exaggerated prurience. 'What of it?' She threw this down as a challenge.

'I'm fairly certain Tony has seen a recording where your nanny, Jane Whiting, states you've been sleeping with him—'

'Oh no, that's not right,' she interjected. 'I've been fucking him, not sleeping with him.' She challenged Teàrlach to continue.

'Fucking him then. Your husband probably knows you've been fucking your gardener. The same gardener whose body was found with a face smashed to pulp and his heart ripped out of his chest.'

She sobered at that, face angled down towards the floor.

'He knew the risks,' she said quietly. She faced him directly, anger in her eyes. 'That bloody stupid girl thought he was in love with her, didn't she?'

'I don't claim to know anything about...'

'She did this out of spite! Doesn't matter, she should have saved her breath. Tony doesn't care what I do. Sometimes, he doesn't even know I exist.' She swung alarmingly from hysterical to furious to maudlin with the ease of a functioning alcoholic.

Teàrlach doubted that was true. If Tony really didn't care what his wife did, then chances were the gardener would still be alive. Of course, there was wounded pride at stake as well. There was always that.

'There's something else I have to tell you before your husband gets home.'

'What?' Samantha stared morosely into her empty glass.

'In the same interview, Jane said that she'd warned you Lilybet wasn't safe to be left out unattended on the decking. She said you'd ignored her when she told you she'd caught Lilybet climbing over the balustrade, that she was in danger of falling into the loch.' Teàrlach used the word interview instead of interrogation as if that might mitigate what he was telling her.

She raised her head up from the empty glass, glaring at him with defiance.

'That never happened!'

Teàrlach held his hands up in surrender. 'That's as may be, but that's what Tony will have seen on the recording. Jane said you'd prevented the police from searching the loch at first because you'd told them she couldn't have climbed over.'

He saw fear replacing anger. 'That's not true.' Her voice was quieter now, almost desperate.

'She also said you'd stopped her from informing the police she'd seen Lilybet climbing the balustrade before. That you were frightened of Tony holding you responsible for your daughter's death by leaving her on her own when you knew how dangerous that was.'

Teàrlach made one last effort to persuade Samantha to leave. "In the video Jane said you'd told Richard that Lilybet was his child. How do you think Tony will react to that?"

Samantha's face drained of colour, leaving patches of rouge on her cheeks so she appeared as a porcelain doll. A doll in fear of its life.

'That's not true. I didn't – he wouldn't believe her.' The colour returned as she convinced herself.

Teàrlach saw the lies, heard the untruths as they tumbled out of her painted mouth.

'You should probably leave before he gets back.'

She shook her head in denial. 'Tony wouldn't harm me.' Samantha stood suddenly, staggered as the drink affected her balance. She made a grab for the chair, dropping her glass which exploded into sharp, crystalline shards on the polished concrete floor. 'She was my daughter too!' Her features reflected the anguish of her cry, followed by loud sobbing as she buried her face in her hands.

'I can take you with me, put you up in the hotel whilst you decide what you want to do.' Teàrlach's outstretched arm was angrily shrugged off.

'Haven't you done enough damage?' Her bitterness turned on him with the twisted logic of a poisoned mind. 'Just fuck off! FUCK OFF!'

Teàrlach left. He'd done all that he could. His phone screen lit up with a message as soon as he sat in the driving seat.

> That went well! Tony's ten minutes away, he must have just switched on his phone. D x

He'd taken the phone Dee had hacked. Making a mental note to leave it in his hotel room in future, Teàrlach exited the gates and left the house. He'd tried to take Samantha away from danger. Whatever happened next wasn't his fault. Even unvoiced, his words sounded hollow, but apart from forcibly removing her from the house, there was little else he could do.

TWENTY

SILVER BULLET

When Teàrlach returned to the hotel, his parking space was occupied by a silver airstream caravan, large enough to give him difficulties in negotiating around it and into another vacant space. Dee's motorbike remained outside the entrance, a heavy chain woven through the front wheel. He could hear her laughter before he opened the door. She propped up the bar, exchanging ribald comments with the barman who looked as happy as a lark to have her undivided attention.

'You're back then.' He noticed Dee was working her way through a line of shots, eight empty glasses on her right, two full on her left.

'Whisky?' The barman expectantly held up the bottle of Lagavulin, whisky glass in his other hand.

'No, I'll try a pint of...' Teàrlach scanned the meagre row of pumps. 'Blond Bombshell.'

The selected pump spat air and bubbles into a glass. 'I'll have to change the barrel, unless you want to try something else?' The barman hung hopefully on Teàrlach's response.

'I can wait.'

The lark plummeted back to ground. Teàrlach waited until the barman left the bar and they were alone.

'I don't suppose you'd stop listening in on my mobile if I asked you nicely?'

She smiled sweetly. 'Nope. I was asked to keep an eye on you and help you with anything you asked for. That's what I'm doing.' Dee picked up another shot glass, tipped the contents down her neck and grimaced.

'You drinking to remember or to forget?'

She slid the empty glass over to join the others. 'I'm drinking to drink. Nothing else doing here.' She pointedly looked around at the empty bar. 'She's staying put then?'

He nodded. 'Doesn't think he'll do anything.'

'Rather her than me!' Dee reached for the last glass. 'I know what he's capable of.' It followed the others. 'Where's Blair fucked off to?'

Teàrlach put a name to the barman. Barman Blair. It helped having mnemonics to associate people and names, came in useful in his line of work. Blair returned to work the pump, froth and air preceding a steady amber stream. He placed the pint glass in front of Teàrlach, waiting for a reaction. Teàrlach wasn't sure if he was expected to be grateful he'd changed a barrel or if the barman was waiting for him to opine on the ale. He sipped it, cool hop saturated beer sat pleasantly on his tongue. He swallowed, nodding appreciatively.

Blair appeared satisfied with that, wiping the pump nozzle with a cloth that must have significantly added to the bacteria count rather than reduced it.

'It's one of our better beers,' he commented.

The bar door opened, allowing in a small flood of people. Leading the party was a thin man, pointy features and cloth cap like a budget Peaky Blinder; following him was a wad of muscle, thick neck balancing an equally thick expression. A slim woman followed in their wake, watchful eyes taking in everything.

They dressed as if the last twenty years or so had never happened.

'Good day to you.' The thin man touched his cloth cap in deference. 'Awful cold outside.' He deviated towards the open fire, rubbing his hands together. 'Now that's what a man needs on a cold winter's night.' He motioned the others in his party towards the seats by the fire, and they dutifully obeyed.

'I'll have two pints of whatever yer man's drinking, and a whisky Mac for the lady.' He pointed at Teàrlach.

Blair the barman hesitated, long enough for an awkward silence to fill the bar, before he took glasses off the shelf behind him and started filling them.

Cloth Cap gave every indication of having won a battle he'd fought countless times before.

'You wouldn't happen to know anything about the terrible murder happened just a way up the road?' Peaky Blinder's finger left no doubt that he was aiming the question at Teàrlach.

'Who's asking?' Teàrlach countered. An antagonism between the two men could be felt, an electrical charge in the air.

'That's a fair enough question,' Peaky Blinder acknowledged. He lifted his pint from the tray Blair had set on their table, returning promptly to his refuge behind the bar in case of any trouble. 'We're family. Family of yer man Richard Tavistock.'

Teàrlach sipped his pint, catching Dee's eye and trying to warn her to keep quiet. He couldn't help noticing her eyes no longer properly focussed. She was grinning at him like an idiot.

'The police are investigating his murder, up on Hell's Glen. Best speak to them if you're family,' Teàrlach advised.

'I'll be sure to do that, thanks.' His glass raised in salute. 'Did you happen to hear that the fella's heart had been cut out of his body?'

'That's the rumour.' Dee made a grab for the counter, steadying herself before turning to face the table of newcomers.

'A terrible business.' Peaky Blinder shook his head in sorrow at the cruelty of mankind. 'And the heart. Do they have the heart? It wouldn't be right to bury the man without it.' A chorus of disapproving noises and shaking heads followed his words.

'As I said, best ask the police. We're just tourists.' Teàrlach attempted to close the questioning down.

'Are ye now?' Peaky Blinder managed to express complete disbelief. 'Well, there's a thing.'

Dee returned her focus, such as it was, back to the bar. She gesticulated towards her row of empty glasses and mimed filling them up as if unsure of using her voice.

Teàrlach held up his palm towards Blair. 'I think she's had enough.'

Dee made to stand, seemingly forgot how high the bar stool was and fell into Teàrlach's waiting arms.

'I think that's us for the day.' He started half carrying her to the bar exit, ignoring her protestations that she wanted another drink.

'Have you seen the Tinkers' Heart yet?' Peaky called after them. 'There's an awful lot of blood lying there. Thought the polis ought to take a good look.'

Teàrlach paused, one foot holding the door ajar and turned his head to inspect Peaky Blinder at close quarters. He saw cool intelligence, calculation behind bright blue eyes. Now someone else was looking for answers, and if he wasn't mistaken, looking for retribution.

'I'll be sure to pass that on, if I happen to meet a policeman.' He let the door swing shut behind them and helped Dee up to her room. She remained propped against the corridor wall as he retrieved her room key, guiding her towards the bed where she fell backwards like a felled tree.

'Aren't you going to undress me?'

Teàrlach pulled a blanket up to her neck.

'Good night, Dee.' He left her key on the bedside table, pulled the door closed and listened until the lock clicked securely into place.

Once back in his own room, Teàrlach mulled over the arrival of the caravan and the unwelcome party ensconced in the downstairs bar. If they were from Richard Tavistock's extended family, and he was Lilybet's real father, then his search for the missing girl and the circumstances around her disappearance had just become that more complicated. Had the girl been taken by the travelling people as one of their own – and if so, whose body had been found in the loch?

What had Peaky called after him, as he wrestled Dee's drunk body out of the bar before she passed out completely? Had he seen the Tinkers' Heart, there was an awful lot of blood lying there? Initially, he'd taken it as poetic licence, but Peaky had spoken factually, as if there was a place with that name. Teàrlach searched the internet, found the Tinkers' Heart and unobtrusively slipped out of the hotel. The web page had informed him this was a tribute to the Travellers who died in the Jacobite uprising and was now a place where they solemnised marriages. He drove a few miles back up the road, parking opposite the turning to Hell's Glen. A farm gate led to a short section of orphaned tarmac. Embedded within the road was a heart-shaped outline of white stones, protected by a low fence. Teàrlach took photographs with his phone, the flash reflecting off crystals in the stones and leaving the image of a heart emblazoned on his retina. In the centre of the design the ground was stained darker than the night itself.

Teàrlach climbed back into his car, glad to be out of the cutting salt-laden winter wind. He'd felt observed whilst he stood at the site, although when he looked around, there was nothing to be seen but oppressive darkness. The map had shown the loch to be five hundred metres or so to the north-west, but the wet sound of waves slapping against stone had sounded much closer. More disturbed than enlightened, Teàrlach span the steering wheel around and headed back to the warmth of the hotel.

TWENTY-ONE
TINKERS' HEART

Dee was late down for breakfast, so late that she was only reluctantly offered toast and coffee by the receptionist who deserted her position at the front desk with an ill grace. The thought of a fried breakfast threatened what delicate equilibrium she possessed so the toast was a welcome alternative. She sat alone in a sea of deserted tables, willing the lights to dim before her headache exploded. Dee had imprecise memories of the previous evening. A row of shots. Teàrlach carrying her up the stairs to bed. Thereafter everything was at best hazy. The fact that she had woken fully dressed and covered with a blanket gave her reassurance. There had been a group of strangers in the bar, something odd about them even for the west coast of Scotland. They hovered around the edges of her memory like Hogarth engravings. The coffee didn't help, more homeopathic than the full-strength Italian the sign outside advertised. She could see right through the cafetière glass, the room beyond turned into a bromide print. What the hell – she needed hydrating.

As far as she could remember, it had been a good night. Plenty of craic with Blair when Teàrlach had left, then the new arrivals promised to liven things up until she'd all but passed out. Dee scrunched her eyes closed, willing her memory to work. There was something the guy in the cloth cap had said as Teàrlach helped her out of the bar... Whatever it was had gone, drowned along with a bunch of brain cells. She finished the coffee, wiping her mouth with the back of her hand and advised herself to pace the drinks in future – especially the shots now she was no longer a teenager. Back then shots were self-medication to make life more bearable – better that than the harder drugs doing the rounds.

Once her blood had stopped painfully pulsing against the back of her eyelids, Dee checked her phone. No contact from Tony Masterton which was a good thing, Teàrlach's location showing as still in his room. A chime sounded from her laptop, displaying forensics as the message header. Dee sobered up rapidly. Someone had just placed a report on the police server, one she had managed to insert an insignificant virus into yesterday via an anonymous online report.

The message contained an analysis of the child's skeleton found in the loch. Dee skimmed the science, picking out the relevant passages. Female, age between two and four. That put her bang in the centre of Lilybet's age at the time of her disappearance. Dee kept reading, finding a section detailing the DNA analysis of material collected from inside the child's femur. No match to Tony Masterton or Samantha. She read it again, willing her mind to focus. No match.

It wasn't their child's skeleton in the loch. Dee blew the air she'd been holding out between pursed lips. She had been convinced they'd found Lilybet. She kept reading, more information relating to DNA which she skimmed until a paragraph caught her eye.

...match to DNA extracted from the body of Richard Tavistock showing greater than 98% probability that he is the father.

Degradation of the submerged sample prevents our making a
99.9% accurate identification...

The Hogarth engravings, her clouded memory from last night informed her, said they were related to the gardener. She needed to inform Tony Masterton – or she could wait for the police to do that job for her. Dee made a swift decision. Always better to be the bearer of good news rather than bad. She shot off a text to his mobile, added the confidential police forensics report for good measure. That should ensure she stayed on his Christmas card list. The alternative being a very cold and dark place.

She tried Teàrlach's door, knocking when she found it locked. He wasn't there – which meant that he'd taken her advice and ditched his mobile again. So, what could she do now? Samantha had been warned that Tony might have seen incriminating evidence relating to her infidelity and childcaring skills. If she chose to ignore where that road led, then that was her choice. The nanny and her uncle were still fair game, and Tony might see them that way. Richard Tavistock and these new arrivals – it would be better to have an idea of who and what they were. She decided not to bother Tony with extraneous information unless they turned out to be relevant to the ongoing search for Lilybet.

Satisfied she had enough to be getting on with, Dee set back to work on her keyboard. She started by installing an image search with Jane Whiting's face, set to run as a background activity on remote servers that specialised in searching hacked CCTV cameras using artificial intelligence. Once that was in place, she began looking for the online trail that Richard Tavistock and almost everyone else leaves behind on the internet. As an afterthought, Dee sent the hacked forensics report to Teàrlach's PA in Glasgow. Chloe would be able to reach him via burner phone or whatever the two of them had put in place to prevent her from eavesdropping. It would slow her down, nothing else.

* * *

Teàrlach had made another early start, driving over the mountain pass to the local police station. It had snowed on the summits overnight, just a light fall but enough to make the driving treacherous. The weather was turning again, grey cloud wrapped around the higher peaks, concealing yesterday's powder blue sky. An ice-warning light had come on as soon as he'd turned on the ignition, the instrument panel informing him the outside temperature was two degrees. That had dropped down to zero once he'd motored up the final hill, tyres losing purchase on the ungritted road surface. He cursed his own stupidity in attempting the journey; a phone call would have sufficed, but he could learn more by reading a face.

Sergeant Jock Daniels lived up to the sobriquet his constables used behind his back. Jock had the ruddy complexion and bloated physique of a habitual alcoholic. He wheezed into the police station reception like a man desperately in need of oiling.

'You're the fellow nosing around for Tony Masterton.' The accusation was accompanied by bushy eyebrows drawing down in disapproval. 'What do you want?'

'My name's Teàrlach Paterson. Here's my card.'

Swollen red fingers plucked a business card from his hand, earned another frown.

'So, what have you got that's so important you come to see me? We've a lot on our plate, so don't waste my time.'

Teàrlach kept his expression neutral as he faced down the wheezing sergeant. 'Richard Tavistock's heart – have you found it yet?'

The policeman's bushy eyebrows travelled in the opposite direction, raised almost comically in surprise. 'What makes you think I'm about to share confidential information with a private investigator?' He imbued the words 'private investigator' with derision.

'I'm not expecting anything, officer. It's just that a group of Travellers came into the Lochside Hotel last evening and suggested you look at the Tinkers' Heart. I'm just passing that on in case it helps you in your investigations.'

Teàrlach could see the mental gears turning. It took a few seconds.

'Who told you that?' The sergeant didn't wait for an answer, opening a door that allowed a glimpse of a back office. A solitary uniform looked up from a desk, a sandwich frozen midway to the policeman's mouth. 'Spence. Take yourself to the Tinkers' Heart. We've had a report that Tavistock's missing remains might be there.'

He shut the door, but not before Teàrlach saw the sandwich complete its objective.

'Come into the interview room. We can't talk out here.'

Sergeant Daniels held open another door, and Teàrlach followed the wheezing policeman into a room that smelled strongly of sick and disinfectant. A table divided the space into two, four chairs waited patiently for the accused and his brief, for good cop and bad cop. A digital voice recorder blinked an unseeing red eye as they entered.

Teàrlach took a seat, waited patiently as the sergeant struggled to remove a notebook from a straining jacket pocket.

'Now, who told you to look for Richard Tavistock's missing organ at the Tinkers' Heart?'

'I don't know their names, officer. There were three of them, two men and a woman. They came into the Lochside Hotel bar yesterday evening – asked if anyone knew anything about Tavistock's murder. They said they were relatives.'

The sergeant's rheumy eyes engaged moistly with his. 'Relatives?'

Teàrlach nodded. 'That's right. I didn't have anything to tell them so suggested they speak to yourselves.' He paused, as if just realising something. 'They asked me to pass on the information about the Tinkers' Heart. Can't imagine why they didn't contact you directly.'

'These three people, can you provide descriptions, know what they're driving? Anything at all useful?'

'One was around five foot nine, slim build, age around forty. Sharp-featured – looked like he spent a lot of time outdoors. The other guy similar age but built like a tank. Near as damn six foot, didn't say anything but then his brain was probably muscle as well. The woman was small and skinny.'

Sergeant Daniels wheezed as he wrote. The scratch of biro on paper added to the symphony.

'Car, accent, clothing, distinguishing marks or tattoos?'

'I'm no expert, but I'd say they were Travellers. Old school if you know what I mean?'

The word TRAVELLERS appeared under the scratching pen, block capitals. The policeman underlined it, twice.

'Are they staying near there, by the hotel?' He sounded hesitant, like he didn't want to know.

'There was one of those cigar-shaped caravans there last night. It wasn't there this morning when I left. I get the impression they wanted to find out who killed Richard Tavistock.' Teàrlach left the rest of the sentence unspoken.

Rheumy eyes understood alright.

'I don't suppose you've had a look yourself – at the Tinkers' Heart?'

'I went there last night. Kept out of the fenced area. I only had my phone torch so couldn't see much, but something had been left in the middle of the stones. Something that stained them dark.' Teàrlach reached for his mobile, remembered he'd left that one in his hotel room and let his hand return to his lap.

'There's nothing there now?'

Teàrlach shook his head. 'Nothing I could see. Forensics may be able to find something.'

The sergeant gave him a look that said he didn't like being given advice. 'Thank you for bringing this to my attention. I'd advise you keep your distance from the Travellers. One murder is enough.'

'Thanks, officer. I'll bear that in mind.' Teàrlach felt the vibration as his burner phone alerted him to a message. 'I'll be on my way then. Just thought you should know – about the Tinkers' Heart.'

'Aye. We'll see what's there. If that's where his heart was left, then a wild animal or the gulls would have taken it by now. Be lucky to find anything.'

TWENTY-TWO

OFF THE GRID

Once settled in the driving seat, Teàrlach read Chloe's text with the latest from forensics. Lilybet was still out there, somewhere, waiting to be found. He breathed deeply, like a man facing a long and arduous climb. Either the nanny, Jane Whiting, was leading them all on a wild goose chase and knew something she wanted kept a secret or she truly believed that Lilybet had died in the loch. The interrogation, though – the first part was pre-arranged, acting more than anything else, but the second part hadn't been planned. The woman was clearly terrified, and that's when she had spilt the story about Richard's affair with Samantha and Lilybet being his child. She had never meant it to come out, he was convinced of that. If Jane had truly loved Richard Tavistock, then that made sense, if only to keep him safe from Tony Masterton.

He opened the attached forensics report, cursing the small screen. It confirmed that the skeletal remains belonged to a young girl but had no genetic link to the Mastertons – only to Richard. Teàrlach stared out of the car windows, seeking inspiration from a tired seaside town whose best days were long since gone, departed along with the Victorian steamships that used to ferry Glaswegians *doon the watter*. No inspiration was forthcoming, just a growing sense of melancholy, which the grey winter weather only added to. According to Jane Whiting, it had been Samantha who had told Richard he was the father. Why would she have done that if Lilybet wasn't his child?

None of this was helping him find the girl. Teàrlach turned the car around, headed along the sea front with its large houses festooned with B&B signs and drove back to the hotel. Whatever answers were out there, they remained at the place the girl went missing. The clouds had lowered since he made the earlier journey, now the roads were cloaked in a fine mist which made driving difficult. Headlights served no useful purpose, so he dropped to a crawl, remembering there were sharp bends and narrow stone bridges to negotiate – never mind the ice and any oncoming traffic.

Meanwhile another girl's bones lay in a forensics lab, yet nobody had come forward to claim her. She remained unreported and unmourned in a country where such things were almost unthinkable, even more so in a small rural community where everyone knew each other's business down to the minutiae of daily life. Someone knew what was going on here, he just had to find out who.

He reached the hotel at lunchtime. The silver bullet caravan hadn't returned to clog up the parking spaces, and he manoeuvred back into his favoured slot. The bar was deserted, even Barman Blair hadn't bothered showing up for his shift. It was little wonder; he and Dee were apparently the only people staying there, and the lunchtime trade was non-existent.

'There you are,' Dee's voice came from a table in the breakfast bar. Teàrlach squinted to see her outline, lost in the gloom of drawn curtains and only illuminated by the ghostly blue glow from her laptop screen.

He wandered through to join her, pulling open the nearest curtain to allow what grey light there was to penetrate. Dee shrank back like a vampire fearing the sun. Her hand had automatically shielded her face, only to be slowly lowered as the threatened headache failed to materialise.

'Ah, so I'm over my hangover.' She smiled encouragingly. 'Sit here, Sherlock. Let me show you what I've found.'

Teàrlach sat obediently, curious despite himself to see what she had to offer. Dee helpfully spun her laptop around so they could both view the screen. It was blank.

'I don't understand.' Teàrlach looked again, wondering if he might have missed something, some small writing in one corner.

'Me neither.'

He wondered if Dee might be playing some sort of game, but her face was uncharacteristically serious for once.

'This is the result of a comprehensive search for any data on Richard Tavistock. I've covered social media, tax, national insurance, births, schools, universities, newspapers. I've even searched using his face as a search term and nothing, nada, zip, jack.'

She saw his confusion, realised he didn't know what this meant.

'And that isn't possible, Sherlock. Even MI5 and MI6 operatives leave a trace. It's next to impossible to live any length of time in the twenty-first century in a G7 economy without leaving a digital footprint. Can't be done!'

'What's that mean?' Teàrlach knew where she was coming from, he just couldn't work out where she was going to.

'It means he either doesn't exist – and there's a body that proves he did – or he's somehow either kept off the grid or been erased from it.'

'How do you mean, erased?'

Dee gave him a pitying look. 'There are countries out there

who have the resources to erase every trace a person leaves online. It's expensive, incredibly labour intensive and no way is it foolproof. You'd only use it if you had an asset you want to keep under wraps, a sleeper agent if you like.'

'You think he was a spy?'

'No, Sherlock, I don't. What the fuck use is a gardener working on a gangster's garden and bedding his wife more often than his plants on the banks of some loch in the west of Scotland?'

Teàrlach had to admit he struggled to see what benefit that could offer anyone, even someone wanting detailed knowledge of Tony Masterton's business dealings.

'Off the grid then,' he ventured.

'Aye. Off the fucking grid.' She slammed the lid of her laptop down triumphantly.

'I still don't see how that helps us look for the girl.' Teàrlach hadn't felt as lost as this since the first time he'd ran away from home.

'Because Fagin, Mr Bloody Bumble and Mrs Corney are all off grid as well!'

'Am I meant to know who these people are?' Teàrlach had a dim recollection of a musical about a pickpocket – this wasn't a strong subject for him.

'The bunch of characters that were in here last night. None of them show up, none of them are likely to show up – unless they've been arrested. The Travellers are the only people who can evade bureaucracy if they want to. Remember Fagin said they were related to Richard Tavistock?'

Teàrlach nodded, putting the names she'd given them to each of the characters sat by the fire last evening.

'Well, that at least was probably true,' Dee continued. 'Then the connection to the Tinkers' Heart – you've been there, right?'

'Aye. Last night after you passed out.'

She flashed him a look of annoyance. 'I was just getting into my stride.' Dee regained her chain of thought. 'Well, that's connected to the Travellers. It's where they celebrate weddings for one thing. It seems a bit too coincidental that his heart was left there – if that's where it ended up.'

'Might not have been Tony or his guys then?' Teàrlach worked through the alternatives; they weren't encouraging.

'Jesus, and you do this private investigating for a living?' Dee was enjoying herself at his expense.

'Nothing is ever as easy as it seems.' He drummed his fingers on the table, sounding like a distant calvary charge. If Richard's death was a result of internecine Traveller conflict, then they'd just arrived in the middle of a war zone, with the hotel as near to ground zero as made no difference. Alternatively, Tony might have deliberately had the gardener's heart placed in such a symbolic location to put the local police off the most obvious scent – his own. If so, he had made a big mistake as Richard's extended family had come looking for his murderer and him being a bigshot Glasgow gangster wouldn't bother them at all.

In the middle of all this, Teàrlach had to try and find where Lilybet was. He shook his head. This was turning out to be a lot more complex than he liked.

'You may be safer going back to Glasgow,' he suggested. 'If they get wind of the fact you're working for Tony, then that might put you in danger.'

She studied him from underneath red curls. Her cool eyes remained unconcerned.

'I can look after myself,' Dee said eventually. 'You're the one they'll be wanting answers from – the famous private eye.' She unplugged her laptop from the wall, tucked it under her arm.

'I'll be in my room if you want me.'

Teàrlach tried not to read anything into her parting comment and failed. She may be able to look after herself, but not if things turned ugly. It was time to pay Richard Tavistock's mother another visit — Annie Tavistock. If that's who she really was.

TWENTY-THREE
CAST-IRON CASTE

At least Teàrlach knew where the silver bullet caravan had gone; it was parked at the end of Annie Tavistock's drive occupying a space someone had recently cleared from the encroaching jungle. A small fire burned in the centre of a ring of blackened stones, black kettle suspended on a wire frame and lid bouncing energetically, clattering in the escaping steam. He was being observed by a large woman framed in the caravan doorway, arms folded across her chest. She didn't appear happy to see him. There was no sign of the three Travellers he'd met in the pub last night.

'What the feck do you want?'

Teàrlach made a point of locking the car, looking around him for the other characters. It appeared to just be the two of them, for now. The woman moved her bulk with deceptive ease down the caravan steps and towards him. She carried a large skillet, and he suspected it wasn't for any culinary intent. In a cage fight, he doubted if he'd come off best.

'I'm just here to see Annie.' His hands rose defensively. The pan was cast iron, she could do some serious damage if it made contact. 'She knows me.'

The skillet wavered – five kilos of iron held as lightly as if it were made from aluminium. 'She knows you?'

'We've met before,' he elaborated as her eyes narrowed to a slit. 'I'm trying to find out what I can about the missing girl – the one found in the loch.'

The pan dropped from her grip and met the ground, confirming its solidity with a dull chime.

'They've found her?' She expressed disbelief. There followed several emotions flitting across her face so rapidly that he suspected she shared a face-changing lineage with the old woman inside. 'In the loch?' She took a step back at this point, so close to the fire that Teàrlach prepared to make the Herculean effort of catching her if she fell.

'That can't be,' she added weakly. 'When was this, who found her?'

Teàrlach puzzled over her response until a familiar voice intruded.

'Teàrlach Paterson. I knew we'd be meeting each other again, just wasn't expecting it to be so soon – and here of all places on God's green earth.' Fagin had entered the clearing in complete silence. His overlarge shadow followed until they stood there like a pair of unlikely ghosts.

'Jeremiah, perhaps you could make yourself a nice cup of tea now the kettle's boiling? Mr Paterson and I need to talk. Why don't you come into the house?' Fagin made an elaborate gesture towards the bungalow, Mr Bumble blocked off any retreat.

Teàrlach stepped inside the cottage. Annie Tavistock watched him from her bed as the trio walked by her open doorway.

'Annie, how are you holding up?' Teàrlach paused in full view of the bed.

She regarded him silently, holding the three of them in stasis. Mr Bumble tried encouraging Teàrlach to move by shoving him none too gently in the back, but he had braced in readiness and remained solidly in place.

'I'll be better when you've all buggered off.' She returned to staring into space, his cue to move on.

They entered the kitchen.

'Have a seat, Mr Paterson, no standing on formalities with the likes of us.'

'What are your names?' Teàrlach asked.

'Why do you want to know that?' Fagin responded. He filled an electric kettle, placing it on its base and flicking the switch. A bright blue LED attempted to add some cheer to the otherwise unlit room.

'No particular reason, but you have my name.'

Fagin opened a cupboard and picked a tin of teabags in the manner of someone who knew the house intimately.

'Sure, why not? My name's Mick. This here is my brother, Brian.'

He caught Teàrlach's dubious comparison as he switched from one to the other.

'Brian's my brother by another lover,' he confided. 'He doesn't say much, but he's blessed with a lovely singing voice. Haven't you so?'

Brian's smile grew more pronounced.

'Now we've all been properly introduced, what the feck are you doing here, Mr Paterson? I thought your job was to find the missing girl, and unless my ears are needing a good old clean, you've found her.'

Brian's smile had been replaced with an altogether uglier expression.

'That's not the girl I'm looking for. I was hoping Annie might be able to assist.' Teàrlach saw the two half-brothers exchange a meaningful glance.

Mick poured boiling water into three mugs, stirring the tea bags for good measure.

'How is it the *wrong* girl, Mr Paterson? Exactly how many young girls are in that loch, do you suppose?'

Teàrlach shrugged. 'Who knows? All I do know is that whoever the girl was whose bones were pulled out of the water, she isn't the Mastertons' daughter.'

'How do you know that – sure they'll be bones and nothing else this many years later.' Mick spoke quietly, setting three mugs down on the table. 'Do you take milk?'

'Aye, just a splash,' Teàrlach replied. This had all the makings of as mad a tea party as he could remember being part of. He waited until the other two sat down, leaning towards him so close that he could see every healed scar on their faces. A history of bare-knuckle fights laid out in jagged detail. 'Because they ran a genetic test to identify the parents. Neither of the Mastertons had any link to that child.'

Two disbelieving faces stared at him from scant inches away. Teàrlach blew steam off the surface of his mug before taking a noisy sip.

'What they did find, though...' He sipped thoughtfully whilst considering his next move and deciding against throwing scalding tea in their faces. 'They found that Richard Tavistock was almost certainly the father of that wee dead girl.'

Now he had their attention. Mick looked dumbfounded. Brian's face adopted a confused expression which Teàrlach suspected was habitual. He took the opportunity of a lull in proceedings to lean back in his chair and adopt a more relaxed attitude – it also gave him more time to react if they decided to come at him. He looked around him on the off chance there was something he could use as a weapon. His eyes lit on a photograph, a young woman with a child on her knee. He'd not seen it on his previous visit.

'They said it was Richard's?' Mick finally spoke. 'How can they be sure?'

'I've seen the report from forensics. They said it was almost certainly his. As certain as you can be with the bones being under water for three years.'

'Well now. You've given us a lot to think about, and that's for sure. See Mr Paterson back to his car, Brian. We'll no doubt be in touch again.'

'I wanted a word with Annie,' Teàrlach protested, but Brian's vice-like grip lifted him bodily out of his chair as he stood up beside him.

'Another time, Mr Paterson. I think that would be best,' Mick advised. 'We need some family time, alone with Annie.' There was a hint of menace to the words.

Teàrlach had no choice but to exit the way he came in, his feet scarcely touching the floor. Brian had the strength of an ox – there was no way he'd win in a fair fight if it came to it. Annie ignored him, still staring blankly into space as he floated past her doorway. Out in the courtyard, Jeremiah was apparently rooted in the same spot by the open fire, but he'd seen her moving fast, away from the cottage door.

'You daft bugger. Do ye know what you've done?' She spoke quietly, just for his benefit. Brian ignored her, fixing Teàrlach in his sight until he'd reversed back out into the road and out of view.

He drove slowly back to the hotel, his mind whirring over the ramifications of what had just transpired. In truth, he hadn't any idea what it was that Jeremiah had just accused him of. Whatever it was, it was too late now to be undone.

TWENTY-FOUR

FAGIN'S SECRETS

I am the mother
Sold my soul so she could live
I deserve to die

Teàrlach pulled the files out of his overnight bag and searched until he found the picture of Lilybet. It had been taken weeks before she went missing, standing in the garden next to the elaborate Japanese treehouse. It was early summer, meadow grass reached almost to her shoulders. She faced the camera full on, sun catching her blond hair and laughing without a care in the world. He studied the shape of her face, the space between her eyes, the waves in her hair. It had been dimly lit in Annie's kitchen, only a meagre amount of grey daylight had managed to penetrate the foliage and grimy windows, so his viewing of the photograph wasn't great. But he'd say it was the same girl.

If the girl's skeleton belonged to Richard Tavistock's daughter, then it wasn't that unlikely that Annie Tavistock would have a photograph of the child in her house. Which could only mean that Annie knew a lot more than she was letting on. Teàrlach's mind whirled with it all: the skeleton in the loch; Lilybet's whereabouts; the murder of Richard Tavistock and the arrival of the Travellers; the bizarre, filmed confession and then Jane Whiting's faked death. Something had to link all this together – unless these events happened purely by happenchance. Teàrlach could accept coincidence, even serendipity could make an appearance. But everything pointed back to the big house overlooking the loch and Tony Masterton.

He headed down the corridor to Dee's room, tapped on the door. Bedsprings creaked a welcome, then he heard the door being unlocked. She opened the door a crack, stretched to peer over his shoulder, checked he was on his own.

'Just a minute. I have to shift this before I can open the door.' The door closed in his face, only to be flung wide open again.

'Come in.' Dee held a metal doorstop in one hand. She caught him looking at it. 'Always travel with one of these. The more someone tries to force their way in, the more difficult it gets. Simple but effective.'

'You expecting trouble?' Teàrlach asked.

'I seem to attract it,' she countered. Dee sauntered back to her bed, sitting with her back propped up on a pile of pillows. Her laptop lay within easy reach, the lid closed. 'How's the detective work going?'

Teàrlach searched in vain for a chair whilst Dee curled her legs up underneath her. 'Plenty of room here if you're looking for a seat?'

'I'll not stay.'

She gave him a look that said *suit yourself*. He stood there feeling like he was an awkward teenager again. Why did this woman have such an effect on him?

'I went to Annie Tavistock's cottage, further down the loch. The Travellers have taken it over, had me in for a chat.'

Dee scanned his face for any damage, flicked her attention down his body looking for any sign he'd been roughed up.

'Just a chat, then?'

Teàrlach nodded. 'I wanted to talk to Richard Tavistock's mother again. The police interrupted me last time, so I was hoping we'd have a proper chat together.'

'Did you talk with her this time?'

'No, apart from a word as Brian tried shoving me down the corridor.'

'Brian?'

'The one you called Mr Bumble. His half-brother – Fagin – his name's Mick.'

'Sure it is,' Dee interjected, trying out an Irish accent.

'Anyway, apart from wishing everyone would leave her alone, I didn't have much of an opportunity to exchange any more pleasantries with her. Mick was more interested in what I knew about Richard.'

'Did you work out what relation they are to the gardener?'

He shook his head. 'We didn't get around to that. When I first arrived, there was another woman there, armed with a bloody great skillet which she had designs on wrapping around my skull.' Teàrlach caught Dee's confusion. 'There's at least four Travellers,' he elaborated. 'This one, Jeremiah, hadn't heard about the child's remains being found in the loch. She took it quite badly, said that it couldn't be.'

'What did she mean by that?' Dee asked.

'I don't know. She asked who found it, when they found it – but didn't ask exactly whereabouts.' He puzzled over the omission again.

'Then what?'

'Then Mick and Brian slid out of the undergrowth like they were fresh back from a tour of duty in Vietnam and encouraged me to have a chat in the kitchen.'

'Did they threaten you?' Dee was suitably put out on his behalf.

'Not as such. They asked why I was still here if the missing child had been found, and that's when it got interesting. I let them know that forensics confirmed that the child found in the loch wasn't Tony or Samantha's child, but Richard Tavistock was almost certainly the father. Mick looked like he was in shock.'

'They didn't know Richard had been shagging his way around the glen?' Dee asked.

'I don't know about that, but I touched a raw nerve when they heard it was his child in the loch. Couldn't get rid of me soon enough.' Teàrlach replayed the scene in his memory. 'Said they needed family time alone with Annie.'

'Do you think they're going to harm her?'

'No. If they're family, I'd have thought she'd be as safe as houses.' He spoke with more conviction than he felt. Mick hadn't sounded too friendly when he said they needed a quiet word with Annie.

Dee looked unconvinced too but held her tongue. 'So, where do you go from here?'

Teàrlach had one more thing to mention. 'There was a photograph in the kitchen, propped up on the counter. I'm sure it wasn't there the last time I visited. A picture of a young woman and a kid. I couldn't see it too well as they left the lights off, but it looked a lot like Lilybet.'

Dee considered for a few seconds; mouth twisted in concentration.

'Seems kosher if he was the dad. Makes sense that his mum would want a picture of her granddaughter.'

'I guess,' he agreed reluctantly. 'But something doesn't add up. If Richard was Lilybet's father, why keep that a secret? Sure, don't let Tony Masterton know – I get that. But wouldn't Richard's family be told?'

'Maybe they can't be trusted to keep schtum when they have a drink in them. Too much of a risk for Richard if word got out. Annie wouldn't want the local gangster finding out the gardener's been planting his aubergine in amongst his wife's azaleas!'

Teàrlach gave her a pained look. 'I suppose you're right. The two men certainly didn't know anything about it. Jeremiah though, she knew something. I'm sure of it.'

'Wouldn't be the first time the womenfolk run rings around the men, so?' Dee adopted the same lilt the Travellers used, her eyes returning to laughter.

He thought for a few seconds. 'If that's not Lilybet in the loch, then it's another of Richard Tavistock's kids.'

'You want me to start digging around the hatched, matched and dispatched notices?'

'It would be a help. So far, all we have to go on is a video recording and my main witness is in a morgue minus his heart. I'll have another attempt at talking to Annie once her campers have gone.'

'Who do *you* think killed the gardener?' Dee's eyes drilled into his.

'My money's on Tony Masterton – or he ordered the hit. He had reason to do so after seeing Jane's video accusing Richard Tavistock of not only having a long-term affair with his wife but being the father of his child. That had to hurt. So far, the only Travellers I've seen are looking for Richard's murderer, which rules them out in my mind.'

'Unless there's another bunch of them roaming around the countryside,' Dee countered.

'Maybe. I'd still put my money on Tony.'

'Awkward. He's the one paying your wages.'

'And yours.' Teàrlach reached for the door.

'There's only so far I can help you if I turn up anything incriminating on Tony, you know that?'

Teàrlach paused at the threshold, turned back to see her opening her laptop.

'Aye, I know. My only interest is in finding Lilybet – or

finding out what happened to her. All these other things going on, they're not my concern.'

'Glad we understand each other.' Dee sent him a sweet smile as he shut the door behind him. He could hear the sound of a doorstop being kicked back under as he walked away, deep in thought.

He'd told Dee his only interest was in finding out what had happened to Lilybet. Her story had filled the news for months – was it his ego that had made the decision for him? To be the one investigator who found the missing girl when everyone else had failed? The danger in working for someone like Tony Masterton was clear from the outset, and he'd already been pulled closer to the man's orbit than was advisable. Richard Tavistock's murder was almost certainly down to Tony, and the police would have no hesitation accusing him of withholding evidence at best. Then there was Samantha. He'd warned her, but if Tony decided to take matters into his own hands, then her death would be at least partly on his conscience.

The further he went into this swamp, the more difficult it would be to escape. It was the same for Dee, he could see she was scared of Tony even through her bravado. And with good reason. If only half of the stories of brutality associated with the man were true, he was still someone you wouldn't want to cross. Yet despite all this, Tony cared deeply for Lilybet and needed closure of some kind, quite at odds to the psychopath personae everyone assumed was the real him.

He could walk away now, give Tony back his money and leave Dee to walk the circus tightrope alone. He owed her nothing despite the unsettling physical pull she had on him. Or he could focus on the job in hand, find out what happened to Lilybet. The key, he was increasingly sure, lay firmly in Annie Tavistock's hands. He opened the door to his hotel room, decision made.

TWENTY-FIVE

SNAP, CRACKLE AND WALLOP

The light was already fading. This close to the winter solstice it would be properly dark by the back of four. A mist had rolled in over the loch, spectral fingers reaching towards the shore. Distant lights erased one by one as a bank of sea fog spread towards land. Teàrlach stared out over the loch, his thoughts about as clear as the view. The arrival of the Travellers had played to Tony Masterton's advantage, he knew that much. The local police were wary of tangling with a big time Glasgow gangster, too large a prey for them to handle. The Travellers, however – they fitted neatly into the narrative of being responsible for every crime that occurred in the locality. Poaching, theft, assault – even murder. Especially murder. He could see it in the sergeant's face as soon as he'd mentioned them, particularly when they had suggested having a closer look at the Tinkers' Heart. Why would anyone think to look there for Richard's heart unless they were somehow involved?

Had forensics been to look at that dark stain in the centre of the monument? He felt a moment's fleeting frustration that he didn't know the answers to any of these questions, then took a deep breath to let it all go. Dee would know as soon as anyone if the police found any evidence that the gardener's heart had been left there. These were all distractions. His job was deceptively simple – find the girl, or whatever had happened to her. Nothing else, as he'd just unconvincingly told Dee, was of any concern.

There were precious few avenues left for him to explore. The nanny had gone to ground, probably still somewhere in Europe. Dee was running a search for her using hacked CCTV cameras – he didn't need to know the detail. If Jane Whiting turned up, then he could ask her what she knew, but if she had any sense, she'd keep a low profile. The other people there on the day, apart from the Mastertons, were staff – the helicopter pilot, later the gardener. Then the local bobbies and whatever detectives they'd sent from Glasgow. There was little to no hope of having them talk to him. That left Annie, Richard's mother. Teàrlach couldn't see a way of having a quiet talk with her whilst the Travellers were there.

A slow smile appeared on his face. Teàrlach keyed the number for the police station, asked to speak directly to Sergeant Jock Daniels.

'What do you want? We're in the middle of a murder investigation.' The sergeant's unmistakable wheezy tones sounded over the phone.

'Just so, officer. You asked me to let you know if I found where the Travellers were staying – the ones who suggested you look at the Tinkers' Heart.'

'Where are they?' The wheezing stopped, the sergeant holding his breath for an answer.

Teàrlach waited longer than was kind. 'They're staying at Annie Tavistock's bungalow. Do you know where that is?'

'Oh, we know where she lives. Don't worry. Thanks for your assistance, PI Paterson.'

'Doing my civic duty,' Teàrlach replied. 'You may want to go there quietly if you want to question them.'

'We know how to handle them, thank you.' The reply was terse. He could imagine the sergeant beckoning his team of constables even as they spoke.

'Well, good luck.' Teàrlach realised he was speaking to himself as the phone had cut off. He lay down on the bed, flicked on the small TV and prepared to wait the next couple of hours out. Long enough for a couple of patrol cars to arrive at Annie Tavistock's cottage and take away her family members. She had asked for them to bugger off and leave her in peace after all.

The wait gave him time to think. If the bones in the loch weren't Lilybet's, then someone else was missing a child and more to the point had managed to keep that a secret. In his experience, that child's mother was either going to be one of the few female psychopaths in the population or dead. It was possible the child belonged to the Travellers and the birth hadn't been registered – and the fact that Richard Tavistock was the likely father added credence to that theory. Then Richard's murder and the gruesome details of his death – was Tony enough of a madman to have been the killer, and if so, what were Samantha's chances now he knew she was at least partly negligent in caring for their daughter? Lastly, there was the nanny and her naïve attempt to earn the reward. She was probably next in line for Tony's vengeance. Teàrlach felt events were moving too fast, and he still had no real leads on Lilybet, just a string of people whose lives were now in danger. Annie Tavistock was his only hope of finding out what really happened to Lilybet, and who had ripped out her son's heart.

The bungalow was in darkness when he returned, except for a single outdoor bulb shining a baleful glow over the driveway. Teàrlach made a cautious approach on foot, not wanting to be on the receiving end of a cast-iron skillet. The small fire had all but gone out, wisps of smoke curling out of the cinders and being absorbed by the enveloping cold mist. There were no signs of life from the caravan, no sound apart from an increasingly bitter wind rustling the tops of the pine trees surrounding the bungalow.

'Hello, anyone here?' Teàrlach called out, his breath turning to ice crystals in the chill early evening air.

He was met with silence. Emboldened by the absence of any Travellers, Teàrlach knocked on the cottage door. There was the sound of glass breaking, followed by a hushed curse from inside and the outside light going dark. Teàrlach put his head to one side, listening intently.

'Is that you, Annie? Are you alright?' The house could have been otherwise deserted. 'It's Teàrlach Paterson, the private investigator. I was here earlier. I just want a word.'

The air hung motionless at ground level, a grey shroud hugging the cold ground and scarcely affected by the stronger wind moaning through the branches higher up.

'I'm going to open the door, Annie. Check you're alright in there.'

Teàrlach turned the handle. The door wasn't locked. Inside he was met by pitch darkness. He could taste the sour aroma he'd noticed on the air during his first visit. Teàrlach felt along the wall for a light switch, fingers encountering every lump and bulge under the wallpaper. Where was it?

'You OK, Annie?' He called out again, blindly inching his way forward until he must have been about level with the door to Annie's room. Changing tack, Teàrlach left the wall and put both hands out to feel for the doorway. The creak of a floor-board alerted him, sensing that someone was standing there in front of him. He didn't see whatever hit the side of his head, just the flashing lights that signalled concussion. His arms went up protectively but too slowly. He heard the whistle of air as another blow landed heavily on the side of his forehead and his legs buckled underneath him. Face down on the floor, his nostrils confirmed the source of ammonia before a third blow came crashing down on the back of his head and even that strong aroma faded away.

Teàrlach came round to feel someone pulling at his arms. He tried opening his eyes only to be beaten back by waves of pain splitting his head. Smoke stung his eyes, caught in his throat. He was dimly aware of someone coughing before realising the sound originated from his own chest.

'Come on, big man. Help me out here.' A woman's voice, agitated to the point of panic.

The indignity of being hauled face down over carpet began to win over the lethargy affecting his limbs. He heard himself make an unintelligible groan as he forced his legs to help propel his body forward. Flames licked around the periphery of his vision, orange and yellow and growing larger.

'You're going to die here if you don't help me!'

Teàrlach began to realise the danger he was in. Down on the floor he had escaped most of the acrid smoke filling the hallway. His rescuer wasn't so fortunate, taking deep breaths to fuel the effort of heaving his unconscious body away from the fire. His hands fell to the floor as she let them go, her body bent double as she fought for air. He made a monumental effort to rise, only managing to raise himself onto hands and knees. There was fresh air in front, a dim rectangle indicating an open door to the night sky.

'That's it, come on. You're almost there.' She encouraged him between wracking coughs and painful gasps for fresh air.

Flames licking at his leg gave him encouragement, the fight for survival overriding everything else. Teàrlach crawled like a toddler out into the open, the house at his back erupting into fire and illuminating the silver caravan with dancing sparks. Dee fought for breath, backing away from the heat.

'Annie.' He croaked, a hand raised, pointing back at the inferno, and he collapsed, unstable on three limbs.

'Too late. That's where it started. No chance. She's gone.' Dee only managed a few words before coughing into incoherence.

He rolled over into a sitting position, hand gingerly exploring his head and coming away sticky with blood. His skull seemed intact at least, no telltale indentations that signified the blows that landed had caused major damage.

'What happened. How did you...?' The pain issuing from his head made him stop. Something substantial collapsed inside the bungalow, sending a cloud of sparks through the open doorway and covering his clothes and hair.

'We have to leave. Now!' Dee straightened up, wiping the hair from her face and revealing sooty streaks across her face. 'Here, you have to stand.' She flourished a makeshift crutch in his direction, a stout stick pulled from the pile by the open campfire.

Teàrlach staggered to his feet, Dee's arms under his, pulling him up with more strength than he thought possible.

'Lean on me. Use the stick.' She took most of his weight on her right shoulder, forcing him forward and away from the burning cottage. The sound of glass windows shattering made him look back. Curtains newly liberated billowed in the updraft, fire licking them into tortured shapes. Now the conflagration had been given access to oxygen, it redoubled its efforts, feeding on the freezing night air. Trees loomed overhead, caught in the leaping lights as if waiting for their own chance to join the dance.

'This whole fucking place is going to catch fire!' Dee saw the danger even as the nearest conifer caught a leaping flame, hungrily spreading through the needles and towards the main branches as the newly liberated resin fed the fire. The wind caught the flames as they reached higher, spreading the conflagration from treetop to treetop. A muted roar joined the crackle and small explosive pops coming from the trees.

The sight was enough for Dee and Teàrlach to redouble their efforts, staggering crablike down the drive with Dante's inferno at their heels. They reached his car, Dee propping him up against the passenger door as she searched his pockets for keys.

'Get in. Hurry – this will bring everyone from miles around once they see it.'

Teàrlach collapsed into the passenger seat, dragged the seatbelt over his chest. His lungs were on fire, his head felt like a war zone. He pulled down the sunshade to see himself in the vanity mirror as Dee jumped in, pulling away from the side of the road and forcing him back into his seat.

'Fuck's sake, Sherlock! You would have been barbequed if I hadn't shown up.'

His hand automatically returned to his forehead, felt the blood congealing.

'What happened?' he heard himself ask through the pain.

Dee spared him a glance as she straightened up from a bend, treating the single-track road like a racetrack.

'I was hoping you'd be able to tell me.' Dee coughed again, wound down her window to let the freezing night air access. She breathed deeply a few times which set her coughing off again.

Teàrlach joined her, coughing from deep in his lungs. Each cough was accompanied by an increasingly severe stab of pain from his head until he began to feel being burned alive might have been the more humane option.

'Who hit me?' He asked the question without expecting an answer. It had been pitch-dark inside the cottage and whoever had been there had been silent. Too strong a blow for it to have been Annie. Maybe the cage-fighting woman with a skillet?

'We can work on that once you're patched up. First thing is

to get back in the hotel without being seen. Too far to the nearest hospital – and neither of us want to be in the frame for what happened back there!' Dee scanned the dash, searching for the time. 'Nine-forty. There wasn't anyone in the bar when I left. We may be lucky.'

They drove in silence, Teàrlach feeling himself being flung around as Dee threw the car into curves and corners. He dimly realised she was wearing her leathers.

'Your bike?'

'Left it off road. Going to be a bitch to pull it back out of the hedgerow. Shit! Hope the fire doesn't reach it.'

'I need a drink.' Teàrlach's throat made the words heartfelt.

'That makes two of us, but we need to clean up. Even the local police may work out we were at the cottage if they catch us both covered in soot.'

The hotel came into sight. Dee parked up and climbed out.

'Stay here. I'll check it's clear.'

She was gone for a lot longer than he liked. Dee returned wearing clean clothes and carrying a towel.

'OK. Place is deserted – one advantage of being here in the middle of winter I suppose. Wipe your head.' She offered him the towel. 'Dry the blood off your hands, otherwise you'll leave a trail. Keep it over your face if we meet anyone. I'll say you walked into a tree or something.'

Teàrlach doubted her explanation would fool anyone but followed her back into the hotel. He needed her help more than he cared to admit, his legs had turned to jelly and hardly supported his weight. Once they'd reached his room, she started undressing him, ignoring his objections.

'You need to clean up. I'm not after your body in this state.'

He helped shrug off his shirt until his top half was exposed, then reached for his trousers.

'Whoa tiger,' Dee admonished. 'Leave that for another day. It's your head we need to look at.'

In the harsh bathroom light, he looked a sight. A heavy gash showed red under his hairline, dried blood covered his face. Dee carefully washed it away, patting his skin dry as she went.

'You're a lucky bastard,' she announced. 'You've a skull as thick as concrete. That would explain how there's not much room in there for a brain.'

Teàrlach didn't appreciate the joke.

'I'm putting butterfly bandages over this wound.' She dabbed at his head, making him wince with pain. 'Has to be clean, stop being such a baby!'

There followed the sensation of his scalp being pulled together, tape pressed into skin and hair.'

'Not sure how good this will be with all your hair in the way, but I haven't any needle or thread.' She patted his head with a towel, stained red with his blood. 'That will have to do.'

Dee left him looking at himself in the mirror. The blood and soot had gone but bruising was already colouring purple blotches around his eyes.

'I may have to apply make-up tomorrow.' Dee eyed him critically. 'Paracetamol and water, get it down you.' She held out two tablets and a glass of water.

'We should tell the police. Fire department. Annie's still in there.'

Dee shook her head. 'It's too late. She'd have died before we left the house. If you hadn't been stretched out on the floor near the open door and with fresh air...' She helped him over to his bed without finishing the sentence. 'The less we're connected to the fire, the better.'

She bent down, removed his shoes and socks. 'Give me your trousers. We need rid of anything that smells of smoke.'

Teàrlach found he couldn't manage that simple task without help.

'OK, Sherlock. Into bed and try not to have any convulsions in the night, otherwise you may not see the morning.'

'Thanks.' He lay down, feeling his head pound with each heartbeat.

'Sweet dreams.' Dee turned off the light, he heard her footsteps fade down the corridor before falling back into a darkness so intense it felt like death.

TWENTY-SIX

PLAYBACK

The companionable sound of a spoon stirring against china woke him, metamorphosing from the fire engine's urgent clamour in his nightmare. He'd been in the sheltered housing with his mother and brother, the smell of petrol saturating the air as a hand carelessly dropped a lighter through the hall letter box and turning a supposedly safe place into a fiery hell. They'd screamed at him to help, ineffectually stamping at the flames and backing up to a rear bedroom with their bedclothes catching fire. He'd stood like a statue, incapable of movement, untouched by the fire reaching a crescendo around him, watching helplessly as their bodies crisped to an agonising death with blackened hands curling towards him in a final plea for life. This was a dream that had haunted his teenage years, one he thought he'd managed to leave behind.

Dee perched on the side of his bed holding a cup of coffee. Teàrlach struggled to an upright position, ignoring the warning pain from his head.

'How am I looking?' His voice didn't sound like his own, he was croaking like a habitual smoker.

'You look a mess,' Dee replied honestly. 'Have some coffee.

It's hot, wet and vaguely brown-coloured. Whether it's ever seen a coffee bean is a moot question.'

He received the cup gratefully, holding it in both hands.

'My head,' he complained.

'Like I say. You're a mess. Still, at least you're alive.' Dee sounded too chirpy, Teàrlach's radar picked up on it even with the mother of a headache pounding behind his eyes.

'What's happened?'

She cocked her head to one side, working out how well he was.

'Well, to start with, Annie Tavistock's bungalow no longer has even a ground floor.'

'She's dead?'

Dee nodded. 'One way of saving on cremation costs.'

'What are the police saying?'

'Do you think I spend every waking hour spying on Scotland's finest?' she asked, faux outrage in her expression. 'They believe it was an accident. According to the lead fireman, the fire started in her bedroom. He said it looked like she'd fallen asleep, and a dropped cigarette set fire to her bedding. There was a broken bottle of gin by her bed which would have acted as an accelerant. Everyone knew she was almost bed-bound – she didn't stand a chance.'

'What about the Travellers?' Teàrlach remembered the sound of breaking glass, the hushed exclamation from inside the cottage.

She pulled a face. 'They're out of the picture because your pet sergeant had them in for questioning at the station when the fire started. Don't think they'll be too happy about their caravan, though.'

'Is that the official conclusion then – this soon?'

'No. Just the prelim. The firemen are all volunteers, took them a while to arrive by which time I gather there wasn't much left. They spent most of the time preventing a forest fire –

although how anything burns in this weather I don't know.' Dee glanced out of the window.

Teàrlach realised the background hiss wasn't from his concussion but rain ricocheting off the windowpanes. He took an exploratory sip from the cup, failed to detect any coffee flavour, but the liquid soothed his raw throat. Teàrlach resisted the urge to cough, fearful it would split his head apart.

'You were tracking me.' He'd come to the only conclusion that could explain Dee's miraculous appearance at his hour of need.

'Lucky for you. I did tell you to leave that phone behind if you didn't want to risk me listening in,' she said defensively.

'Aye. I guess. Thanks for... well, just thanks.'

Dee had the grace to look slightly embarrassed.

'There's something else.' She recovered her demeanour quickly. 'Something you should listen to.'

Dee opened her laptop, selected an application and played an audio file. Teàrlach recognised his own voice, the sound muffled from his pocketed iPhone.

'I'm going to open the door, Annie. Check you're alright in there.'

He heard the door handle being turned, the door being opened followed by the sound of his breathing and the drag of his own feet on worn carpet. Fingers scraped over wallpaper searching for a light switch.

'You OK, Annie?'

Teàrlach tensed involuntarily as the unmistakable squeak of a floorboard sounded, followed by the dull thwack of something hitting his head with force. There was an outpouring of air as his lungs emptied in a silent cry of pain, then another equally solid thump. He could hear his body hitting the floor, bones and face impacting thin carpet stretched over wooden boards. Then the final sickening thud that knocked him unconscious.

'And fucking stay down, you nosey bastard.'

Teàrlach locked eyes with Dee. It was a woman's voice – one he couldn't place.

'Who...'

Dee motioned him to be silent, pointed at the laptop. They heard liquid being poured, a bottle glugging as it emptied. Heavy breathing, then a match being struck.

'Goodbye, Annie, you grasping cow. Take your secrets to the grave, you'll not be ruining any more lives.'

There was a whoosh as the match flame took hold. Teàrlach imagined Annie's bed soaked in alcohol, blue flames reaching out.

Footsteps faded away until all he could hear was the sound of a fire taking hold.

Dee stopped the recording. 'And that's when I figured you might need help.'

Teàrlach realised he'd been holding his cup all the time without taking another sip, engrossed in the playback. He drank to sooth his throat.

'A woman?' He spoke like someone disbelieving their own voice. 'She hit me pretty hard for a woman.'

Dee shook her head in sorrow. 'She was about to be discovered attempting to murder Annie. I didn't hear a peep from the old lady, so she must have been out for the count before you arrived. If I had a choice of whacking a big guy hard with a baseball bat or going to prison, I'd hit him pretty hard! Last thing you want is for him to be able to come back at you.'

'Aye, I can see the logic in that.' Teàrlach's fingers touched his scalp tenderly, feeling the plasters stuck to his skin. There was a large lump forming at the back of his skull.

'You're going to have to lie low for a few days, at least until the bruising's gone.'

'Can't do that,' Teàrlach countered. 'There might be evidence at the cottage. Something that will lead us to whoever it was that killed Annie and had a bloody good attempt at me as well.'

He attempted to swing his legs out of bed, felt the room spinning and belatedly realised he was completely naked. Teàrlach hurriedly pulled the sheets back over himself.

Dee regarded him completely unabashed. 'No need to be shy. How do you think I managed to get you in bed in the first place?' She grinned broadly. 'At least she didn't kick you in the balls, then you'd really have something to moan about.'

She made for the door. 'Stay in bed for a few hours. I'll bring you breakfast, or whatever I can liberate from the kitchens. There's a glass of water next to your bed and a packet of paracetamol.' She threw a glance back over her shoulder. 'Any other witnesses in mind? Because I think it's only fair to let them know their lives are in danger.'

Teàrlach couldn't be sure if she was being serious or joking with him.

'There's just the one. The woman that used to be a cop. She was the first on the scene.'

He pointed Dee towards the case file, asked her to have a chat with Helen Chadwell on the other side of the loch and warn her to look out for herself.

'Sure thing, Sherlock. Soon as I've managed to retrieve my bike.'

'I'll drive you.' Teàrlach protested, struggling again to leave his bed.

'Don't be daft. You can't even stand by yourself much less drive a car. I'll walk, it's not that far.'

She closed the door as he sank back into the pillows. Dee was right, he wasn't much use to anyone until he'd had a chance to recover from last night. He grabbed a couple more tablets, washed them down with water and lay back trying to concentrate on the case. He'd known Annie was holding something back, a secret that the Travellers and last night's assailant wanted buried for good. Teàrlach's head span with theory after theory until the pain made his eyes close.

Outside, the rain fell steadily, whipped in heavy squalls against the hotel windows. The sound of a passing motorbike drifted out of his consciousness as sleep took hold once more.

TWENTY-SEVEN
A UNICORN CALLED LILYBET

Dee turned her bike into Helen Chadwell's drive. She recognised the church and the kid's goalposts that Teàrlach had described, parked up as near to the house as she could and rested the bike on its kickstand. Smoke blew almost horizontally out of a chimney, shredded by the wind until all that was left was a tang of woodsmoke in the air. Seahorses played across the loch's agitated surface, galloping away until erased by the rain and mist.

'Can I help you?' Helen Chadwell held the door protectively, one hand in readiness to slam it shut.

Dee removed her helmet, offering the reassurance that she was another woman. She brushed her red hair back from her face.

'Teàrlach Paterson asked me to have a chat. About the Masterton girl?'

Helen eyed her suspiciously. 'Why didn't he come himself – he let me know he was going to visit last time he was here?'

Dee pointedly looked skywards, wiped rain from her face. 'He's had a bit of an accident. I can come back another time if now isn't convenient for you. I would have called, but he forgot to give me your number, sorry.' She tried her most winning smile, mixed with real regret. It must have worked for the door opened wider, and Helen gestured her in.

'Come out of the rain. It's terrible weather, isn't it?'

She led Dee into the kitchen, where a young girl with cropped blond hair was sitting at the table, colouring in a unicorn with great concentration, pink tongue held between her small white teeth.

'This is Alana.' The girl gave her a disinterested look, then back to her colouring. 'Sorry, I didn't catch your name?'

'Dee. Dee Fairlie. I'm working with Sherlock – I'm sorry, Teàrlach, on this case.'

Helen laughed in response. 'Yes, it does sound like that. You'll be Watson then, I presume.'

Dee smiled dutifully in response. 'Guess so.'

'What can I help you with then? I told Teàrlach already that I couldn't add much to what's already on file. It was three years ago.' Helen reached for the kettle, filled it up at the sink. 'Tea, coffee?'

'Coffee please, thanks.' Dee was lacking a caffeine hit, and just the thought of a proper coffee had her salivating. She thought rapidly. Teàrlach hadn't briefed her before she came, he'd been all but unconscious in the hotel room but wanted Helen warned. Easier said than done without scaring her to death – her and her daughter.

'Did you hear about the fire last night?' Dee attempted as an opener.

'No, was anyone injured?' Helen had her back to the table, plugging the kettle into the mains and filling a coffee pot.

Dee spared a glance towards the young girl, Alana. 'Yes, someone called Annie Tavistock?'

Helen paused momentarily, then selected two mugs from the counter. 'That's a shame. Nothing serious I hope?' She turned to face Dee directly.

Dee made a point of looking towards her daughter before answering. 'Terminal, I'm afraid.'

Helen's skin whitened in shock. 'That's awful.'

'What's awful, Mum?' Alana's attention switched from her colouring to her mother.

'Nothing, dear. Just someone hurt in a fire. We must be careful with fire, mustn't we?'

Alana nodded wisely, then bent back to her colouring.

'Teàrlach had gone to ask her some questions – about the Masterton case.' Dee carefully omitted mentioning the missing girl. 'Her son was the gardener. You probably heard about him?'

Helen nodded once, turning back to deal with the coffee.

'Everyone Teàrlach has tried to question has been involved in an accident. He asked me to let you know.'

Helen returned with two mugs of coffee, placing them on the table along with milk and sugar.

'Alana's eaten all the biscuits,' she said apologetically, earning a cheeky grin from her daughter. She appeared unconcerned by Dee's warning.

Dee tasted the coffee, relieved to find it as strong as it looked. She puzzled what to do next since her warning had all but been ignored. Alana provided inspiration by shyly showing her picture.

'Oh, that's lovely. Aren't you good at colouring? Is it a unicorn?'

Alana gave her a disappointed look. 'Of course. Look, there's a horn growing out of its head. I've painted it green and blue.'

Dee admired the picture whilst Helen looked on. 'Does it have a name?' she asked the child, pointing at the unicorn.

'Lilybet. I'm calling it Lilybet.'

Dee caught the startled expression on Helen's face before she was able to conceal it.

'That's a lovely name, darling,' Helen said. 'Do they know what caused the fire?'

Helen's change of subject was transparent. She sipped from her mug, unconcern personified.

'No idea,' Dee lied. 'Dare say it will all come out eventually.'

They exchanged reflective glances over the coffee.

'Did you know the woman at all – Annie Tavistock? You interviewed her son, Richard, at the Mastertons'.'

Helen adopted an air of concentration, searching the air above her head for memories.

'No. I never met the lady,' she eventually acknowledged.

'But you have heard of her?' Dee persevered.

Helen smiled tightly, finished her drink and laid it back on the table. She pointedly glanced at Dee's mug, looked to see how much longer she had before it was empty.

'Just the odd word.' The smile appeared stuck in position.

'Good words, or bad?' Dee was beginning to enjoy herself.

'Oh, you know what small communities are like. Always gossip for those that like that sort of thing.'

Dee inclined her head wisely. 'So, what was the gossip about Annie?'

Helen's smile lost its rigidity, her expression turning towards irritation.

'I really don't like to talk about other people behind their backs. It's not a pleasant habit and one I've taught Alana not to indulge – despite the delight weak-minded people derive from it.'

The rebuke was aimed squarely at Dee.

'What sort of man was Richard? You said you had interviewed him at the house.' Dee vaguely gesticulated across the loch, which by now was almost completely lost in mist and drizzle.

'I said I *didn't* interview him,' Helen answered curtly.

Her daughter looked up from her colouring, alerted by the change in tone. Helen smiled reassuringly towards her.

'Anyway, we have to get on.' Helen stood, collecting her mug and staring quite openly at Dee's. 'It's our day to go shopping, isn't it, Alana?'

The girl shut her colouring book with excitement. 'Can I have an ice cream?'

'If you like. Put on your jacket, it's cold, remember.'

Alana ran across the kitchen, retrieving a coat from hooks and struggling to feed arms through the sleeves.

'Sorry.' The thin smile returned. 'But we have to get going.'

Dee finished her coffee. 'Can I use your toilet? Came here straight after breakfast and the combination of cold and a motorbike plays havoc with a girl's bladder.'

'Sure. First left.'

Dee followed Helen's instructions and shut herself into a small downstairs loo. Her request wasn't entirely fictional, and she took the time to think over Helen's reactions. There was more not being said, that was without doubt. The girl calling her unicorn Lilybet – she was certain that was more than coincidence.

Dee returned to the kitchen. Helen and Alana both stood in coats, anxious to leave.

'Thanks for the coffee.' Dee attempted to defuse the newly arrived tension that filled the air between the two women like an electric charge. She pulled her helmet over her head, secured fastenings then hands into gloves.

At the front door she paused, feeling very much like she was being herded out of the cottage. Leaning against the wall of the small porch was a heavy shinty stick, its curved head scrubbed clean.

'You could do someone a mischief with one of those,' Dee's muffled voice issued from underneath her helmet. Her gloved hand stretched towards the stick. 'Do you play?'

Helen's eyes became glacial. 'I used to. It was nice meeting you,' she added. Her features gave lie to the words.

'Likewise,' Dee shot back.

She pressed the electric start, pulled away from the cottage and out onto the road snaking around the loch. Helen and Alana stayed motionless in front of their cottage until they were lost to sight.

TWENTY-EIGHT

MIT

Tony Masterton stared out of his home office window, watching the rain erase the white-topped waters of the loch from view. Water streamed down the glass in rivulets, causing the world to twist and distort until the view outside matched his inner mood. He'd had a call from the Major Investigation Team in Glasgow, advising him two of their unit would be with him in the next few minutes. They were so close he couldn't avoid them, and they'd already confirmed he was at the house. The gate intercom buzzed, a woman standing in full view of the camera and ineffectually attempting to shelter her face from the driving rain. He left her there for a few minutes before activating the gates.

A man stood at the door when he opened it, dressed in a cheap suit and holding an umbrella in his left hand. His right hand was outstretched for a welcome that he wasn't going to receive. His partner sprinted from the car, seeking shelter under the porch.

'Mr Masterton, I'm DI Johnson. This is DS Franklin. Do you mind if we come in for a chat?'

The wind was erratic here in the lee of the building,

random draughts catching at the rain and playfully spraying it under the porch cover to wet the two police officers. DI Johnson wiped his face clear of moisture as he waited for an invitation.

'You'd better come in,' Tony Masterton relented. He led them down the hall, into the room that faced over the decking. He sat, invited them to do the same.

'Is your wife here, Samantha? What we have to say involves her as well.' The DI did all the talking, as his sidekick watched in silence.

'What is it you have to tell me? Us,' Tony corrected.

'We've had the forensics report back, from the girl's body found in the loch. It would be better if you both heard this together.'

Tony already knew what the report had to say. 'I'll fetch her.'

Samantha entered the room behind Tony, taking a seat next to her husband. They both looked expectantly at the two police officers.

'Thank you for joining us, Mrs Masterton.'

Samantha inclined her head. 'Just tell us what you have to say, officer.'

DI Johnson looked from one to the other.

'The genetic analysis has come back negative. Whoever the girl was, she's not your daughter, Lilybet.'

Samantha clutched the arm of her chair, let loose a long shuddering breath.

'Thank you. Thank you, officer. That means there's still hope. That Lilybet might still be out there, waiting to be found.'

'It's been three years, Mrs Masterton. I don't want to raise any hopes, but of course we are continuing enquiries into her disappearance. As soon as we have anything, we will be in touch.'

Samantha nodded, dabbing under each eye with the edge of

a handkerchief. Tony sat impassively, aware of the female detective watching him closely.

'The strange thing is,' the DI continued, 'there haven't been any reports of a missing child in this area apart from Lilybet. It's given us a bit of a puzzle if I'm honest. No missing person reports, no child reported absent from school or tourists losing a member of their party. Can you shed any light on this? Any thoughts as to who the girl could be?'

Tony Masterton's expression remained neutral. Samantha's handkerchief returned to her face, muffling her words.

'Oh, the poor child. Some mother must know she's missing. I hope you find her and put her mind at rest.' She raised her head from her hands. 'There's nothing worse than not knowing. She could be anywhere. With anyone.'

She sobbed, body shaking with grief whilst Tony ignored her.

'You don't have anything belonging to Lilybet, do you?' The female detective spoke at last, focussed on Samantha. 'Any clothes, bedding, towels, a toy she played with?'

'Why? We've not kept her clothes – she'd be too large for them now,' Samantha explained, shaking her head. 'The nanny cleaned everything. She wasn't herself the day Lilybet disappeared. Scrubbing her room, washing all her clothes and belongings again and again as if that would somehow bring her back. I wasn't able... I was in grief for weeks and when I realised how unstable Jane had become, we had to let her go.'

'Jane Whiting, your nanny?' The policewoman looked for confirmation.

'Yes. She was very badly affected by what happened. I advised her to seek psychiatric help.'

The two police detectives exchanged a look.

'Do you happen to know where we can reach Jane?' the DI asked.

'It's been three years since she left our employment, officer,'

Tony interjected. 'We didn't bother keeping in touch.'

'And there's nothing you can think of that might still have a strand of Lilybet's hair, or do you still have her toothbrush?' DS Franklin persevered.

'There's nothing left of her here. Do you think we want to be reminded every day that our child has gone missing, that someone could have taken her?' Tony's voice raised in anger.

'We're here to help. We are not the enemy, Mr Masterton. It's just the original enquiry never took a proper sample of Lilybet's DNA, which is contrary to our procedures. It would help immensely if you had anything used by your daughter that we could take away for analysis. You'd have it back within days, I assure you.'

'I said we no longer have anything of Lilybet's.' Tony's voice was dangerously low. 'By the time one of your detectives thought to ask for Lilybet's hairbrush, the nanny had cleaned every last hair from it and bleached the brush, so it was no use. Or that's what they told me at the time.'

'Do you know what she did with the hair?' DS Franklin questioned. 'Once she cleaned the brush.'

Tony fixed his eyes on hers. 'I was too busy looking for my daughter instead of ensuring your officers did the job they should have done three years ago.'

DI Johnson took over. 'I'm going to make sure that whoever was responsible for not doing their job on the day will be reprimanded. You have my word on that. However, we have enough genetic information from you both to state without any doubt that the body in the loch was not related to either of you.'

Samantha gave a small smile of thanks, dabbing at her eyes once more.

'I do have some other questions on a different topic if you don't mind my asking?' DI Johnson asked.

'Will I need my lawyer?'

'I'm sure it won't come to that, Mr Masterton.' The DI

dropped his bedside manner and became more business-like in his questioning.

'Your gardener, Richard Tavistock. You'll be aware his body has been found not too far away from here?'

'One of your lot called me, said something about it,' Tony answered. 'I spend a lot of time in Glasgow, so I'm not that well up on all the local news.'

'Slightly more than local news, Mr Masterton. This was reported on all the TV channels and provided newspapers with lurid headlines.'

Tony shrugged unconcernedly. 'What more can I tell you? I don't really pay much attention to the news – you only hear what they want you to hear after all.'

'I thought you might have had an interest, seeing as how Richard was your gardener?'

'No. He's not needed so much this time of year. Haven't seen him for a couple of months – if this is going where I think it is?'

'We're just trying to eliminate anyone that knew him from our enquiries.' Both detectives had focussed in on him. 'Do you know of any reason someone might have wanted to hurt him – do you know if he had any enemies, had upset anyone?' The DI talked in generalities, but Tony knew he was the target.

'As I said, officers. He worked for me, keeping the grounds. I hardly ever saw the man even when he *was* here. There's nothing I can add.'

'How about you, Mrs Masterton?' The DS took over the questioning. 'You would have had more dealings with him, on a more regular basis whilst your husband worked in Glasgow.'

Samantha kept her face deadpan. 'He was a part-time employee. He knew what he had to do, did the job adequately and was paid direct by bank transfer. I really had no more contact with him than Tony, and I have no idea who might have wanted him dead.'

There was a pause as the two police officers focussed on Samantha, the unasked question unanswered.

The DI spoke directly to Tony. 'Can you tell us where you were on November 28th, early evening?'

'I was here all day, officer, and all night. I had to make a few business calls. I had an appointment with my private investigator, Teàrlach Paterson, around teatime, then worked in my office here until Samantha and I had dinner at around seven. You made your beef wellington, do you remember?'

'Your favourite,' Samantha responded. They held hands like any loving couple.

'Do you have contact details for this Teàrlach Paterson?' The DI looked pointedly at his sidekick. She pulled a notebook and pen out of her pocket and sat expectantly.

'He's staying at the Lochside Hotel, just a few miles down the road.' Tony Masterton's voice expressed unconcern.

'And what about yesterday? Were you in the area?'

'If you're trying to accuse me of something, I really will have to ask you to leave until I have a solicitor present,' Tony coolly countered.

'We're just trying to get a picture of who was around. Nobody is accusing you of anything.' The DI gave the impression this was all routine, boring work but someone had to do it.

Tony heard the unvoiced 'yet' missing off the end of his statement.

'I was at my Glasgow office all day, stayed over in my town flat. Why do you ask?'

He sounded genuinely interested, which threw the two detectives.

'Richard's mother – Annie Tavistock. She died in a house fire yesterday evening. By the time the emergency services arrived, it was too late.'

'I'm sorry to hear that,' Tony managed with a complete lack of feeling.

'How terrible. The poor woman,' Samantha added.

'Do you think there's a connection between Richard's death and that of his mother?' Tony put the question bluntly.

'That's something we're looking at, Mr Masterton.' DI Johnson stood, followed immediately by the DS. 'Thank you for your time. If we think of anything else, or of course if we find any leads regarding your daughter's disappearance, we'll be in touch.'

Tony escorted them both to the front door, then watched them through the glass as the car headed back down the drive.

They could see his figure outlined against the light, standing motionless behind the door.

'What did you make of them, boss?'

'He's a difficult one to read, that Tony Masterton. But I think he had something to do with both these recent deaths. Look into corroborating his statements on the day of Richard Tavistock's murder. He'll show up on the street cameras if he was in town.'

'What about the woman, Samantha?'

'What about her?'

'She tried hiding it, but I'd swear she was surprised to hear about the old woman – Annie Tavistock.'

'You think she hadn't heard about it?'

'No, I think it came as a surprise to her. An unpleasant surprise.'

The DI considered her comment. In front of them the electric gates swung back noiselessly, an invitation to leave.

'We'll pay a visit to this Teàrlach Paterson. Take his statement and see if it lines up with Mr Masterton's.' He swung the wheel to take them further away from Glasgow, down towards the Lochside Hotel.

TWENTY-NINE

THE BRIGADOON MASSIF

Teàrlach was climbing out of his bed at the exact moment the two detectives turned their car towards the hotel. He'd spent the morning alternating between sleeping and coughing up soot-laden phlegm, each cough reminding him how much his head hurt. Now he sat on the edge of the bed and wondered if he'd be capable of standing. He stood, swayed like a tree in a storm, then staggered to the bathroom to inspect the damage.

Two bruised and bloodshot eyes reproached him from sunken sockets. A plaster hung loosely from his forehead, trapped in an unholy amalgam of hair and dried blood. An exploratory hand retreated quickly from a lump the size of an orange at the back of his head, the sharp pain advising he leave it well alone.

'Shit.' He spoke with feeling, then proceeded to dab away the worst of the mess with a towel and warm water. His clothes had gone missing whilst he slept, he remembered Dee had said something about getting rid of them. Teàrlach regarded his naked reflection in the wardrobe mirror, bruised, battered and looking stupid. How could he leave his room stark bollock naked?

The door opened, leaving him no choice but to cup his genitals in response. Dee's bright smile grew wider.

'I've brought you some clothes.' She threw carrier bags at the bed. 'Not a lot of choice around here, so you'll have to make do.'

A Harris Tweed jacket spilled out of one bag. Something suspiciously like tartan trews threatened to join the jacket.

'You're kidding me?'

'That's your lot. You better get a wriggle on; Tony's warned me there's two detectives on their way to see you. Wanting you to corroborate seeing him November 28th – best not fuck that up!'

She left as abruptly as she had arrived. Teàrlach emptied the bags, his worst expectations realised. He started pulling on the most innocuous clothes he could find, out of those that fitted. Each movement identifying new pains and aches he hadn't been aware that he was suffering from. He tried to avoid seeing himself in the mirror.

They were waiting for him in the bar, a tall guy not carrying much weight so his suit looked better on him than it should and a woman who stood deferentially beside him. She carried a notebook, pen in the other hand. Two no-nonsense expressions turned to incredulity as he entered.

'You the PI working for Tony Masterton?' the male detective asked. A note of disbelief had entered his voice, as the two detectives shared a look.

'Yes. Will this take long?' Teàrlach took one of the bar stools, untrusting of his ability to prise himself up from anything lower.

'Do you want to report an assault?'

Teàrlach saw that the DI apparently couldn't decide whether to stare at the bruising on his face or the Harris Tweed, tartan shirt/tartan trews combo. He hoped they didn't notice his shoes were two sizes too big for him and had flapped loosely around his feet as he cautiously took the stairs. He felt like a clown.

'No. Had a bit of an accident, that's all.'

The two detectives expressed disbelief as only detectives can.

'Had a run in with the Brigadoon Massif, have we, sir?' The woman displayed a talent for comedy, he reluctantly gave her that.

Teàrlach remained silent, watching them as they smirked.

'OK, to business.' The DI gave Teàrlach another look over, from his oversized brogues to the plaster still clinging valiantly to his forehead, probably committing the vision to memory for future ribaldry. 'Where were you on November 28th?'

He gave it a while, as if referring to memory. 'I booked in here at six o'clock. Stayed in this bar all evening and then went to bed. One of your constables was interviewing a guy about a murder. You can check with the hotel staff or the local police. They came from the local police station,' he added helpfully.

The woman detective's pen scratched away in response.

'And earlier that day?' the DI probed.

Teàrlach's head was pounding, two small wooden mallets beating a tattoo against his forehead.

'I drove up from my Glasgow office.' He searched the Harris Tweed jacket in vain for a card. 'Then had tea with Helen Chadwell around 2pm on the other side of the loch – she used to be one of your lot. Then drove to see Tony Masterton and his wife, stayed there until coming here.'

'What exactly are you doing for Mr Masterton, if I might ask?'

'I'm searching for his daughter, Lilybet. She went missing from their house just over three years ago. He's asked me to try and find out what happened to her.'

'I see. You have experience with this sort of thing – missing children?'

'It's one of the things I do. You can search me on the internet if you like – Teàrlach Paterson. I've had some successes.'

The detectives both looked unconvinced.

'And what happened to your face, Mr Paterson? Those look like nasty cuts to your head.' The woman decided to join in.

'As I say, accident.'

The DI looked him directly in the eye. 'You'd be well advised to be more careful then, Mr Paterson. If your accident had been any worse, you might not still be here to talk about it.'

Teàrlach nodded in agreement, then wished he hadn't.

'I don't suppose *you* know anything about the two deaths that have occurred around here?' the DI asked.

'At the same time you just happened to arrive in the area.' DS Franklin added for good measure.

'Sorry officers, I can't help you. As I said, I'm here looking into their daughter's disappearance. Nothing else.'

'Bit of a coincidence a girl's body has been found, of the same age and as far as our forensics team are able to judge, from around the same time that Lilybet went missing?' the DI probed, unerringly finding the exact same issue that had been giving Teàrlach doubts.

'Not their child, so I've been informed.'

'No. So it would seem.' The DI motioned towards reception. 'Corroborate Mr Paterson's story with the staff, will you?'

DS Franklin obediently left the two men alone. DI Johnson moved closer to Teàrlach, bending closer so he couldn't be overheard.

'I don't know what's going on here, Mr Paterson, but I'd be careful how you go.' He sniffed suspiciously. 'Is that smoke I can smell on you?'

Teàrlach jerked a thumb behind him. The detective craned his neck to view the fireplace, ash and soot in the grate.

'Be a shame if you had another accident,' DI Johnson

advised, giving Teàrlach the benefit of the doubt before joining the other detective in reception. Teàrlach couldn't make out their conversation, just the tapping of a computer keyboard as the receptionist confirmed his arrival date and time. The female detective's voice came back into focus as they headed towards the entrance.

'Sartorial vigilantes caught him!' The sound of laughter drifted back down the corridor before the closing door shut the sound off.

Teàrlach wondered if he stayed on the stool for long enough whether Barman Blair would make an appearance. His throat felt like the bottom of a parrot's cage, and he could murder a pint of Blond Bombshell.

'Hoots mon!' Dee's head poked around the door, followed by the rest of her once she saw the police had gone.

'Don't,' Teàrlach cautioned, before she came out with anything else.

'Kinda suits you.'

Teàrlach's glare must have struck home. Dee held her hands up in mock surrender.

'It's really all I could find, sorry.' Her face expressed every emotion but sorrow. 'I went to see your Helen Chadwell like you asked.' She checked that Teàrlach was giving her his full attention before continuing. 'I warned her to look after herself, best as I could with her daughter sitting at the same table, but she didn't seem too bothered. Then when I asked her about Annie, she clammed up – said she didn't approve of spreading malicious gossip or something...'

Teàrlach held his hand up to stop her. 'Her daughter?'

'Aye. Cute kid, around seven. She was colouring in a unicorn – you'll never guess what she named it?'

Teàrlach took a wild guess. 'Lilybet?'

Dee looked suitably impressed. 'How did you do that? You

ever thought of going on stage?' Her smile came back stronger than before. 'Now you're dressed for it,' she added.

'I'm going to head back to Glasgow, if only so I can wear my own clothes again.' Teàrlach sighed deeply and with feeling. 'What else did you get from her?'

Dee scrunched her face in concentration. He found it strangely appealing.

'Nothing really. I think she knows something about Annie Tavistock, but whatever it is should be common knowledge if it's the talk of the steamie.'

'I thought Helen had a boy,' Teàrlach mused, more to himself than to Dee.

'Because of the goalposts?'

Teàrlach nodded.

'You should be over those tired stereotypes by now. Aren't you keeping up with societal trends?' Dee sounded genuinely cross. 'Oh, and another thing. Helen keeps a shinty stick by her front door. It had been cleaned recently.'

'I don't think that was Helen's voice on the recording, but the sound's so muffled it's hard to tell,' Teàrlach mused. 'Could have been a shinty stick, though.' His hand unconsciously returned to feel his head. 'What did her daughter look like?'

'Blond. Blue eyes. I didn't really pay much attention.'

'How much does she look like Lilybet?'

Dee frowned, reached for her mobile and swiped through until she found a photograph. 'Kinda similar, but it's not the same girl. Did you think that because she called her unicorn Lilybet?'

Teàrlach shook his head gently. 'I don't know. I'm clutching at straws here.'

He ran through the conversation with the detectives in his mind. They had him marked as a potential suspect for the two murders, that was for sure. His alibi was fairly sound for Richard

Tavistock's death – unless they believed he and Tony Masterton had planned and executed it together. The other thing the DI had mentioned – about it being one hell of a coincidence that a girl's body had been found in the loch from around the time and place that Lilybet had gone missing – that needed investigating.

'Can you do me another favour?' he asked.

'What do you want?'

'How easy is it for you to find out where Lilybet was born?'

'Why do you want that information – can't you just ask the Mastertons?' Dee expressed surprise at the question.

'I'd prefer to keep this line of research just between us, for the time being. If that's not going to give you a conflict of interest?'

Dee thought for a second. 'No, should be OK. I'll see what I can do. What are you hoping to find?'

'I'm not sure. Let's just say I'm being thorough.' He stood, holding onto the bar for support. His legs felt stronger already. 'I'm heading back to Glasgow.'

'Not in that state, Sherlock. You'll go off the road and kill yourself,' Dee protested.

It was Teàrlach's turn to smile. 'Remember, my head is like concrete.' He took note of her concern. 'Seriously, it's OK. I wouldn't risk it if I didn't feel up to it. Anyway, I can't be seen in public wearing these any longer.'

Dee's gaze travelled from his battered head down to his overlarge shoes.

'Fair enough,' she laughed. 'Drive safely.'

Teàrlach staggered slightly, turned to hold a hand up in farewell and left the hotel.

THIRTY

WOKE WAKE

Dee spent the rest of the afternoon looking into the multiple searches she had been running. The nanny hadn't surfaced. Her best guess was that she was still in Europe somewhere, where there were fewer CCTV cameras to find her. She'd be wise to stay there. Tony had already hinted that he'd like a word with Jane Whiting if he came across her whereabouts. She'd better stay hidden. Jane's uncle was keeping a low profile as well. His company was in even greater financial difficulty than when she first looked at his books. Whatever reward he had hoped to win from the deception he and Jane played on Tony was lost when the film company decided to try the same trick themselves. Dee considered opening Tony's accounts to see if he'd paid any money out for the video, then decided the risk wasn't worth the effort. All the extended video had accomplished was to have Richard Tavistock murdered and possibly his mother. It also put Jane and Samantha at risk of retribution but hadn't moved the search any further forward for the girl.

The police had departed the diving site at the Oitir, which meant they'd collected as much of the mystery girl's skeleton as they could find. She viewed the police files, which were nominally secure, but once Dee had a way in, they might as well have been on public display. There were no matches to the skeleton DNA apart from Richard Tavistock being the most likely father. Samantha was most definitely not the mother – a fact that had almost certainly saved her life. Had the results come back with her and Richard as the parents, then Tony would have dealt with them both the same way. Who could the girl in the loch be if she wasn't Lilybet?

It had become apparent that Richard Tavistock was something of a one-man stud servicing the women around the loch. His reputation had been hinted at, and here at least was proof of one of his children. How could they identify the mother if no one was missing a child? Out of all the questions the investigation had raised, this was the strangest.

Teàrlach had asked her to investigate Lilybet's birth, look for the certificate, which hospital she was born in. At least she could understand why he wanted that information. If Lilybet's trail finished at the house, he could start the search at the very beginning. Dee followed a legal route for once, paying a fee to an online genealogy site and viewing the registrar of births, marriages and deaths for Lilybet Masterton. It took no time to find her birth certificate, Samantha and Tony down as the mother and father. The place of birth was a private hospital in Glasgow. She sent Teàrlach a copy of the certificate in case he wanted to look into it, but as far as she could see, everything was as she'd have expected.

On a whim Dee searched for Helen Chadwell and her daughter's birth. Alana's father was listed as unknown, place of birth Lochgilphead Community Hospital. She wondered about the missing father's details – that must have caused some debate amongst her police colleagues. Could that be the reason she left the force? Alana's birthdate was within weeks of Lilybet's. Both girls shared the same blond hair and blue eyes, could there be a link? She made a note of the similarities in looks and closeness in age. Teàrlach could chase it up if he thought it was at all relevant – she didn't see how this was going to get them any closer to finding Lilybet.

Whilst Dee had the genealogy site open, she searched for the Tavistocks. This proved to be a lot more difficult. Richard Tavistock's birth certificate was registered a good five years after his actual birth, under the different surname of Brazil which was his father's name, occupation horse-dealer. Place of birth was listed simply as Argyll. Mother Annie Tavistock. Dee looked at the time. Half past six. The only light outside the window came from the floodlights illuminating the white walls of the hotel. She realised it had taken two hours to find Richard Tavistock's birth certificate. The thought of attempting to track down any of his children was too much of an effort. Maybe Helen Chadwell's child was his too. Did that move them any further forward?

Frustrated at not being able to find anything of note, Dee turned to Annie Tavistock. Helen had hinted at Annie's reputation, about not wanting to spread gossip. She started digging, tracing Annie's first mention in the Scottish census of 2011. She was listed as being on a Traveller site in Perthshire, working as a strawberry picker on one of the large soft fruit farms that pervaded the rolling hills north of Perth. On the most recent census, from 2022, Annie was registered as the sole homeowner at her bungalow, with Richard as a resident. Intrigued how a farm labourer made the leap from caravan to owning a bungalow, Dee sought the title deeds of the property. Annie had bought the property recently, back in 2015. The details she really needed weren't online – the title deeds and how the purchase was financed must be gathering dust in some solicitor's filing cabinet. Either that or they went up in smoke with the cottage.

Dee's stomach let her know she hadn't eaten for hours. She closed down her laptop, headed towards the bar in the hope that

Blair would be there, and she'd be able to order a meal. The sound of voices coming from the bar gave her encouragement, and she strode in to see the Travellers gathered around the fireplace. Their voices stopped as she entered, all four of them giving her their full attention.

'Good evening to you.' The thin-faced man who'd given his name as Mick broke the silence.

'Evening,' she replied. Dee marched purposefully over to the bar, ordered a glass of white wine and scampi and chips. Blair served her, his eyes continually drawn to the four of them sitting at the table then quickly flicking back to Dee. She could feel the intensity of their gaze on her back.

'Will Sherlock be joining you?' Blair sounded hopeful, but whether that was because he wanted Teàrlach there for backup or fancied his chances she couldn't say.

'No, he's gone through to Glasgow. Had some work to catch up on.' She sipped at her wine. 'He may be back later tonight,' she added, more for the benefit of the Travellers than anything else.

'That's a pity,' Mick intoned from his table. 'I was hoping to have a word with him, friendly like,' he said encouragingly, as if there was another way to exchange words. 'Do you think he'll be back before too long?'

Dee turned to face them, keeping her expression neutral. 'I don't know when he'll be back. I don't even know him that well – certainly not well enough that he leaves me with a full itinerary before driving off.'

'Right, so.' Mick responded, his eyes not leaving her face.

She turned back to Blair. 'I'll eat here at the bar. Be good to have a chat with you.'

Blair's face lit up at the prospect. He seemed at a loss for words, pouring himself a drink for Dutch courage before responding.

'Are you enjoying your holiday then, now the rain's eased off?'

Dee hadn't been out of her room all afternoon. Now that he mentioned the fact, she realised the windows no longer played a soft percussive sound, waves of fine moisture hitting the glass on random gusts of winter wind.

'More of a working break. A chance to concentrate away from all the distractions of city life.'

'What is it you do?' Blair's curiosity loosened his tongue. The table behind her ceased their low murmur as they waited on her response.

'I write software. Code for computers.' Dee expected this would be boring enough for them all to lose interest. She was right – the Travellers re-kindled their subdued conversation, Blair tried to look interested but failed to follow through.

'Oh,' Blair managed. 'I always wanted to be in a band. Tour the world, that sort of thing.'

'What do you play?'

'I don't. Least, not well enough to be in a band. If I play anything, then it's the guitar. I can strum a few chords – the easy ones, like.'

'Do you sing?' Dee asked, grateful she was no longer the subject of questioning.

'Well, a bit.'

Dee could swear Blair was starting to blush.

'Do yer have a guitar there, son?' Mick called across from his table. The rest of his entourage craned their heads around to face the barman.

'It's in its case, in the store,' Blair replied, puzzlement etched in his face.

'Go get it then. If you don't mind me playing a few tunes. It's in memory of the family we've lost, our way of marking their passing.' Mick lost his permanently hardened cynical expression, exchanging it for something altogether softer, more hopeful.

'Sure, I'll fetch it now. I don't know if it's in tune or not.' Blair hurried off, coming back seconds later with a guitar case which he handed over.

Dee's interest quickened as Mick handled the case almost reverentially, took out the guitar and rested it on his knee before trying a practice chord. The sound was discordant, causing him to tweak the tuning pegs with practised ease, playing individual notes and adjusting them until the instrument produced a minor chord.

'Winter... that's... the terror time. No place to go nor doesn't know where to go. Doesn't know any place to go and sit. And it doesn't matter whether it's snowing or blowing, you've got to go.' Mick played the chord again and four voices erupted in full harmony, the big man's voice taking the lead and the others wrapping around so perfectly that Dee could imagine she was in a cathedral rather than a small country bar.

When the last voice died away, the only sound came from the crackling of embers in the fire.

'That was beautiful,' Dee managed. Something in the words spoke to her of the hardships of being a Traveller when winter froze the ground, when every man's hand was turned against you and the police moved you on from place to place.

Mick inclined his head in thanks.

'In memory of Dick and Annie!' They raised their glasses into the air, Dee and Blair joined in the toast.

'Now, we'd better be having a few bottles on the table.' Mick directed this towards Blair. 'Here's a hundred pounds to be starting with. You keep us topped up.' He looked at Dee as if seeing her for the first time. 'And you're a fair drinker too. You're welcome to try and keep up with us.'

Dee knew a challenge when she heard one and pushed her newly emptied glass to Blair for a refill. Now that the natives appeared to be friendly, this gave her a chance to find out more about them, maybe tease out some information that would help Teàrlach when he returned.

'That song, what was it?'

'A song for the Travelling people,' Mick answered. 'Written by a friend to us, Ewan MacColl. It's called "The Terror Time".' He swivelled back towards his table.

'To Ewan!'

They echoed his words, drinking another toast.

Dee considered the song title. It was an appropriate enough song for the time of year, and for the deaths that had brought them all to this lonely place beside the loch. She sat there, joining in where she could, demolishing the scampi and chips and drinking the evening away until the night enveloped them all.

THIRTY-ONE
DIVORCE

Teàrlach arrived at his Glasgow office, glad to be out of his Brigadoon outfit and back into something more normal. The bruising had darkened; rich purples and dark reds surrounded his eyes, so he resembled a survivor from a bad car crash. At least he'd removed the bandage which had hung annoyingly in front of his eye every time it lost adhesion on his forehead.

'Jesus, Sherlock! What the fuck have you been involved in this time?' Chloe's eyes couldn't have opened any wider as he entered the office.

'Looks worse than it is.' His words didn't even convince himself. 'Don't worry, I'll live.'

'Who did that to you?' Chloe sounded angry enough to sort them out single-handedly.

'Didn't see. I was in a dark building when they clobbered me with something hard. Then they landed a couple more blows until I passed out on the floor.' He decided not to mention the bit about almost being burned alive. 'What have you got for me; did you manage to find anything more on the nanny?'

Chloe saw right through his attempt to steer the conversation away from himself. She ran a practised eye over him, saw he wasn't too badly injured.

'Not much more than you've had already.' She ruffled through paperwork strewn over her desk, moving cans of soft drinks to retrieve buried documents.

'She's been with the Mastertons pretty much from the start. They hired her a few weeks after Lilybet was born. I think the reality of having her own kid must have come as a shock to Samantha – missing out on her beauty sleep and everything. She left their employment a few weeks after Lilybet went missing. Looks to me as if she was sacked because they gave her six months' pay to leave without a fuss.'

'Not bothering about due notice or anything?'

'Nah. Just kicked her out, basically. That's when she went to live with her parents in Aberfoyle.'

'And she's not done anything much since?'

'No. Few odd jobs – she didn't stick at anything and then this trip off to Amsterdam paid for by her uncle.' She put the papers back down on her crowded desktop. 'How are you getting on with this hacker?' Chloe asked rather too nonchalantly.

'Hmmm. She's being quite useful,' Teàrlach admitted. 'I don't know how much she feeds back to Tony Masterton, but she's proving to be a help.' He thought back to her pulling him out of the burning cottage, risking her own life for his. 'We're actually getting along like a house on fire.'

Chloe's mouth turned down in displeasure. 'After nosing around our computers?'

Teàrlach had to smile at Chloe's obvious dislike of a woman she hadn't met. 'She's just doing her job, same way we're doing ours.'

Chloe snorted in derision.

'This is where we're at with this investigation,' Teàrlach continued. 'The gardener I wanted to question...'

'Richard Tavistock,' Chloe butted in.

'Aye. He's not been much use since someone extracted his heart – nothing more on that, I take it?'

Chloe shook her head. 'I've been keeping an eye on the news. Nothing's been mentioned except they've sent in a Major Investigation Team looking for his murderer.'

'They came to the hotel and questioned me – think I'm a suspect.'

Chloe edged away from him. 'You got previous you haven't told me about?'

'No.' He could see she was enjoying having him portrayed as a murder suspect. 'It won't be amusing if they lock me away for ten years. I'll not be paying your salary from Barlinnie.'

'What about this fire? I saw it on the news. A woman died?'

Teàrlach realised he hadn't been in touch since the fire and gave Chloe a sanitised version of events.

'That was his mother?'

'Aye, Richard lived with her. I was trying to find out more information about Richard and who might have killed him, but someone's making damn sure every source I try is closed down.'

'Who could be doing that? And why? All you're doing is trying to find a missing girl. These deaths must be a coincidence, surely?'

Teàrlach didn't have much faith in coincidence. 'I think Tony Masterton either killed Richard himself or had him killed.'

'For shagging his wife?'

'Poetically put. Yes – or at least being told he was shagging his wife.'

'Fair comment,' Chloe admitted. 'But he wouldn't get in the way of the investigation he's paying for?'

Teàrlach had already considered this. 'He wouldn't have known how important it was that I needed to talk to everyone who was at the scene. From his point of view, Richard Tavistock was just a hired help. One who was helping himself to things he should have left well alone.'

'You really think he was having an affair with Samantha?'

'I don't know. Maybe. Who cares?'

'Tony Masterton.'

'Aye, right enough,' Teàrlach agreed. 'He's not the type you mess around with.'

'But he wouldn't have the guy's mother killed as well? That's a bit excessive.'

Teàrlach had to agree. 'There's something else. Dee managed to record my phone when I was knocked out. There's a woman's voice. I think she was the one who hit me.'

Chloe narrowed her eyes. 'Were you anywhere near the house when it went up in flames?'

'Keep it to yourself, or you really will be needing another job.' Teàrlach inwardly cursed for giving away too much information.

Chloe regarded him for a moment. He felt he was being judged.

She brightened, then returned to lifting paper off her desk, flourishing a document in front of his face.

'You'll find this interesting.'

It took him a while to work out what she'd given him. He was looking at an initial writ, a divorce proceeding raised by Samantha Masterton against Tony Masterton. The date was today, 4th December.

Teàrlach's breath whistled out from between his lips. 'Shit!'

'That will set the cat amongst the pigeons,' Chloe said brightly.

He looked at her. 'It will do a damn sight more than that. He'll probably go ballistic!'

'Do you think she's still in the house? The writ will be served on him today.'

'I suspect she's packing her bags now.' Teàrlach thought

carefully. If he alerted Dee, she was likely to tell Tony what was coming down the line. He wasn't employed as a marriage counsellor or to be responsible for whatever went on between the two of them.

'Why now?' Chloe asked. 'Do you think it's connected to the murders?'

'Maybe she's getting in first before he divorces her. Their marriage didn't strike me as a bed of roses.'

'He'd fight it, wouldn't he? And there's still the possibility that Lilybet is alive.'

Teàrlach read the writ again, noting the mention of an irretrievable breakdown. 'If he fought her in court, then they'd want to see his financials. I suspect Tony Masterton would prefer to keep those hidden, so chances are he'd either agree a payoff or...'

'She has an "accident".' Chloe filled in the pause.

He nodded. 'I'd say she's playing a dangerous game, but with two deaths already Tony may not want to draw any more attention to himself than he has already. As for the girl, I think Samantha's given up all hope. It's Tony who still clings to the possibility she's still out there somewhere. Either way, doesn't have much bearing on the divorce. Makes it easier to deal with without a child.'

'The court isn't going to assume she's dead, though, they can't – can they?' Chloe sounded unsure.

'There's a seven-year rule. If there hasn't been any contact or sighting during that time, then they can presume death – raise an action for declarator for the court to grant a decree. It's not a hard and fast rule. Without a body you're left with probability that someone missing is dead.'

'You think she's dead, don't you?' Chloe spoke quietly.

Teàrlach nodded. 'I told them as much when I took the case.'

'So, what do *you* think happened to her?'

He fixed Chloe with tired eyes. 'That's what we're being

paid to find out.' He pulled his phone out of his jeans pocket, swiped through to Dee's last message referencing Lilybet's maternity hospital. 'Find out what you can about this place. It's where Lilybet was born.'

A printer came to life in the corner of the office, mechanical whirrs announcing it had resurrected, then the swiping sound of paper being sprayed with precision ink droplets as Lilybet's birth certificate was born afresh.

'I'll pay them a visit before heading back to the Mastertons.'

Chloe pulled a face, lifted the finished sheet out of the printer. 'Why bother with her birth?'

'Because I'm running out of options. Each lead I try to follow has ended up dead so far, so I'll try another angle. Track Lilybet's life from the cradle.'

Chloe didn't need to fill in the rest of the phrase for him.

'And see what you can find out about Annie Tavistock. Someone wanted her dead, some woman. I've a feeling this is all connected to Lilybet. I just don't know how.'

Chloe sent him a text as he drove to the private hospital, detailing the major shareholders of the company whose name it was registered to. The names meant nothing to him, although he could tell the two main beneficiaries were both doctors. The building was an anonymous Georgian pile in the West End, a modest brass plaque on the gate pillar displaying the same names he had on his phone. Teàrlach parked in the drive, rang the brass doorbell, and waited.

A woman in a starched nurse's uniform answered the door, smile as fixed as a Stepford wife.

'Good morning, do you have an appointment?'

'Good morning,' Teàrlach dutifully responded. He handed her a business card as he introduced himself. 'My name is Teàrlach Paterson. I'm investigating Lilybet Masterton, the three-year-old girl who went missing three years ago?'

The nurse gave him a quizzical look. 'I'm sorry, but I don't see how I can help you.'

'I'm working for her parents, Tony and Samantha Masterton. Samantha gave birth to the girl here. I was hoping that you may have some records, or someone I could speak to?'

She looked affronted. 'We cannot give out any medical details. Everything is on a strictly patient confidential basis – you must know that?'

Teàrlach leaned in closer. 'Of course, I was just hoping for a word with one of the doctors who was present at the birth. I realise it's unconventional, but it may help in my search for the child.'

The Stepford smile wiped from her face. 'I don't see how discussing a mother's birth can assist in your search. I'm going to have to ask you to make an appointment if you want to take this any further, although quite frankly you'll be wasting your time.'

She shut the solid door in his face, leaving him with his nose almost pressed against a glazed panel. Further down the corridor he could see a worried face peer around an open door, and as quickly pull back out of view. He committed the face to memory, made a mental note to search for the two doctors online. It was no great surprise that they hadn't invited him in. These private hospitals made a comfortable living from keeping everything they did confidential – from stretching the sagging jowls of TV personalities to removing the more obvious effects of indiscretions before partners discovered an STI or unwanted pregnancy.

They were concealing something; he was sure of that. Teàrlach climbed back into his car, catching a curtain twitch on the ground floor. Here was another job for Dee. The thought of seeing her later that day brought a smile to his face. Teàrlach studied his expression in the mirror, saw past the bruising and into his troubled eyes. He recognised that telltale trickle of endorphins coursing through his brain and warned himself off catching anything too serious. Love was for freshly minted teenagers, not people like him.

Thoughts of love brought back his time at Glasgow university, everything so new and intense that when he fell in love with Cassie, it had felt like he'd been reborn. They were inseparable from the start, losing themselves in each other until he never wanted to be alone again. Convinced with the certainty of youth that they'd be together for eternity – only eternity faded during his first tour of duty. The phone calls lessening until she said it was over and was going back to New Zealand. Teàrlach let her image fade into the background, another memory of what might have been.

THIRTY-TWO

PURGATORY

Teàrlach's mobile rang as he turned his car north and away from Glasgow, Chloe's name displayed on the dash.

'You been to that private hospital yet?'

'Just leaving. I don't think they liked the look of me. Asked me to make an appointment.'

Chloe's laugh echoed over the car speakers. 'Not really surprised with you looking like that. Do you want me to set one up for you?'

He considered her offer. 'No, don't bother. I'll make use of my hacker – whilst she's still working with us.'

Chloe left a non-committal silence.

'Was there something you wanted?' Teàrlach prompted.

'Aye, it's your father's care home. They asked if you could visit in the next few days or so.'

Teàrlach features set hard. 'They say what it's about?'

'No. Don't think it's anything urgent, but as you're heading in that general direction...'

Chloe left the words hanging. What little she knew of Teàrlach's relationship with his father was enough to advise caution. He'd spent more time living with a family relation on Mull than with his parents, going to high school at Tobermory before setting out on his own. He'd never given reasons for it, apart from alluding to 'a difficult home life'.

'OK, thanks. I'll swing by the home on the way out.'

The connection died. A song started playing over the car sound system and he hit the button to turn it off. Teàrlach had yet to find the idiosyncratic setting that insisted he listen to a random track from his iPhone every time a call finished. Most times he let it play – but not today.

The care home was in Milngavie, off his route, but at least it was on the right side of town. He drove there on autopilot, scarcely registering the change of tempo as city centre was replaced by suburbs, then by shabby greenery that announced he'd reached the city outskirts. Greenplace Care Home shared a common vernacular with every other similar establishment – two-storey, new brick, a garden area hemmed in by a high, link-metal fence. Security cameras patrolled the environs instead of guards. The only thing differentiating the place from a prison was the absence of watchtowers and abandonment of hope for any parole being granted. These residents were in for life. Teàrlach parked in a visitor bay, saw the twinkling lights of an artificial Christmas tree shining a welcome from a window.

Once inside, his nose quickly accustomed to the sharp tang of disinfectant that did little to mask the underlying and pervasive smell of urine. White-coated staff escorted him through to the residents' lounge, loitering at the periphery of the room as if expecting the place to erupt in violence at any minute. Teàrlach exchanged waves and nods with chairbound inmates, their rheumy eyes engaging his with the same hope he'd seen in a dog home on the one occasion he'd been promised a dog himself. Like most things from his childhood, that promise turned to dust. A bit like the inhabitants of this place, Teàrlach thought. Marking days towards an appointment none of them wanted.

His father sat apart, blanket draped over legs turned skeletal thin. The light of recognition appeared in eyes disconcertingly similar to his own.

'You bothered to come and see me then?' The voice was querulous, weak.

Teàrlach remembered when that voice was so much louder, threatening. He should still feel anger. Demand retribution. But what was the point? Life had marched inexorably on. Only the heaviest footprints left a trace and even those would erode in time.

'How you keeping, Dad?' He cast around for a spare chair, pulling one over from where it kept company with the wall.

His father coughed in response, a long, hacking cough sufficiently prolonged to attract the attention of a white-jacketed nurse.

'Are we alright, John?' A hand the size of a dinner plate held a tissue in a blue glove stretched to the limitations of nitrile.

His father wiped his mouth, tissue streaked with blood. Blue nitrile removed it, took himself off without comment.

What comment could you make? Old man dying of lung cancer, coughing up blood and bits of lung. Feed him morphine when the pain's too bad, tea and cake when the pain's away so it's like they're all playing roles in some staged simulation where death doesn't walk the boards. Teàrlach looked around him, seeing death everywhere – in the rattle of air in his father's lungs, in the dull eyes of the woman opposite staring at the silent TV screen, in the futile protest of a man arguing with his own imaginary demons. If death was a destination, this was the waiting room. Was purgatory still a thing?

'I'm dying, Teàrlach.'

'I know, Dad.'

'You know I've always loved you, son. Despite... you know, everything.'

No, Dad. I don't think you ever loved me. Or my mother. Or my young brother – especially not him.

'Aye.'

Teàrlach played his part. Their eyes met, acknowledged the lie. There was pain in his father's eyes. 'What did you want to see me for? What do you want?'

His father sipped from a plastic straw that remained fixed in place behind his chair. Self-medication. An instant ticket to heaven, bypassing this hellhole of a waiting room. What was the point of purgatory again? Teàrlach had a dim recollection of a place of purification, a place where the sins of mankind were expunged from the soul before entering the kingdom of heaven. Seven levels that had to be climbed: Pride, Envy, Wrath, Sloth, Greed, Gluttony and Lust. He watched the pain dissolve from his father's face as the drug took hold. It was too easy – a stairlift up to paradise.

A crucifix was fixed to the wall. It was the only indication that this was a Catholic care home. How his father had wrangled a place here would be a secret he'd take to the grave. He'd had no time for religion except as a convenient dumping ground for Teàrlach whenever being a father proved too demanding. Too busy racking up his scores in Pride through to Lust to care about a son bereft of any other family. He'd be away for another few minutes, soaring in heaven with angels.

Teàrlach stared impassively at his father. The man who had brought him into being, then left him to fend for himself after his mother and brother had died. A Catholic care home provided a fitting comedic touch to a life ill-lived. Teàrlach was reminded of Dante's *Divine Comedy* wherein it's stated all the seven sins derived from love. The second book of that series, *Purgatorio*, takes the reader on an allegorical climb towards Paradise. Now a morphine drip would do the job for you without requiring any effort at all. It was also Dante who qualified that love could be perverted, turned into evil by excess or putrefaction. The love his father declared came from Dante's more catholic palette.

'I wanted to say I'm sorry.' His voice was so weak Teàrlach thought he might have imagined it except for the pleading in his father's tone. 'I don't know how long I've got left, son. I wanted you to know.'

Teàrlach felt nothing. The words rang as true as a deathbed declaration of belief in God. Clearing the slate. Expunging the past. Sealing the pain and hurt of a child's life into a neat sarcophagus and tying the whole rotten thing up with a pretty, pink bow. The stage was set, the other actors played their parts – the white-coated nurses weaving slowly through the chairs with pills, teas, kind words. The old waiting for God or whatever came next as long as this interminable waiting came to an end. Around him human clocks slowed down, memories faded, dust was shed. The room held a collective breath for Teàrlach's touching soliloquy.

'Bye, Dad. Don't call me again.'

Teàrlach replaced his seat back into position against the wall, walked out of the resident's lounge under the same hopeful eyes of the inmates. Jesus spared a sorrowful look from his spreadeagled stance, frozen into place on the wall, and Teàrlach left purgatory behind.

THIRTY-THREE
THE FISH THAT NEVER SWAM

Tony Masterton read the legal text again. A bank of freezing fog lay draped above the loch, stretching cold tendrils towards the house, encompassing concrete and steel in insubstantial fingers and reaching ineffectually for his heart. Samantha had finally plucked up the courage to leave him. She'd left yesterday afternoon, not long after the two detectives had departed. She'd said something about shopping but had never returned. Sent a text informing him she was leaving and not to try finding her. He'd found that amusing at least. Truth was that love and longing no longer held sway between the two of them. Their relationship hadn't survived more than a few days beyond Lilybet's disappearance. Days where time held no meaning. Days when they'd held each other in fear that they, too, could vanish in broad daylight and never be seen again. Possessively clutching at the substantial until even that lost form and meaning, until in the end they found they were clutching at shadows – turned into wraiths by Lilybet's absence. Bereft of her love and warmth and laughter until all that was left was memory and the hard polished concrete, steel and glass of their house. More tomb than home.

Why now? Why wait three and a half years before making her move? Tony gazed into the greyness surrounding his eyrie. The discovery of the girl's remains in the loch had been the catalyst. They were both so certain that it would be Lilybet when the skeleton had been found, no amount of preparation could have been sufficient to face the truth that it was another girl, another lost child taken by the loch.

He couldn't see the water surface through the mist. It hung like a shroud over the loch, concealing the child's watery grave in mystery. The dream came back to haunt him, the fall into darker and colder water until he came face to face with that sinuous creature, a woman's face on a snakelike body. He'd heard the stories of course – the garrulous barman at the Lochside Hotel had determined it was his duty to warn these new residents of the danger in the loch. The shape-shifting creature they called a kaelpie, how it lured children, cattle and occasionally men into the deep and fed on their flesh until nothing was left except bones.

He'd laughed it off, local folklore that the natives used to frighten the children and keep them away from the deceptively calm waters of the loch. But then he'd heard reports of missing sheep and cattle, seen shapes in the water himself that couldn't be explained rationally. Under its shifting grey shroud, he could believe the loch still held secrets. In places it plunged more than two hundred metres deep, stretching seventy kilometres out towards the sea. The gardener had demonstrated a wary respect for the loch, often standing like a statue looking out over the waters for minutes at a time. Had he seen the same dark shapes, twisting and turning under the surface like smoke? He dismissed the thought even as it occurred. Richard Tavistock was born of Traveller stock, their people full of superstitions and strange beliefs.

When he'd viewed the Belgium video, he believed the nanny without question. There was no need to face Samantha with allegations once the gardener admitted he'd been having an affair with her.

The gardener's last moments replayed in his mind. The surprise when he landed the first blow to Richard's handsome face, the gardener's head spinning around and spraying blood in an arc. The kick to his kneecap when arms belatedly raised in a futile defence. The patella had popped like a champagne cork, and he'd celebrated by felling Richard with a crashing blow to the temple, leaving him poleaxed and concussed on the ground where he hammered blow after blow until the face Samantha had kissed was no more. He'd left him bubbling frothy blood from his ruined face, then fetched the hole saw from his car. It had been surprisingly difficult to cut through the sternum and ribs. Flesh and sinew sprayed along with the blood until he felt he was holding a bloody Catherine wheel. Richard had tried fighting back once the pain brought him around, so there had been some sport in the endeavour. Tony remembered the exultation when he held the heart above his head, presented as a sacrifice to the night. It had been more difficult to remove than he'd expected, slippery to hold and secured in place by rubbery veins which he'd had to cut through. He'd thrown it onto the Tinkers' Heart, a poetic touch and a fitting place for it to be found – except it hadn't been found. Taken by some scavenging animal or eaten by crows, only a dark stain remained which the police forensics had pored over in their white suits. There'd be no trace of him for them to find – forensics suits cut both ways.

The legal letter he put to one side. He'd have to pay Samantha what she asked, otherwise the courts would be taking too much of an interest in his business dealings. She knew that of course. Samantha was anything but stupid. Maybe that had been the attraction? Two cold-hearted individuals recognising each other's qualities from opposing sides of a room. He remembered the event he'd been attending; a charitable venture for Glasgow's homeless held in Glasgow City Chambers

Banqueting Hall – Empire profits manifested in stone and opulence. Under crystal chandeliers and murals by the Glasgow Boys, the liberal classes wrung their hands in sorrow for the dispossessed, drank wine and contributed meagre amounts from the wealth they'd accumulated on the backs of the very people they pitied. She'd sent him a card after the event, suggesting they meet again. Unusually, he'd kept the missive, a postcard depicting the entrance hall and a verse describing the city's coat of arms:

Here's the Bird that never flew

Here's the Tree that never grew

Here's the Bell that never rang

Here's the Fish that never swam

Tony made a mental note to clear out her things and destroy the card. Things were less complicated before Samantha entered his life. If it hadn't been for Lilybet, they would have parted ways much sooner.

The thought of the girl brought back a familiar hollow feeling in his chest. He had begun to suspect he was incapable of love, of those simple emotions others take for granted. There was a good chance that he was borderline psychotic – or so a shrink had once told him with nervous looks towards the door as she'd pronounced the words. He'd laughed it off, but he knew it to be true. True until the day that Lily had been born. He'd been abroad, flying back to Glasgow Airport when Samantha had left him a panicked text – said her waters had broken. The child wasn't due for weeks. Snow blocked the road. He couldn't even immediately reach the pilot to pick her up in the helicopter. He'd raised three kinds of hell to get a snowplough diverted down their road, but by the time the medical team arrived, she'd already given birth and was airborne. He'd arrived at the Glasgow hospital to find mother and child both well after being dropped there by the helicopter.

She'd told him what had happened. How she'd called Richard in desperation as the contractions increased with no help arriving. How Richard had taken a boat up the loch carrying his mother. Describing how his mother acted as midwife to the Travellers and had brought Lilybet into the world. Had she been fucking Richard even then? Was Lilybet even *really* his child?

The forensics report had come back with neither he nor Samantha being the parents of the child in the loch, but Dee had let him know Richard was the likely father based on DNA analysis from the skeletal remains. A wry smile curled his lips upwards. They wouldn't have made that connection if Richard's body wasn't lying on a slab in the mortuary. He'd paid the midwife for her trouble – Anne or Annie, he forgot which. She'd been reluctant to take any payment at all, standing in the doorway of her bungalow as if it was somehow beneath her to be paid. He knew how these things worked. Nobody does anything for free – least of all the Travellers. And now she was dead too. Burned on the funeral pyre of her own bungalow.

Lilybet's picture adorned the wall of his study. Taken mere weeks before she vanished, she stood in the meadow – hair as yellow as summer daisies, eyes as blue as cornflowers. How could he be psychotic when she filled his heart with so much love that it physically hurt? She was the single good thing he had ever done in a life full of violence and death. If there was any karma in the universe, any ying or yang, then Lilybet provided all the good to counteract a lifetime of evil. And now she was gone.

They'd released a picture of what she'd look like now – AI sleight of hand to show a six-year-old Lilybet standing in the same spot. It had been shown on all the news channels at the private investigator's insistence. Said it could help. It didn't help him. All the picture did was remind them both how many years had gone by without her, years that could never be replaced or returned no matter how much money he threw at it. A six-year-old Lilybet stared back at him from his computer screen, mute pleading from blue eyes to find her. A sad, lost smile on her lips.

The PI had told him to expect the worst. He knew that already. If she was still alive, then someone would have demanded money by now – and he'd have gladly paid everything he had just to have her back. Then whoever had taken her would pay. Tony had envisaged many scenarios where he'd exacted revenge, each one dismissed as being too lenient until his mind held tortures sufficient for hell itself.

It was the lack of knowing that wounded him the most. If she was dead, if there was a body to mourn and bury, then the pain would eventually lessen to something more bearable. Instead, he was forced to conjure Lilybet out of the circling mist, imagine her enduring a life where death would be a release. What had the creature from his dream said when he'd asked who the child in the loch belonged to?

'*Your child's mother.*' The creature's harsh voice sounded so clearly in his mind he could see the leering face, more reptilian than human. He shrugged it off, the mind's ramblings in a dream, the words nonsense.

His phone rang, the number displayed as the private hospital he used.

'Tony Masterton.' He waited for a response, puzzled why the medical centre should be calling.

'Good morning, Mr Masterton, sorry to disturb you, but we've had a private investigator call here. Says he's working for you?'

'What did he want?'

'He said he wanted to see your daughter's birth records. Talk to someone who was present at the birth.'

Tony looked into the circling mist, saw patterns appear and disappear.

'Did he leave a card or his name?'

'He left a business card. PI Teàrlach Paterson. Looked a rough sort, like he's been in a fight recently.'

'Give him anything he needs.' Tony closed the call. Outside his window the freezing fog curled in on itself, reminiscent of the creature from his dream. He faced it impassively, ready for whatever would come.

'I'll collect my dues. I always do.'

THIRTY-FOUR

TEA LEAVES

Jane Whiting stared at the charred remains of Richard Tavistock's home with horror. She hadn't thought about what she would say to his mother beyond offering a few words of condolence, which went nowhere in easing the burden of guilt she carried. She'd seen the reports of a man's body being found in Hell's Glen with his heart torn out of his chest – put two and two together and came up with Richard's name before forensics had worked their magic.

She'd run off to the south of France after the Bruges filming debacle. Of course, the film studio had looked into why a young Scottish woman wanted to enact a fake kidnap and murder scene. A simple search for Tony's name brought forth the money he was offering for information about his missing daughter. Why be the middleman when they could deal directly with the source? She'd been stupid enough to set the whole thing up for them, even to the point of letting herself be tied to the chair. So much for her uncle's great idea for making money off the back of Tony Masterton's reward. Neither of them had received a single penny and now Richard had been murdered. To top it all, the police had found a girl's remains in the loch – they had to be Lilybet's no matter what the news said. The last few weeks she'd spent nervously expecting either Tony's henchmen or the Gendarmerie to knock on the door of the holiday cottage that was her temporary home. She was responsible for Richard's murder, however unwillingly, and Tony could easily take issue with her trying to scam him. Eventually the waiting proved more nerve-racking than facing the truth of her actions, and she headed back to the Lochside bungalow to pay her respects and exorcise her demons. Except the bungalow and Richard's mother were no more.

A silver bullet caravan was parked nearby, the surface streaked with soot from the fire. Jane stood facing the cottage, the smell of burning still pervading the chilled air. A mist had risen from the loch's surface, spread over the fir treetops and laying damp fingers on her. A shiver ran down her back and she spun around in fear, convinced that someone was watching. The driveway remained empty apart from her hire car and the caravan. Was this Tony's doing as well – burning down the cottage with Annie inside? She knew enough about him to know that he could. That meant she now had two deaths on her hands.

Jane held her palms up towards her face in bewilderment. How had she allowed herself to be talked into all this? Her uncle's financial woes were well known in the family. He was full of madcap ideas to clear his debts, turn the corner, start afresh. The lure of the Masterton millions had proven too tempting for him and the only way to access them was by involving her. Like a naïve fool she'd agreed – thought it might bring closure to them both as well as making enough money so she'd never need to work again. She'd dreamed of buying her own place, a small house in the Borders where she could tend to her cats and garden. And then she'd have something to offer Richard: an escape from his controlling mother and the poisonous relationship with Samantha. A new life with her. Maybe a baby with him, another blond child brought into the world but this time with her.

A plump tear fell onto her palm. Her hands went to her face, wiped the tears away. The life she dreamed of would never be. Standing by the charred ruins of Richard's cottage, she felt the reality of her own situation – alone, unloved, her lover murdered by her own words. Even Lilybet might have still been alive if she only had the courage to insist the decking be made more secure, or if she'd told the police to search the loch first before anywhere else. Then the desperate rush to clear any trace of Lilybet's DNA before they found she was Richard's daughter. She was trying to protect him even then, aided by Samantha who only ever looked out for herself.

Jane turned away from the ruin. It was too painful a reminder of the pain she had caused, the deaths she was responsible for. The desolation of the scene too perfect a mirror to her own failed dreams. She placed a hand on her car when the caravan door opened, making her jump back in fright.

'What do you want?' The voice cut as sharp as the winter air. A middle-aged woman stood outlined in the caravan doorway, her features set as harsh as the weather.

'I'm sorry, I thought it was empty – I mean, I didn't know anyone was here.' Jane stumbled over her words, a surge of adrenaline making her incoherent.

'So, what are you doing here – looking for things to steal?'

Much to Jane's discomfort, the woman started down the caravan steps, a determined expression fixing Jane in her sights.

'No, I... I know Richard. Knew,' she corrected herself.

The woman switched from Jane's eyes to surveying her womb.

'You pregnant?' She searched for confirmation.

'No. I haven't... It's been three years since I last... since I last saw him.'

The woman nodded in understanding. 'You'll be one of the lucky ones then.'

Jane stared blankly in response.

'Dick has left a string of bastards around this loch.' She laughed as if this was of some amusement to her. 'It's the one thing he was good at. Knew it would be the end of him.' She measured Jane in a glance. 'You used to love him.'

Jane felt the tears building afresh, was grateful for the mist coating her cheeks with moisture.

'I still do,' she said quietly.

'Aye. Well, you and the Mother knows how many others. The whole area is full of little blond kids – every one of them likely his.'

This unlikely revelation proved too much. The sobs escaped before she could hold them back. Tears falling for the death of her dreams, for Lilybet, for Richard and his mother, for a future without hope.

'Come on, lass. I'll make you a cup of tea.' She started back towards the caravan, stopping as Jane spoke.

'I'm sorry. I didn't mean to intrude. I'll go. I'm sorry.' Jane found she'd lost the use of her legs. Rooted to the spot, she tried concealing her tears behind her hands as her chest convulsed.

An arm encircled her waist. 'Come on, come and have a sit-down inside. You're no use driving like this.'

Jane allowed herself to be escorted into the caravan, the spotless interior in striking contrast to the grime and soot outside.

'Sit here.' The woman indicated an upholstered bench lining one wall.

Jane sat, dabbing at her eyes and feeling foolish.

'I'm sorry...' she started.

'You spend too much time being sorry.' A kettle sang on a gas hob, teapot stood waiting. 'What's your name, girl?'

'Jane. Jane Whiting.'

'I'm Mercy.' She poured boiling water into the teapot. 'Do you take milk, sugar?'

Jane felt dislocated, sitting on a chintz seat in a gypsy caravan next to a burned-out cottage as if this was an entirely normal event.

'Just milk, thanks.'

'So.' A bone china cup and saucer were placed into her hands, then just as quickly taken away again and placed on a table as the tea threatened to spill out of the cup. 'How did you know him, you live around here?'

Jane shook her head, untrusting of her voice. Mercy fetched her a tissue, the box concealed within a furry pink container that resembled a toy cat. She blew her nose, then held the sodden tissue in her hands with no bin anywhere in sight.

'I used to work at the big house on the loch, at the Mastertons' as a nanny.'

Mercy's eyes narrowed, but she made no comment, sipping her tea as she watched Jane closely.

'I had to leave after Lilybet – their daughter – went missing.' Jane lifted the teacup, took a noisy sip before replacing it on the saucer. 'Richard was their gardener. We became friends. More than friends.' Her eyes engaged with Mercy's. 'He said he wanted us to live together. To be married.'

Mercy nodded in response. 'Aye, Dick had a heart big enough to hold every woman he met. Don't get me wrong, I'm sure he *did* love you – same as he loved all the other poor girls he met.'

'It wasn't like that.' Jane flashed back. 'We were in love. Richard was planning on leaving the Mastertons, leaving his mother.'

'Why didn't he then? Where have you been the last three years when you could have been with him?'

'I had nowhere to live. No income.' She sniffed noisily, dabbing at her nose with an already sodden tissue. 'Tony made it clear he didn't want to see me around. I think he blamed me for his daughter's disappearance, even though I wasn't there on that day.'

'So, why are you here now? Now that Richard's dead.'

Jane's eyes darted from Mercy to focus on the various ornaments that took possession of every spare shelf and surface inside the caravan. It was a mishmash of china cats and dogs, religious icons, fading sepia photographs of country folk from a previous century.

'I wanted to pay my respects to his mother. To Annie. To tell her I was sorry.'

'Why are you sorry? Did you kill him?' Mercy's gaze was unflinching.

'No. Of course not. I... I've come from France. On holiday,' Jane added lamely.

Mercy's attention was drawn to the window, offering Jane some respite from the interrogation. She sipped her tea, comforted that her hands had stopped shaking. The cup was drained, returned to the saucer. Tea leaves caught in her teeth, and she worried about picking at them in front of this stranger.

'Do you know who killed Richard?' Mercy's voice was pitched dangerously low.

Jane's eyes automatically went to the door, seeking an exit as if her own life was at risk. She scolded herself for being overdramatic and faced Mercy with more confidence than she felt. Mercy's eyes bored into hers, as intense as a hypnotist as she waited for an answer.

'I think it was Tony Masterton. Richard was sleeping with his wife. He found out.' The words blurted out before she could rein them in. She felt faint, losing herself under Mercy's unblinking stare. What had just happened – was the tea drugged?

'Give me your cup.'

Jane dutifully obliged, wondering how to leave as quickly as possible. She hadn't meant to say anything.

Mercy held the cup up to the skylight, peered inside. Jane realised she was reading the tea leaves, and felt strangely reassured by such a harmless gypsy tradition being performed in front of her. She worried that there weren't any coins in her purse – wasn't she meant to cross her palm with silver?

'You've been on a journey,' Mercy intoned.

Jane didn't know what to do, sitting there as if in a fairground tent hearing her repeating what she'd already told her mere moments ago. She fidgeted, waiting for the moment when she could leave without causing offence.

'There was danger, you escaped death.' Mercy remained fixated on the inside of the cup. 'There is a child.' The reading paused as the cup was tilted from side to side, the first shadow of confusion crossing Mercy's otherwise confident expression.

Jane's heart leapt. Did this mean she was going to have a child? Could her dream still become real? Despite her cynicism she leaned forward, keen to hear the next words.

'You and the dead child will see each other before too long. There's death and blood on the path ahead.' Mercy suddenly put the cup down, her face paling.

'What is it? What did you see?' Jane felt the fear that had suddenly gripped Mercy, squeezing her heart in icy fingers.

'It's nothing. Just a bit of fun.' Mercy's voice betrayed her words. 'You're best to leave now. There's nothing for you here now.'

She stood, opening the caravan door as if anxious for Jane to depart. Somehow, their roles had been reversed. Now Mercy was on edge, frightened of Jane.

'What did you see?'

Mercy looked like she was going to argue, insist that Jane leave. The struggle was written so clearly on her face that Jane could plainly see the moment when Mercy acquiesced.

'The reading is never clear, but you bring death with you.'

'How do you mean, I bring death?'

Mercy bit her lip, her eyes troubled. 'There's darkness and water. Something unspeakably evil is coming. I can't tell what it is, but you should not stay here. Go. Go now.'

She pulled Jane up out of the seat, propelled her towards the door and almost flung her down the steps. 'Go far away from here and don't come near me or my family again!' she shouted from the caravan doorway as Jane fumbled with the car keys, suddenly gripped with the same sense of dread that she'd felt when she had first seen the cottage. As she drove away, she caught Mercy making warding gestures with her fingers – sending her away with a blessing or a curse until the creeping mist erased her.

THIRTY-FIVE

CRAIC

Dee raised her head from the pillow and set off a headache bad enough to force it down again. She spent what was left of the morning feeling sorry for herself and debating whether to be sick. When she finally struggled to her feet, the face that greeted her in the mirror was in a sorry state. She groaned in sympathy with her reflection, splashed cold water over her face and started tugging the knots out of her hair. The bedside clock admonished her in dull red numerals letting her know she'd slept through to mid-afternoon.

Mick, Jeremiah, Brian and Mercy – she realised they were all now on first name terms – had consumed industrial quantities of alcohol. What had turned into a wake for Richard and Annie had been a long and musical one, their lives encompassed by anecdote and laughter. Theirs had been a peripatetic life, travelling from farm to farm, fair to fair. Nobody knew who Richard's father was, a scandalous situation within the Travelling community and the reason Annie was eventually exiled to the cottage by the loch. She would have been ostracised completely if it wasn't for her skills with gynaecological instruments, not always for the good of the foetus. Instead, a steady stream of pregnant visitors were deposited at Annie's door, conveniently removed from Traveller society until ready to be collected. Sometimes, babies were admired and fussed over. At other times ashen-faced women were fetched in secrecy and swapped for bulging envelopes. It was an arrangement that suited everyone – the Gorger hospitals were a refuge of last resort to be avoided like all institutions favoured by the settled people.

Dee hadn't been so drunk that she didn't pick up on the insistent questioning about Teàrlach – what he was doing there, why he'd been to see Annie, how he'd arrived the same day that Richard was murdered. Mick remained sober despite the amount of drink that passed his lips, his attention never wavering. The two women flanking him were sharp as well, casting furtive glances to read her face every time she answered. Brian had sat there like a mute mountain, only coming to life whenever the guitar launched into another ballad and his voice filled the space with sound.

There was now no doubt in her mind that they had come looking for Richard Tavistock's killer, and by extension whomsoever had set Annie's cottage on fire. Dee hoped she'd done enough to clear Teàrlach as a potential suspect – although the local police still eyed him suspiciously. The Travellers had been nothing but welcoming last night, drawing her into their small group and treating her as one of their own – but there was a sharp edge underneath the bonhomie, a blade concealed behind the craic. Dee knew they intended dispensing their own form of justice on the perpetrator, once they'd found out who it was. She'd remained silent on Tony Masterton despite repeated attempts to ask her what she knew of him. He was a suspect, that had become clear during unguarded comments, although only through reputation rather than motive. If they discovered Tony knew Richard had been having an affair with his wife, was suspected of fathering his child...

Dee took herself unsteadily down the stairs in search of a late breakfast. The hotel retained the feeling of a land-locked Mary Celeste, glasses and bottles left on breakfast tables. The guitar had been returned to its case and left propped against a wall. The sounds of an argument drifted through from reception, resolving into more of a one-sided diatribe as she approached.

'The state of the place. You could have lost me my licence. What if the guests had wanted breakfast? What were you thinking?'

'We took more money last night than we made in the last month.' Blair's voice.

'And that's another thing – we don't want those sorts of people here. I had to call the police to get them to move that caravan from the car park. Next thing you know there'll be whole families of them cooking outside and leaving rubbish everywhere. This is a respectable establishment.'

The voices stopped as they caught sight of Dee standing in the hallway.

'Hi.' Dee offered a smile which did little to soften the hard expression worn by the receptionist. 'Any chance of a sandwich or something?' She felt her eyes attempting to blink in sympathy with each pounding wave of pain from somewhere behind her eyes.

'Blair will see to you,' the receptionist replied sniffily.

'What can I get you?' Blair escaped reception with alacrity, the receptionist's laser eyes boring into his back.

'Bacon butty?'

'I'm on it. Take a seat in the bar, and I'll bring it through.'

The fire had been lit, flames dancing up the chimney and bringing much needed warmth to the room. The place was deserted, and not for the first time Dee wondered how the business managed to survive through the tourist-free winter months. Even last night there had only been the five of them in the bar performing an impromptu wake for the departed. Outside, the mist was finally beginning to lift, retreating to hold a last stand on the loch. She imagined there must be a practical explanation for the mist holding sway above the water, latent heat stored in the loch's water against the insistent chill of the air. Shapes shifted as she stared mesmerised out of the bar windows, sinuous curls like some sea monster had raised itself out of the water and was heading towards land.

Blair broke her reverie, a plate wafting the smell of bacon towards her nose.

'Do you want a coffee as well?' Blair asked, appraising her with a practised eye.

'You're a mind reader.'

'Barkeeper,' Blair corrected. The coffee machine sounded like it was taking a final breath as he placed a cup under the machine's nozzle. He left it to gasp and splutter whilst he collected the glasses and bottles from last night, the rattle of glass against glass coming from the next room.

'You'll never guess who made an appearance over lunch.' Blair reappeared with her cup.

Dee almost grabbed it out of his hands, washing down the bacon with weak coffee. She was on the verge of complaining about the lack of any coffee flavour when natural curiosity took over.

'I don't know, surprise me.'

'Jane Whiting – the Masterton nanny.'

'What's she doing here? She's meant to be in France somewhere.'

Blair frowned in puzzlement. 'Why do you think she's in France?'

'Oh, nothing. Something I'd heard. Is she staying here, at the hotel?'

'No, just passing through. She'd been to Annie's house –

hadn't heard she'd died in the fire. I think the Travellers must have spooked her, she seemed pretty shook up.'

Dee thoughtfully sipped the insipid coffee. 'Where's she going, did she say?'

'Why are you so interested?'

'Teàrlach wanted to ask her about the Masterton girl. See if she could remember anything that could help him find Lilybet.' She looked directly at him.

'I don't know, she didn't say. Don't think she's keen to stay around here now Richard's been murdered. She was sweet on him – like most of the women around here.' His last words sounded bitter. 'I better clear up, after last night,' he added hurriedly, almost running off to the breakfast room to cover his embarrassment.

Dee contemplated her half-drunk coffee, pushed it away in resignation. She needed to clear her head, and the coffee wasn't helping. The view outside decided her, now the mist was receding a brisk walk would work off the worst of the hangover. She fetched her leather bike jacket, made for the front door only to be confronted by Blair.

'You going for a walk?' He'd scanned her for the rest of her motorbike paraphernalia and had come up missing helmet, gloves, leather trousers.

'Aye, thought I'd see the sights.' A thought struck her. 'Where's this Tinkers' Heart place? It's near here, isn't it – back up the road towards Hell's Glen?'

Blair couldn't conceal his discomfort. 'It's not good weather for a walk. Why not wait until tomorrow, the forecast is for sun?'

Dee frowned. 'I don't think the mist will kill me.'

Blair fidgeted on the spot, his hands nervously feeding a cloth between his fingers. 'It's not the mist.' He looked over her shoulder, out to the loch still shrouded in secrecy. 'I told your man, Teàrlach, but he didn't listen.'

Dee was about to correct his assumption about her relationship with Teàrlach, but curiosity stayed her tongue.

'Told him what?' she asked impatiently.

One hand went to tug at his ginger beard. She could see a battle being fought behind his eyes.

'I warned him there's something dangerous in the loch, a kaelpie.' He spoke hesitantly, not wishing to be perceived as a superstitious teuchter.

He saw the grin forming as Dee's eyes opened wider in surprised amusement.

'It's not a joke!'

Dee's grin froze, Blair was being serious. Did he really believe such things existed? One look at his face showed her the truth of it.

'And is this a commonly held view, around here?' Dee's amusement still held in her voice.

'There are things people have seen, those of us who live here on the shore. They can't be explained, not by anything rational.' Blair's tone shifted from defensive to combative. 'You want to know who took the Masterton girl?'

Dee nodded, unsure of the barman's sanity and feeling for the front door handle.

'We told them not to build there. Not such a big, modern building right on the shore. We tried to warn them but no! Big city folk know everything. It was only a matter of time before the kaelpie took their girl, and now it's thirsty for more. Go out if you want, I can't stop you – but stay away from the shoreline. It can move freely without being seen, hunting in the mist. Any sane person stays inside on a day like this.'

He turned his back on her, walked towards the bar. Dee stood rooted to the spot, astonished to hear such a ridiculous story told with no hint of anything other than true belief. She shook her head in denial of such an implausible tale and left the hotel, turning right and following the road with senses attuned for any road traffic. On her left the sound of small waves impacted the shore, muffled by the shifting mist. On her right pine trees creaked like arthritic pensioners straightening their backs as the light darkened towards evening. Cold air worked its magic, searing her nose and throat and clearing a muddled head. It was only as her mind cleared from the effects of her own internal fog that she began to consider that the barman may have had a point – this was not the most opportune time to take a lonely walk along a deserted road as night approached.

THIRTY-SIX

NO SHIT, SHERLOCK

The location of the Tinkers' Heart was easily identified by shredded police tape hanging limply from a farm gate. Dee had thought about turning back, seeking the refuge of the hotel bar and its welcoming fire as dusk fell. Blair's warning about a monster poised to drag unsuspecting victims into the loch preyed on her mind, every muted splash coming from the shrouded loch sending her imagination into overdrive. She knew it was errant nonsense – talk of sea monsters, kaelpies, mythological creatures from ages past when the unexplained could be neatly encapsulated into folklore. Even so, with the light fading and tendrils of freezing fog reaching inland once more, Dee felt less certain than she had been when leaving the hotel. The dusk and mist conspired to turn everything liminal, to erase reality and replace it with ambiguity. She hesitated at the gate. Somewhere in that direction lay the loch and whatever sixth sense still served duty in the twenty-first century strongly advised her to go in any other direction but this. Dee shrugged off the feeling with irritation and opened the gate, hinges squealing a protest and advertising her presence to anyone within a half-kilometre radius.

ANDREW JAMES GREIG

The Tinkers' Heart was a disappointing monument – even the term monument was working overtime to describe the unsophisticated arrangement of white quartz pebbles sunk into tarmac in the shape of a heart. Abandoned in an orphaned patch of road and bordered by a triangular fence, Dee felt this mark of Traveller heritage had suffered the same fate as the people themselves. Uprooted and moved somewhere more convenient, out of sight and out of mind. There was still enough light to make out the darker stain surrounding the central stone, the alleged resting place for Richard Tavistock's heart. The symbolism of the site was unequivocable, the placing of his heart there sent a clear message both as to the rationale for his murder and as an insult to his people. If that had been the intention, then the challenge had been accepted by Mick and his small party. She shivered in the cold, started back to the road. From the direction of the loch came a frantic lowing, a cow repeating the same panicked call again and again. Dee stopped in her tracks, tried to pierce the encircling gloom to find the source of the noise, considered walking towards it in case the animal was trapped or needed help. The cow stopped midbellow, cut-off as efficiently as if by an abattoir bolt gun.

She remained frozen, a sixth sense clamouring urgently for her to run. That part of her mind dedicated to cold reason and logic argued she should stay, dismissive of fear engendered by the approaching darkness. Her ears caught the sound of leaves rustling in a breeze, or tall grasses rubbing against each other in a gentle summer eddy. There were no leaves mid-winter, her reason told her, any grasses frozen rigid and encapsulated in ice. The unidentifiable sound drew closer, fear gibbered in her mind until she gave in to madness and ran back to the road. Dee pulled the gate shut behind her in a desperate attempt to stop whatever it was that haunted her, cursing when the hinges announced her position with rusting shrieks.

The road was almost invisible now, lost to the encroaching

236

night and encircling mist. Dee felt the comforting solidity of tarmac under her feet, held an arm out protectively in front of her face to ward off stray branches as she ran. The darkness that threatened an end to the weak daylight now ruled oppressively, no starlight or moon to take on the sun's role. The road impacting her feet was barely discernible, only the ghost of its surface giving hint to its existence. The fog was denser now, great billowing banks rolling across the shoreline and adding to her sense of dislocation. She couldn't explain the reason for her panicked flight, this headlong rush into blackness. A primitive part of her brain had taken control, desperate to escape the nameless fear drawing ever closer.

Only when the mist captured car headlights and flung them back in her face, broken into luminous halos by a thousand miniature water lenses, did she stop. Now another danger presented itself as the car bore down on her. Dee inched across the road to feel for the margins with her feet, then faced the oncoming source of the light and held both hands up in a plea for help. The driver must have only seen her at the last moment, applying brakes and swerving violently away from her. Dee ran towards the red glow of rear lights, recognised the number plate with relief and pulled on the passenger door to collapse breathless in the seat.

Teàrlach regarded her with astonishment.

'Drive! Just drive!' she managed, casting a look behind her in sheer terror.

Teàrlach obeyed, checking his rear-view mirror with concern.

'What is it, is someone after you?'

Dee didn't know how to respond. How could she admit to being chased by some featureless creature conjured out of darkness and mist.

'I don't know,' she eventually managed. 'I had a feeling something was out there. Something evil.'

He drove without comment. The night mist made driving conditions difficult, especially on this road with its random twists and turns. The headlights caught strange shapes in their beams, bands of thicker fog assumed solidity, created fantastical creatures.

'You've been listening to that barman, haven't you?' Teàrlach's tone was flippant.

She scarcely listened to him. To react how she had was completely out of character. Dee felt foolish now that she was securely belted into a warm car, Teàrlach at her side. But all the same, something had spooked her, the same something that had spooked the Highland cow.

'Aye, you're probably right.' She imagined he saw her as a city girl out of her comfort zone. If so, he was damn right. Night never arrives this quickly or as completely as it did here. No lights anywhere, just the creeping mist and a lone cow bellowing its abrupt death into the approaching darkness. 'Blair did say something you'd be interested to hear.' She took comfort in discussing the mundane, if mundane now stretched to cover ripped out hearts and being burned alive.

'What?' Teàrlach kept his eyes fixed forward, scanning for the hotel sign.

'He said Jane Whiting turned up at the bar this lunchtime. She'd been to see Annie, met her extended family instead.'

'She's come back?' He risked an incredulous glance in her direction. 'Does she have any idea how dangerous that is for her? Did you speak with her?'

'No, I was late up. Had a bit of a session with Mick and co last night.' Dee wondered if her latent hangover may have conspired to create the feeling of panic she'd just experienced. The shiver running down her back told her otherwise.

'Ah! Here we are.' He pulled into a parking bay, stretched behind his seat to hoist an overnight bag. 'Tell me more about it when we're inside.'

Dee followed him to his room, sat on the bed as he unpacked.

'Do you know where Jane is now?' Teàrlach called through from the bathroom.

'She didn't say. Blair said she seemed upset, thought the Travellers had scared her off.'

'They weren't particularly welcoming when I saw them at the cottage.' Teàrlach returned to the bedroom, stood with his back to the window.

'That may have had something to do with suspecting you of murdering Richard and then finishing off his mother.'

Teàrlach's expression remained neutral. 'I rather got that from them. Were you able to convince them otherwise?'

Dee nodded. 'They thought it unlikely that you'd stick around if you'd been the killer. Also lack of motive.' She winked. 'And I put in a good word for you.'

'Who *do* they think killed them?' he said quietly.

'I get the impression that Tony's very much in the frame. His reputation alone makes him a suspect – if they hear talk of Richard shagging Samantha...'

'Is that public knowledge?'

'Everything's public knowledge around here. Mick as much as admitted that Richard's responsible for fathering a lot of the children here. Any kid with blond hair is likely his.' Dee thought of the ex-policewoman on the other side of the loch – of Alana with the drawing of the unicorn she named Lilybet. 'There's something else I learned.'

'Go on.' Teàrlach reached for his bag, withdrew a notepad and pen. Stood ready like a reporter.

'Annie wasn't just a midwife for the Travellers. They let slip that her services sometimes included abortions for any Traveller woman who wanted mistakes quietly put right. She'd been all but banished from their society for having a child out of wedlock, forced to live alone in a cottage, but they all used to come to her. It's how she earned her living. They avoided Gorger hospitals and doctors whenever possible.'

'Is that true, they threw her out because she had a kid out of marriage?'

'Evidently. The Travellers keep to the old ways – in every respect.'

Teàrlach added the information to his notes. It didn't offer much in the way of insight and didn't lead him any closer to finding out whatever had happened to Lilybet.

'I wanted to have a closer look at that photograph in Annie's house.' Teàrlach shut his notebook in frustration. 'I could see a woman with a young girl on her knee. It was in her kitchen. I thought it was Lilybet and Jane Whiting, but Mick and Brian weren't in the mood for me to try for a closer look.'

'It will have burned to a cinder in the fire,' Dee said. 'Why would she have a picture of those two in her house?'

Teàrlach looked out of the bedroom window, could only see his imperfect reflection staring back through the blackness outside.

'I thought it was because Lilybet was her granddaughter. Now I'm not so sure.'

'But the girl in the loch wasn't Samantha's, the DNA proved it.'

'It proved Richard was the father. We still don't know who the mother was,' Teàrlach corrected.

'But maybe Annie would have known.' Dee started to follow his train of thought.

'And maybe that's why she was killed.' Teàrlach turned his back to the window once more. 'And it was a woman's voice we heard on my phone at the cottage. A woman who burned Annie alive and almost did for me.'

'We need to find who that is.' Dee stood, looking straight into Teàrlach's troubled eyes.

'Aye. And we need to speak to Jane. There are secrets

buried under secrets and one by one those that know anything are being killed. She's right to get away from here, it's not safe.'

Dee thought of the loch, of the feeling of dread she'd experienced at the Tinkers' Heart, of Blair's warning that the kaelpie would take the Mastertons' girl, of missing hearts and immolation.

'No shit, Sherlock.'

THIRTY-SEVEN

INVERNESS

Jane Whiting finished breakfast in an Inverness café. Plastic Santas were strung in lines from the ceiling, holding hands in chains and swaying to the incessantly cheery Christmas songs playing tinnily from a radio behind the counter. She didn't know where else to go. Staying anywhere near the Mastertons would have been suicidal – Tony wouldn't have appreciated her attempted scam and would want to ask her for more detail about Samantha's indiscretions before most likely doing away with them both. Like he did with Richard and Annie. She couldn't go anywhere near her parents or uncle without being easily found. A tear escaped before she was able to reach for a handkerchief, falling onto the wooden table and shattering like crystal to form minute droplets on the waxed surface. Where had it all gone so horribly wrong for her?

She had always loved children. Found she was in demand as a babysitter even as a young teen, and faced with poor academic results, decided this is what she'd do for a living. One day she wanted her own children, once she'd found a man whom she loved and who loved her in return. Her handkerchief dabbed delicately at each eye whilst she surreptitiously looked around in case anyone caught her openly weeping. The other customers were too engrossed in newspapers, laptops or mobiles to pay her any attention.

The Masterton job had been her first. Big house, wealthy family. The isolated location didn't bother her at all. She fondly imagined taking baby Lilybet on country walks, teaching her the names of plants and animals, making daisy chains together. By the time she realised the source of Tony's wealth, it was too late. She'd heard too much, seen too much. She became complicit in his organisation the same way as Samantha, drawn by money and held by fear. He ignored her for the most part, saw her as part of the house. Tony lived up to his cold-blooded reputation except where Lilybet was concerned. She could swear he loved the child more than Samantha ever had; a transformation took place in front of her every time he saw her, holding his daughter close with such love and tenderness that sometimes she doubted her eyes.

Samantha treated Lilybet as an unwelcome responsibility, one she was grateful to relinquish to the nanny. Jane knew there were cases where a mother rejected their child, including postpartum depression – she'd covered the subject on her nursery course. Samantha's rejection went far beyond those first few months after birth when raging hormones excused her fluctuating feelings for the new baby. Jane had joined the family when Lilybet was a few weeks old, thought this was how rich people were. Now she understood Samantha had what was popularly termed Cold Mother Syndrome. Through a quirk of fate Tony compensated by shrugging off his psychopathic personality whenever the child drew near, giving her the hugs and love her mother was unable to offer.

It was a family dynamic nursery classes had not allowed for, and Jane had to plot her own course through two dysfunctional relationships. She'd managed well, she thought. Forming a bond with Lilybet as strong as a mother's. Through those first few years Lily had learned to walk and talk, became her own wee person with a lightness of being that brought life and joy to an otherwise sterile house. And then Richard...

She'd seen him around, of course. During the summer months he tended to the garden and grounds, riding the mower over the helicopter pad and lawns, fussing around the flowerbeds that were Samantha's fiefdom. They'd scarcely exchanged more than pleasantries during the first year, then she found her attention drifting from Lilybet whenever he came into view – fixing up the decking, cleaning the glass, stripping off to his torso when the Scottish sun reached summer tempera-tures. He had gypsy blood running through his veins, or so Samantha had once told her. She'd said how romantic it was to have a gypsy gardener. If only Jane hadn't been so naïve, she would have seen what was always in front of her; the shared looks they exchanged, the possessive touch of Samantha's hand on Richard's olive skin. Tony spent too much time abroad or in Glasgow. The time he did spend in the house was always in his study or focussed on Lilybet. She knew whatever force had orig-inally drawn them together had long since lost potency – they now existed in separate worlds.

By the second year, she and Richard were well on the way to becoming an item. But their courtship had to remain hidden from the Mastertons, Richard explained. She'd thought at the time this was because he wanted to protect her job, and by this was showing how much he cared for her. She now knew Richard was more interested in protecting his own life. Samantha must have noticed their growing relationship. Women often see what men cannot.

It was only a matter of weeks before Lilybet went missing when Richard had indicated she meet him by the treehouse.

She'd taken Lilybet with her of course, armed with a colouring book and pencil, she'd left her comfortably ensconced on the cushions absorbed in her task. Richard met her around the back where they were both hidden from view of the house windows.

'Samantha knows we've been seeing each other.' She could still picture his concerned face framed in unruly black locks, a face she dearly wanted to kiss.

'But that's all we've been doing. I mean, just talking.'

He had smiled sadly at her, his hand caressing the hair back from her face. She should have kissed him then, pulled him closer until he understood the raw animal intensity of longing she felt for him. Instead, he told her that he'd been having an affair with Samantha, wanted it to stop, but she'd said Lilybet was his child. Jane remembered the pain of the moment as clearly as if she'd been stabbed in the heart. She had run away from him, buried herself inside the treehouse with Lilybet and cried silently as the young girl coloured in, oblivious. Jane studied the child through blurred vision, wiping eyes to see the similarities in Lilybet's features – the shape of his eyes, the curve of his ears.

On her day off, she'd taken the spare car to Inverness, to this same café where she had met the other nannies and pretended everything was fine. They bitched about the mothers, complained about the work and pay, fantasised over which knight in shining armour would carry them off to another life. Jane knew she'd have to leave Lilybet and the Mastertons. The house had become as dangerous as a powder keg – one small spark was all it required before the whole place blew up. And then her phone had rung with the news of Lilybet's disappearance and her world fell apart.

Tears again filled her eyes. She tried blinking them away but only succeeded in making the world turn as blurry as a Monet landscape. Outside the café windows, life continued as normal, shoppers wrapped up against the cold stooped in on themselves as if the entire population of Inverness had aged overnight. All except the young girl being tugged along behind her mother, blond hair shining in the light from the café lights.

Jane's breath caught in her throat. The girl looked so much like Lilybet that she did a double take, wiping both eyes with the back of her hand to clear away the tears. The girl and woman had gone. She jumped to her feet, pulled on a coat and left without bothering to do up the buttons, so she resembled a crow with broken wings flapping uselessly as she exited the café. There, further along the road.

She followed the pair whilst questioning herself. That couldn't be Lilybet. It had been three years, and she'd look different now even if it was her. Besides, the girl in the loch. It had to be her. Lilybet was dead.

Despite her internal protestations, she stayed close, angling for a better view. The two of them entered a supermarket, and she followed close on their heels, taking another aisle so she could approach them head on. The girl's hood had been pulled up over her head, almost completely obscuring the blond hair. They came closer, the woman agitated, pushing a trolley and arguing with the girl. Jane pretended to select pasta, picking up a packet and replacing it for another. As they drew level, she stepped backwards, barging into the trolley and forcing them to stop.

'Oh, sorry, I didn't see you.' Jane gave an apologetic smile.

'My fault. We're in a rush.' The woman straightened her trolley, flashed a harassed look at Jane and turned to the girl, voice tight with irritation. 'Come on, stop dragging behind. Look what you've made me do!'

The girl lifted her gaze up from the floor, looked directly at Jane. There were those same eyes, the same face. Why had Lilybet not recognised her? She suddenly doubted herself – this couldn't be the same girl. Was this what she'd look like as a six-year-old? Children change so much over the first years. Losing that soft plumpness, the scaffolding of bones and muscle rearranging in readiness to form adult features.

'Excuse me.' The mother's voice was sharp with impatience.

Jane stood to one side, clearing a way for the mother to push past with a belligerent look. The girl's hood caught on Jane's open coat, exposing blond hair and ears. Those were Lilybet's ears, she'd swear to God!

'And keep your bloody hood up!' the woman she took to be the mother hissed, glaring angrily at Jane for having not moved completely out of the way. They moved quickly up the aisle, the mother grabbing items off the shelves with practised ease. She shot a look back as they turned the corner, saw Jane still watching, then they were out of sight.

Jane didn't know what to do – was this a kind of daytime illusion? Was she starting to see Lilybet in every blond-haired young girl that passed by? She searched on her phone, found the press article with an artist's rendering of Lilybet as she might look today. The picture was of the same girl, the likeness so accurate it might have been a photograph. The only difference was the hair – in the missing person press release her hair remained as long as it had been when she was three. This girl had a short crop.

Jane held her phone in her hand, started back down the aisle. They were almost at the end of the next section, and both looked at her as she took the snap. She heard the woman shout in anger and ran, furious footsteps sounding close behind her as she passed the puzzled checkout operator in a panic and headed for the exit and out into the street. When she no longer heard running feet behind her, Jane stopped, gasping for air with legs weak from adrenaline. The woman was heading back to the store and back to Lilybet. She had no doubt as to the girl's identity now. Secure from pursuit for the moment, Jane checked the photograph she'd just taken. The mother's features held a complex mix of emotions: shock, anger and fear. The girl merely looked puzzled but in clear enough focus to make it a close match to the missing person drawing. Close enough to clear the air with Tony Masterton. Close enough to earn the reward and start again.

THIRTY-EIGHT

LIQUIDATE

Tony Masterton was not expecting the call. His secretary had patched it through from his home number after screening the caller for him. It was Jane Whiting.

'You've some nerve calling me after playing that stunt with the film crew.'

Jane swallowed nervously before she found her voice would work. 'I'm sorry, Mr Masterton. It wasn't my idea – my uncle wanted me to do it, to earn the reward. I thought it might help put your mind at ease if you knew she'd died in the loch.'

He remained silent, waiting for more.

'I didn't know they planned on really torturing me. I didn't mean to say anything else, about Samantha I mean. I'm really sorry.'

Tony snorted in derision. To think he'd even considered going after this weak-minded girl. None of that mattered since Samantha had left him. Still, she might be of some use to him in the divorce settlement. 'You have any proof my wife was sleeping with the gardener?'

'Only what Richard told me. That Samantha had said

Lilybet was his child. I didn't mean for any of that to come out or for anyone to get hurt. I'm sorry.'

Tony heard her sobs before she was able to muffle them. What a pathetic excuse for a woman. What did she think was going to happen once she told him about Richard Tavistock?

'You might as well have killed him yourself.' Tony enjoyed twisting the knife. If the stupid girl thought Richard loved her, then she deserved all the pain he could give her. He didn't even have to go to the bother of tracking her down, and she was paying for the phone call. Tony felt his spirits lift for the first time since ripping out the gardener's heart.

'I think I've found Lilybet.'

Tony's face darkened. If she thought she was going to play him along again, then he would finish her.

'What the fuck are you playing at?' He motioned for the chauffeur to pull into the side of the road.

'I saw a woman with Lilybet. I'm sure it was Lilybet. I took a photo.' Jane's voice betrayed her nervousness.

Tony squashed the first glimmer of hope before it could surface. 'Where?'

Jane delayed before finding the courage to speak again. 'What about the reward?'

Tony stared at his mobile with incredulity. Did this woman not learn anything from those years with him?

'You remember who I am?'

'I remember. I'm sending the photo to your WhatsApp address. If you think it's Lilybet as well and you want to know where they are, then you'll have to pay me, and I'll disappear forever.'

He nodded in agreement – she was right about that. 'I'll look at what you've got. What's your number?'

'I'll call again, this time tomorrow. If you want to know where they live, I want half the money paid up front, the rest when you get her back.' It seemed Jane had learned a few things working at the Mastertons that weren't included in the nursery syllabus.

The phone cut off, leaving Tony in a swirl of emotions. He made another two calls; one to his office to forward the photograph to his mobile, the second call to Dee.

'Forget whatever you're doing. I want you to track down Jane Whiting, find out where she is.' He viewed the picture newly arrived on the screen, leaned in for a closer look. 'It can't be.' The hope he'd thought was lost forever, rekindled in his heart.

'Sorry, didn't catch that last bit?' Dee's query was ignored.

'She's just called me, sent me a photograph of someone who looks exactly like Lilybet. I need to know where she saw her, where she is now. I don't care how you do it, just find her.'

'Teàrlach's here with me. You want him on this as well?'

'Sure. He's not exactly doing anything useful chasing down Samantha's maternity suite. Tell him to prioritise finding Jane. If that is Lilybet, then I want to know where she is and who has her. Don't fuck this up!'

'Teàrlach says can you send us the photograph? We may be able to work out where it was taken.'

'Sending it now.'

Tony threw his mobile down on the seat, opened his laptop to view the photograph on a larger screen, zooming in until the girl's face filled the picture. Even allowing for a girl three years older than Lilybet had been the last time he'd seen her, that was her.

'Carry on to the office.' He tapped the privacy glass for emphasis, motioning for the driver to continue. There were funds he needed to liquidate to pay the nanny. It was a temporary loan, nothing more. Then he'd liquidate Jane Whiting.

. . .

ANDREW JAMES GREIG

The subject of Tony's focus took a seat at the fast-food outlet at Inverness Railway Station. Her hands holding the burger shook so much she could barely eat. She'd just gone head-to-head with one of Glasgow's most notorious gangsters – a man who she knew for sure had ripped out Richard's heart and probably enjoyed the experience. The least he owed her was the reward money, but she knew he'd now be placing all his considerable resources on finding her. The train left in ten minutes. She left a barely eaten burger on the table, left her mobile there as well. This was the most dangerous thing she'd ever done and if she made a mistake, it was only going to end one way. The same way it had for Richard and his mother.

THIRTY-NINE

CO-OP

Dee and Teàrlach studied the photograph on her laptop. The girl in the supermarket bore a striking resemblance to the artist's interpretation of how a six-year-old Lilybet might look, if you disregarded the short hair.

'Fuck me!' Dee exclaimed for the second time. She'd used the same expression after Tony's brief phone call.

'She looks just like Lilybet,' Teàrlach studied the picture closely. 'It's been taken in a Co-op, see the sign there?' He pointed at the top right corner of the hastily snapped photograph, telltale corporate branding coming into view as he zoomed in.

'We just need to find which town that supermarket's in, and we're close to finding her.' Dee retrieved her laptop, started analysing the frame pixel by pixel.

'If it *is* her,' Teàrlach cautioned.

'Tony doesn't sound too impressed with your snooping around that private hospital in Glasgow. Did you find anything?' Dee asked, still staring intently at the photograph.

'No. I was going to ask if you could search their computers – see if you could find out anything about the birth.'

'Not now, Sherlock. We've been given our orders. Find Jane Whiting, and these two.'

'If she hasn't spooked them. Look at them, they're both staring directly at the camera. They know they've been snapped – and the woman doesn't appear too pleased.'

Dee opened a new app on her laptop, entered a long number and scrolled upwards as a sea of digits appeared. 'That's his office number, which probably means Jane called his home and was patched through.' She reset the app, typed Tony's home number into the search field.

'OK. Here it is.'

Teàrlach saw a telephone number with a timestamp, ten minutes ago. 'Is this where she called from?'

Dee nodded. 'Didn't withhold the number. Rookie error.' She continued typing rapidly, brought up another window. 'This is a reverse look-up site. Only available on Tor.' She pasted the same number into a search field, came back with a destination.

'That's not so helpful.' She angled the screen so Teàrlach could read it.

Inverness Railway Station Public mast, station concourse.

'Can you find a live feed from Inverness Co-op?'

Dee looked at him with a pained expression. 'Do you think I can walk on water as well?' She thought for a few seconds, then brought up a map of Inverness. 'There are only a few car hire companies with a branch there. I'll call them as Jane Whiting and say I left a bag on the back seat when I returned the car. If she's taken a train out of Inverness, then there's a good chance she left a car there.'

Teàrlach watched Dee as she worked the phone, giving him a thumbs-up as the second call confirmed Jane had hired from them.

'Nothing there? Never mind, it was a long shot anyway. Thanks for looking.' She ended the call with a triumphant smile.

'OK. Inverness it is. I'll drive there now, see if I can match this shot to the same store.' Teàrlach started pulling on his coat.

'I'll see what trains are running around the time of the call from Inverness. May be able to have a guess where she's heading. I'll send the snap to your phone.'

Teàrlach hadn't made the door before Dee cursed again. He turned around, saw her brows pulled down in frustration.

'The woman's not as stupid as I thought. There are trains to Wick, Edinburgh, Aberdeen and Kyle of Lochalsh all departing within eleven minutes after her call. She could be anywhere.'

He left her with the almost impossible task of finding Jane, taking the road back up the glen and north to Inverness. Yesterday's mist had cleared, burned off by welcome sunshine. The loch no longer appeared dark and sinister, turning turquoise underneath a cerulean winter sky and framed by golden tree-clad hills catching the low morning light. Driving past the Tinkers' Heart, he replayed the events of last night. Dee's panicked face as she threw herself in front of his car, the almost palpable sense of dread they'd both experienced as the mist closed in. They hadn't talked of it again, both too embarrassed to admit they'd been spooked by the claustrophobic fog, the oppressive darkness. The inexplicable feeling that *something* was there and coming closer.

The remainder of last night had been spent in the bar, sharing the space with a few locals whose presence helped provide a feeling of much-needed normality. They'd talked about the Travellers, the likelihood that they were there to exact revenge, the apparent absence of any police activity since the initial flurry. Lilybet was the unspoken presence at their table – a three-year-old girl who had seemingly vanished into thin air. The body in the loch hadn't been hers, and so far, no one was any the wiser as to who the bones belonged to. Richard Tavistock and his mother were the only keys they had to unlocking this mystery, and they'd both been murdered.

Teàrlach shrugged off the paranoia from last night, put it down to the murders and his suspicion that worse was yet to come. He checked the time – 11:32. If the roads were clear, he should reach Inverness around 3pm, giving him enough time to check the supermarket and start a search for Lilybet – or the girl who looked very much like her.

A call came in from Chloe, and he flicked accept on the steering column.

'Hi, Sherlock. I've had a call from that maternity hospital you visited. Seems Tony Masterton has told them to give you anything you wanted from Lilybet's birth. You want me to follow up from this end?'

'That's odd. Had instruction from him this morning to drop that line of enquiry and concentrate on finding Jane Whiting.' He provided Chloe with an update since they'd last spoken.

'The hospital called yesterday evening. Thought I'd wait until this morning – wasn't anything urgent, was it?' Chloe asked.

'No, it's OK, just trying another approach.' He thought rapidly as he drove. 'If Tony hasn't been back in touch with them, then they'll still be willing to divulge case notes. Ask the hospital to send us any medical records they have concerning Lilybet's birth, any pre-natal, post-natal stuff. I'm just looking for anything that doesn't look right – bit of a long shot.'

'OK. I'm on it. Good luck in Inverness.'

'Aye, think I'm going to need it the way this case is going.'

He ended the call without much expectation. Going after Samantha's medical records was unlikely to bring up anything other than she'd given birth to Lilybet without any complications. If something unusual did come up, then how was he even going to be able to question Samantha? She had gone to ground as soon the divorce settlement proceedings began – she knew her husband well enough to remain out of his reach. Finding her would be as difficult as finding Jane Whiteman – two women deliberately keeping themselves hidden from the same man for much the same reason.

Teàrlach had the sense he was clutching at straws. The only solid lead he had in this case was Jane Whiting, who had sufficient survival instinct to keep herself out of sight. Tony hadn't explained why Jane had been in touch with him, but it didn't take a genius to work out that she would be offering Lilybet's location for money. If so, then Tony would pay anything to get Lilybet back – if this girl *was* Lilybet. And there was the next problem. Even if Jane led him to find his daughter, he was not the type of man who appreciated being shaken down for money. If she turned out to be wrong...

He had to find Jane Whiting before Tony or Dee. Firstly, because she was his last remaining hope to find out what really happened to Lilybet and to have any chance of returning the girl to her parents. Secondly, because Tony would use more primitive methods to gain the same information, and once she'd been questioned, she was of no further use to him. Then Jane Whiting was destined to become just another statistic. Another missing woman too unimportant for an overstretched police service to investigate. Another body in the loch.

The Inverness Co-op was easy to find, a large supermarket in one of those industrial parks that border city centres like leeches, sucking in the trade that once kept the city shops alive. Teàrlach tried matching the limited view of the shelves showing in the photograph, taking each aisle in turn until admitting defeat. Like every other lead in his enquiry, it looked like he'd driven for hours on another wild goose chase. Jane had most likely realised her call could be traced, so where had she taken the snap?

Teàrlach grabbed a packet of sandwiches and bottle of water, made for one of the few manned tills.

'Is there another Co-op in town?' he asked the cashier as he swiped his card.

The woman behind the counter looked up from her contemplation of the conveyor belt bringing another load of shopping towards the till.

'Church Street, old town centre. They won't have anything we haven't got.'

Teàrlach didn't bother responding apart from a quick thanks. He entered the street name into the satnav and followed a twisting route into the old town centre. There was a parking space directly outside the supermarket, and for the first time, he allowed himself to hope that maybe things were at last starting to go his way. He entered the shop, saw shelves that were a direct match to the picture on his phone.

This was where Jane had taken the photograph. This was where the girl and woman had been standing. Now all he had to do was find them.

FORTY

A LONG LIFE

As Teàrlach started on the road to Inverness, Dee concentrated on finding Jane Whiting. Teàrlach was on Lilybet's trail and best placed to find her, assuming the photograph was taken in Inverness. If only the photograph had been sent as an email attachment, then she would have been able to access the geolocation from the metadata. Sending it via encrypted social media meant all the personal metadata had been stripped out, more to protect users from themselves – or from the prying eyes of state. All it took was a right button click on the mouse and everything from the camera model number, exact time of day to GPS co-ordinates appear on every digital photograph, unless basic security steps are taken.

Hacking into the station CCTV could take days, especially if they'd installed the popular Chinese cameras with firewalls that only leaked in one direction – back to China. That left identifying Jane's mobile and setting up a search for it. Again, not an easy task but one within her expertise. She had a shortcut to identifying Jane's mobile number. The WhatsApp message had been sent from her phone, and she had the time and location set as Inverness railway station. That would more than likely reside on a local dedicated 4G cell. She sat hunched over her keyboard, oblivious to the sunshine outside her hotel bedroom.

One hour later and she had the phone's location, tracked to a vehicle driving around Inverness. The signal so clear she could pinpoint it within a ten-metre radius. The satisfied smile on her face changed as her own phone announced Tony Masterton wanted to talk.

'Hello, Tony.'

'How are you getting on with finding this girl and Jane Whiting?'

'Teàrlach is looking for the girl now. We think she might be in Inverness, that's where he's heading and should get there in a few hours. I've just managed to track Jane Whiting's mobile, looks like she's still there.'

'Good.' He almost purred down the line. 'Send me a live link to her phone. I'll have her collected before the PI gets there. Good work.'

She held her mobile, biting her lower lip as she considered what her next move should be. There really wasn't any other alternative but to send Tony the link that would allow him to track Jane's mobile. Trouble was, once Tony had her collected, then Jane Whiting wasn't going to have a good time. Teàrlach was still hours away and couldn't help, and she couldn't risk warning her. Dee sent the link, trying to ignore the sick feeling in her stomach as she consigned the nanny to an uncertain fate. She made for the public bar, asked Blair to set up a line of shots and proceeded to deaden her conscience, slowly and deliberately.

Outside the bar windows, the sun glinted off the loch surface, turning the waters deep blue. She could have been abroad, in some exotic holiday destination and far away from the threat Tony held. Caught between the devil and the deep blue sea, Dee sought sanctuary as so many times before with the genie in the bottle. She didn't want any of this – the murders, the missing children, the responsibility for casually handing another woman's life over to a man like Tony.

The arrival of Mick and his entourage was all the encouragement she needed to down all the shots in a hurry. Mick stood next to her seat at the bar, a questioning expression appearing as he eyed up the row of empty glasses.

'Starting early?'

'Same again,' she spoke to Blair, then twisted on her bar stool to face Mick. 'Not much point living above the bar if you don't make use of it.'

He inclined his head in agreement, then placed an order himself. 'I was hoping to have a word with yer man.' Mick straddled the bar stool next to hers.

Dee could smell wood smoke on his clothes, saw stubble he'd missed shaving. Brian and the two women took the table they'd appropriated as their own, next to the open fire. They sat and watched her like she was about to entertain them.

'Like I said before, he's not *my* man. He's away, had work to do.'

Mick nodded sadly. 'Sure, he's not around much, I'll give you that.'

Blair placed the beers down on the bar, stood waiting for payment, then remained in place after he had been given the money. Dee considered the newly refilled row of shot glasses. She needed to keep her wits about her dealing with this lot.

'Why don't you come and join us at the table? Sure, you're almost family now.'

She caught the questioning look in Blair's face, gave him a quick smile to reassure him everything was alright and took two glasses over to the table. Brian reached over, lifted a spare chair without effort and placed it down for her.

'Slàinte mhath!' Mick raised his pint glass, and they all followed in unison.

'So...' Mick held her gaze. 'We'll be moving on soon enough. Once we've sorted out a few things that remain to be sorted.'

Dee sank a shot, feeling the heat burn its way down her throat. Insufficient to remove the bile collecting in her stomach.

'What things are those then?'

'I think you know,' Mick replied cryptically. He shot a warning look at Blair, standing behind the bar and unconvincingly cleaning glasses whilst listening to the conversation. 'Can you get us a few packets of crisps – the sweet chilli ones you keep in the store?'

He waited until the barman had left them to talk in privacy. 'You work for Tony Masterton, isn't that so? You and that private detective fella.'

Dee eyed up the last shot glass, decided to finish it. 'What of it? He asked us to find out what happened to his daughter. She went missing from here three years ago.'

'Aye. I heard about that. A terrible business.' The others nodded in agreement. 'You kept that awful quiet the other night – I was asking you about him.'

Dee left her seat, collected the rest of the shot glasses from the bar. She was going to need them.

'It's nobody's business who I work for but mine.' Dee set the glasses up as a defensive perimeter on the table, sat back down with one in her hand. 'I didn't ask any of you how you earned a living now, did I?' She upended the glass, reached for the next only for her hand to be intercepted by Mercy.

'That's true,' Mercy joined the conversation. 'Can I read your palm?'

The question was so unexpected that Dee allowed her hand to be turned palm upwards and pulled towards Mercy's face. A finger traced delicately across the hand, exploring creases and folds. Dee spared a glance at the others, they all looked intently at Mercy as she weaved her spell.

'You've had a hard life,' she intoned. 'This line here.' Her tracing finger halted mid-palm. 'This is your blood line.' She looked up to stare directly into Dee's eyes. 'You've a good while to live.'

'That's reassuring,' Dee answered flippantly. It *was* good to know. Between this bunch of Travellers and Tony Masterton, she was beginning to feel her life might be measured in days rather than years.

Mercy's eyes narrowed in concentration as she returned to looking at Dee's palm. 'You've felt her, haven't you?'

Dee shook her head in confusion. 'Felt who?' The drink was beginning to take effect, wrapping fog around her brain.

'The creature in the loch. She's been watching you.'

Dee's hand shook involuntarily. 'I don't know what you mean.'

Mercy shrugged. 'As you will. I'd stay away from the loch – that's all I'm saying.' Mercy stroked her hand in a calming gesture, three fingers drawing across the skin in repeated circles. 'We know Tony Masterton killed Richard.'

Dee rocked back in her seat, shocked. Four pairs of eyes bore into hers as she struggled to answer. This hadn't been a good idea, coming down to the bar. Much less drinking herself stupid when she needed to keep sharp.

'I don't know – I mean, I can't say anything about that. Teàrlach and me, we're just looking for the girl. I don't know how Richard died or who murdered him.'

'So,' Mick responded. He stopped whilst Blair dropped a packet of crisps onto the table.

'One packet enough?' Blair asked. He hesitated at their table, sensing the tension.

'One's fine, can you fetch us all another round?' Mick

pulled out a couple of crisp twenty-pound notes, put them into Blair's hand. 'There's a good lad.'

Mick waited until Blair was out of earshot before continuing. 'The nanny, Jane Whiting, told us herself. We know Tony has a reputation as a bit of a hard man. Wouldn't be that unusual, wanting to kill someone you found out was having sex with your wife?'

Dee attempted to appear nonchalant whilst all the time wanting to run off and barricade herself into her room. 'I don't know anything about that.'

Mick gave her a pitying look. 'What I haven't been able to work out is why Tony would want Annie dead. Unless someone else did that?'

'It was an accident. A house fire. That's what I heard.'

Mick's face hardened. 'A fire that happened after somebody let the polis know where we were camped, and Annie was left on her own. Bit convenient, don't you think?'

Dee thought of the woman's voice on Teàrlach's phone recording. Whoever it was had killed Annie, it wasn't Tony. Not this time.

'I can't help you. I've hardly left this hotel since I arrived. My job is to try and find what happened to his daughter. You're best talking to the police if you have any concerns.'

'The polis!' Mick spat the words out in distaste. 'As much use as a one-legged man at an arse kicking contest.'

Nobody smiled.

Mick lowered his voice to a whisper. 'You can tell your boss that I'm coming for him. I don't care if he's a bigshot Glasgow gangster, he's still flesh and blood. If I can't find who did for Annie, then he can pay for that as well.' He downed his pint as Blair arrived with fresh glasses. 'Give them to the girl. She's developing an awful thirst.'

They stood as one and left the pub. Blair remained like a statue with the change still in his outstretched hand.

'Best put that where it will do the most good,' Dee said philosophically. 'Want to join me in a pint?'

Blair's pleased expression answered that question. Dee was just grateful to have someone distract her as she tried to stop the thoughts whirling through her mind. She had to let Tony know they wanted to kill him – it was only too obvious how that would turn out.

FORTY-ONE

HOME DELIVERY

Chloe read the medical reports from the private hospital as soon as they appeared in her email. The laptop she was using was such an old model that everything took ten times as long as it should. She sent another unvoiced curse to Dee for snooping around their network, causing her to use this museum piece and a new Gmail account merely to avoid letting Dee see everything they did. She wasn't missing much – so far Teàrlach was getting nowhere fast – but this information was interesting. Chloe called him on the burner phone – another inconvenience they both suffered due to that bloody hacker woman!

'Hi, Chloe. Just a minute, getting back in the car.' The sound of a car door opening and closing was accompanied by heavy breathing. 'What have you got?'

Chloe wasn't sure what she had, or what it meant for the investigation.

'The medical reports came in. In short, Samantha gave birth at home, not at the hospital. Seems the baby was a few weeks earlier than expected and she was on her own. The roads were blocked with snow, so Tony sent a helicopter to collect her, but she'd already had the child. All the hospital did was check them both over and give them a clean bill of health. Mother and child were back home in a week.'

Teàrlach digested the information. 'So, she definitely had the baby – it wasn't adopted or anything?'

'I'm no nurse, but the report goes into some detail about stitching her up afterwards and colostrum, so yeah, I'm guessing she had the baby.'

'OK, I was just trying to work out if the kid they found in the loch could have been hers. Theirs.'

He corrected as he thought it through, pictured her on her own in the big house without Tony and no way out except by helicopter. 'Did she deliver it by herself?'

Chloe shuffled through the printout. 'There's no mention, except a line here that states "baby delivered normally, afterbirth was disposed of at home".'

'Is that something a new mother would know how to do?' He instantly regretted the question, wished there was some way of stopping the words that had just been uttered with such harsh insensitivity to a woman who'd only recently lost her own child.

'I don't know.' This was getting to be an uncomfortable conversation. 'Nature takes its course. If there's not a problem, then the baby's not going to hang around for the ambulance to arrive. I think they give you an injection to speed up expelling the afterbirth – I can't honestly remember.'

He listened for the pain in her voice, relieved when she responded naturally. Dee's conversation with the Travellers came into his memory. About Annie being a midwife.

'Do you think Annie could have delivered Lilybet?'

'I suppose. Does she live near enough to reach the house if the roads were snowed in?'

'Not by road. She could by boat. Her house is close to the loch. The Masterton house is right on the loch.' He decided. 'Look, I'm in Inverness. I'm sending you a picture the nanny sent to Tony Masterton earlier today. It might be Lilybet. See what you can find online – try primary school year photographs, all that stuff. She looks about the right age, around six. Only difference is her hair's short, but that might be on purpose following the missing girl press release.'

'I could try local hairdressers as well, see if anyone's brought their daughter in for a crop in the last couple of weeks.'

'Good idea. Go carefully, we don't want her running. I'm planning on staying here tonight, see if I can track her down and the woman she's pictured with. In the meantime, I'm going to call Tony Masterton. See if he can shed any light on what happened at Lilybet's birth.'

Tony picked up the call immediately. 'You found them?'

'We've tracked the location to Inverness. I'm having a search made right now for both the girl and the woman and plan to stay here until I've found them.'

'OK. Good. Better luck than Dee had with tracking Jane Whiting.'

'How do you mean?' Teàrlach asked.

'She identified the phone Jane used to send the message, sent a tracking link, but when my boys stopped the car, it was some burger joint employee who thought he'd struck lucky. He found the phone left on a table at Inverness train station and took it for himself. Lucky he wasn't taught a lesson.'

Teàrlach refrained from explaining the irony of a big-time gangster taking any kind of moral high ground with an opportunistic thief. 'Jane used a burner?'

'Yes. Learned something whilst she was working for me. You concentrate on finding Lilybet and the woman with her – do *you* think that's Lilybet?'

The question stopped him dead. 'It looks a lot like her, but until someone's spoken with her, tested her DNA, I think you shouldn't get too invested.'

'Shouldn't get too invested?' Tony spoke quietly.

'I'll let you know as soon as I find anything, but there's something you can help me with.'

'What?' Tony answered curtly.

'When Lilybet was born, at home. Did Samantha have any help – did Richard Tavistock's mother act as the midwife?'

There was a silence that stretched on for seconds, long enough that he doubted the call was still connected.

'Yes, she delivered the baby. The roads were blocked, so there wasn't a hope for the ambulance reaching her in time. Why do you ask?'

'I'm just trying to get a clear picture—'

'Leave getting a clear picture to the photographers, understand? You're being paid to find Lilybet. Nothing else. Am I making myself clear?'

'Crystal.'

'Good. I'll give you until tomorrow, then I'm putting my guys onto it.'

Teàrlach was left listening to silence. He sat back in the car seat, put his hands behind his head and thought. The girl here could be Lilybet. The likeness to the artist's drawing was uncanny, but you could see the resemblance to the three-year-old girl just by comparing photographs of then and now. The fact that she was blond added a layer of complication. Neither Tony nor Samantha was blond, and every child Richard Tavistock fathered had that characteristic. According to Jane, Samantha had said Richard was the father. How would Tony react if they found Lilybet only for him to discover she wasn't his child all along?

Then the admission that Tony's men had grabbed the current owner of Jane's mobile. That meant Dee had tracked her phone and given Tony the tracking data. Dee must have known what the likely outcome for Jane Whiting was going to be once Tony had her in his hands. He sighed heavily. Dee was working for Tony, she didn't have much other choice but to pass on everything she found. What he couldn't allow was for Lilybet – or the girl who looked like her – and the woman to be picked up by Tony's thugs. He needed Dee's help, that was becoming clear, but how could he trust her when she reported everything back to Tony? The answer to that question was clear – he couldn't. He had no choice but to go to the police and social workers once he found them, if only for their protection. This was turning into a shitshow no matter what outcome he envisaged.

The final problem was Annie being the midwife. Was that why she was killed? And who was the unidentified woman who had attempted to burn him alive? He had no answers. The time was approaching 3:30pm, mothers and schoolchildren walked past his car. Struck with an idea, Teàrlach searched his phone for the local primary school. If the woman shopped here, chances were they used the local school. He waited until 4:00pm and the smaller kids were replaced by adolescents wearing different uniforms and displaying a total disregard for how cold the day was. At least he had a plan for tomorrow.

Home for the night was a Victorian pile close to the primary school, the retired owners making capital out of three high-ceilinged bedrooms they had no other use for. He brushed off their inquisitive questioning about what he was doing in Inverness, gave them some story about being a writer and researching a plot, then locked himself away saying he needed peace. The window looked out over the street, net curtains providing a degree of privacy. The sun was already hidden behind the houses opposite, his bedroom beginning to darken as the short day came to an end. He sat on the bed, felt the springs sag and fired up the laptop, entering the Wi-Fi code left on a bedside table.

First, he needed to touch base with Dee.

'Sherlock.' She answered his call brusquely. He imagined her bent over her own laptop, searching for Jane.

'Hi, Dee. The Co-op here is the same as in the photo. We're close.'

'Aye, I managed to track Jane Whiting's mobile there as well, but she'd dumped it at the station.'

'I talked to Tony, he told me a couple of his associates had pulled over some young guy who'd taken a fancy to a free mobile.'

'I didn't have any choice, Teàrlach.' Dee spoke more quietly. 'What Tony wants, Tony gets. One way or another. You were still driving there when he called me.'

'He said he'd give me until tomorrow to find the girl, then he was planning on finding her his way.'

Dee remained silent.

'I think she may go to the local primary. Do you think you can find out who's on the school roll for P1 or P2?' Teàrlach confirmed the school name and address to her after checking his laptop.

'Aye, should be easy enough. She's not going to be listed as Lilybet Masterton, though, is she?'

'You have her photograph. Schools always sell these class group photos every year, should be easy enough to look for Lilybet on last year's selection.'

'Yep, I can do that. I have to put my main focus on finding Jane Whiting though, just so we're straight.'

'Can you let me know before Tony?' He waited for Dee to respond.

'You think he'll go in heavy-handed?'

'What do you think?'

She snorted. 'Aye, I'll delay as long as I can. I'll see if I can confirm this girl's identity at the school.'

'I'm going there tomorrow morning. I'll park up and watch for her. If I don't see her, then I'll dream up some excuse for visiting the school.'

'That's easier said than done.'

'Aye, right enough. Well, must hope that between the two of us we can find the lass.' He paused, wondering whether to share the other information. 'Tony told me that Annie Tavistock was the midwife at Lilybet's birth, at the house. She was a couple of weeks premature and the roads impassable with snow, so Annie was fetched by boat. Samantha had already had the child by the time the helicopter arrived to take her to hospital.'

'Is that significant? Does it explain why Annie was murdered as well?' Dee put voice to the same thoughts that had been troubling him.

'There's something I must be missing. No one in their right mind kidnaps the daughter of a Glasgow gangster. I suppose a three-year-old can be brainwashed into having a new mother – especially if her real mother had nothing much to do with her in the first place – but why go to the risk? It doesn't add up.'

'And there's the other little girl they found in the loch. Do you think there's a connection?'

Teàrlach thought it through. 'It's not unknown when a mother has lost a child that she's driven to taking another. It's like a biological imperative sends some people over the edge.'

'Is it worth looking at births six years ago in the area? See if there are any unexplained disappearances or deaths?'

'The police are already on that. You'd have seen something come up on the reports if there was anything to find. Assuming the birth was properly registered,' he added as an afterthought.

'You think Annie may have delivered a child without noti-fying the authorities?'

'I'd say anything's possible where she was concerned. There's no way you could raise a kid without all the relevant paperwork, though,' Teàrlach said decisively.

'But what about a three-year-old living the life of a Trav-eller? They wouldn't have to bother with any paperwork until they needed hospital treatment or schooling.'

Teàrlach didn't have an answer to that. 'How's the search for Jane Whiting going?'

'Bloody impossible. Who'd have thought she'd know to use a burner phone and ditch it after first use? It's like looking for a needle in a haystack – unless she makes a mistake.'

'Aye, a mistake that could mean her death.'

This time it was Dee unable to respond.

'I'll talk to you tomorrow morning, after I've watched the school gates. Let me know if you're able to find anything on the school roll or photos.'

'Sure, will do. I'll keep in touch.'

FORTY-TWO

AGAMI KARMA

I am the boatman
I ferried my own child, torn
From death's cold fingers

Tony Masterton was losing patience. The possibility that Lilybet had been found in Inverness made everything else inconsequential. Even the unwelcome news that Samantha was divorcing him had faded into a minor irritation, something to throw money at until it went away. Samantha had hidden herself away somewhere, when the time was right, he'd have her found and dealt with. There hadn't been an update since Dee had last been in touch at lunchtime, now it was almost 6pm. He stared into black glass, reflecting his mood back at him. Dee had called to warn him that there were two travellers threatening to kill him. It was the only good news to have come his way since learning that his daughter may have been discovered. Two men coming to murder him to avenge family – that was something he could understand and deal with. Something he'd enjoy dealing with. The shotgun lay within easy reach, both barrels loaded and waiting to blow a dinner plate sized hole in anyone foolish enough to come looking for trouble.

At the stroke of six, his mobile vibrated, alerting him to an unknown number. He answered.

'Hi, Mr Masterton, it's me, Jane.'

'Hello, Jane. What have you got for me?' His gentle tone always put people ill at ease – confirmed by the wet sound of Jane biting her lips before being able to speak again.

'I've the address for Lilybet, but I want the money first.'

Tony kept his voice conciliatory whilst his free hand caressed the shotgun's polished stock. 'I'll give you £100,000 now, the rest when I've confirmed it's really her. If you're wrong, then you're going to have to pay me back. You understand?'

'I'm sending you the bank details. Once the money's been transferred, I'll send her address.'

His screen displayed an account.

'I have it. You have the address ready?'

'Yes. It's written on a WhatsApp message. I only need to press send.'

'You know what's going to happen if you mess me around, don't you?'

'I wouldn't do that.' Jane could hardly bring herself to speak, the fear evident in each word issued from her lips.

'No, I don't think you're that stupid. Wait whilst I send you the down payment.' Tony entered the bank details, transferred across his money. 'You should have it.'

He could hear the sound of keys being tapped, silence followed by a sharp intake of air.

'It's here.' Jane's voice gave away her disbelief. 'I'm sending you the address now. She's in one of those apartments, I could only follow them to the shared entrance.'

She cut the call before he had time to ask her what she meant. An address showed on his screen. He saved it, checked the details online, saw it was one of three flats. His need to see Lilybet again was overpowering. Tony wandered through his empty house, footsteps echoing hollowly down the concrete hall. He felt submerged in an air of unreality. He had resigned himself to believing Lilybet was dead – had been dead for years. And now this.

Jane's hastily taken snap filled his phone screen, his fingers magnifying the image until the girl looked straight at him. There was no question in his mind that this was Lilybet. Three years might have elapsed, but he knew his own daughter. Tony was tempted to just have the girl taken. One phone call – that's all it would need, and the girl and the woman could be with him within an hour. He had people he trusted there, a helicopter on standby.

Tony's finger hovered over the speed dial before reluctantly withdrawing. No, he had no choice but to do this by the book. The police had him in the frame as a suspect for the gardener's death, probably that of Annie as well. A rash move involving child abduction could cost him Lilybet forever. He dialled a different number.

'Dee. I have the girl's address in Inverness. Coming your way now.'

'That's great news. How do you want Teàrlach to play it?'

'By the book. Involve the local police, social workers, what-ever it takes. Just don't lose her.'

'Understood. Anything else you want me to do? I'm still no closer to finding Jane Whiting – you want me to carry on looking?'

'She's not a priority, now I have what I want. I'll track her eventually.' There was a thoughtful pause. 'You have the girl's address. Find out everything you can about her, whether the woman is registered as the mother of this girl, birth certificate, names. If she has taken Lilybet, then I want any documentation checked so she can be exposed. That's your priority now.'

'I'll get on it now. Should be easy enough to find her birth certificate online, I'll follow that trail.'

'Thanks, Dee. Keep me updated.'

His next call was to the local police letting them know there was a credible threat to his life. He was patched through to Sergeant Jock Daniels.

'Who do you believe is threatening you, sir?' Jock Daniels could hardly keep his tone civil. This was the man he knew was responsible for the murder of Richard Tavistock, probably his mother as well, and here he was having the audacity to call for help.

'I'm reliably informed these are relatives of Richard Tavistock who want me dead. I've no idea if they killed Richard as well, but I'm letting you know, officially, that I'm requesting a police presence around my home until these people are caught.'

'We've already questioned the people concerned. They have an alibi for the murders of both Richard Tavistock and his mother, and unless further evidence comes to light, I cannot act against them. Do you have any witnesses who can testify they wanted to kill you?'

Tony smiled. 'No, but I'm sending you a follow-up email in the next few minutes advising my life is in danger and I have requested an immediate police presence.'

He cut the call. Now they'd have little option but to hang around his property and arrest the two Travellers when they turned up. The smile broadened. And having two potential murderers on his doorstep would help deflect suspicion for Richard's murder away from him. It had been a rash move, on his home turf, but he needed an outlet for his anger and Richard Tavistock was in the wrong place at the wrong time. Besides which, Tavistock had been working the gardens for years – he knew the risk he was taking. Now he was shot of both of his wife and the gardener. It was agami karma.

Once the girl had been confirmed to be his daughter, then

the nanny could be dealt with. He opened a bottle of cabernet sauvignon, didn't bother checking the label or waiting for the bottle to breathe, pouring a generous measure into a glass and held it up to the light like a priest inspecting Christ's blood for impurities. Wine connoisseurs missed the point. The colour, clarity, afternotes of cassis, blackberry and vanilla – all this was mental foreplay. The act of drinking the liquid was the point. A tradition extending down the centuries, even beyond Rome's empire. Generation after generation where the rich enjoyed the spoils and the poor worked until they died. The symbolism of raising a glass to whichever god was flavour of the day and saying fuck you and your eternal afterlife. Sell that to the masses. There could only be one certainty amongst the pantheon of religions and that was *now* I am alive, *now* I exist and tomorrow I will become dust.

Tony left the bottle uncorked. He'd not risk any more than one glass in case the Travellers came for him tonight. He picked up the shotgun in his spare hand, headed up the cantilevered stairs to his office and bedroom. For safety, he operated the electric blinds, closing off the view across the loch – nothing but impenetrable blackness at this hour. Even the few houses and marine navigation lights couldn't pierce the dark, although he couldn't shake off the feeling something was watching him from the loch. He pulled on a bullet-proof vest, picked a larger shirt out of the wardrobe to wear over it and checked his reflection in the mirror with satisfaction. Tony watched a computer screen, a small window in one corner displaying the view from the gate camera with mist already coiling into view.

'Come on then, you bastards. Have a go!' He sat back to enjoy the night.

FORTY-THREE

BIN AND GONE

Teàrlach reacted to Dee's call with incredulity.

'She's given him the girl's address. Just like that?'

'I think there's likely more to it than he told me. He probably paid her for the information,' Dee elaborated. 'Can't be sure, but it would make sense.'

Teàrlach nodded. 'I'll let Chloe know, she's still trying to track the girl down. Tony knows I'll be doing this by the book? I can't just force my way in and take a girl because she looks like Lilybet.'

'That's what he wants. Involve the police, social workers. However you want to do it. Just don't lose her!'

'What will you be doing now, still searching for Jane?'

'No. Tony wants me to run a check on the woman and girl you're about to collect. If this *is* Lilybet, he wants any potential legal obstructions dealt with, so I'll be looking for anything unusual with birth certificates, adoption papers, that sort of thing.'

'If it is Lilybet, then she may remember enough to confirm it herself. Anyway, a simple DNA test will prove parenthood.'

'Aye,' Dee commented drily. 'Things have moved on from Solomon threatening to cut a disputed child in half.'

Teàrlach checked the time after Dee ended the call. It was after eight o'clock at night, not the most opportune moment to contact the Inverness police about Lilybet, but he had no choice. As expected, his initial calls were met with polite refusal to engage – until he dropped the names of some high-ranking detectives. That earned him a conversation with the duty sergeant.

'I'm sorry, sir, but what do you expect us to do?'

Teàrlach tried explaining for the third time. 'You remember the three-year-old girl went missing just over three years ago? Her father is Tony Masterton...'

'*That* Tony Masterton?' the sergeant interrupted. 'I remember. Blond-haired lass. Didn't I see they'd found her body in the loch?'

At last, he felt he was making progress.

'It wasn't her body. It was another, as yet unidentified girl. Lilybet is still missing, and we've had a reported sighting of her here. At this address.'

'Well, you know we can't just go marching in and take a girl away from her mother just because of a passing resemblance to an artist's drawing? We'd need proof it was her: DNA, a confession, faked documents. The social will need to be involved and the emergency out of hours worker won't be any help. It will have to wait until the morning when everyone's back at their desks.'

Teàrlach clenched his fist and told himself to stay calm. 'All I'm asking is for you to send a patrol round to talk to the woman – check on the girl and make sure everything's OK. If there's a problem, they can be taken in for questioning or for safeguarding the child or whatever. Do you want to be the one who has to explain how the missing girl slipped through your fingers?'

The ramifications of being the one whose perceived incompetence would make the headlines eventually hit home. 'I'll send a patrol round to the house, and they can see what's what. You know this is most likely an innocent parent and child?'

'Thank you, officer. Thanks for your help. We're making investigations our end with regard to the legality of their relationship, but I'd appreciate it if you could prime everyone to be ready tomorrow morning so we can confirm the girl's identity. Glasgow MIT have both parents' DNA on file, I'll send them a message asking if they can get in touch first thing.'

Teàrlach pulled on his coat and headed out of the B&B. He needed to be there when the police arrived.

Number twelve Chambers Court sounded a lot grander than it looked. A stack of 1960s social housing maisonette flats occupied a patch of no-man's land, sandwiched between once-grand Victorian shops on the one side, and warehouses catering to a random collection of businesses whose only common defining factor lay in a desperation to cling on to solvency. He stood in the doorway, viewing the choice of three doorbells unhelpfully marked a, b and c in faded print. They looked as if they'd been printed on a typewriter and pasted there when the flats were first built, the letters almost invisible in the meagre glow thrown by the porch light. Teàrlach found a location on the other side of the road, far enough away from the nearest streetlight, and searched the flat windows for clues. Diffuse light showed through the ground floor curtains, drawn tight against the winter night. The second floor was in complete darkness. The third floor was well-lit, but frustratingly at too acute an angle for him to view inside.

'Can I ask what you're doing, sir?'

Teàrlach staggered, caught unawares and on tiptoe as he'd craned his neck for a better view of the top floor windows.

'Evening officers. I'm Teàrlach Paterson – I called ten minutes ago about the girl living here at number twelve.'

ANDREW JAMES GREIG

Two constables viewed him with suspicion, the WPC narrowing her eyes as she caught sight of the bruising still evident around his head.

'Do you have any ID, sir?' she asked in that particular tone which must be inculcated at police college, an obnoxious blend of civility and insolence.

Teàrlach handed over his driving licence and business card, both items handled as if they came from a plague victim and handed back with distaste.

'Which flat is the girl in?' the PC asked. Unlike his partner, he appeared disinterested in the exchange, bored before his shift had even begun.

'I don't know. One of these at number twelve.'

The PC looked at him, a glimmer of hope that Teàrlach might kick off or run away dissipating as he stood calmly facing them.

'And what exactly do you expect us to do?' The WPC dropped any pretence of calling him sir.

Teàrlach could sympathise, he really could. The sergeant would have contacted them on the radio, given them some story and almost certainly had used the phrase 'make it look as if we're doing something'. He brought up Lilybet's likeness on his phone, showed it to the two police officers.

'I'm searching for this girl. She went missing three years ago and her father was provided with information just thirty minutes ago that she may be living at this address with a woman purporting to be her mother. The MIT in Glasgow are providing DNA samples so we can match the girl to her real parents. I just want someone to check the girl's OK, not being held against her will or anything.'

'You're not expecting us to take her or the mother into custody?' the WPC asked.

'Only if it becomes apparent that the girl's been kidnapped.'

The WPC and her partner exchanged a look, cynicism

distilled to its purist form. 'You stay here,' she advised. 'We'll have a word. Have a look at the girl if she lets us inside. There's nothing else we can do without a warrant or due cause. It's really a job for the social workers – or detectives.'

They crossed the road, rang the first doorbell. From his vantage point, Teàrlach saw the heavy curtains twitch on the ground floor. An old lady opened the door, framed in the shared hallway light. There followed a brief conversation and the woman leaned out, pointing her finger at the top bell. She wandered back down the hallway and was lost to view. The PC's leg extended to catch the door before it closed, rang the top bell. Teàrlach saw a woman approaching the door, stopping in obvious shock at seeing two police officers there. He took a few steps towards the flats for a better view, made out a few random words. She could be the woman in the photograph – they needed to see the girl. The conversation appeared relaxed, unhurried – more like a social call than an investigation into a kidnapped child.

Teàrlach's phone vibrated in his hand. He went to turn it off, saw it was Dee and answered.

'Not now, Dee. I'm at the house with the police – they're questioning the woman now.'

'It's not her. She's been living there for the last five years with her daughter. I've seen her social security file. It can't be Lilybet.'

'I'll call you back.' Teàrlach focussed on the woman opposite as the import of Dee's words struck home. He stared at the girl who had joined her mother, standing out in the open with her face tilted up towards the PC and the porch light illuminating her features. If this wasn't Lilybet, then she looked so much like her, sufficiently identical to fool her nanny of three years.

The officers said their goodbyes, the girl skipped back

inside, and the door closed. They came back over the road, stood facing him with an air of tired resignation.

'That can't be the girl you're looking for,' the WPC said. 'I've seen her out shopping with her wee girl for well over four years – she'd only just had the wean when she moved in.'

The PC wrote in his notebook, then stood to one side as he called the station. Teàrlach listened with half an ear as his reputation as the PI who finds missing children was shredded.

'We'll do a follow-up of course. Ask the social services to confirm dates, but that's not your wee lassie.' The WPC almost allowed a note of pity to slide into her voice. Almost.

'Thanks. I'm sorry to have wasted your time.'

The WPC nodded an acknowledgement. 'That's what we're here for. Good evening, Mr Paterson.' She touched her cap and started towards her partner, sending a last comment back to Teàrlach over her shoulder. 'I hope you find her, I really do.'

He waited until the two constables turned towards the main road and were lost to sight, then quickly crossed over to the flat entrance again. There was an alleyway at the side of the flats leading to a courtyard, bins lining a wall. He searched until he found a bin marked '12c', using his phone torch to retrieve a bin bag. The ground floor curtains gave another twitch as he passed by, the old woman looking from his face to the bin bag he carried, and back again. Teàrlach ignored her and headed back to his car.

FORTY-FOUR
HAS SOMETHING DIED?

It was well past midnight when Teàrlach returned to the Lochside Hotel. He'd left the B&B in Inverness with the excuse of a personal tragedy requiring his immediate attention – close enough to the truth in this instance. Even from a distance he could have sworn the girl was Tony Masterton's daughter, older but with facial features so similar she could have been her doppelganger. He could well understand how Jane Whiting had made the same mistake – one that Tony was unlikely to forgive.

The inside of his car smelled like a curry house – whatever the other contents were in the bin bag, they had been effectively masked by the remnants of a festering takeaway. Teàrlach gave silent thanks to the winter weather, any warmer and his car would have been full of flies by now. As it was, he'd had to drive with windows open and a scarf wrapped around his mouth and nose to reduce the stench.

He slipped on latex gloves and opened the bin bag in his en-suite, the detritus of a week or two laid out in a pungent mess. A final demand utility bill emerged soggily from under his exploring fingers, the paper threatening to fall apart as gravity placed additional strain on sodden fibres. Now he had a name, one he could confirm with Dee in the morning. The exploration continued, lifting potato peelings and wet wipes out of an unidentifiable brown/grey sludge that adhered to everything like glue. Teàrlach continued until he had what he was looking for – several clumps of hair that looked as if they'd been pulled from a hairbrush. One clump was blond, or as close as he could tell through the grey slime that coated it. He put the results of his investigations into sanitary bags ready for the morning, carrying the newly sealed bin bag out into the hotel car park and depositing it in the industrial waste container around the back.

He was woken by Dee coming into his room unannounced.

'Jesus! Has something died in here?' Her hand covered her nose. 'I thought you'd still be in Inverness,' she added as she attempted to open the bedroom window beyond Teàrlach's best endeavours of last night.

'No point. The police said she'd lived there along with her daughter from before Lilybet's disappearance. And you confirmed the same.' He stretched, tentatively sniffed the air without any due ill-effect. He must have become inured to the smell overnight. 'I took one of their bin bags,' he added as way of an explanation.

'Plenty of takeaways in Inverness if you were hungry.'

Teàrlach didn't dignify Dee's comment with a response. 'Found a utility bill. I left it on the side of the sink. Her name's Cordilia, Simone or something.'

'Selina Cordona,' Dee called through from his en-suite. 'That's the same name I had.'

'Can you stay there for a minute whilst I get dressed?' Teàrlach climbed out of bed, made for his overnight bag and hastily pulled on a fresh set of underwear. He grabbed his trousers off the chair only to be faced with Dee's wry grin. 'You know anything about personal space, boundaries, privacy?'

She laughed. 'Don't be so coy. So, what else have you brought back?' Dee held floral-printed sanitary bags delicately in each hand, her nose wrinkling up in distaste.

'Hair. Hers and her mother's – if that's who she is.' He took the bags out of her hands, maintaining as much dignity as a man can muster stood only in his boxers.

'Ocean,' Dee stated simply. 'The girl's name is Ocean.'

'Unusual names.' He held the bags up above his head. 'Paperwork is one thing, but DNA doesn't lie.'

'You have someone to test it for you?' Dee quizzed.

'Aye, but I'll need Tony and Samantha's samples. I'm going to try the same forensics lab that have their DNA. Tony may be willing to provide another sample, but Samantha has gone off grid.'

'So where does that leave us with finding Lilybet?' Dee watched him unconcernedly as he finished dressing. 'We're no further forward, are we? And Tony will have to be informed this girl isn't his.'

'I'll tell him,' Teàrlach said. 'He needs to hear it from me, from someone stood in front of him, not as an email or phone call.'

Dee nodded acceptance. 'He's not likely to take it well,' she warned.

'I can handle Tony Masterton.'

'Not if he's armed, you can't.'

Teàrlach finished dressing. 'He won't shoot the messenger.' He spoke with more confidence than he felt. Men like Tony were unpredictable, and difficult to read. 'I'll let him know I've told the police I'm on my way to update him, that should stop him doing anything too rash.'

'Have you – told the police?'

'No, but I will. Listen, how well do you know the Travellers? You've been in their company a few times now.'

Dee crossed to the window. Morning sun angled down the length of the loch, turning the waters red like a premonition.

'I know them well enough to get pissed with them. Why do you ask?'

'Because they were after something at Annie Tavistock's house. Either information, or something else. I'd like to know what they found, if they found anything before she died.'

'I'll see what I can do. You know they suspect you for her death, as well as Tony?'

Teàrlach pulled on a jacket, had a quick look at the weather. 'I'd be more surprised if they didn't. Have they decided who to blame?' He asked the question already knowing what Dee was about to say.

'Tony. Not so much for Annie's death, but he had a strong enough motive for killing Richard. I've warned him they're coming for him.'

'Is he concerned?'

'Don't think so. If anything, he's quite looking forward to them paying him a visit.'

'OK, I'm off to see him now. Be careful around Mick, I've met his type before. He's more dangerous than he appears underneath the blarney.'

'I can take care of myself, Sherlock,' Dee sounded affronted. 'You're going to be the one needing to take care.'

Dee's words still rang in his head as he pressed the intercom at the gates to Tony's house. They opened without any word from inside. Tony stood in the doorway much as he had the first time Teàrlach had visited.

'I don't see the girl,' Tony called softly.

'That's why I'm here.' Teàrlach approached until they stood face to face. 'Are you going to invite me in?'

Tony considered his question, searching him up and down

before walking back inside. A shotgun lay propped against the wall within easy reach. Teàrlach made no comment as he followed him back to the lounge, seeing the unmistakable outline of body armour under his oversized shirt.

'Take a seat.' Tony indicated the same settee as before, facing out through the French windows and over the loch. Early sunlight caught the tops of small waves, painting them in reddish hues. A faint mist hung patchily in the air, burning away even in the small heat offered by a wintry sun.

'That's not your girl. Dee's searched her social security data and she gave birth the same year Lilybet was born, but it's definitely her daughter, not yours. The local police confirmed the two of them have been living there since well before Lilybet's disappearance. I managed to source samples of their hair – if you don't mind, I intend to ask the police forensics to check it against yours and Samantha's DNA. So there's no room for any doubt.'

Tony inclined his head, his expression neutral.

'I'm still looking for her – if that's what you want?'

'Do what you have to do, Mr Paterson.' He looked away, out over the loch. 'Did you see her? The girl?'

'From a distance. The police wanted me to keep back, but she came out into the open, under the light. She looks very much like Lilybet was expected to look like now. I can see how the nanny made a mistake.'

The smile Tony returned sent a shiver down his back. 'Oh, she made a mistake. I think we can agree on that.'

'Do you mind if I look at the treehouse again? Before I take my samples to the police?'

Tony's eyebrows raised in surprise. 'If you want. Why?'

Teàrlach didn't have a ready answer. 'I'm not sure. I just wanted another look – in daylight.'

Tony nodded. 'I told you to look around in the daylight.' He opened the French windows, waited for Teàrlach to exit, then called after him. 'Make your own way round the front. I'm locking up. Best keep the house secure.'

The sound of deadbolts sliding metallically home echoed off the glass balustrade. Teàrlach retraced his steps to the strange-looking treehouse, blocks of wood giving the impression a half-finished game of giant Jenga had been left on the lawn. He opened the entrance door, pushed past the cobwebs again to reach the oasis of calm in the centre. Here he squatted on the rug, fingers exploring the surface whilst his phone torch illuminated the rug at ground level. After a few minutes, he had what he needed, berating himself for not having the foresight to do this on his initial visit.

The house windows all appeared blank as Teàrlach circled around the front drive and to his vehicle, sightless glass eyes watching the loch darken even this early in the day as the low sun dipped behind mountains. The mist, emboldened by the absence of heat, regrouped and sent exploring fingers inland once more.

FORTY-FIVE

GRAVES

Dee cautiously angled her motorbike around the narrow bends, wary of the invisible patches of black ice that stubbornly refused to shift from roads enveloped in shadow. All the evidence she'd been able to uncover about Selina and her daughter in Inverness proved that Ocean Cordona had lived there since she was one year old. There were still questions to be answered, but the mere fact Ocean lived in Inverness at the same time Lilybet lived with her parents in the lochside house ruled the girl out of the search.

She turned into Annie's driveway, carefully in case her front tyre slid on the loose gravel and pulled to a halt in front of the ruined building. Only the remnants of a campfire remained, the silver bullet caravan had vanished as if it had never really been there. She dismounted, pulled off her helmet and stood facing the sorry remnants of Annie's home. Someone, police or fire brigade she surmised, had attached a sign to the brickwork stating, 'Dangerous Building, Keep Out'. The roof sagged along the main ridge, red tiles scattered randomly on the ground leaving dark gaps behind like a bare knuckle boxer's smile. The front door was missing, burned or smashed by firefighters gaining entry. In its place, insubstantial tape criss-crossed the entrance advising this was a crime scene, do not cross. Dee accepted the challenge, pulled the tape away and entered the hall.

Could it only be five days since she'd dragged Teàrlach out of here, smoke choking her and flames threatening to grill them both alive? The wooden floor was treacherous underfoot. In places only the main joists remained, blackened by fire so she had to step from one to the next, feeling the charcoal crunch beneath her boots. The whole place smelled like a bonfire which had been piled high with plastic, furnishings, and garbage. She tried to ignore the barbequed pork scent that hinted at Annie's death – trapped in her bed as the flames took her like a witch.

The house grew darker as she picked her way through to the kitchen. The windows had all shattered, glass breaking underneath her feet like ice. Teàrlach had mentioned a photograph he'd seen and wanted a closer look at. One of a woman and a child – he thought it could have been the nanny with Lilybet. One glance at the room told her there'd be nothing left. This looked like the epicentre of the blaze that had consumed the cottage. A gas cooker lay as deformed and twisted as a Dali painting, fallen into the floor like a partial burial. The remnants of table and chairs stood as silent and unmoving as mourners, blackened stumps hinting at their original purpose. It was a miracle anything remained at all given how fiercely the fire had taken hold.

A doorway off the kitchen opened out into another space, most likely a utility room of some kind. A cracked Belfast sink lay on the concrete floor, pipes warped by the heat corkscrewed out of the wall. One still supplied water, dripping randomly into a large, dark puddle topped with grey scum. A cabinet had spilt its contents, metal tools which she took for kitchen or garden implements at first – before their real purpose became apparent. She was looking at medical instruments metamorphosed by intense heat into tools for torture: forceps gleamed in the light piercing through holes in the roof; speculum; clamps; long-handled scissors; bent probes ending in vicious hooks. This was where Annie must have performed her trade, here or in one of the bedrooms.

Dee suddenly felt ill and made her way back through the narrow hallway and out towards the lure of fresh air. The smell of death and images of distorted gynaecological implements accompanied her through the blackened interior until she stepped outside. She threw back her head and drew a breath of pure, cold air deep into her lungs, expelling the stale stench of death that had permeated deep inside her.

Annie had made the trip to the Mastertons' house by boat, according to Teàrlach. There was no sign of the loch from the house, just the creeping tendrils of winter mist coiling through the trees behind the charred bungalow. Dee resolved to find the loch if only to confirm whether Annie could have travelled by water.

The rear of the bungalow had once held a vegetable garden and a patch of lawn. Now the forest was encroaching, saplings reaching out of abandoned raised beds. A greenhouse stood some distance away from the house, missing panes of glass and leaning drunkenly in readiness for collapse. If Richard had been a gardener, surely he'd keep his own patch of land in better shape? A whirligig occupied the exact centre of what used to be the lawn, plastic threads drooping from each metal arm where the heat from the fire must have melted them. A newly cleared path led away, into the trees.

Dee entered the forest. Someone had recently cut back the branches and brambles from the path, possibly Mick or one of the others. It was dark under the pines, branches linked above her head giving the impression of an outdoor cathedral. At least the scent was sweeter here. The path climbed a small rise and then dropped down via a zig zag towards the loch. She smelled the water before she saw it – a seaweed tang of iodine and taste of salt coating her lips. At the end of the path lay a small wooden jetty, jutting out into the loch. There was no sign of a boat, but at least it gave credence to Annie using this route to travel around. In many ways it was a superior method of transportation, avoiding the narrow, twisting roads and taking direct routes across the loch to reach other settlements. Standing at the very end of the jetty, she could make out Tony's house, large rectangular shapes unable to be fully erased by the white mist hugging the loch's surface. She guessed it would only take fifteen minutes or so to reach his house with an outboard motor.

Dee looked down, into the dark water. There was no telling how deep the loch was at this point – it may have only been a metre or she could be standing above a drop of two hundred metres. The thought made her skin prickle and she shivered involuntarily. What was it about this loch that made her feel so uneasy? The water had a character all of its own – one minute sparkling azure blue and welcoming and then dark and threatening with a cloak of mist wrapped so heavily around that she felt herself being erased from the world. She shook her head in irritation, told herself to get a grip. It was just a bloody loch, like all the others that filled this shattered western coast. Only she knew this wasn't true. On a rational level she could poke fun at herself, but standing here, alone...

She left the jetty in a hurry, trying not to run as she took the zigzag trail back up into the trees. A small, newly cleared track led off to the left, unnoticed on the way down. Dee was anxious to leave the lochside, to climb back on her bike and roar back to the hotel and its welcoming fire and normality, but the new path called to her. Reluctantly, she gave in to the siren call and let her feet take her along this new, almost invisible track. It turned, parallel to the shoreline, some 10m above the water. She was close enough to hear each muted splash as waves spent their energy on the rounded rocks of the foreshore, and the drag of small pebbles as each wave retreated. It sounded so much like someone keeping pace with her, staying just out of sight in the mist that she stopped, holding her breath in concentration. The sounds continued, repeating with each wave. Reassured, Dee continued.

When the path ended, Dee wasn't sure what she was looking at. Five angular lumps of rock stood haphazardly in the frozen ground, poking jagged fingers upwards like fingers escaping a grave. A small offering of pinecones and frayed ribbons in front of each miniature megalith confirmed her suspicions. These *were* graves. Small graves. The size of newborn babies.

Dee took a photograph with her phone, pocketing it and almost running back to the burned cottage and her motorbike. The feeling that she was being watched, being followed, accompanied her all the way back through the dark forest until she reached the clearing and jumped on her bike. She pressed the electric start, felt insanely relieved as the engine roared into life, and headed back up the road without a thought for loose gravel or black ice – just the need to get away from whatever she'd left behind her.

Back in the hotel, she sent Teàrlach a message telling him what she'd found, attaching the photograph of five sad graves. Dee tried convincing herself these were pet burials, favourite animals given a plot of their own where they could be remembered, but the reality of what the graves contained lay in the twisted surgical instruments scattered on the concrete floor. She added a comment that the police would be informed and pressed send. Teàrlach was on his way to Glasgow with the hair samples. He must have some plan or leverage to have the DNA analysis done, but between that and whatever lay in the ground at Annie's cottage, Dee hoped the mystery of Lilybet's disappearance was close to being answered.

The local police were almost nonchalant in their response to Dee's call, saying they'd send someone to have a look after they'd ascertained she hadn't attempted digging anything up herself.

'Don't go back there,' the duty sergeant had ordered. 'It's still a crime scene and having the public stamping all over the site helps no one.'

She attempted to sound suitably chastised and ended the call. A herd of wild horses wouldn't have been able to drag her back to Annie's house – much less to the creepy little graves above the loch. Whatever lay underground could wait for the police, and then the forensics team in their ghostly white suits once the babies' bones had been uncovered. She had no doubt that's what they'd find there, purposely hidden from prying eyes. The results of miscarriages or mistakes, stillbirths or bungled deliveries. She tried not to think they may have been abortions. Annie would not have wanted to advertise her failures – not with a steady income from Traveller mothers at stake. Dee wondered how many children Annie had delivered over the years in that small cottage, and how many had been delivered as normal, healthy babies? Without any proper medical care or supervision, the stillbirth rate could be expected to be far worse than the one in two hundred average – and that figure was with properly trained midwives and well-equipped hospitals, not with someone who picked it up as she went along in a less than sterile cottage.

Dee felt tears pricking her eyelids in preparation for the grief she felt towards those tiny graves and their rough unmarked stone markers. The bar would be open, Blair standing behind the bar and longing for company, the fire lit. She closed her laptop, locked her room behind her and headed downstairs.

FORTY-SIX

EVERY GENOME TELLS A STORY

The Scottish police forensics laboratory at Gartcosh, a few miles east of Glasgow, resembled Russian utilitarian tower blocks from a cold-war era building project. Great hulking concrete towers riven with vertical windows screened from the road by a row of identical Lego trees. A high wire fence surrounded the entire estate, visible through the hedges planted there in a failed attempt to soften the brutal architecture.

Teàrlach blagged his way past the first checkpoint, and now waited in an air-conditioned entrance foyer under the suspicious gaze of a uniformed receptionist. His paper sanitary waste bags containing samples of hair had been inspected before he was allowed inside, but at least he didn't have to remind them to wear protective gloves before handling the contents. They still exuded an aroma of vindaloo – some of those spices and aromatic oils were long-lasting.

'Teàrlach Paterson?' the receptionist asked as if he hadn't been the only person waiting there.

'Yes.'

'Walk this way please.' She motioned him through the only door, swiping a pass to allow entrance. Teàrlach resisted the urge to swing his hips. A white-coated lab technician waited for him on the other side.

'You have samples relevant to the Tinkers' Heart murder?'

'I believe them to be relevant, as I explained to the Major Investigation Team leader. They are hair samples I collected yesterday. This one is from the girl who looks identical to Lilybet Masterton. She went missing three and a half years ago and her body was never found.'

The technician wrinkled his nose as he took a closer look inside the paper bag.

'Sorry,' Teàrlach explained, 'I retrieved it out of a bin bag full of takeaway curry.'

The technician didn't seem overjoyed, slipping the bag inside a more hygienic clear plastic bag and marking it with a permanent pen.

'This one I think is from the girl's mother. I'm looking for mitochondrial DNA linking her to the girl and nuclear DNA in case there's a link to anyone else in the database.'

The technician repeated the process with the second bag, sending a look that clearly expressed Teàrlach should stick to his own area of expertise and leave forensics to theirs.

'And this small sample, I think is Lilybet's own hair. I scraped it off the floor of her playhouse. When she went missing, the nanny removed every last trace of her from the house, so there wasn't a sample available during the original investigation. He handed over a sticking plaster, gold hairs trailing from it.

'Sorry, I didn't have any sample containers. Had to make do with what was to hand.'

It was duly dealt with the same as the others.

'And you want the results when?'

'Soon as you can,' Teàrlach replied.

'I don't immediately see what relevance this has to the murder investigation?'

'It's complicated.'

The technician held the samples in surgical gloved fingers, eyebrows raised in enquiry.

Teàrlach took a deep breath. 'I'm working for Tony Masterton, searching for his missing daughter, Lilybet. The child's body they found in the loch last week was the right age and sex, but the DNA didn't match either parent. What was found was a direct link between the skeleton in the loch and Richard Tavistock's DNA, giving high probability that the murder victim was the dead girl's father. Tony Masterton believes that Richard may have fathered Lilybet, and even if that wasn't true, he had no doubt that Richard was sleeping with his wife.'

'Yes, yes. We have all that already – but why are you providing motive if you're meant to be working for Tony?'

'As far as I know, Tony has an alibi so wasn't involved in Richard's murder – at least, not directly.' He hurried on. 'We've identified a girl who looks identical to Lilybet, I need to rule her out from my search. It shouldn't take long for you to provide proof that she's someone totally unrelated to the family and I can close that line of research down. In addition, the small hair sample is the only DNA we have for Lilybet and that missing person case is still open.'

'This isn't standard procedure. I'll have to go back to the lead investigator before we commit resources.'

'That's fine. That's all I ask.' Teàrlach stood aside as a key fob swiped and the door opened back into reception.

'We'll be in touch, Mr Paterson.'

The door closed with a solid click. He could see the receptionist holding a hand out for his temporary lanyard out of the corner of his eye. There was nothing else he could accomplish here. Teàrlach signed out and climbed back into his car. There was a message waiting for him from Dee, together with a photograph of five jagged stones set into a piece of rough ground. He read the note with care, shaking his head in denial. Could Annie really have buried five dead infants by the loch without notifying the authorities? He had to admit it was entirely possible. The Travellers actively avoided any contact with settled people together with their paperwork and regulations unless strictly necessary. If a mother lost a child during labour, then the parents wouldn't have wanted the fact disseminated – fear of infertility, or something wrong with the child, or judgement from God. Whatever reason, it suited both parties to pretend nothing untoward had happened and only celebrate the mothers who left with a healthy child.

Could this be where the child in the loch came from? Teàrlach dismissed the idea before it was fully formed. The bones in the loch belonged to a three-year-old girl, not a newborn. Besides, now that Dee had notified the police, the site would be swarming with forensics soon enough. He hastily forwarded Dee's text to the MIT, asking them to check any remains in case they matched the Mastertons' DNA. He might as well cover all the angles in case that's where Lilybet's body had finally ended up.

He had intended to visit his office, see if Chloe had discovered anything new before heading back to Dee and the hotel. Instead, Teàrlach found himself taking a well-trodden route along familiar Glasgow roads where memories refused to fade and die. This was the primary school he attended, the only change being the addition of a higher link fence in a futile attempt to keep the horrors of the world at bay. He saw himself in the playground, long shorts flapping around scabbed knees as he careered round in a gang of shrieking boys. The girls' playground was segregated to protect them from the rough and tumble, but their games were just as rough, albeit not so physical.

There were the shops he trailed around with his mother, fighting with his younger brother to be the one holding her hand and feeling the raw injustice as his sibling always took precedence. 'You're a big boy now, Teàrlach. You have to look after us both.' Aye, he didn't do such a good job of that.

His destination was always the same, a crematorium with uniform gravestones laid out in precise rows so the council lawnmowers had an easy time of it. Each small plot designed to take the ashes from the incinerator and topped with a domed metal flower holder which invariably held plastic blooms. The nearest thing to immortality in this grey and depressed part of the city.

Teàrlach stood in front of a grave, reading an inscription he knew by heart.

'Hi, Mum, Jamie.' He scuffed the pink gravel covering the grave, turning it over with his foot to remove the moss that worked ceaselessly to colonise each plot. There must be something that encouraged moss to grow on these stones, you didn't see it anywhere else. Teàrlach stared uselessly at the headstone, waiting for words to come. They never did, but true to form the tears did. This was a ritual he performed less and less often, standing in silent commemoration of the dead. There weren't even any bones under his feet, no relics over which to properly grieve. Their ashes had either blown away by now or been consumed by the creatures who made this soil their own. He imagined them – the beetles and worms ingesting the ashes over and over again until every last scrap of nutrition or essential minerals had been extracted, leaving behind what?

Not his mum. Not his young brother either. They were both frozen in time whilst Teàrlach aged and lived on. Him and his dad, although soon enough it would just be him. He turned away, wiping tears with the back of his hand until the world returned to sharp focus.

When his dad died, he didn't give a flying fuck where his ashes ended up. As long as it was miles away from here.

FORTY-SEVEN

HAIR TODAY

Chloe's research was taking her in an altogether unexpected direction. She'd paid for a copy of Ocean Cordona's birth certificate, her date of birth only ten days after Lilybet's. That coincidence wasn't what had caused her to whistle in astonishment. The father was listed as Richard Tavistock! When she magnified the birth certificate until it filled the screen to confirm the mother's name, it was listed as Clementina Cordona – not Selina Cordona. Had Selina changed her name? Perhaps she didn't like Clementina and preferred to call herself Selina. Chloe knew a few people who preferred alternative names to the ones they were given at birth – never mind the issues surrounding how individuals later identified sexually and how they wanted to present. Personally, she could sympathise with having a name sounding so much like an orange and the potential for teasing that would present. Ocean was born in Dundee, sufficiently far enough away from Annie's home to allay any suspicions in that regard.

She continued digging into Selina's past, finding references to her and Ocean at that address years before Lilybet's disappearance. She had booked Ocean into a nursery as a one-year-old whilst working a variety of low-paid jobs: cleaner, bar staff, agency worker, fruit picker. There was nothing in her life that raised any warning flags. She apparently worked hard as a single mum bringing up her only child, taking less benefit payments than she would have been entitled to. Something didn't feel right; the birth certificate was one thing, but Chloe was developing what Teàrlach referred to as a 'nose'.

Chloe exhausted all the legal means she could think of researching the girl and her mother. Maybe that Dee woman could do better with her hacking experience, but Chloe wasn't prepared to give in that easily. So far, Selina and her daughter appeared honest, normal and altogether unremarkable people. The sort of people whose lives leave no trace except in the hearts and minds of those they meet. With no court appearances or newsworthy escapades, Selina and Ocean might as well not exist. Almost erased from life even as they lived through it.

There was still another hour to go before she clocked off, not that Teàrlach took any notice of the hours she put in during the week. Another band of rain was moving in, dark clouds ominous on the western horizon against a stormy orange sky. At least she was working from home this week, that was one thing Dee had accomplished with her hacking of the office. Now she didn't have to worry about getting soaked on the way home. Chloe decided to make herself a cup of tea whilst she considered her next move. What little she'd unearthed was of interest, but like a dog with a bone she knew there were still tasty morsels waiting to be found.

When she sat back down at her laptop, she had a new search term in mind. Clementina Cordona was not a common name, yet the few suggestions coming up on social media were definitely not her. If anything, Clementina was even more invisible under that name than the one she now used. Chloe sent Teàrlach an update before closing the laptop in frustration. She *knew* there was more to find, but without the right tools, she was operating blind. Besides, Ocean couldn't be Lilybet, and as far as Teàrlach was concerned, Clementina or Selina or whatever she called herself was no longer of any interest.

* * *

Teàrlach would have been in complete agreement with Chloe's analysis if it wasn't for the call he was having.

'We've fast-tracked the DNA for you. Not sure what you're going to make of the results if I'm honest.' It sounded like the same taciturn individual he'd given the samples to just four hours previously at the Glasgow forensics labs.

'What have you got?' Teàrlach couldn't keep the surprise out of his voice. Forensics usually took a few weeks or longer, although with modern techniques the process could be completed within the four hours since he'd dropped off the samples. He was back on the single-track roads in the dark and the mist had spilled off the loch again. It was like driving into an insubstantial grey wall with visibility down to tens of metres and his concentration was focussed on the road ahead.

'The small sample you provided, the one of the missing girl... Lilybet. I started with that as we have both parents' DNA on file.'

Teàrlach urged him on. 'Yes?'

'Well, I can tell you the hair didn't belong to their daughter. Could it be contaminated with another sample, or belong to someone else?'

'It's possible. As I said, I took it off the rug in Lilybet's tree-house. I don't think anyone's been in there since the day she went missing – the place was full of cobwebs. Could well be three years' worth of cobwebs, and I can't see either of her parents setting foot in there.'

'Hmm.' The lab technician sounded doubtful. 'I do have a

match, and it relates directly to one of the cases we're working on.'

Teàrlach wished there was a way of shaking him violently via 4G. 'Which case is that?'

'The girl in the loch. The hair is a complete DNA match to the sample we were able to extract from the skeleton. Whoever the girl was, that's her hair.'

He cursed under his breath, searching in vain for somewhere to pull over in the heavy fog so he could give his full attention to the call.

The technician continued. 'Could the hair be from a friend she had over? A playmate? Whoever she was, we need to search the property. Looks like your client has more questions to answer.'

'Could you hold for a minute?' Teàrlach requested. 'I'm going to park, there's a turn-off ahead.' He recognised the turn-off to Hell's Glen and pulled into the side of the road. The ramifications of the forensics report had set his mind whirling.

'That's not all. The sample from the girl you wanted us to rule out of your search, from Inverness?'

'Ocean Cordona,' Teàrlach clarified.

'Yes, Ocean Cordona. She shares identical DNA with the hairs you provided from the treehouse and the body in the loch. Are you sure you haven't contaminated the samples because that would only be possible—'

'If they were identical twins,' Teàrlach butted in.

'Yes, identical twins.' The technician sounded put-out now that his thunder had been stolen.

'How could that be?' Teàrlach put voice to the question that had sprung to mind.

'Well, if the girl in Inverness—'

'Ocean Cordona.' He interrupted again, desperate to add clarity to the doubts circling like the mist outside the car windows.

'If Ocean had a twin sister, who played in the treehouse, that would explain why the identical DNA was in both locations – or you somehow used the same hair for both samples,' the technician added reasonably. It was, after all, the most obvious conclusion.

'I didn't mix the samples,' Teàrlach said quietly.

'No matter. We have to send a team back there tomorrow to inspect the graves. We'll pay a visit to your Mr Masterton's property whilst we're at it – with a warrant if we need one.'

'Tony Masterton is as keen to understand what happened to his daughter as you are. There won't be any need for a warrant.'

'That's for the MIT team leader to decide. He's still a suspect for the murder of Richard Tavistock, alibi or not. There's also the unexplained fire at Annie Tavistock's house and her death to investigate. Now we have a direct link to a child's body found in the loch. He has some explaining to do.'

'Are you taking a fresh DNA sample from Ocean Cordona and her mother as well?' Teàrlach asked.

'The local police surgeon will be with them anytime soon. Your samples weren't the best, and the Inverness detectives will want to question her about a potential twin daughter. Oh – one last thing.'

Teàrlach's head was spinning with the information that had already been provided. He wasn't sure he was prepared to hear anything else. 'What?' He hoped his voice didn't sound so despairing at the other end of this call.

'The mother, Ocean's mother.'

God, this guy loved to spin things out. 'Selina Cordona,' Teàrlach reminded him.

'Yes, Selina Cordona. She's not the girl's mother, at least not according to the sample you gave me. She's close, could be a sister. But she isn't Ocean's mother.'

Teàrlach heard himself thanking the technician for supplying the preliminary information over the phone, said he'd wait for the official report once they'd obtained pristine samples and had run the comparative analysis again. The mist was denser, pressing against the car as if it was alive. He could see air currents as the mist eddied in the car headlights. Finding his way to the hotel was going to be a slow and laborious task. He engaged gear, and turned the wheel into a tight turn, hoping the front tyres didn't fall into a ditch as he did so. Back on the loch road he inched along, almost blind to the way ahead.

FORTY-EIGHT

CHANGELING

Dee resisted the urge to drink herself into oblivion at lunchtime. She still had work to do, and the sooner she finished, the sooner she could leave this isolated hotel and its unsettling loch. The area was popular with tourists in the summer months, evidenced by the large caravan park she'd glimpsed on her journeys up and down the glen. Under blue skies the loch could appear inviting – she'd caught sunlight dancing on the surface, reflecting the hills on rare moments when the surface lay as placid as glass. But this was winter and underneath dark, grey clouds the loch exuded an air of menace, of mystery. Something about it spoke of death and she knew that feeling hadn't originated with the discovery of the child's skeleton at the Oitir. The environment had worked its way under her skin, leaving her paranoid and imagining she was continually being watched or followed.

Her dreams had changed as well. Dee would never normally remember whatever world she inhabited in her sleep. The dreams she'd been having here were so vivid and other-worldly she had trouble forgetting them. The loch always featured, changed into some transparent element other than water such that she found herself walking over the surface or sinking slowly down into the glassy depths. Underwater she found she could breathe as easily as on land, reaching the bottom where sea grass grew as green as a spring meadow under her bare feet, fish diving for shelter whenever larger fish appeared. The light here was green and yellow, the water warm and clear. As dreams go, these had an aimless quality where she floated freely without any destination in mind, no task waiting to be finished. They always ended the same way – something coming towards her, snakelike and hungry for her flesh. She tried to run, but she could only move slowly, limbs sluggish in the water as her panic built and the creature rapidly approached, cutting through the water like a knife. For the last week, she'd had the same dream, woken every night drenched in sweat. It was time to leave this place.

Tony had tasked her with finding out everything she could about the girl in Inverness and her mother, and that's what she worked on. She'd spent the afternoon bent over her laptop, fuelled by instant coffees made from the replenished stock in her hotel bedroom. Like Chloe, she had uncovered Ocean and Selina Cordona's names. She had seen Richard Tavistock was the father and had identified the discrepancy in the mother's name on the birth certificate and then searched for any record of Clementina. She found her in the 2011 Scottish Census – though not the publicly available data which is stripped of any personal identifiers; Dee had to worm her way deeper into the datasets without setting off any alarms.

Clementina had been living at the caravan park a few miles down the road on the 27th March when the census was taken. Her occupation was listed as waitress, working at a nearby restaurant, age twenty-two. The other occupier of the caravan was her younger sister, Selina, age nineteen. Why had the younger sister taken care of the child, and where did Clementina go? Dee tried other sources, opening social security files and applying Clementina's National Insurance number to searches. The tax offices were more difficult to crack, layer upon layer of protection over which she eventually had to admit defeat. It would require insider knowledge before being able to access the information she required. Even so, she had a picture of Clementina's life, however vague and imperfect. She had worked in a succession of short-term jobs since leaving school in Dundee at sixteen, spending more time off the radar than being visible to the relevant authorities – that meant she was mostly paid in cash and kept a low profile. It was the sort of life a Traveller would lead, and their unusual names lent credence to that theory.

Living a peripatetic life meant both women would prove well-nigh impossible to track, but from the little Dee had been able to piece together, one inescapable fact stood out. Clementina had left no trace of her existence since giving birth to Ocean six years ago, and that usually meant bad news. Her sister surfaced a year after Ocean's birth, renting a flat in Inverness where she'd lived ever since with the daughter.

A knock at the door startled her. She quickly checked to see if the security doorstop was securely in place before hearing the reassuring sound of Teàrlach's voice asking if he could come in.

'Just a sec, I have to shift this first.'

He entered the room, looking around helplessly for a place to sit like he had the last time and then sank onto her bed, slumped into himself.

'You look as if you've got the world's problems on your shoulders,' Dee quipped. 'What's up?'

Teàrlach brought her up to date.

'Jesus!'

'Aye, and it will take a miracle to unravel this lot,' Teàrlach replied. 'As usual, everyone we need to speak to who knows anything about this are dead.'

'Except for the sister, Selina.'

'I don't think she's going to open up about this, not if it risks losing Ocean.' Teàrlach stood, took his favoured place at the window and frowned at his bruised reflection and the freezing fog outside. 'I'm going to have to give Tony an update, except all I have for him are questions.'

'You have to let him know the police will be coming tomorrow, and forensics too,' Dee cautioned.

He turned to face her, knowing Dee would keep Tony advised of any police activity; it was an unwritten part of her job description.

'You let him know about the police – and that he's still a suspect for Richard's murder. I don't think they buy the alibi.'

Dee remained unreadable.

'I'll provide an update on the provisional forensics. Maybe I did mix up the samples,' he added doubtfully. 'Either way they'll be running the tests again.'

'What if Ocean *is* Lilybet's twin. Could Tony and Samantha have been bringing up the wrong child all along and the girl's bones are Lilybet's?' Dee asked the question that had been troubling Teàrlach.

'I can't see how Samantha wouldn't know her own baby. They were both airlifted to the Glasgow hospital within minutes of the birth – it doesn't make sense.'

'Except the midwife was Annie Tavistock, the father was Richard Tavistock, and we don't know how long it was between the delivery and Samantha being flown to Glasgow.' Dee started piecing the jigsaw together in her mind.

'Unless Samantha *did* know that wasn't her baby. But why would she – how could that even be possible?' Teàrlach shook his head in confusion. 'Why would a woman swap her newborn baby immediately after birth, and who has a spare baby just lying around miles from the nearest maternity ward?'

'Annie, maybe?' Dee's quiet voice replied.

Teàrlach nodded thoughtfully. 'I guess it's a possibility.' He stared out at the mist, turned into yellow muslin by the hotel lights as it wrapped ever closer to the stone walls. 'If ever there's a place where changelings are real, it would be here.'

FORTY-NINE

THE BOATMAN

I am the mother
Whose child was ripped out of me
And died in my arms

The next morning Teàrlach called Tony straight away, explained what forensics had found and reminded him this was only preliminary. Until they'd collected their own samples, it would be best to assume contamination and ignore the first set of results. He'd sounded disinterested, thanked Teàrlach for his contribution and effectively thrown him off the case. Chloe let him know the bank balance was once more healthily into the black, so his time hadn't been completely wasted. But he couldn't let the case go. Not until the forensics tests had been rerun with controlled samples.

He knocked on Dee's door.

'You in there?'

'Just a moment, have to shift this doorstop.' Dee blinked away the tiredness in her eyes, rubbing them with the back of her hand for good measure. 'Have a seat.'

Teàrlach tried unsuccessfully to find something else to look at as Dee changed her T-shirt, staring a hole into the worn carpet until she was decent.

'Had a rough night?' He tried for inconsequential chat, aiming for mundanity in an atmosphere charged with electricity.

Dee's eyes met his with amusement.

'Aye. Tony's had me working most of the night.' She walked into the bathroom, pulling the door shut behind her. He could still hear everything, up to the point when she'd finished brushing her teeth and made a reappearance.

'Come on,' Dee commanded. 'I need a coffee, even if it's the stuff they serve here.'

As usual, they were the only guests in the breakfast room.

'I think this is the first time we've had breakfast together.' Dee's nonchalance belied the glint in her eye. 'Could turn into a habit if we're not careful.'

Teàrlach felt he was being played like a fiddle. He was beginning to enjoy it.

'What's he had you doing?' Teàrlach looked around in vain for any serving staff. 'He's just thrown me off the case.' He observed her reaction carefully.

'Yeah. I know.' Dee didn't show any surprise. 'I think he wants you out of the picture for a while. Until he's sorted out a few things.'

The arrival of the grumpy receptionist stopped any further discussion until she'd taken their orders, returning almost immediately with two coffees. Dee drank hers with an appreciative slurp.

'Think this has been brewing all night. It actually tastes of coffee.'

'So, anything you want to share?' Teàrlach tried a second time.

Dee's expression was uncharacteristically solemn.

'No.'

Breakfast passed in silence, the easy exchange between them suddenly snuffed out with that single word.

'I'll be off then, leave you to it.' He stood, feeling as lost as he had the first time he'd met her.

'Guess so, Sherlock.' Dee kept her eyes down until Teàrlach left the table. When he reappeared, heading back through to reception with his overnight bag, Dee called out.

'I've stopped tracking you.'

Teàrlach hesitated, looked as if he was about to speak, then gave a curt nod of acknowledgement.

Teàrlach returned to his office the next morning and things were beginning to return to normal. Dee had withdrawn her spyware, or so she said. He was willing to give her the benefit of the doubt. Besides, as he was no longer officially working for Tony Masterton, she had no reason to keep an eye on him. The arrival of the completed forensics report, expected as it was, grabbed his interest immediately.

He skimmed the text until he came to the pertinent information. The fresh samples obtained by forensics from the treehouse confirmed Teàrlach's original findings. He sat back in his chair, breathed out slowly. That had been Lilybet's body they'd found in the loch. But whoever Lilybet was, she wasn't the Mastertons' real daughter.

Teàrlach read on, reaching the analysis of the five graves found on Annie's land. Four had been children – all newborn. The accompanying photographs showed bones that could have been small animals except Teàrlach knew enough to recognise human bones when he saw them. The fifth grave contained a fully grown adult female's remains. The coroner's investigation was ongoing, but he could guess the results.

Forensics spelt out the missing jigsaw pieces. One of the infants matched both the Mastertons' DNA profile. He'd found

Lilybet, except she'd never survived the birth or had ever been given a name. Somehow, Annie had swapped their infant with Ocean's twin sister. The reason for that might never be known – perhaps the Masterton baby was a stillbirth? Annie wasn't expecting to be any part of Samantha's birth. If it wasn't for the fact the baby came early and the roads had been impassable, the two of them might never have met. He could imagine the panic if there were complications during the delivery. By all accounts, Annie had no professional training, just a set of gynaecological instruments which she probably didn't know how to use properly or safely. It wouldn't take much for the birth to go horribly wrong, especially a premature birth.

What would Annie have done then? The father already had a reputation as a Glasgow hard man, and she must have known she could well be the focus of his rage if his daughter died. Was it coincidence that another mother had died during childbirth, leaving two healthy twin motherless girls in her cottage? Clementina's grave dated to around the time of Ocean's birth, as did the Mastertons' baby. Even the proximity of Annie's house and the Masterton house fitted the theory, especially if Annie and her son, Richard, used a boat to travel back and forth unseen between the two houses.

There was no way of knowing how the events of that day had played out. The only people left alive and who might know anything were Samantha – whose whereabouts were unknown – and Clementina's younger sister, Selina. Teàrlach added the forensics to his box file and closed the lid with a sigh. Tony Masterton now knew what had happened to his daughter, what had happened to Lilybet. Left in the wake of his investigation were at least two murders, Richard Tavistock and his mother. God knows what had happened to the Travellers, they'd vanished off the face of the earth. As for Samantha and the nanny, the clock was ticking. In the front office, Chloe was taking a call.

'That's Tony Masterton on the line, wants to see you at his house at 3:30pm today sharp to wrap things up. What shall I tell him?'

'Tell him I'll be there,' Teàrlach called to Chloe as he picked up his coat. He'd see the job through to the end, whether he was on Tony Masterton's payroll or not.

* * *

Dee was still very much on Tony's payroll and facing the biggest dilemma of her life. He'd tasked her with finding Samantha, honeyed the words with the suggestion that he only wanted to talk to his wife about the divorce proceedings before it went to court. She'd taken his words at face value; it was easier that way. Samantha had been planning her escape for a while, pre-booked hotels and taxis liberally scattered through her timeline; banks accounts opened and closed; change of name. None of it helped in the end, not when her biometrics matched those of a Diane Waterman. Some things you can change – appearances can be altered – but fingerprints and facial geometric measurements remain the same.

She parked the bike outside the country house hotel deep in the Scottish Highlands, took a deep breath and walked into reception. The search had taken her all night, following twists and turns as Samantha took great trouble to conceal her trail, ditching her phone, using cash. Dee could have told her not to bother.

'Good morning, how can I help you?' The receptionist couldn't help looking at Dee askance, taking in the leathers and the motorbike parked outside and failing to make any connection to someone who would enter an establishment such as theirs.

'Good morning,' Dee replied brightly. 'I'm here to see Diane Waterman. She's staying here as a guest.'

The receptionist played a delaying tactic by consulting her screen. 'And who can I say is visiting?'

'Tell her Annie Tavistock sent me. I'll wait over there.'

'Is she expecting you?'

'Oh yes, she most certainly is.' Dee spoke encouragingly, adding a friendly smile.

Dee sat on an armchair commanding a view of the sweeping staircase and waited to meet Samantha Masterton for the first time.

Tony Masterton wanted to find Samantha to have her killed, despite his protestations of peaceful intent. Samantha had not only been screwing around but had passed off another child as his own. Now Dee was about to issue the death sentence and her stomach felt hollow. She desperately wanted to talk to Teàrlach, ask his advice. It was only yesterday morning they'd last seen each other, an awkward goodbye at the Lochside Hotel and a promise that she'd stop hacking him. Now she felt more alone than during a lifetime spent being passed from one orphanage to the next, too difficult to be fostered, too much trouble for everyone. Teàrlach had turned out to be yet another ship in the night. She'd felt herself growing closer to him, tried to fight it, but she'd let him get under her skin only to be rejected when Tony threw him off the case. He'd made no attempt to contact her, and she was dammed if she'd be the first to make a move. It was the story of her life, repeating over and over again.

Samantha came down the stairs like a movie star, catching sight of Dee with a fleeting look of relief as the expected hitman faded back into her imagination. She took the adjacent chair, sizing her up with evident curiosity.

'What can I do for you, Miss...?'

'Is there somewhere we can talk, in private?' Dee replied.

'There's a reading room, we won't be disturbed there. Would you like a drink or anything?' Her eyes made a deliberate traverse from Dee's boots up to her leather jacket before settling on her face.

'Coffee, splash of milk.'

Samantha gave the order to the receptionist, leading Dee through to a back room where a fire provided a warm welcome. They shared a settee, Samantha relaxing into the cushions.

'How much do you know?' Samantha opened. 'Who sent you?'

'I know Lilybet wasn't your daughter, that you swapped your own dead child at birth.'

Samantha nodded, a single fatalistic acknowledgement that the truth had found her out.

'Does he know?' Her face had paled despite her attempt at remaining calm. 'No, you don't need to answer. Of course, he does.'

A member of staff brought a tray with coffee and short-bread, moving a small table to place the tray within easy reach. They waited until the waiter had left them alone before Samantha spoke again.

'Are you Izanami?' She saw Dee's confusion. 'She brings death in Japanese mythology. Did he send you to kill me?'

Dee shook her head. 'No, that's not what I do. I just find things for him.'

Samantha breathed heavily. 'I thought that was it. I was expecting you to point a gun at my head, end it with the pull of a trigger.' She appeared almost disappointed. 'Do you have children?'

'No.' Dee replied.

'No, I didn't think so. You're a woman though, so you should be able to understand.' Samantha paused as Dee reached for her coffee. 'I've not seen you before. How long have you been working for my husband?'

'A year, slightly longer. I stay in Glasgow. He's never asked me to visit your home here. Hasn't mentioned you before to be honest – until recently.'

'I was on my own, in that house. My baby wasn't due for almost a month and when my waters broke, there was no one I could call on for help. We were snowed in. Tony didn't answer my calls – still on the plane headed for Glasgow. I called the emergency services of course, once my contractions had started. They said it would be hours before anyone could reach me and to get neighbours to help. I only had Richard.'

She stopped, gathered herself before continuing. 'He came on the boat with his mother. I'd heard something about her being a midwife – it's not as if I had any choice,' she said defensively, watching Dee for any sign of judgement.

Dee remained impassive, watching Samantha intently as she bared her soul to this stranger, the words tumbling over each other in her eagerness to speak the truth she'd had to conceal for so many years.

'She botched the whole thing. The pain...' Plump tears fell silently onto her lap. 'She ripped my baby out of me. My wee girl died in her arms, and she offered my baby to me. She gave me my dead child as if she was a lump of meat.' Samantha convulsed into tears, silently grieving like she must have done so many times before.

Dee put down her cup, moved closer to hold her shaking body in her arms. When the shaking stopped, she spoke words of comfort to her.

'I'm so sorry. That must have been horrific. I can't imagine.'

Samantha dabbed at her eyes, sniffing for good measure. 'If Tony had found out, he would have gone mad. You've no idea.'

Dee didn't contradict her, but she knew what he was capable of, was still capable of.

'Richard said there were newborn twins at the house. Something had happened, but Annie shut him up before he could tell me about it. Annie said it was God's will that I take one as my own. I didn't know what else to do. I needed a baby – I had to have a baby. Annie and Richard took care of everything, took my own child's body away, gave me Lilybet. I know it was wrong, but I loved her. I really loved her even though she wasn't my own flesh and blood – she was Richard's baby.'

'Tony knows all this. The police found your child's body along with Lilybet's real mother. They'd been buried in shallow graves on Annie's property, along with some other babies. The police let him know about Lilybet and his own child. I have to tell him where you are, I'm sorry.' Dee's words sounded inadequate even to herself. 'I'll give you as long as I can. You'll have to leave today, change your name again.'

Samantha nodded silently, gave a small smile of thanks. Dee left her crumpled on the settee, broken and frightened. She retraced her journey back to the Lochside Hotel with the same sick feeling deep in her stomach. There was more in the police forensics than she'd passed on to Teàrlach, something she'd had to give to Tony. Whatever he had in mind, he needed her close by and focussed on the police.

* * *

Mick and Brian waited for dusk to fall. Richard's boat was moored on the far side of the loch, somewhere where it was unlikely to be recognised. A white mist had formed in the middle of the water, spreading out towards the shores as what little of the day's heat surrendered to the night. The engine started easily, the regular throb echoing across the water and held there by the newly forming inversion layer.

'Shit!' Mick's voice was urgent and low. 'First the bloody fog and then the motor's loud enough to wake the dead.' He squinted into the dusk, focussed on the diffuse light from Tony's house lights which still showed above the low-lying mist. 'Keep us pointed straight at the house – and keep the speed down.

Lucky for us he's got the place lit up like a bloody Christmas Tree.'

The characteristic sound of a helicopter came from over the hills, heading for the same destination. The two of them exchanged a worried look.

'Do you think he's going away in that thing?' Brian pointed towards the triangle of red, green and white lights moving above them, the body of the helicopter obscured by mist as it passed over their heads.

'If he is, then we'll have to come back another day.' Mick opened the rifle case slung over his shoulder, produced a Winchester .270. 'I don't want to be taking down a helicopter with this.'

Brian smiled mirthlessly. The hunting rifle was effective against deer at 140 metres, lethal against the smaller target of a man with the Viper scope fitted.

'You'll need to get me within a hundred metres,' Mick cautioned. 'And keep the boat as steady as you can.' The helicopter made a descent on the opposite shore, landing behind Tony's house. 'Wait just out of sight of the house, the noise from that thing will hide the racket from Richard's engine.'

Brian lowered the engine speed to a tick over. Around them the mist reluctantly parted as the small boat coasted, concealing them in a cold, grey blanket until the only reference point they had was the diffuse glow from the house. They remained silent, rocked in a slight swell with the light fading to darkness each passing minute. When the helicopter eventually took off, they were completely hidden from view.

FIFTY

THE CHOSEN

The Masterton house entrance came into view. Teàrlach pressed the intercom and the gates opened noiselessly, inviting him to drive in.

Tony Masterton stood in the doorway in his customary position, arms folded against the chill winter air. The drive lights were lit against the coming of the night, this close to the winter solstice it would be dark within the next hour.

'Charlie. I was wondering if you'd make an appearance in time.' He gestured for Teàrlach to follow him inside, leading the way through to the back of the house and the lounge overlooking the loch. 'This is actually quite serendipitous,' he added as they each took a seat.

'I guess you've read the report, from forensics.' Teàrlach opened.

Tony looked straight at him, his expression, as always, unreadable. 'Yes.'

He waited an uncomfortable time for Tony to add something. Nothing else was forthcoming.

'I'm sorry. About your daughter.'

Tony's eyes flicked downwards for a second, a look of pain

flashed across his face so briefly Teàrlach wondered if he'd imagined it.

'Sometimes, we're given a second chance.' Tony regained his composure, but the pain remained behind his eyes.

'I'm sorry, I don't know what you mean.' Teàrlach struggled to understand.

'You know why I moved here, Teàrlach?' For the first time, Tony pronounced his name properly, as if all the previous attempts had been in jest. He waved an arm out expressively over the misty loch, distant mountaintops catching the dying embers of the sun and painting the sky in vivid red hues.

'The view?' Teàrlach hazarded a guess.

'Yes, the view. But there's more to it.' He stood, moved closer to the French windows as if to search the sky. The sun had almost set, and the light outside was already dimming. At least the evening mist remained in the centre of the loch, not spreading out to cover the roads and houses dotted around the shore as it had so often the week he had stayed there.

'This is an ancient place, the loch.' Tony continued. 'Generations of people have lived, fought and died here. The land holds secrets, the loch holds ghosts.'

Teàrlach didn't know how to respond to this, so remained silent.

'I knew my daughter was dead before I hired you. I could feel it – here!' Tony held a clenched fist tight against his heart. 'I didn't know how, or why, or where. That was your job, and one in which you excelled.'

Tony opened a cabinet, brought out a bottle of whisky and tilted it towards Teàrlach with a questioning expression.

'No thanks, I have to drive.'

Tony smiled. 'Of course. I'm going nowhere, so if you don't mind...'

He poured himself a generous measure, held a crystal glass

towards an overhead light so the glass threw rainbows from cut facets. 'To second chances,' he toasted.

'Second chances,' Teàrlach echoed, wondering what to do with his empty hands.

'I wasn't as surprised by the discovery of my child in that unmarked grave as you may have thought. Samantha never really loved Lilybet. She was always relieved when the baby was taken away – had me find a nanny when she was still only a few weeks old. Lilybet died because Samantha couldn't bring herself to watch her for the few minutes she played outside that day, then misdirected the police and search teams anywhere except the one obvious place to look. The loch.'

'I don't think you can blame Samantha...'

Tony cut across Teàrlach's defence. 'Oh yes, I can blame her. I blame her for swapping the babies at the start. Are you seriously suggesting she didn't know what had happened, hadn't realised that girl wasn't ours?'

Teàrlach didn't have a ready answer.

'No matter. Our changeling was loved – by me at least. Lilybet was the one saving grace I had. The only good thing I ever did in a life so full of pain and shit I would otherwise rather not have lived it at all. You of all men must know what I mean by that?'

Teàrlach wondered how much Tony knew about his past, his alcoholic, abusive father. His mother and brother burned alive. Again, he felt unable to answer.

'It doesn't matter.' Tony wasn't bothered by Teàrlach's silence.

A searchlight appeared in the sky, hovering above the house as if a modern-day nativity miracle was about to unfold. Tony's eyes narrowed against the beam, a smile once more appearing.

'Good, they're here.' He almost ran to the front door, calling over his shoulder for Teàrlach to follow.

A helicopter dropped towards the lawn, rotors cutting the

chill air like scythes until the engines died. The pilot emerged, held out a hand to assist a woman and child down onto solid ground. Tony positively bounded towards them, arms outstretched in welcome. The woman instinctively pulled the girl behind her as Tony approached.

'I'm sorry, too enthusiastic. Please, come in out of the cold. I'm Tony Masterton, we talked on the phone.'

The woman sent an enquiring glance towards Teàrlach.

'Oh, and this is my private investigator, Teàrlach Paterson. He's the one I have to thank for finding you.'

'Pleased to meet you at last,' Teàrlach said quietly. He recognised them of course, Ocean and Selina Cordona. What on earth was going on?

'Here, come through to the lounge.' Tony led them back along the same route. They followed in bewilderment, still recovering from the novelty of being flown there by helicopter and now having to adjust to the house.

'I don't know how long I have.' Tony spared a glance at his watch, a flash of gold showing as he raised a cuff. 'Let me look at you.'

He directed this towards the girl, shyly standing beside her guardian. Selina switched her focus from Tony to Teàrlach, then encouraged Ocean forward with obvious reservations.

'Ocean.' Tony's voice broke. There were tears running down his cheeks – so at odds with the Glasgow hard-man image that Teàrlach had to do a double take. The tears were real.

'You're so much like her. Can I hold you – just once?' He directed this at Selina. She nodded, standing ready to snatch the girl away.

'Do I have to?' Ocean asked, taking a step back in alarm.

'It's alright, darling. I'm here.' Selina encouraged the girl forward.

Ocean reluctantly allowed herself to be enveloped in Tony's

arms, her face screwed up in displeasure. He released her, standing back to view her again as if he couldn't believe his eyes.

'You said you had something for us?' Selina asked. There was a hard edge to her voice, brought on by nerves or the hardship of bringing up her sister's child, it was difficult to say.

'Yes, that's right.' His phone chirruped and Tony frowned as he read a message. 'So soon? Excuse me a minute, will you?'

Tony left the three of them standing awkwardly in the lounge.

'What's this about?' Selina posed the question to Teàrlach.

'I'm sorry, I'm not sure what's going on here. Did Mr Masterton say anything about this to you?'

'Said he had something to give us, to give Ocean. In memoriam he said.'

'And I do,' Tony added as he re-entered the room. He laid a sheaf of papers down on a coffee table, followed by a pen. 'I've had these drawn up by my solicitor. They hand over this house and a substantial amount of money to you and Ocean. You can choose to stay here or sell up and live wherever you want, I won't mind.'

Three people stood rooted to the spot in shock.

'Teàrlach, if you can witness each page where marked; Selina, you need to sign these as well.' He noticed the disbelief etched on Selina's face. 'There's no catch, I promise. I'm giving everything I possess to you both, passing to Ocean when she's of age. You'll want for nothing.'

A buzz sounded from the gate intercom. He ignored it.

'I have to ask you to hurry if you will, there's not a lot of time left.' Tony held the pen out to Selina, who began reading the papers with eyes growing larger by the minute. 'We have about ten minutes before they start forcing the gates. I'd rather they didn't.'

'Who will be forcing the gates?' Teàrlach asked. He was

beginning to feel like an actor in a play without a script. It was little comfort that Selina apparently was in a similar position.

'Police,' Tony said simply. 'Dee let me know they've found DNA linking me to Richard Tavistock. My fault, evidently, he managed to scratch me.' He glanced towards Ocean, placed a finger on his lips. She smiled at the pantomime, unaware of what he was keeping secret. 'Should have been more thorough, but my hands were full enough without adding another pair to my haul.'

Teàrlach made the connection to the armless swimmers in the Clyde, Tony's modus operandi to avoid any risk of evidence being unwittingly retained by his victims. He pictured Richard's still warm heart dripping blood over Tony's hands in Hell's Glen, wondered how safe any of them were in his presence.

Selina started signing the papers whilst Tony looked on.

'What about Samantha?' Teàrlach couldn't help asking.

'She'll not have a penny. Won't be needing anything where she's going.' A hint of Glaswegian hard man returned.

Selina completed signing the papers, looked enquiringly towards Teàrlach. He picked up the pen and started signing each page as a witness.

'Good!' Tony exclaimed. 'And on these too.' He pointed at sheets Teàrlach had missed.

'Give these to the pilot, he knows what to do.' Tony handed the papers to Selina, guided her back towards the entrance.

'I don't understand.' Her voice echoed down the hall towards Teàrlach.

'You don't have to. Consider this recompense for the loss of your sister, Clementina. And for bringing up her child. Good-bye, Ocean, Selina. I'm glad we had this one chance to meet.' The door closed with a solid click. Outside, Teàrlach could hear a helicopter engine starting up. Tony re-appeared with a look of complete satisfaction written across his face.

'Just a minute,' he forestalled Teàrlach's question, pressing a switch on a wall panel. A group of uniformed officers could be seen milling around the entrance to the drive. Their attention was fixed towards the sky as the helicopter lifted off into the dusk.

'Evening, officers. Do come in, the front door is unlocked.' As one, the police switched their attention to looking at the intercom, then rushed back to their cars as the gates started to open.

'Teàrlach, I'm sorry I couldn't share everything with you – about my intentions towards Ocean and her mother – guardian,' he corrected. 'I do want to thank you for everything you did, what you discovered.' He crossed over to a sideboard, picked up an antique leather-bound book and placed it in Teàrlach's hands.

Teàrlach read the title which only added to his confusion – *The Waste Land* by T.S Eliot.

'What's this?'

'When we first met, in your office, I saw the books arranged on the shelf behind you. It may surprise you to know that I'm also a lover of poetry.'

Teàrlach could only nod in agreement. Never in a thousand years would he have associated the Glasgow hard man with poetry. His own meagre selection of books had belonged to his aunt, passed onto him when she died a year ago.

'My parting gift. You may find it instructive.' Tony looked out to the loch, lost in thought. 'We don't actually fear death, we fear that no one will notice our absence, that we will disappear without a trace.'

He opened the French windows, letting the cold night air enter the room. Teàrlach caught the tang of iodine, salt forming on his lips. He tasted the sea.

'You know the story of Charon?' Tony asked.

Teàrlach hadn't felt so lost since the day he was told his mother had died.

'I don't know, the boatman? The guy who ferried souls across the sea?' He searched his memory for references. It sounded about right.

'Aye. The guy who ferries the dead across the Styx.' Tony nodded towards the loch. 'Sometimes, I wonder if this loch *is* the Styx.' He started towards the decking, casually collecting a shotgun concealed behind curtains and swinging it to point at Teàrlach.

'Only the chosen, Teàrlach. Only the chosen.' The shotgun angled away as Teàrlach stopped following.

Teàrlach watched in bewilderment as Tony walked over to the glass balustrade to stare out over the loch, standing floodlit in the same place where Lilybet had left her daisies. As the noise from the helicopter engine faded into the night sky, another mechanical throb began to replace it, coming out of the mist. Tony's head turned in search of the source, aiming his gun out over the loch. A policeman's heavy knock sounded from the front door, accompanied soon after by the sound of running feet. Teàrlach turned around, only to raise his hands as armed police levelled weapons at him.

'Armed police! Hands where I can see them! Lie down, down on the floor, arms outstretched!' Shouts came from the police, red laser dots played across his vision as Teàrlach sank to his knees.

'I told Dee you made a good team. Goodbye, Teàrlach.' They were the last words Tony would speak.

A single shot hit Tony's chest causing him to spin away from the loch, his shotgun veering towards trigger happy police high on adrenaline. Two armed officers reacted instinctively, the kinetic energy from multiple bullets threw him backwards through the glass balustrade shattered by stray rounds, and he fell into the loch with a heavy splash. Above the ringing in his ears, Teàrlach made out the sound of an outboard motor fading into the mist.

'Cease fire! Cease fire!' The order came too late for Tony.

Teàrlach risked raising his head off the polished concrete, saw armed officers fan out onto the decking, crouching low to minimise target size. Multiple red lasers sent enquiring beams into the fog, down into the loch.

'Can't see him. He must be under water.'

'The shot came from that boat. They've gone into the mist.'

Radios crackled with urgent questions. Rapid-fire answers responded with requests for medical assistance, divers, patrol cars, marine police. It was dark, the loch was spilling freezing fog inland. Teàrlach could imagine Mick and Brian speeding across the loch and to freedom.

In the water, Tony found he had no need to breathe anymore. He might be dreaming except the water was cold, so dark and cold. He couldn't tell if he was sinking, or floating face down – nothing mattered anymore. He saw Lilybet's face, stretched out his arms to hold the soft warmth of her. She was coming for him even as darkness wrapped its coils around him, promising absolution in her touch.

FIFTY-ONE

TOAST

'Happy Christmas.' Teàrlach had to raise his voice to cut through the noise.

Chloe tried not to look too pleased as Teàrlach handed her a present. They were sitting in one of Glasgow's finest Indian restaurants, the table full of assorted dishes and drink. Every table was the same, the place filled to capacity with people finishing up for another year. Ravi Shankar played sitar over the speakers, barely audible but a welcome change from the constant diet of festive hits.

'What is it?' Chloe pulled at the inexpertly wrapped parcel with the eagerness of a child to reveal the latest iPhone. 'You're kidding me?'

'Don't get too excited, it's a company phone. Unlimited data and calls. Even dials out for help if you're in a crash.'

'Aw, thanks, Teàrlach.' She planted a kiss on his cheek before he could react. 'Is it hacker-proof?'

She directed this frostily to the redhead sitting beside him.

'Peace on earth ladies.' Teàrlach held both hands up in supplication. 'Play nicely for once – it's Christmas for fuck's sake.'

'I can make it hacker-proof if you like?' Dee's conciliatory tone earned a sharp look from Chloe.

'And this is for you,' he placed a parcel with identical dimensions into Dee's hand.

'What can it be?' The sarcasm was evident, but Dee's face still lit up as she unwrapped another iPhone. Her kiss landed on his other cheek, leaving him with two red blotches so he resembled a blushing boy – one who'd recently been in a fight.

'Personal space,' he muttered. 'No idea of personal space.'

Over a week had passed since the events at the Masterton house. Teàrlach had been taken back to Glasgow for a 'debrief' by the MIT, which mostly consisted of them desperately trying to cover themselves for the shooting of Tony Masterton. His body had still not been found, even though dive teams searched the loch daily – some quirk of underwater currents had swept him away from the vicinity of the house. He wondered if Tony was making slow progress towards Lilybet's resting place on the Oitir, whether his bones would be found picked clean there in years to come.

'So that's it – as far as the police are concerned?' Chloe's indignant tone brought Teàrlach back from his musings.

'Case closed,' he replied. 'Tony's directly linked to Richard's murder since they matched the DNA under Richard's nails, and he had motive.'

'Aye, but what about Annie?' Dee questioned.

'And whoever tried to kill you as well,' Chloe added.

Teàrlach nodded thoughtfully. 'They're laying that at Tony's door too.'

'Convenient, now he can't answer back.' Dee still felt anger on Tony's behalf. He'd frightened the bejesus out of her when alive, but now he was gone, she missed him in a way she wouldn't have been able to articulate. A steady presence, an immoveable rock, a landmark you only realise you needed when it's gone. 'It was a woman who killed Annie.'

'I didn't see the need to tell them everything.' Teàrlach finished his drink, attracted a waiter's attention for refills. 'There's more than enough suffering as it is, why add to it?'

Chloe's eyes narrowed. 'You know who she is, don't you? The woman who left you for dead.'

He sighed heavily, viewed the table contents with a full stomach and decided against another helping.

'Aye, there's only the one likely contender.' He sounded tired.

'Come on then, you can tell us,' Dee encouraged.

'I don't know if the police took all the Travellers back to the station when they picked them up from Annie's cottage. I'd only told them about the three I saw in the bar. My suspicion is that Jeremiah managed to avoid being discovered and they either couldn't be bothered searching or didn't know about her – it was Mick and Brian they wanted. I must have disturbed her when I arrived that evening.'

Teàrlach took a sip of his beer, remembering inching his way along the corridor towards Annie's bedroom.

'She'd turned off the power, probably when she heard my car coming up the drive. I can imagine she panicked – thinking the police had returned to look for her and there she was in the house with a dead woman. Setting the place on fire was more of an attempt to cover her tracks after I turned up. I don't think she planned on killing me as well, but I'd make a useful suspect if I was found there.'

'But why? Why would she want to kill Annie? I thought they were family?' Chloe's attention wandered as fresh drinks arrived.

'Because they'd discovered the graves. You said the path had only been recently cleared. Annie certainly wasn't capable of physical labour and Richard was dead. I suspect they started putting it together themselves, Clementina's disappearance and the row of gravestones. Mick was after the truth when I left them with Annie, I think she told him enough to seal her fate.'

'You think she told them the truth about Clementina? That she died during childbirth?' Chloe asked.

'Once they'd found the graves, I don't think she had much choice. I still don't know how closely related they were to Clementina and Selina – but close enough for Jeremiah to want revenge. If I had to guess, then I'd say Jeremiah was Clementina's mother, and she's been looking for her daughter for years with each search ending up at Annie's door. Whether she killed Annie or not... that evidence went up in flames and she's unlikely to confess. All I can say with any certainty is that Annie was still alive when the police picked up her visitors, otherwise they'd have held them on suspicion of her murder.'

'So, the Travellers were looking for Clementina, not just to find Richard's killer?' Dee frowned over her glass, tipping the contents down, so she could start work on the next.

'You'd have to look into how they are all related. Mick and Brian are half-brothers so good luck with that! Maybe Richard was seen as family because he'd fathered Clementina's daughters. I don't think they'd realised she'd had twins and certainly not that one of the babies had been swapped with the Mastertons' stillborn child, much less that Clementina had actually died during childbirth and was buried by the lochside. My guess is they'd been looking for Clementina for years and kept coming back to the place she'd last been seen.'

The three of them sat in silent contemplation. Around them the hubbub increased in volume, inhibitions lost and people relieved they had holidays ahead to be with family and friends, away from the drudgery of work and early starts.

'I wouldn't like to be in Samantha's shoes.' Dee broke the silence. 'Tony wanted her dead.'

Teàrlach grimaced. 'She's under witness protection, until she's of no more use to the police. I feel sorry for her.'

'How can you feel sorry for her?' Chloe almost slammed her glass down on the table. 'She took another woman's child for her own, for God's sake. Then couldn't be bothered to look after her, so the wee girl drowned without anyone being there to save her.'

Teàrlach heard the same self-righteous tone the more sensationalist press had plastered over the front pages. It was never that simple, never that black and white.

'Samantha had her own demons to fight. Lilybet's death wasn't anyone's fault, it was just a dreadful accident and one that will haunt her to the end.'

'She still took another woman's child,' Dee said softly.

'Yes, and she'll regret that forever. Now she has no money, no friends and more than likely a contract on her head. She lost a child too that day, remember? She lost two children. Is it fair to add to that hurt?'

'So, you'll not be telling the police?' Chloe asked.

He shook his head. 'No point. Samantha can spin whatever story she likes, the only other people who were present at the birth and could tell us exactly what happened are dead. I'm certain the police have their suspicions regarding Samantha, the Travellers, even Jane Whiting, but nothing I can add will change what's happened. Nothing will bring them back from the dead.'

Teàrlach took another swig from his pint, only too keenly aware of his last words. Samantha might have escaped lightly with Tony gone, but she carried the burden of two children's deaths on her shoulders. Jane had also dodged Tony's retribution and had enough to make a new start, despite the naivety of her attempt to take the reward. Annie's death would remain an accident – he didn't have the proof but was certain Jeremiah killed her and set fire to the house. She and her fellow Travellers had been looking for Clementina ever since she'd last been seen at Annie's. Once her daughter's grave was discovered, Annie's fate was sealed.

Dee shivered beside him, her thigh pressed closely against his.

'You cold?' Teàrlach's concerned face turned towards her, the bruising almost away except around his eyes.

'No, just felt a chill, that's all. I was thinking of what Tony said to you, about the boatman and the Styx. He knew what was coming, didn't he? He knew he was going to die in that loch.'

'I don't know. Maybe he did. Everything happened so fast at the end. I don't see how he could have arranged everything that happened that night.' Teàrlach shook his head. 'There was a lot more to the man than he ever let on. Did you know he liked poetry?'

Dee's wide-open eyes gave away her answer before she could speak. 'That's why he gave you that book?'

Teàrlach nodded. They sat in silence, an uncomfortable oasis of quiet in amongst the revelry.

Dee raised her glass. 'To Teàrlach Paterson, my new employer, and Chloe, my new friend. And to a case closed!'

Three glasses rang together as they met over the table. 'Sláinte!'

'And to Ocean and Selina!' Chloe added. Three glasses raised in unison.

And to the dead, with no one left to say their names. Teàrlach's silent words accompanied the last toast of the evening. He replayed the events at Tony's house, the shots from the loch and then the police instinctively returning fire – Tony's body tumbling into the dark water. Whilst Chloe and Dee finished their drinks, Teàrlach remembered Tony's last words – only the chosen, and Charon the boatman ferrying lost souls across the Styx. Teàrlach had recently finished *The Waste Land*, Tony's parting gift which he had said might be instructive. A poem in which water represented both death and rebirth whilst man is a wasteland waiting to be reborn. Water lapped at the very foundations of Tony's life, took his Lilybet and in the end clasped his lost soul to its cold and hidden depths.

They exited into the cold of the night, exchanged drunken hugs and took taxis to three separate destinations. Outside Teàrlach's cab windows Glasgow had turned into one large party, one he was happy to leave to the young.

> *I am the boatman*
> *Whose song is sung, I loved too*
> *Much. Is that a sin?*

A LETTER FROM THE AUTHOR

Thanks so much for reading *The Girl in the Loch*. If you want to join other readers in hearing all about my new releases, you can sign up for my newsletter here.

www.stormpublishing.co/andrew-james-greig

Please consider leaving a review. This can help new readers discover a book you've enjoyed and gives us all a big boost!

I find inspiration for my stories in the beautiful dramatic landscapes around my home in Scotland. The loch with the starring role in this book is nothing like as dark and mist-covered as I describe, but then I did visit in the height of summer! I enjoy having the freedom to work with a PI, his character can work outside the rigid boundaries of a police procedural and use unorthodox methods to find the truth. At heart, this is a story about love and death, and how a single wrong decision can destroy lives. My fascination with Scottish mythology weaves a thin thread throughout.

I very much look forward to sharing my next book with you. You can peer under this author's bonnet at:

andrewjgreig.wordpress.com

KEEP IN TOUCH WITH THE AUTHOR

facebook.com/andrewjamesgreig

x.com/AndrewJamesGre3

instagram.com/andrew_james_greig

tiktok.com/@andrewjamesgreig

mastodon.scot/@ajg

ACKNOWLEDGEMENTS

My thanks to Claire Bord and the team at Storm Publishing for their enthusiasm and expertise. I would also like to thank Pete Bicheno for his diving experience in Scottish lochs, my family and friends for their support, especially Shona, Dr Peadar Morgan of Bòrd na Gàidhlig for his help with Gaelic. Finally, my thanks to the booksellers, reviewers and most importantly of all to you, the reader.

Printed in Great Britain
by Amazon

44469202R00199